RIBBLESTROP

LIFE IS DANGEROUS

Andy Mulligan

SIMON AND SCHUSTER

First published in Great Britain in 2009 by
Simon and Schuster UK Ltd
A CBS COMPANY.

Simon & Schuster UK Ltd
1st Floor, 222 Gray's Inn Road
London WC1X 8HB

A CIP catalogue record for this book
is available from the British Library.

ISBN 978-1-47112-153-1

1 3 5 7 9 10 8 6 4 2

Printed and bound by CPI Group (UK) Ltd, Croydon, CR0 4YY.

www.simonandschuster.co.uk

To Mum and Dad

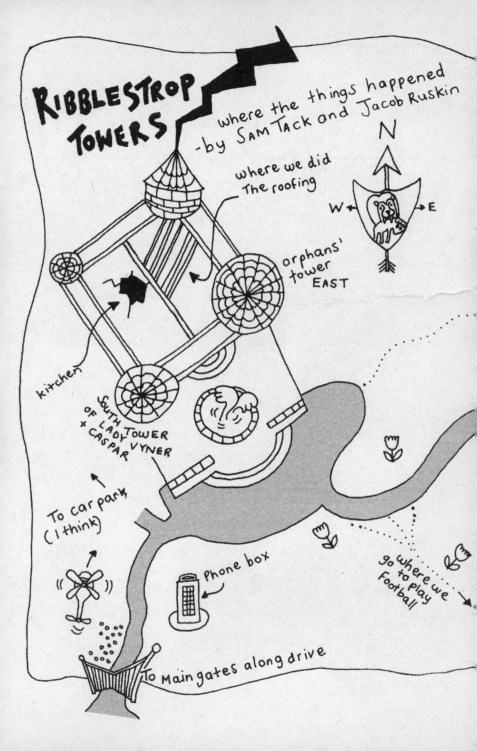

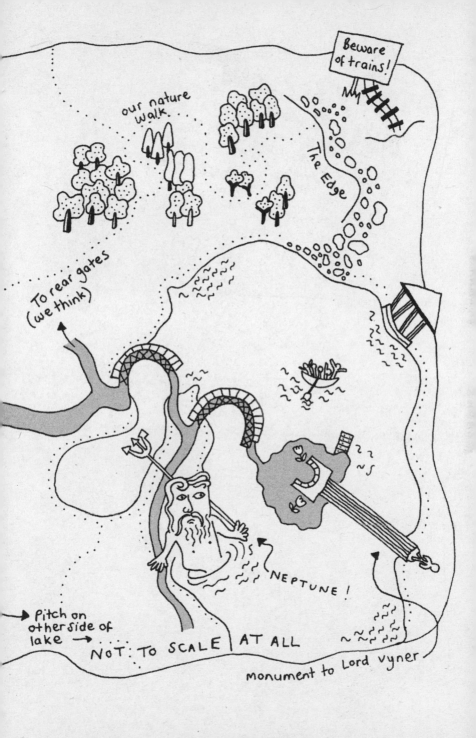

Chapter One

Sam Arthur Tack knew that he was on the threshold of an adventure: the biggest adventure of his life. In fact it was his first adventure, being as he was only twelve years old. He wasn't to know just how dark and dangerous his adventure would be, but he was still close to tears.

'Be brave, son,' said his father.

His mother had tears rolling down both cheeks. 'You make sure you write,' she said. 'As soon as you get there.'

'I can't, though, I—'

'As best you can, love. Draw a picture.'

'I will.' Sam's voice was a cracked whisper and his lips were wobbling.

'It's an opportunity,' said his mother. Her voice was swerving and shaking too: she tried hard to steady it. 'If anything goes wrong, I want you to promise me—'

'Nothing will go wrong,' said his father. 'He's only off to school. Now, where's that pound I gave you?'

'In my pocket.'

'You buy a sandwich when you get to Exeter. We're going to miss you, son.' He shook his son's hand. 'Good luck. Goodbye.'

The train should have left then, to avoid further embarrassment. But trains never leave conveniently and this one was already six minutes late due to a mix up over staff in the buffet car. The sad farewell had a little while yet to run. Sam rested his chin on the window of the carriage door and let his hands disappear into two long blazer sleeves. He was wearing brand new clothes: jacket, cap, shorts, shoes, all of them too big. The only thing that fitted him was the black-and-gold striped tie, which roped in an oversized grey shirt collar. He pushed the window a little lower, and everyone tried to think of something to say.

It was lucky for one and all that just at this moment a fat boy, in the same unmistakable school colours – the black and gold of a bee – should cross the platform lugging a well-stocked briefcase, plus various parcels.

'Darling, look!' said Mrs Tack. 'A Ribblestrop blazer!'

It was true. The boy was wearing the very same garment as her son: the same vivid stripes that caused the eye to jar slightly as if a mild hallucination was taking place.

'Hello. Are you *Ribblestrop*?' said Mr Tack.

The fat boy looked up. He was breathing heavily. 'Yes I am,' he said. 'Jacob Ruskin, I'm a second year – I thought I'd missed this train!' He had a cheery voice and was full of beaming confidence. 'Can I get in here? Is this your boy? I say, a new recruit!'

'This is Sam.'

'I thought I'd missed this train. I'll just—'

'Watch out!' cried Mr Tack.

The boy yanked open the door and Sam immediately fell on top of him. His parents watched as their son's two bare knees smacked onto the concrete platform and the new school cap, grabbed at and scrabbled for, rolled between platform and train.

There was a moment of silence.

'I'm sorry,' said the fat boy. 'I didn't realise he was leaning – I thought he was . . . oh Lord. Is he alright?'

'Blast it,' said Mr Tack. Mr Tack was lowering himself painfully and was staring into the dark space under the train.

'Nobody wears those caps,' said the fat boy. 'I wore mine

2

once for the school photo: I couldn't tell you where it is now. I say, your son's very brave ... Do you need a handkerchief? Look ...'

The boy climbed up into the carriage and offered Sam, who'd staggered to his feet, a chubby little hand.

'What a gaffe. Sam, do you need a hand up?'

'His knees are bleeding,' said Mrs Tack.

'Excuse me,' said a voice.

'I think I ...'

Sam was more worried about the fact that his left eye had hit the fat boy's head when he fell, and he now felt as dizzy as if he'd been punched. There was a throbbing in his skull and the station was swimming.

'I'll get it, Sam,' said his father. 'I'm worried this blasted train will set off and—'

'Excuse me!' said the voice again. It was pitched high, but had a strange grating sound under the shrillness. 'Excuse me please, do you mind? What's that? No, no – I can't hear you ... Could you ...' It was an elderly woman; severe, tall and thin. She was sweating with the strain of dragging a large suitcase-on-wheels whilst trying to talk into a cellphone. The strap of a handbag had become coiled around one arm, and she was also carrying a large, box-like briefcase that appeared to be metal. She wore a high-necked white blouse under a grey suit and, as she fought her way forward, she gave off the powerful scent of cigarettes, perspiration and heavy perfume. Mrs Tack, Sam and Ruskin tried to move out of the way as a wheel of the suitcase rolled over Sam's toes. They cowered back as best they could, and the woman grunted her way up into the train. Her metal case tipped dangerously, and Ruskin moved in to assist. 'Leave it, thank you!' rasped the woman. 'I can manage. What's that?' The case crunched against the side of the train, scratching the paintwork. 'No,' she barked into the cellphone. 'No, no, no ...'

Mr Tack was still on his knees trying to locate the fallen cap.

'When the train leaves,' said Ruskin, 'you could hop down onto the tracks. Then you could send it on.'

'Blast it!' muttered Mr Tack.

'He won't need it, honestly,' continued Ruskin.

'Go on, darling,' said Mrs Tack. 'You'd better get a seat, both of you.'

Sam let the fat boy lead him shakily down the carriage. He pressed two handkerchiefs to his knees. It hadn't been a hard fall, and he wasn't a frail boy. But he did suddenly feel rather faint: the result, he knew, from eating no breakfast. It was also, he knew, a result of the tension of the morning. From his parents' loving attentions as they admired his silly clothes, carried his trunk out to the car, and drove earnestly through the South London traffic to get to Paddington way too early. They'd sat in a café for an hour not eating anything. When the train finally moved and the platform slipped away, Sam's faintness turned to sickness. He pressed one hanky to his mouth and waved the other.

'You blub if you want to,' said the fat boy. 'I did. I thought your gran seemed rather nice.'

'That's my mother, actually.'

'Oh. Are you their only one?'

'Yes.'

Ruskin pressed his cheek to the glass to get a final view. 'Yes, she's crying her eyes out, poor thing. I expect you'll get a bit homesick, won't you? The new boys always do. We had two leave last term, they just couldn't stand the place. And another boy fled. Boarding isn't for everyone, I suppose, though Dr Norcross-Webb tries to make it jolly. I love it!'

'Who's Dr Nor—?'

'Norcross-Webb's the headmaster. He founded the school and does everything. Or he did last term. We're supposed to have a load more teachers now, after the accident – and that includes a new headmistress, which'll be fun. I just hope there's enough boys, it's *boys* we really need. Five wasn't enough for anything.'

Sam looked at his sleeves and wondered where his hands were. Ruskin sat back with his arms folded. 'I love it,' he said. 'It wasn't at all what I expected, so I just hope it hasn't closed. Money's pretty tight and everyone's on these scholarships, so no one really pays full fees – I'm on a singing scholarship.'

'Singing what?'

'Dr Norcross-Webb wants to start a choir. There's an organ in the chapel – or there was. No one knew how to turn it on, thank goodness, because I can't sing a note. It was out of bounds anyway, the roof was so dangerous. After the fire, well . . . that was that. What made you choose Ribblestrop? It's a good school, but . . . what on earth made you choose it?'

Sam stared at Ruskin. He'd had to make several adjustments very quickly and at least it had taken his mind off feeling sick. Ruskin was built like a ball and his thick glasses were round as well, as if there were two marbles stuck to his eyes. He had short, jet-black hair that seemed to be painted on his head like a helmet. His mouth, when it wasn't talking, settled into a friendly, wise smile. He was smiling now, waiting for Sam to answer.

'We saw an advert,' said Sam. 'The fees were low and my parents don't have much money.'

'Nor do mine.'

'They wanted to send me to private school, you see. The school where we live is quite rough and they promised they'd send me to a private one if they could find one cheap enough.'

'I got bullied at my last school,' said Ruskin. 'And the food was bad. It was chips every day. My father used to be a boxer, in the army – so they wanted a school with a good sporting tradition.'

'I love sport, it's the only thing I'm good at. Is there lots?'

'No. None at all.'

'Oh. I thought you—'

'There *will* be. Dr Norcross-Webb says we're pioneers, like in the Wild West. We can do anything and everything, if we put our minds to it.'

'It is a *real* school, isn't it? We saw the brochure and we thought it looked quite posh.'

'Yes, I saw that. It's called "marketing", Sam. He spent lots of money on the brochure because it was a *calculated investment*.'

'I was worried it would be too posh.'

'Well, the building's pretty grand, if you stand at the other side of the park and look at where Lady Vyner lives. It was falling down when I arrived, and then Miles set fire to the dining hall, so we lost the library and the chapel. He was expelled, so that meant we were down to four, because two had left; and then poor old Tomaz ran away. That's why he had the brochure made, you see, because we needed more boys. By the time we get there, there could be loads! There's Lord Caspar – he's the grandson of the owner – but he doesn't come all the time. He's a law unto himself quite honestly and he may not come back, he says he hates the place – but then, to tell you the truth, he's just a teeny-weeny bit spoilt.'

'Who set fire to it? One of the boys?'

'Yes, I told you – Miles. He was one of those rather disturbed children that can't really fit in. He was friends with Tomaz, and Tomaz was the orphan who ran away. Miles got really upset, so he splashed a load of petrol around and the fire went right through the roof. We had five fire engines; it took ages to get under control. One of the things we're supposed to be doing this term, actually, is rebuilding. The headmaster sent off for a book on DIY, and our summer project . . . well. Take a look at this.'

Ruskin was delving among his parcels. The train was speeding along now and Sam knew there was no turning back. He watched the fat boy untie some string and gingerly withdraw something from brown paper.

'We had to build a model. You had to calculate the maximum span of a timber beam, bearing in mind a load of – I can't remember – one hundred thousand kilos, I think. Ever so complicated. My brother helped me a bit, but it took ages . . . What do you think?'

Sam wasn't sure what to think. Ruskin's model had four walls and was then a mass of struts and beams. It was exquisitely built and reminded Sam of a cathedral in miniature.

'You could probably get away without some of the purlins,' said Ruskin. 'But we decided to be better safe than sorry. It took most of the holiday, but the best project wins a rosette.'

'And that's the roof we're going to build?'

'If there's enough of us. It's not as complicated as it looks, actually. The principles are pretty straightforward; it all works in triangles. Do you want some tea, Sam?'

Sam didn't know what he wanted. Thoughts and feelings were getting more confused than ever, so he nodded gratefully. Ruskin smiled happily and attended to the other items in his bag. In a short while he'd laid out a flask and two plastic cups. The train was juddering, so pouring was tricky, but soon there were two steaming cups of boiling water. He produced two tea bags from his breast pocket and dunked vigorously. He had cubed sugar, a whisky miniature that held fresh milk, and a plastic teaspoon. Finally, he set down a lunchbox and opened it to reveal a stack of homemade biscuits.

'I expect you want to know about the other boys,' he said.

'Yes.'

'Well, they're both good fellows. Do you take sugar? One of them is from South America. He's a funny one, I'll tell you about him – ever so nice, I really hope he's coming back. The other boy's quite old. Sixteen, he says. But he looks older, and he doesn't really talk. We so need eleven! The only game I'm any good at is football.'

'I thought it was a big school. I thought I was lucky to get in.'

7

'Oh, you are! It is! It's a smashing place, really! It's got such an interesting history, too – it was a research base in the Second World War. You know how these stately homes got taken over by the army? They built bunkers and everything – there's tunnels underground. So after the war, it became a donkey sanctuary, I believe. Then the monks arrived, and they're still there, but you don't see them – am I talking too much? I'll just tell you this. The story goes that our headmaster bought the place in *one* day. He made "the offer" in the morning and took the cash round in a suitcase that afternoon. He bought the donkeys too. They live on what used to be tennis courts, but what *will* be the football pitch – not that you can really play, not with three people, even when the headmaster goes in goal. And Sanchez can't run too well, because he lost a toe.'

'Sanchez . . .? Hang on, is he one of the other boys?'

'Sorry, yes. The South American boy. He was injured, so he can't really do games, though he does try. When you lose your big toe your balance goes, so he's got a limp.'

'How did he lose his toe?'

'It's a secret, but I'll tell you. You're bound to find out.' Ruskin leaned forward and his voice became a whisper. 'This is true, apparently. Though it sounds like I'm making it up. He was kidnapped and held for ransom. And the kidnappers, to show they meant business . . .'

Sam winced.

'Yes. With pliers.'

'Did his parents pay the ransom?'

'Sanchez said they didn't. When the toe fell out of the envelope, they sent the bodyguards in. There was a shoot-out.'

'And Sanchez escaped?'

'He's a very tough boy. I wouldn't want to mess with Sanchez. He's not a show-off, but he can wrestle a donkey to the ground. I saw him do it after Miles had bet he couldn't – admittedly, it was Peter Pan, the oldest donkey, but even so . . .'

8

'Who kidnapped him?' said Sam. His eyes were wider than they'd ever been. His mouth was slightly open.

'I don't know. His family are from South America, rolling in money. All his clothes are tailor-made. But he's not a show-off, honestly.' Ruskin lowered his voice and leaned in over the table. 'The reason he's at Ribblestrop is so no one can find him. He keeps a gun under his bed, just in case: there's a little hole in the wall. Seriously. Dr Norcross-Webb knows his father, and my father thinks that's where the first lot of money came from. You see, nobody would dream a boy like Sanchez would go to a school like Ribblestrop. So he's safe.'

Chapter Two

It was at this point that Sam experienced his second accident of the day. He was destined to suffer three. It was not serious in itself, but it would set off a chain of interesting events. Ruskin had the dangerous habit of resting his eyes on occasions. This involved removing and pocketing his glasses – he'd been advised to do this by a teacher who'd despaired of the boy's painfully slow reading. The effect of this 'eye-resting' was that for short periods Ruskin was almost blind. He would grope and grab – and that could be lethal. He was now seeking to pour more tea.

The same complex ritual started: tea bag and cup, spoon to tea bag, hot-water flask standing by. Sam went to finish the cup he'd hardly touched: there was a flurry of hands as Ruskin tried to organise the table, and the large, heavy flask inevitably tipped over. A lake of boiling water swept wave-like over the edge of the train table onto Sam's shorts. He suppressed the scream, turning it into a long high-pitched gasp. Ruskin grabbed at the flask, upsetting the cup. Thus the wave was joined by a short geyser and Sam gasped again. Ruskin rushed to help. But what could he do? Sam's thighs and tender regions sizzled in scalding water; the boy fought to keep cloth from flesh.

'This is totally my fault,' cried Ruskin. 'I cannot believe this.'

'It's alright.'

'It's not. Hang on . . . glasses. Hold on, Sam. Oh my word, you're soaking!'

'Oh no.' Sam was whispering.

'Are you burned? I'm so sorry . . .'

'It's alright.'

'Stand up, Sam. No, sit down. Oh my! Have you any spare shorts?'

'No. I only . . . Ow. Help.'

'Look. I have. They're in my trunk, which is down in the—'

'I think I'll stand up.'

'You're completely red, look at your legs! Should I stop the train?'

Ruskin flapped while Sam dabbed at himself with two soaking handkerchiefs. He was feeling sick again and the fire round his thighs was fading to hot clamminess. The seat was wet as well.

'Such bad luck. Look: let's go down to the baggage car and see if my trunk can be got at. Then you can have my spares – and I've got a towel as well. Can you walk?'

Sam peeled himself off the seat and stood dripping in the aisle. A handful of other passengers were staring, icily, as if the boys were seeking attention.

'I'd better take our stuff. Follow me.'

Ruskin packed the bags and, when he'd done so, Sam managed a bow-legged, dripping hobble down the carriage. The first toilet was engaged, but the second one was vacant. Sam dried himself as best he could and emerged slowly.

'I'm a clumsy oaf,' said Ruskin. 'I do apologise.'

'It doesn't matter.'

'Follow me. I'm fairly sure we can get at my trunk – it's in the baggage car, which is right down the end. If we can get to it, we can do a quick change; I mean obviously they'll be a bit big, but you're wearing a belt. If it was the other way round we wouldn't stand a chance – oh my word, look!'

Sam was still prising wet cloth from his thighs, so he didn't look up. The dividing door closed as Ruskin barged excitedly forward, and Sam's thin body was crushed in the steel frame. An angry-looking businessman leaned from his seat. 'Don't play with the doors! Sit down!'

'I can't really. I'm—'

'You boys are a blessed nuisance. Up and down, up and down!'

Sam shoved the door back as hard as he could and staggered out of the carriage. A train conductor was heaving his way through, looking haggard. Sam's 'Excuse me' was lost as the big man wrenched open the door. Then there was a clatter of points and Sam was thrown forward, catching his forehead on the luggage shelves. His friend was way down the far end of the next carriage, so Sam hobbled after him, realising that had this happened a few hours ago, he would have undoubtedly started to cry. Perhaps he was growing up already, he wondered, just as his father had promised. Perhaps he was a man and was responding to burns and blows the way a man would do. Double vision was the price you paid.

When he caught up with Ruskin, the boy seemed at a loss: he was staring at a passenger, in a trance-like state. At length, he managed two words: 'I say . . .'

Sam saw a blurred version of what Ruskin was looking at. Sitting in a seat was another child, in the identical black-and-gold stripes of their own uniforms. But this child was slumped low, with its feet on the empty seat opposite, and was listening to music through headphones. It was unaware it had an audience; it was gazing at the scrubland of outer London. This was just as well: Ruskin's scrutiny had gone on now for a full minute. The child's head nodded to the beat of the music; its mouth was chewing. Ruskin seemed dazed.

'Oh my word,' he finally said.

'What?' said Sam. 'What's the matter?'

'Look at this.'

The child in the seat turned at last. A frown spread instantly across its features.

'What?' it said. Aggressive. Confident.

'Hello,' said Ruskin.

The child clicked off its music and yanked the earphones out of its ears.

'Why are you staring at me? What do you want?'

'I'm so sorry,' said Ruskin. Apologies seemed to tumble out of his mouth. 'I didn't mean to stare, it's just we saw your . . . blazer. We thought – I thought – I'm so sorry, I thought you were *Ribblestrop*.'

The child's frown turned to confusion. 'What are you talking about?'

'Same colours, everything. From the other end, you see, you looked like you were on your way to Ribblestrop Towers, my school, but—'

'I am,' said the child. 'I think. Don't say you're there as well.'

'I'm a second year,' whispered Ruskin.

'I'm new,' said Sam, over Ruskin's shoulder.

The child's eyes flickered back and forth as if it were watching fast tennis.

'Look, I don't mean to be rude,' said Ruskin. 'I don't mean to be rude at all. But . . . you're a girl, aren't you?'

The child's face scrunched into a wizened glare. Her hair, brushed hard back from her forehead and ears, was drawn into a short plait. She'd put on a little lipstick. There was just a hint of glittery eye shadow as well, on her eyelids. A jewel gleamed in the left earlobe and there was a ring on one finger. Ruskin was looking at her legs, half hidden by the table, but still stretched up onto the opposite seat. They were covered to the knee by shorts, and this was confusing.

'I mean, you *are* a girl. You're a girl, and Ribblestrop's a boys' school,' he said. 'Well, it was,' he added, weakly.

'Are you seriously telling me *you* go to it?'

'It's a boys' school,' said Ruskin, faintly. The girl had a rather gravelly voice. Her cheeks were ghostly pale and striking because of sharp cheekbones. 'But it can't be. I suppose it isn't. What I mean is, it used to be a boys' school. Can we sit down?'

'Here? Why?'

Ruskin started to slide into the seat, forcing the girl to remove her feet.

'We were on our way to the baggage car.'

'Oh no.' The girl was sitting forward. 'Your friend's wet himself.' She was pointing rudely at Sam's soaking shorts.

'No,' said Sam. 'There was an accident.'

'What do you mean, it's a boys' school? No one said to me it was a boys' school, I was told it was for girls. Look, you – if you untuck your shirt, no one will see. Look at the state of you! Seriously, what is that?'

'Tea,' said Sam.

'Mainly hot water,' said Ruskin. 'Look, shall I go down to the baggage car and get the spares?'

'You'll have to take them off,' said the girl. 'You can't sit in soaking-wet shorts, you'll get shrivelled. No one'll see, we'll dry them out of the window.'

'I can't really do that,' said Sam.

'I had to do this once with a scarf when someone was sick – I had to wash it in the loo and then we tied it to the door handle between Bristol and Tiverton. It's a warm day, you'll be fine.'

Ruskin nodded and smiled: 'You know, that's not a bad plan, Sam. Because I'm not sure they'll let us in the baggage car and even if they do, my shorts won't fit you. This is all my fault, you know.'

'Then you can dry them,' said the girl. 'What's your name? Sam?'

'Yes.'

'Take them off and give them to your friend. Come on,

14

nobody can see.' The girl was standing up, taking control. Her hand was thrust out and the train was slowing.

Sam feared disaster was on its way. After all, he'd lost a cap, he'd been bruised and scalded. The day had more bad luck in store, that was for certain. But he was one of those boys who found it hard to resist strong-minded people for fear of being thought rude. He struggled out of his shorts, pulling his shirt-tails down to his knees.

'Give us your tie as well. Then we can tie the shorts to the door just in case fat boy lets them go – a little safety device.'

This husky-voiced confident girl: Sam just couldn't disobey. He took off his tie, feeling as if the world was conspiring to steal his whole uniform. At least he had the blazer – and that was the item his parents had saved for hardest. There was only one store in London where you could get them, and they'd only had an unclaimed special order in stock – a blazer, it seemed, that had been made for a small bear. 'He'll grow into it,' said the bored salesman, who'd realised straight away that the Tack family was virtually penniless. The other option had been buying a small dinner jacket and stitching gold ribbons onto it. Sam's mother was keen but her son had managed, politely, to make his opin-ion known, and they'd come home with the overcoat model. It was quite useful now, to wrap himself up in. He curled into the seat and watched the approach of Reading.

'Your friend is very strange,' said the girl.

Ruskin had disappeared into the toilet. He was intending to give the shorts a scrub and then devise the clothes drier.

'I was warned this was a freaky school,' said the girl. 'I guess I should be glad if he's the least freaky. What's his name?'

'Jacob Ruskin.'

'My name's Millie Roads. This is going to be my fifth school. Dad phoned the headmaster and told him the government would put a year's fees up front if they'd take me straight away.'

'Oh.'

'How old are you? You look like a gnome.'

'I'm twelve.'

'You've got a black eye coming – are you a fighter? I had this friend called Katie who could beat up anyone. I was trying to persuade her to come to this *Ribblestrip* place, because she got kicked out of the last school, same as me. She did aikido and flattened our housemaster. Then we trashed the place. I think you've got the skinniest legs I've ever seen.'

'I know.'

'I'm thirteen, by the way, so we won't be in the same class. Katie was amazing! She could make bombs from soap powder. We put lighter fuel on a pillow, OK? And the pillow had a label saying: *This pillow comes up to fire safety standards*, which was a joke. I said in court that the school should sue whoever makes its pillows, because it went up like a torch, and we'd put it in the laundry trolley with these bags of salt and soap powder. The laundry room was in the basement, just under the girls' common room, so in our opinion it was all an accident waiting to happen, and that's what the judge said. What did you get slung out for?'

'Slung out of what?'

Millie snarled with impatience. 'Your last school! The school before Ribbledee-whatever it is. Why did you leave, if it isn't top secret?'

'I haven't been expelled from anywhere.'

Millie stared a moment, then shrugged. 'I thought this dump only took kids who'd been slung out – there's this government scheme, isn't there? My dad was told it had bars on the windows, that's why he was sending me. Twenty-four-hour round-the-clock patrols and all that.'

'Ruskin said it was a normal school.'

'What's he going to know about normal? You think he's normal? Look – do you smoke, Sammy-boy? Silly question. I'm dying . . .'

The train was slowing to a stop. There was a clattering of doors and a few travellers made their way down the corridor.

'Reading,' said Millie. 'Can you imagine living here?' She peered into the grey gloom beyond the station buildings.

'My uncle used to live in Swindon—'

'Set fire to the place, that's what I'd do. A lot of very grateful people. Katie went to jail, by the way. I was the accessory, which just means the best friend – I held the pillow, closed the door. Can I ask you something, Sam? Who cuts your hair?'

'My hair?'

'Is English your first language?'

Sam blinked. 'My mother cuts my hair.'

'Yes, you look a bit like a boy in one of those very old films. Tell you what, when we get to school I'll get my razor and do you a real haircut. Have you visited this school? Have you seen it?'

'No,' said Sam. 'I've seen pictures, but I haven't been there. Look.'

Sam felt around in the folds of his jacket. The school prospectus was in a deep pocket, bent in half. He set it on the table and smoothed it out. It was a comforting sight after all the snippets of information from Ruskin, let alone the dark hints from this terrifying new girl. Sam was reassured to see the same honey-coloured buildings that had impressed his parents so much. And the crest, with a lion and a lamb. The photographer must have been lying in the gravel: the main building loomed up like a cliff, with a fabulous tower climbing up to blue sky. On the next page, in an inset photo, a blond boy sat curled on the lawn reading a book. You could almost hear the birdsong. The headmaster was smiling in another corner, looking totally normal and completely in charge: not a man to let someone down, or dream up an elaborate hoax. A man in a gown, with a wise smile.

'They never sent us one of them,' said Millie. 'The government pays for me, something about investing in me now so they won't go bankrupt later on – that was my father's joke anyway, and everyone laughed a lot. Hey, fat boy – you're back . . .'

Ruskin was back. He wore a forlorn look, but the nickname Millie had invented stung him. He swivelled his head towards her.

'Would you be kind enough not to call me that? I'm not going to call you skinny girl or anything, so I think we could agree basic manners.'

'Basic manners? I'm just trying to be friendly.'

'Sam, there's been an accident.'

Ruskin looked exhausted. He wormed into the chair opposite Millie. 'It's back to Plan B.'

'What Plan B?' said Millie. 'What happened to Plan A?'

'Sam, I'm going to get some shorts for you from the baggage car, but I won't be able to until we get to our station. Apparently, they don't allow access to the freight during transit, or something like that. But I can run down to the baggage car and pretend—'

'What happened to Plan A?' said Millie, again.

Sam said: 'Where are my shorts?'

'I was holding them out of the window.' Ruskin looked pained. 'I had attached the tie. I think my mistake was choosing the very small window – I was using the one in the toilet, which doesn't allow you the space you really need.'

'Oh my . . .' said Millie.

'Did you drop them?' said Sam, quietly.

'Yes, and unfortunately it wasn't the platform side, or one could have just nipped out and picked them up. I chose the other side so as not to draw unwanted attention.'

'So your little friend's shorts are down on the tracks?' said Millie.

'They are down on the tracks,' confirmed Ruskin.

'So jump down and get them.'

'I can't.'

'Why not? You drop the boy's shorts out of a window and you're not going to jump down and get them? What sort of a friend are you?'

'You misunderstand me – the doors on that side of the train are locked.'

'Jump out the window. You can't leave his shorts on the track.'

'I think they went on the electric rail. I really wouldn't like to try to retrieve them – and in any case, there's a hefty fine if you trespass on the railway.'

'This boy has his first day at a new school and he's arriving half naked! Come on, Sam, let's sort this out.'

Sam had sunk into his blazer. He felt the blood draining from his face, neck and even his chest. He felt thin and weightless but surprisingly calm, as if all this had been foretold in a half-remembered dream. 'Sam, get up!'

Millie's hand yanked him to his feet and Ruskin rose to stand out of their way, protesting. 'We're about to leave the station, Sam – I feel awful about this, but is there anything we can do, really?'

'Yes, there is!'

As Millie spoke, the train humped forward: that movement that says: *Sorry, everybody – your last chance to get off has just gone* . . . She hauled Sam into the corridor and wrestled with the window, then leaned out and twisted at the door handle. Rails and sleepers were now rumbling past and, as Sam stared, the station was giving way to a large car park.

'It's alright, Millie—'

'The door's locked. Stop the damn train, it's an emergency!'

'I think Plan B is quite workable, you know,' said Ruskin. 'It's foolproof, really.'

But Millie had one of those brains which gets fixed obsessively on the one idea. No doctor so far had been able to help. She marched back into the carriage and had the presence of mind to pick up her coat and bag. Then she reached up and pulled the emergency lever, holding firmly to the handrail as the train went into an instant spasm of emergency braking. Twenty-five miles an hour, if that – they hadn't been going so very fast, but there was still plenty of dramatic lurching and screeching. Interestingly, the elderly thin woman with the awkward luggage was on her feet at that moment, rooting around in the overhead rack. She was still jabbering into a cellphone, which her chin crushed to her shoulder. But her agitation was increasing, and she was trying to drag the brief-case down from above while keeping the handbag open on her seat. She was already off balance, so the abrupt halt of the train sent her crashing to the floor, jarring her shoulder as she fell. This injury meant she didn't report the disappearance of her purse, with its collection of credit cards, for a full two hours. She was forced to visit Reading General Hospital, and was sep-arated from her luggage: all this meant substantial delay to the train, and was how the new deputy headmistress of Ribblestrop Towers was prevented from taking up her new post for a fur-ther six days.

Of course, Millie, Ruskin and Sam were unaware of this. They stood at the door and, as the locks sprung open, Millie heaved it open. The ground was a long way down, but she leaped nimbly onto the rails and stood staring up at a bewildered Sam.

'Hurry up!' she shouted. So Sam leaped too.

'Is this wise?' said Ruskin, from the doorway. But then, at the other end of the carriage, he caught sight of the train conductor, looking more horrified than any adult he'd ever seen: he was clearly getting ready to scream. Clutching his precious bag and model, Jacob Ruskin launched himself out of the train, head-butting Sam hard on the other side of his temple as he landed. The three children then staggered and stepped carefully over the tracks, making their way to scrubland.

They reached it not a moment too soon.

They hadn't heard the train zooming in from the other direction and they certainly hadn't seen it. The delayed 10:21, a through train from Bristol to London Paddington, was on the very track they'd stepped across, and the driver only saw three blurs of black-and-gold. The train missed the skinniest by ten centimetres. And the passengers in the now-to-be-seriously-delayed stationary train – the 11:14 to Penzance – were so horrified by the accident they thought they'd witnessed, there were several screams. For a full hour most people assumed the three children had been atomised. Because of this misunderstanding, nobody gave chase.

Chapter Three

'Follow me,' said Millie.

'My shorts are back there,' said Sam.

'I don't think we can wait around. I think we need a new plan, a Plan C.'

'I think we need—' said Ruskin.

'And *I* am in charge of Plan C, Mr Ruskin – is that your name?'

'Yes it is.'

'Leave this one to me. We've got shopping to do and I want it done fast. You have not done well, Mr Ruskin. It is only fair to let others have a chance.'

Millie was several paces ahead, her head rotating this way and that as she tried to get her bearings. They stepped over more rails up onto a sloping platform. In a moment they were out onto the main street, close to the station entrance. Millie hailed a taxi and the driver was so surprised he stopped. The children climbed in and the driver was still so surprised he drove on, ignoring the protests from those waiting at the taxi rank some fifty metres on.

'In fact, fat boy,' said Millie, settling into her seat. 'You have done so badly it may make the papers. You have stranded us in a filthy town. I used to come here on a Friday and it was grim. I didn't think it could get much grimmer, but – credit where credit's due – it's hit rock bottom. Just look at it.'

'Where are we?' said Sam.

'*Reading*. Read the signs.'

'I would,' said Sam. 'But I don't really read too well. That's another reason my parents went for Ribblestrop Towers.'

'Are you dyslexic?' said Ruskin.

'Very,' said Sam.

'You know, I was the most dyslexic boy in my region. One teacher told me my brain needed to be totally rewired. I'm dyspraxic too, and something else.'

'Millie, where are we going?' said Sam.

'This is a hole when it comes to nightlife,' said the girl. 'But when it comes to clothes shops, and little bits of tat – it does quite well. Selfridges, please,' she said to the taxi driver. The driver muttered about one-way systems and red zones, so Millie leaned in again. 'Look,' she said. 'We've had a difficult morning. As close as you can, as fast as you can – it's a very big store and the word "Selfridges" is written right on the front. You can find it.'

Then she closed the glass screen on the still-muttering driver.

Ruskin had cash. He grumbled a little, because he'd been looking forward to opening a new account in the Ribblestrop Bank (one of Dr Norcross-Webb's promised innovations for the new term). But he did feel responsible and the taxi driver looked quite threatening. The children hurried through a shopping centre that seemed to think it was a greenhouse, rode an escalator while Sam tried to keep his blazer wrapped tight round his knees – and before long they were in the boyswear department. A very tall lady with very bright lipstick did her very best to help: shorts were no problem at all, and Sam almost cried with relief to be decent again. A new tie was more of a problem, but a local school had something similar. Again, Sam rejoiced in threading it round his collar and straightening the ends. It normalised him. He tucked his shirt in firmly and felt the trauma dropping away like unwanted skin.

'You don't do caps?' he said.

They didn't do caps. This time Millie paid, with a credit card, and three reasonably normal-looking students rode the escalator down.

'Coo,' said Ruskin. 'I wish my parents would give me a credit card. I didn't even realise you could get them till you were eighteen.'

'They're useful things,' said Millie. 'Now, do you boys want to amuse yourselves for an hour? There's a few things I need before my sentence starts. Why don't we meet here, by the sweetie machines?'

'Millie,' said Ruskin.

'What?'

'I think this Plan C of yours has gone incredibly well. My only thought now is getting to Ribblestrop. You *are* intending to go to Ribblestrop, aren't you?'

'Yes.'

'You see, I don't think we'd be very welcome at the station. And to be honest, I'm not sure where we'd get a bus.'

'Could we hitch-hike?' said Sam. 'I did that with my father once when we ran out of petrol.'

'That's not a bad plan,' said Millie. 'If we take a taxi to the motorway, we can join up with the M5. Sam's got that brochure thing, there's a map in there. Give me one hour.' She sailed off up an escalator.

The boys found a burger bar and Ruskin dipped into his cash once again. Sam discovered that his pound – the one his father had pressed onto him for a sandwich – had been in the pocket of the lost shorts. Perhaps some rodent would discover it. Ruskin sighed and decided he owed his new friend rather more than money. They drank fizzy drinks and tried out two different burgers, each with salads, French fries, dips of one sort and another. By the time Millie joined them, laden with shopping, Sam felt triumphant and fat. They strode out of the shopping mall together: but of course, Millie hadn't eaten.

'There's a place my father uses . . . How much cash have you got, Ruski?'

'Pardon? Money? Um, oooh. From my original hundred I now have . . .' He paused to count his banknotes. 'Seventy-four.'

'That should be enough. Keep your eye on the meter: if it goes over that, jump out of the car.'

She was hailing another taxi and, again, the surprise of seeing three school children flagging him down meant another queue was jumped and another driver was soon skimming out of the shopping centre.

'It's a wine bar for the rich and famous. It's called Benders.'

'Benders?' said Sam. He laughed, for the first time that day.

'Benders?' said the taxi driver. 'That's in Frimleigh.'

'Look, Millie—' said Ruskin.

'Exactly right: the Frimleigh Benders. It's the only wine bar with a helipad; my father let me order cocktails, so it's all a bit of a blurred memory.'

'It'll cost you,' said the taxi driver. 'It's twenty miles away.'

Millie relaxed in her seat. 'Nothing is free,' she said. 'And if it was, I wouldn't want it.'

It was nice, she thought, to see Ruskin going paler than Sam. Sam was sitting back, smiling happily.

Chapter Four

Emilio Esteverre Sanchez was not a nervous man: he took such precautions so that he didn't need to be. Inspecting the crops on his mountain ranch in Colombia, he was never without a circle of bodyguards. In any one of his apartments – from London to Bogotá, Bangkok to Istanbul – armed men kept a twenty-four hour vigil. Even in a restaurant – *especially* in a restaurant – a triangle of marksmen stood around him.

'You need two things in this life,' he would say to his son. 'Money – which I have. And peace of mind, which I also have.'

Mr Sanchez actually needed a lot of other things as well, as his son was beginning to realise. For example, at this precise moment, he needed a chocolate-and-fudge cheesecake in brandy cream: the millionaire was spooning it in, unaware of the effect it was having on his thick moustache. Twelve-year-old Andreas Sanchez, in a tailored Ribblestrop uniform, had finished his meal and sat with his hands folded in his lap. He was a slim boy with olive skin and thick dark hair, parted and gelled every morning by the maid who travelled with him; it was cut weekly to keep it off the collar and above the ears. His black-and-gold tie was neatly pressed and bisected a monogrammed, hand-made grey shirt. Black-and-gold cufflinks matched the black-and-gold of his eyes: his father was now looking hard into them, with a love so deep the boy too felt like weeping. His father said softly: 'You ready to go, Andreas?'

'Of course, Father.'

'You feel OK? Everything is good for you?'

'I'm sorry to be leaving my family, Father. Apart from this, I'm happy. I think it's a good school.'

'Ha!' A spray of brandy cream flew across the table. 'Is a good place – a very good place, with a good man in charge. And an English education is the best for you. For me, not so easy!'

He looked around the table and laughed. There were three other men, all in suits, and they laughed politely. Mr Sanchez's hands were a mulch of scar tissue. The left had only three fingers; the right looked as if it had been deep-fried. 'The English school is the best, that is why I send him there, so he mixes with the best. Who's the little boy? Lord Somebody, uh?'

'Lord Caspar, but I don't know if he'll be coming back.'

'Lords and the ladies, eh? The ruling class of England! You make friends, Andreas. Listen to the teachers and study hard.'

'I will study hard.'

'Which school have you chosen, Mr Sanchez?' said one of the dinner guests, politely. 'My own sons went through Pangbourne.'

'I choose my own place, OK? I choose a place nobody knows.'

There was an awkward silence which Mr Sanchez didn't notice. He leaned towards his son and took him gently by the ear. 'No nightmares, uh?' he whispered.

'No, Father, not for a long time.'

'I know, I know . . . the football is important. I also wanted to play for my country. But – you play in goal, is still possible.'

'I can play, Father. It's just the running that's hard. I am learning, though.'

'Andreas . . . If your mother was alive . . . eh?' The man was overcome. 'From Heaven she sees, yes? She is looking down, now. Here. Everywhere. And I say to her, never again! Whatever the business in my life, my son does not suffer. OK, gentlemen?'

The guests were nodding dutifully.

'Let's go. The helicopter's ready, yes? Make sure you keep your eyes like this.' Mr Sanchez stretched his own wide and darted them from side to side. 'I send people fast if you need, OK? And you have the special number in your head, yes? You don't forget, and you still have what I give you last time? Yes? Bullets, also? Good . . .'

Mr Sanchez paused because he'd been distracted. One of his wide eyes had lifted from his son's and had noticed movement on the far side of the room. The restaurant was rarely full this early in the week and the head waiter always faxed a reservation list to Mr Sanchez's PA just before his arrival. Even so, a restaurant was a public place and his own table was not as well screened as he would have liked. They'd put his party by the terrace with a sumptuous view over the lawns, and he was by no means invisible. His son had been snatched in a place not dissimilar.

There seemed to be some kind of quarrel taking place at the main door and he could hear a child's voice cutting through the subdued tones of the staff. 'Oh come on! We could have *that* table!'

'Madam, it's reserved, I'm afraid.'

'Every table's reserved, is it? You think we can't pay?'

'Madam, reservations have to be made in advance, that's our policy. Sir, excuse me, sir! Come back!'

Ruskin had moved away and the waiters were powerless. He didn't want to eat and Millie's outburst was embarrassing. He didn't want to spend any more money, either, having forked out another fifty-five pounds for the taxi. He struck out for the toilets ahead, wondering vaguely how much a cup of water would cost in a place like this. That's when he saw – reflected in the mirrorwork and glass – a boy he *thought* he recognised. Now Ruskin wasn't wearing his glasses again; he was resting his eyes. The vision in the glass was therefore a blur, so it was

28

quite logical that he should stop, blink, and reach for his spectacles.

In the background Millie was warming up: 'Do you know how much money my father has spent here?' she cried. 'More than you make in a year. He brings *me* here, his *friends* here—'

'Madam, please! Sir!'

'My goodness, that's Sanchez,' whispered Ruskin. He could see the black-and-gold of his blazer. 'Andreas! I don't believe it!'

'Sir – that is a private dining area!'

Unfortunately for Ruskin, he didn't hear the warning. A friendly boy, he was keen only to greet the one good friend he'd made last term at Ribblestrop: he had no idea of the danger he was in, nor the impression he gave as he moved quickly forward, his right hand reaching into his blazer.

From Mr Sanchez's point of view, it was all a matter of instinct and action. He didn't have to think: years of survival on the streets of Bogotá made some movements purely reflex.

The bodyguards, too, leaped into action. They saw the figure moving rapidly, having broken through the head waiter's guard. Its eyes were fixed on the boy Sanchez and the hand was gripping something, emerging slowly.

Everyone moved at once. Mr Sanchez up-ended the restaurant table in an avalanche of glass and crockery, rolling it as he did in front of his son. The first bodyguard dived like a swimmer and forward-rolled into a kneeling position beside Sanchez, masking him with his upper body and firing into the air. The second bodyguard was behind Ruskin but ten metres away: his training was in karate and he knew from bitter experience that assassins are better living than dead. He cartwheeled dramatically over the one table that was in his path before landing heavily on Ruskin, feet first. As he fell he pinched the schoolboy's neck and shoulders between his legs, locking his feet in the famous 'Kiss of the Scissors'. The third bodyguard unloaded his machine gun, raking the doors and windows just above the heads of Millie, Sam and the head waiter. The explosions of glass had just the desired effect: everyone dived to the ground and lay still, hands over their heads.

Amazingly, nobody screamed. The shock was so total that apart from the orgy of breaking glass, the whole drama was performed in silence. Andreas Sanchez was the one to break the silence. Luckily for Ruskin, his purple, suffocating face was just in the boy's sightline, and he said simply: 'Hey! It's my friend! It's Ruskin!'

Emilio Esteverre Sanchez was not a man to feel foolish and a millionaire's sense of humour tends to be contagious. When he started to laugh, the other guests started to laugh. Gunfire was not unknown in Benders – the waiters took it in their stride, and a case of champagne hastily distributed round the other tables soon greased the wheels of apology. Like a scene change in a fast-moving play, tables were righted and relaid; brooms swept away debris with lightning efficiency; and Ruskin was soon in a chair, head between his knees.

'¿Qué pasa?' said Mr Sanchez to his son. He switched to Colombian-Spanish when speed was essential.

'Es un buen amigo, padre.'

'El gordito! ¿Un amigo?'

'Si! Empezó el trimestre pasado, como yo. No haría daño a una mosca, es un caballero!'

'Ai, soy un idiota!'

Sam and Millie looked at each other, wondering if they really had entered a movie. Guns were replaced in shoulder holsters, and a man was babbling into a walkie-talkie. A pianist appeared and started to play.

Millie said: 'What the hell is this?'

'I don't know,' Sam replied. 'But I think that's the boy I was hearing about.'

'Ruskin,' said Sanchez. 'You never met my father! Come and meet him.'

Jacob Ruskin looked up but couldn't focus on very much. He was helped to his feet. Hands dusted the dirt and glass from his blazer, and a chair was thrust under his backside.

'Mr Sanchez?' panted Ruskin. 'I'm so sorry I disturbed your meal.'

Mr Sanchez erupted in laughter. 'Look at this!' he shouted. 'Does anybody believe this, eh? He comes all the way to see my son, to say hello, and what do we do? We nearly shoot him in the head! How many lives you got, my friend?'

'I don't know. One less, I suppose!'

'One less, he says!' There were peals of laughter. 'Thank God – imagine! Only, no, let's not even think. Again, you see, God is watching. And friends, more of them. Look, join us here. Everybody, come and eat. Sit!'

Introductions were made. Hands were shaken and cheeks were kissed. The language rippled from English to Spanish and back to English; suddenly there was champagne in everyone's glass, and Ruskin's proper colour slowly returned.

'So you mean,' said Mr Sanchez, 'this is a total coincidence, uh? Absolutely no plan, no rendezvous? And you the boy I wanted to meet, you the very good friend of my son, the one who is looking after him?'

The laughter rose up louder still and spread, it seemed, to other diners. The pianist grew hysterical in his playing.

'Listen, all of you,' he said. 'Sammy, and ... whass your name? I forget, I'm sorry ...' He was looking at Millie.

'Millie,' said Millie.

'Millie also. Jacob – Ruskin. Sammy. Put your glasses in here.'

Sam drained his glass nervously, then realised with delight that for the first time in his life he was drunk. It was instant. A hand snatched the glass. It joined Millie's, Ruskin's, and one each from Mr Sanchez and his son. Five glasses. The man laid a serviette ceremoniously over the top. He tucked in the edges. From his pocket he produced a handgun.

'My son Andreas has one sister now. And two brothers. Yes?'

'Er . . . yes.'

'We meet today, eat today. Today we become family. I don't know your fathers, your mothers. But today, you have one more father – is me. Yes?'

'Thank you,' said Sam.

Mr Sanchez brought the butt of the gun down hard on the pile of glasses, once, twice, three times. The crunching of the glass seemed slightly ominous to Sam. He burped, loudly – nobody noticed. His wrists were grabbed and he managed to find his hands in his blazer sleeves. Everyone had linked hands as if for *Auld Lang Syne*, but Mr Sanchez continued, whispering intensely: 'You look after Andreas and he looks after you. You understand me? Many people in this country, so many bad people – not enough friends. So it's good to make the friend. You hold the friend; you *keep* the friend.'

Sam rather liked being hugged and kissed. Millie was grinning and Ruskin was smiling again, as if bullets whipped past his ears every day.

In the Sanchez helicopter later, Sam tried to piece together the fragments of coincidence that had led him on and off trains, up and down escalators, in and out of taxis and finally onto an aircraft that was now zipping over the countryside of Devon. He looked down onto brown fields and friendly green hills. They were all joined up cleanly like waves in the sea. He was flying over a map: there was the motorway, there was the railway. He was seeing double still – partly from concussion, partly from champagne – but he could see the way the land was divided. A settlement there, by the stream – someone had put a yellow crop there by a greeny-brown one, and there were a whole load of cows. All in all, despite the bruises, the day had been rather good:

and it was still only half-past five. He vaguely remembered, in his letter of acceptance to Ribblestrop, that they had to report to the headmaster between four-thirty and six. So he was well on schedule, with new shorts and some very rich food slurping about with burgers, chips and champagne. He was minus a cap and a pound coin, but that had been a very small price to pay really. And he still hadn't cried. In fact, he was giggling.

'Look,' said Ruskin. 'That's the viaduct near the school! There's the train!'

Mr Sanchez was pilot and was yelling into his headset. Andreas Sanchez was trying to navigate – map on his knee, nose pressed to the glass.

'OK, OK,' shouted Mr Sanchez. 'I think we nearly there!'

'Look!' yelled Ruskin.

Millie and Sam looked.

'That's the road from the station, I think. Yes – look, we turn right there, by the garage. Now, can you see that wall? That's our wall, that goes right up to the gatehouse – there's the gatehouse!'

Mr Sanchez came in low, and Sam caught his first glimpse of real Ribblestrop territory. A high stone wall and behind that mountains of spinach-like hedging, with a driveway through.

'Fly up the driveway, fly up the drive!' yelled Ruskin.

Mr Sanchez was enjoying himself as much as the children. The helicopter banked sickeningly and paused in the air. It dipped and it felt they were skimming the ground.

The driveway was long and turned slowly to the right into open parkland. It passed a vast, glimmering lake.

'There's Neptune!' shouted Ruskin. A huge white statue lay reclining on the bank, its feet in water, its noble face staring ahead.

'There's a donkey!' shouted Sam.

And yes, sure enough, a donkey was staring at them, deeply unimpressed by what it saw.

They were past it in a moment and Sam could contain his excitement no longer. He simply screamed the word, 'Yes! Yes!' repeatedly – for there, rising up from neatly-cropped lawns, was the building from the photograph. The sun was low and softened the ramparts by turning honey-coloured stone into gold. The school was a perfect square, half castle, half mansion; it had battlements and a giant set of timber doors above steps, statues and a courtyard with a dramatic fountain. Four towers, one higher than all the rest, rose from each of the building's corners. And, emerging like a spear from the delicate cone that surmounted that tallest tower, a flag fluttering in black and gold. True, the central section of the house was little more than black ash – and one tower was collapsing where the walls buckled – but Sam was able to ignore such blemishes. The school would be rebuilt, and he would help. He saw everything through watering eyes: the school crest stretching out proudly in the wind . . . the lion and the lamb on a cloth of gold.

'My school,' whispered Sam.

Chapter Five

'Headmaster.'

'Yes, Lady Vyner.'

'I think it's time to be frank.'

'Certainly.'

'I think we've wasted enough time. I think it's time we settled our accounts. The debt, Headmaster – your debts to me – are now running at such an intolerable level—'

'Well, in fairness, Lady Vyner—'

'Don't interrupt me!' Lady Vyner snarled, and her spectacles flashed. She licked away the spit from her lips and proceeded. 'You owe me a hundred thousand pounds, give or take. This debt has been run up through massive mismanagement. You still seem determined to call this crackpot venture "your school", though nobody else considers it to be one. You sit here waiting for the term to start – look at you. You wear a headmaster's gown, you carry a register! You should be packing your bags, man! You should be turning any asset you possess into cash. You should be on your bended knee uttering only . . .'

'Tell him, Gran!'

'Apologies! Cash is what we need. Cash is what we want. And we want it now!'

'But have you read my development plan, Lady Vyner?'

Lady Vyner was a thin, wasted-looking woman, with grey skin. She leaned forward now, her bony fists resting clenched on the coffee table. Lord Caspar, her grandson and heir to the estate, sat on a hard chair beside her. His hands gripped an old, flintlock pistol which he was aiming squarely at the headmaster's face. The two Vyners shared curiously rat-like features, with disconcertingly large, pale eyes. They were perched with their guest – Dr Norcross-Webb, headmaster of Ribblestrop – at the top of the south tower, which was the highest of the four. A grubby tea-set sat between them, the weak tea filmed with the dust that constantly dropped from the broken ceiling. The room was a musty junkyard of the Vyners' salvaged antiques, and the sofa and chairs formed a little island in a wild sea of dressers, cabinets and tables, all of which had been piled high with clutter. There were pots, pans, statues, dismembered suits of armour, and broken-framed paintings. There was a chandelier that had pulled down half the plaster, and there were bundles of clothes even the rats had rejected. Presiding over all of this was the loneliest, shabbiest antique of all: Lady Vyner.

Unfortunately for all concerned, Lady Vyner still owned Ribblestrop Towers – on paper at least. The noble seat had been home to her family since William the Conqueror stole it from somebody, and she was clinging to it with nicotine-stained fingernails. This room was all she had left of a home that must, once upon a time, have been quite splendid. Over the centuries, famous people had worked on both grounds and buildings. Two hundred men had dug the lake. Another two hundred had built railway lines to quarry the stone; grottoes, temples and follies had been added. The south tower had been extended upwards, with gargoyles carved under mock-battlements. It had once been a gorgeous place to live, and Lady Vyner had been born there – delivered squealing onto an eiderdown which she still slept under today. She had danced with two prime ministers, including Mr Winston Churchill, who had planned a small part of World War Two in an underground bunker specially built by the war office. Legend had it that the tunnels beneath Ribblestrop connected these bunkers to Whitehall in London. Legend also said that there had once been a train that ferried Cyril Vyner (her husband) and his wartime cronies backwards and forwards, and that plans of national importance had been incubated deep in the vaults.

All that was in the past. Lady Vyner had vowed never to sell her home unless, she said, 'the family honour is at stake'. Fifteen years ago, soon after her husband's death, the family honour had been very much at stake. The estate had been losing money. Lady Vyner had filled her white Rolls Royce with the last few decent antiques she could find, intending to sell them. Drunk on champagne, she'd got lost in Knightsbridge. Doing a three-point turn outside Harrods, her foot slipped off the brake and she reversed the car straight through a plate-glass window. When the police looked hard at her load, they found that many of the antiques had been pilfered during the Second World War – nothing to do with Mr Churchill, but something very much to do with Lord Vyner and his trips across France and Germany. When the police get their teeth into that sort of scandal, they chew you to pieces – so Lady Vyner decided to sell.

'It's bricks and mortar,' she said. 'Nothing stays the same, we'll put it on the market. Let the bidding begin!'

'I'm not sure it will be so easy,' said Mr Cromby, of Cromby and Cromby, London agent to the Vyner family since seventeen-something. 'It won't be easy in the current climate.'

It wasn't easy. Nobody bought it.

People were interested, of course. They came piling up the drive to inspect. But the problem was Lady Vyner herself, who insisted she be allowed to keep rooms in the south tower on a complex lease agreement. Most buyers turned around quickly, especially as the vast majority were developers, who wanted to sub-divide every cupboard into retirement flats. The price went down and down until eventually, five years prior to the present, it was bought by a donkey sanctuary. For a little while, it was successful and many donkeys enjoyed the happiest years of their lives at Ribblestrop. But the donkey-people gathered debts. They tried to diversify, and leased the west wing to St Frideswide's Brethren-of-the-Lost, a tiny band of monks that dedicated themselves to prayer and fasting.

But the coffers were low and cracks were appearing in the courtyards. Bits of tower would occasionally plummet to the ground and the gardens were turning to jungle. The donkey staff didn't get paid; the donkeys themselves got thinner. The monks moved underground and ran out of rent money. Everyone could see that Ribblestrop Towers was ruined, just as Lady Vyner was ruined.

It was at exactly this time that Dr Norcross-Webb came on the scene.

He had cut a controversial figure in the world of education, pioneering the idea that children learned best *away* from the desk. He ran a small school in Suffolk, and it was – it has to be said – getting smaller under his guidance. He had said, at a packed parents' meeting, that children learned best underwater. It was a chance remark based on an experiment he'd conducted on his own son in the family bathroom, but it was used against him and provoked a vote of no confidence. The next morning, his wife left him, taking his son with her, and he was dismissed.

'One cannot plan for triumph or disaster,' he said, at a press conference on Reading station, attended by a single reporter who'd stopped by for a sandwich. Dr Norcross-Webb was on his way to the West Country, to see an elderly aunt, and his plans had been forming all morning. 'In a way,' he said, 'this is what I have always wanted. The opportunity's arrived and I am going to start my own school. Education in this country is about to change.'

News was slow that week in *The Reading Advertiser*, and the journalist managed five hundred words of cheery optimism. *Sacked head says revolutionary new school opening soon!* ran the headline and, though Dr Norcross-Webb had only got as far as designing the blazers, the newspaper gave the impression that the school already had a waiting list. How fortunate, then, that in the Station Hotel opposite, a certain South American business-man was – that very evening – taking delivery of a large stash of banknotes. How extraordinary that he was planning to confuse the X-ray machines of the local airport by wrapping his bundles of fifties in a newspaper he'd taken from the hotel bar. Mr Sanchez saw the headline and the beaming face of the head-master. The very next day, at an exclusive wine bar known as Benders, a deal was done and a suitcase full of money changed hands. Mr Sanchez had decided *not* to smuggle the cash out of the country, but to invest it in concealing his recently-injured son.

'To get to me, they take him. You see? Andreas, show this man.'

Dr Norcross-Webb peered sympathetically at the boy's foot, swathed in bandages.

'You see what they do? To a child, uh? *To a child!* Start your school, Headmaster. Keep Andreas safe for me.'

'Now?' said the doctor. 'Right away?'

'His mother is dead.' The man had tears in his eyes. 'The shock, you understand? It was all too much, and now I want him *safe!*'

'I'm actually looking for premises at the moment. We've nar-rowed it down, but—'

'Look hard, Doctor. Look fast. You need a down-payment, yes? How much?'

Dr Norcross-Webb visited Ribblestrop Towers on Tuesday

morning. He put in his offer just before lunch and paid cash half an hour later. A one-year lease, renewable. Ribblestrop Towers, with its guest in the south tower, was his.

'There are new pupils on their way, Lady Vyner – they're all listed in that document. The future is looking good and the money will be flooding in very soon.'

Little Caspar pulled the flint of his pistol back on its wheel. 'If this was loaded,' he whispered, 'I could blind you.'

'Hush, darling. Let the man do the one thing he's good at: let him talk.'

'We have a new PE teacher,' he said. He was trying to smile rather than flinch, acutely aware of the child leaning towards him and the dead, fish-like eyes of his landlady. He watched as Lady Vyner picked up the document and put her long grey nose over it. 'Captain Routon's ex-army,' he continued. 'He does PE – and a bit of building . . . he's the one who helped me build the science lab. And Professor Worthington – page two – she's to be our Scientist in Residence, starts in a day or two. Henry's back – that's the boy who broke the fountain. And the exciting news is we've struck a deal with an orphanage in the Himalayas, where I used to go climbing. I'm expecting a number of customers from there.'

'Orphans again? Like the little boy you lost?'

'Well, Tomaz wasn't technically an orphan, and I'm ninety-nine per cent certain he went home to an uncle. The boys arriving today are escaping lives of poverty and misery. You see, a school is a living thing: it grows from a seed. The seed has to be watered, and—'

'Throw him out, Gran! Let me call Crippen!'

'Co-education,' said Lady Vyner. She had balanced a thick pair of spectacles on her nose and had found a paragraph on the third page. 'Wait a moment, Caspar, this is interesting. I was always under the impression that this was a *boys'* school – that's

40

what's in the lease, of course. Which expires, very soon, you know.'

'Only the one girl at the moment, sadly, but a very interesting character.'

'Psychopath or arsonist?'

'I won't deny she's had a few difficulties. But, I like to think my school offers every child a new start. We take the children other schools reject—'

'How attractive you make it sound.'

'We take the children some schools give up on.'

'You take the rubbish the good schools discard. And it sounds like you're now mixing it up with the detritus of the Third World. These are the folk you want my grandson to meet as your miserable seed . . . uncoils. You burn down half my home; you lose a boy – whose body might be buried out in the grounds for all we know – and you bribe the police to stay out of jail— What the devil's that noise?'

'Lady Vyner, those are serious allegations—'

'Crippen! What is that noise?'

The air all around the tower was filled by a hard, metallic throbbing. It seemed to hammer on the roof and, sure enough, a brick-sized lump of plaster crashed from above, smashing an ugly chord from the piano it struck. The headmaster ran to the window and heaved it open. 'It's a helicopter!' he cried. 'It must be . . . Yes! It's the Sanchez helicopter!'

'Crippen!' shouted Lady Vyner again, and her elderly servant who was snoozing outside was jerked awake. 'That thing is not landing in my garden! I never gave permission for helicopters!'

'He's coming down! Look at that, he's circling – he's got . . . Bless my soul! One, two, three . . . they're here!'

The headmaster leaned out and waved frantically. Four boys he could count – they'd spotted him and were waving back, cheerfully. The craft was descending expertly, its tail upraised like a scorpion. You could see the grass shivering in the down-draught as Mr Sanchez selected his spot.

'Perfect landing! What a pilot!'

The noise was deafening.

'Look here, Headmaster. Listen to me!' Lady Vyner pulled at the man's gown, but Dr Norcross-Webb couldn't hear her. Four children scuttled from helicopter to steps, and he heaved himself back into the room, tears in his eyes.

'You must excuse me,' he said. 'I must attend to my students.'

'Listen to me, Doctor!' She stood in the doorway, her fists clenched into tight little balls.

Caspar had the pistol ready, and the servant was in the door-way, covering his ears.

'Listen!' shrieked the old lady. 'Your school is a failure because *you* are a failure. Give it up, while there's dignity!'

'Please, Lady Vyner, I have to go . . .'

'The school was a mistake from first to last . . . Listen to me! Your children are noisy, without respect! Don't you push Caspar, don't you dare! Come back here!'

But Dr Norcross-Webb was leaping, dizzying himself down the south tower's spiral staircase, until he emerged, staggering, into the late sunshine. Four children stood on the terrace, their hair flowing in the gale from the helicopter as it rose again. They looked around them, taking in the grandeur of the park-land, the house, the dream that was Ribblestrop. And as they stared – what was that, coming into view? A car – an expensive car, whistling down the drive. The doctor blinked hard and stared again: there were *two* cars, shiny and purposeful.

'Boys!' he said. 'Andreas Sanchez! Jacob Ruskin! Welcome back, how good to see you!'

Sanchez came forward, disguising his limp as best he could, for a firm handshake.

'I know you,' said the headmaster, looking at Millie. 'I know you from a newspaper cutting . . .'

'Millie Roads,' said Millie.

'Millie Roads – delighted. And there was me saying "boys" when now at last I can say "boys and girls", "girls and boys", as I have dreamed of doing!'

Millie stared hard. Dr Norcross-Webb failed to notice. He moved to the frailest member of the party.

'And you must be Sam – am I right?' The headmaster crouched in front of Sam, levelling their eyeline. 'I know I am, your parents were kind enough to send a photograph along with your swimming certificate. Sam Arthur Tack . . .' The child's hand appeared from his blazer sleeve and clasped the headmaster's. 'We're building a dream here, Sam. Are you a dreamer, or a builder? You need to be both: a school you'll never want to leave. A home! A nation-state! Now how did you manage to come down together? What planning, what foresight! Cool drinks inside, then we'll be meeting for supper. Will you allow me just to . . . to welcome the other new arrivals? – this is such perfect timing!'

The first of the two cars had swung up to the steps. Every door opened and bodies seemed to fall out onto the gravel. But no, the bodies were up onto their feet in no time and a buzz and a birdsong filled the air around them. Everyone stood counting – eleven, twelve, thirteen – one child had skipped round the back, maybe it was twelve in total. Their black-and-gold uniforms were immaculate and they were putting on caps and lining up for inspection: they'd even formed up in order of height, the oldest being a skinny eleven or twelve, the youngest being no more than six. Under the caps dark, anxious eyes faced front and each had a satchel over their left shoulder.

'My orphans . . .' whispered the doctor. 'As promised . . . as prayed for and promised.'

The second car was now unloading: a giant of a boy, elbowing his way out of a Mercedes that suddenly seemed toy-like as it rocked under his weight. Hairy legs, hairy wrists, a satchel like a tiny purse in his fist and a cap so dainty it might have been a skullcap.

'Henry, my dear boy.' The headmaster gripped the hand of the giant. 'Oh, you're exactly punctual . . . Welcome, all of you. Cold drinks in the, er . . . conservatory. I'll help you with your things. Oh, the joys ahead – the joy of an Autumn Term here at—'

There was a sudden moan.

'Henry?'

It was a mixture of alarm and pain. The helicopter had gone. There was silence, broken only by birdsong. But Henry had seen something: he was looking upwards, his face creased in horror.

'Henry, please – what's wrong?' The headmaster stepped towards him, then stopped. He turned and followed the boy's gaze.

Henry had seen what nobody else had noticed: the spectral form of Lady Vyner leaning out of the highest tower window, tea tray in hand. She dropped one side and let the tea service slide gently into space: cups, saucers and spoons seemed to hang in the air. Then it all accelerated cartoon-style: doilies were shed, sugar-lumps scattered. *Smack!* The tea service cracked into the centre of the terrace, exploding china with a sickening crash. The shrapnel flew and everyone leaped backwards, hands to their heads, eyes scanning upwards for the next assault. Little Caspar was throwing scones, one after the other. Sanchez took one on the shoulder. Crumbs burst on a car roof.

It was the headmaster who thought first: 'Into the house, quickly!' he cried. A milk jug exploded at his feet. A biscuit glanced off his arm.

'Pay me my money!' wailed a voice.

Children scattered; an orphan screamed. Sanchez had cat-like reflexes: he grabbed Millie and pinned her behind him with one arm, then he dragged her through the doors of the school building. The other children made a wide run, avoiding the centre of the terrace. Only Ruskin and Sam seemed stuck, and it was Ruskin who made up his mind. Thinking only of his friend, he grabbed Sam by the shoulders and propelled him forwards. 'Move!' he was yelling. 'Move, Sam!'

Ruskin was a loyal, courageous boy and in that split second knew he had to put his friend's life first. He could erase the horrors of spilt tea and lost shorts: he would save Sam whatever the cost.

Sadly, the teapot was on its way: a good old-fashioned heavyweight, from the potteries of Staffordshire. Ruskin drove Sam forwards straight into its path and the teapot landed squarely on the top of the boy's uncapped head.

He went limp in Ruskin's hands.

Ruskin lowered him to the ground, horror-struck. Blood oozed and formed a puddle. The puddle became a pool. Sam was smiling but his eyes were closed.

Chapter Six

'He'll be fine with me! Give us a hand there, lay him out – off the trolley, that's right. Light as a feather, isn't he? Put him on the cooker, I'll clear some space. Out cold. Let's hope it's a flesh wound. Flying teapots and whatnot, oh my word! Now then, let the dog see the rabbit . . . Fetch me some nail scissors, would you, girlie?'

Millie delved in a basket nearby. 'Nothing's broken,' she said. 'I felt all over his head. And his windpipe isn't crushed, I did his airway.'

'Did you, miss? That's good.'

'We had to do all that sort of stuff at my old school. People got beaten up every day.'

Ruskin had gone, too traumatised to be any use. Millie and Sanchez had rushed Sam by tea-trolley to the temporary hospital.

It was actually a temporary kitchen. Once inside the walls of the school – which was an exact, four-turreted square – Millie had been surprised at the extent of the fire damage. Beyond a single corridor, you came into the courtyard and . . . there was nothing really there except ruin. It had once been a dining hall, a library and a chapel: it was now open to the stars but for a series of roped tarpaulins. There was the stink of damp fire-damage still and, though the timbers had been stacked and the fallen stone organised into various piles, the space was still a chaotic mess of ropes, crates, pallets, and trenches. There were ladders and bits of scaffolding, a couple of cement mixers – and here, behind a wall of metal racking, a temporary kitchen.

There was a cooker connected by a hosepipe to a large bottle of gas. Old wooden lockers held the rather battered pots and pans, and a bench on two trestles was littered with onion skins. A couple of desk-lamps had been strung up overhead, the cables running over the mud to a long extension lead looping from a high window. Millie and Sanchez laid Sam on the bench, sweeping the rubbish to the floor. The chef, or the nurse, was a slim, powerful man of six-foot four and he'd been kneading pastry when they hauled the trolley in. His cook's hat made him seem massive, as did his enormous Wellington boots. He wore an apron so splattered with mud and food, you couldn't see much cloth. It was drawn in around his middle by a carpenter's tool-belt, in which sat a couple of meat knives, an adjustable spanner and a pair of pliers. He'd rolled his sleeves up and his forearms were covered in tattoos.

This was Captain Routon and he was good in a crisis. 'You've stopped the flow, miss, that's for sure – we've got a nice little clot forming there. Let's see if we can stitch him . . . give me the scissors. Boil up some water between you and let's get this blazer off. I need to prop him up.'

'Are you a doctor?' asked Millie.

'In a manner of speaking. I've had to deal with a lot worse than this, that's for sure. I've had to hold men's brains in before now: this won't be hard.'

'Will he be OK?' said Sanchez. He had covered Sam with his own blazer and his hand still held the unconscious boy's fingers.

'The skull can take a battering and it's a clean wound, far as I can see . . .'

Sam's hair started to fly from his head as the big man worked away with nail scissors. 'That woman – my word, she's a menace. I've been here a month and I warned him, this is no place for kiddies with that sort of maniac—'

'I'll do that if you want,' said Millie. 'I did promise him a hair cut.'

'If you would I'd be grateful, and I can just throw the pastry . . . you'll find my razor in the bathroom round the corner. What's your name, son?'

'Andreas Sanchez, sir.'

'Ah, you're the Sanchez boy, are you? Right, find a blanket and ask Dr N how many for supper. We've got a meat pie but I don't know how far I can stretch it. Oh, and tell him that the ramble's on for tomorrow . . . That's it, my dear, shave it round. We need a good inch, quick as you can – that'll be sore, that will. Friend of mine did that for me in a much more private place, I can tell you – bullet from a Legionnaire, North Africa. I felt every cut.'

Sam remained unconscious. It was just as well, as there was no anaesthetic and a dry shave is a painful experience. Millie snipped, then rasped away at the scalp: the wound was actually quite small and the skull was undoubtedly intact. A number of people had felt for fractures, including the headmaster himself. He had explained to the assembled students (gathered safely in the hallway) that the sphere, i.e. the skull, was indeed the strongest structure known to man, which was why the brain was kept there. 'Stronger than the ribcage,' he said, 'but of course that has to contract, which the adult skull never has to do. Interestingly, the most vulnerable part of the human anatomy is also the most precious. Gather round, have a look – can you see the blood congealing?' He sat Sam upright and pointed with a pencil. The orphans seemed particularly interested and were soon poking Sam with enthusiasm, twittering and laughing. It was Sanchez who took charge at this point, foreseeing a long lecture. He and Millie left Henry and the orphans listening politely to the headmaster, who had moved on to an explanation of how the human brain is actually afloat. They had carried and wheeled Sam down some steps, into the kitchen by themselves.

'Now we can clean the wound,' said Captain Routon. 'Alcohol's right here, best thing you can use . . . paper towel by the side there, not ideal, so soak it well.'

Millie was quite surprised how easy it all was. Sam might as well have been a football or a cushion. She held him by the ears and the big man rubbed neat rum into the skin and then swished briskly in and out with the needle. It went in so smoothly, knotting the flesh, and soon he pulled the edges together like a pair of smiling lips. The blood was cleaned away and there was a nice little zip spreading five centimetres over the child's cranium – and he had a new haircut too, which Millie vowed to finish as soon as Sam was awake.

'He's less like a geek already,' she said. 'He's like a little monk.'

'Will you put it in the post?' mumbled Sam.

Captain Routon smiled. 'He'll be fine. Bit of a headache, so it'll be best if someone's by when he comes round. Now, what I suggest—'

'Twenty-one for supper, please sir,' said Sanchez, under a pile of blankets.

'Twenty-two, with Sam. Right . . .' He checked the boy's pulse and lifted him into Millie's arms. 'He'll be right as rain. Now wrap that round him and get him into bed. I'm going to talk to that woman, she wants taking away. We could have lost eyes, we could have had arteries cut. I've seen it! Friend of mine was in Londonderry when they let off a nail bomb – there's some wounds you can't stitch up.' He was back at the pastry, crimping merrily with a fork.

'Are you a teacher or a chef?' said Millie. She'd managed to pass the sleeping Sam over to Sanchez, who was wrapping him as best he could on the trolley.

'Oh, bit o' this, bit o' that. Jack of all trades, master of none – I lend a hand where a hand is needed. I did most of the Science Tower with the headmaster.'

'I'm Millie.'

'When we've got more time I'll tell you about the shrapnel I saw in Cyprus.'

'What are you teaching us?' said Millie.

'Anything you want,' said Captain Routon. 'First thing tomorrow, Practical Geography. Walking boots compulsory.'

'I don't have any,' said Millie.

'Nor me,' said Sanchez. 'I didn't know.'

'School shoes then,' said the Captain. 'Rule one, use what's available. Now, listen, if the pain is too much, give me a call – we can knock him out somehow.'

'Sanchez,' said Millie, as they pushed the trolley down one of Ribblestrop's long corridors. 'Is this really a school?'

'Yes,' said Sanchez.

They had carried Sam out of the kitchen-cum-courtyard, up another set of steps made of fruit boxes. A plastic sheet concealed a doorway, where the stone was scorched black. Someone had hung some bulbs on a long, looping wire. It was a bright evening still, but no light got in here, because the windows were boarded over. The bulbs lit the way up a staircase.

'It's a ruin,' said Millie. 'It stinks.'

'Yes. We had a fire. A boy called Miles tried to kill everyone.'

'Can you carry Sam? I'm going to drop him.'

Sanchez took Sam again and they made their way to another door.

'This can't be safe,' muttered Millie. 'Look at it, it's half underwater! They shouldn't allow kids here.'

'Why not?' Sanchez looked baffled. 'We make things better all the time. Me and Henry put the tarpaulins up, last term. This is the west tower; upstairs is our bedroom. It's fine.'

A winding staircase led upwards.

'What about this headmaster?' said Millie.

'What do you mean?'

'He's insane, isn't he?'

'Millie, you've got it wrong – of course he's not insane.'

'He was showing everyone Sam's head! The kid was bleeding to death and he's doing a lecture on . . . anatomy!'

'Yes, he takes the opportunity. He says that "Learning is about opportunities for experience", that's what he does. I think he's good.'

Millie laughed. 'I've just sewn up a boy's head, in the school's so-called kitchen. While I'm doing that, the teacher in charge of first-aid and Geography bakes a pie. Sam could have been killed.'

'But he's fine. Open the door, please.'

'Is it a swindle? He takes money from the government, spends nothing on our education, and walks off with millions. You must have people like that in Colombia.'

Sanchez stopped. He adjusted Sam into a more comfortable position, hoisting him higher over his shoulder. 'All I can say, Millie, is that I was here last term, and – yes, we had problems – but this is a good place.'

'Well, it's better than prison,' said Millie. 'That's where I thought I was going.'

They were going through a low doorway now, which gave onto another, tighter spiral of steps. Sam gave a low whimper and struggled in his blanket. 'I like it,' said Sanchez, after some time. 'In Colombia, I was never at school.'

'Why not?'

'I had one teacher only, OK? Teaching me everything. Here it's the same: one teacher and he teaches everything, but there's nice people. And now there's more of us and I think we have more teachers. It's normal for me, so – yes, I think it's a good school. And you should stop running it down.'

'Where are we actually going?'

'The dormitory.'

'Whose dormitory? Where do I sleep?'

'Millie, just open the door.'

Chapter Seven

'Why don't you damn well knock?' said a voice.

'Who are you?' asked Millie.

Caspar Vyner was sitting on a bed, a snarl of dislike twisting his face.

Sanchez pushed past Millie. Sam was beginning to struggle and Sanchez could feel his weight. 'Hello, Caspie,' he said, as he moved into the bedroom. 'You shouldn't be in here, man. This is our room.'

'You're the one that's trespassing. I own this house, remember? I was looking for your gun – is it true you have one?'

They were high in the tower. The room was timber-panelled with five elegant windows. The park spread out around them, glorious in the sunset. Millie hadn't realised how high they'd climbed. Five beds were set out like the spokes of a wheel, with five little lockers, and five little rugs on the stone flagstones.

'Another thing, Sanchez. I've told you before – don't call me *Caspie*.' He stood and moved to the wall. His voice was reedy with irritation.

Sanchez laid Sam gently down on the nearest bed.

'Hang on a minute!' said Caspar. His eyes went from Sam, to Millie. Back to Sam, then back to Millie. His nose lifted, as if he was trying to catch her scent. 'Oh no. You're the girl!' he shouted.

'What on earth is a girl doing here? And in the boys' room, that's so not allowed!'

Millie looked coolly at the child, her eyes narrowing with dislike. Caspar had a nasal voice; he was skinny, with bad skin, and his tufty hair didn't seem to grow evenly. His school uniform was immaculate, but he had a wizened look, not unlike a little old man.

'That's my bed!' said Caspar, looking at Sam again. 'Move him to another one, Sanchez, I don't want a dirty oik dying on my bed. Is that the one we hit? Full-on strike with a teapot! That was me!'

'Caspar, you don't even sleep here.'

'I can sleep wherever I want. If I want that bed, it's mine. And, look – answer me. What's a girl doing up here? That is so against the rules – and you let her come in! You must be the weirdo-girl that the government's paying for. My granny knows all about you!'

'Who *is* this?' said Millie, moving towards him.

'Caspar Vyner,' said Sanchez.

'*Lord* Vyner, actually,' said the boy. 'I inherit this place in eight years, and if you know what's good for you, you'll damn well remember it.' He stood up and brought his right hand from behind his back. He had the flintlock pistol still, and the boy took great delight in cocking it, and aiming with two hands straight at Millie's face. Millie stood her ground. 'How would you like to lose an eye? You will if you don't get out.'

'Caspar!' barked Sanchez. 'You don't *do* that!'

'Look at her, she's a scaredy!' laughed Caspar, stepping forward. 'A little sissy girl – now why don't you turn around and beat it!'

Millie stared at the pistol and at Caspar's twisted face. Her adrenaline had been rising steadily for the last ten seconds and she knew enough about first encounters to know they were important. Moving fast, she slapped the gun to the side and

54

punched Caspar hard, full in the face. He went backwards, tripping over the bed and onto the floor. Millie followed, kicking,
though the boy's arms were protecting his head so she didn't
connect. She dropped to her knees instead, all her weight on his
stomach. The pistol went skittering across the floor, and Caspar
was gasping and twisting. Millie had him now, though. She
went for his hair, but there wasn't enough to hold on to. As the
boy's head came up, she had to content herself with slamming it
back onto the flagstones with her open palm.

Sanchez was yelling and Caspar had found the air from
somewhere for a long, high-pitched howl.

'Little swine!' hissed Millie. She grabbed the boy's tie and
looped it once round his bare throat, jerking it tight. He was half
on his side, scrabbling to protect himself. Sanchez was between
them, levering her backwards, but she still managed a hard
punch on the child's ear. She was being dragged off now, and all
she could do was kick at the backside that was curling away
from her. Caspar got to his feet, his screams coming in furious
panting sobs.

'You cow!' he whispered. 'You rotten, damn . . .'

He stumbled from the room, clutching his head. He bashed
into the door and nearly fell again. Millie went to kick him once
more, but Sanchez had her from behind and was dragging her
backwards. 'Let him go!' he was shouting. 'It isn't worth it,
Millie, it's just not—'

'Get off me, Sanchez!' hissed Millie. Her voice was trembling.
'Nobody asked you! Get your hands off!' She twisted out of his
grip, and stood ready, fists clenched.

'I'm sorry, but it makes things worse! If he tells his granny, the
headmaster has problems—'

'I'll decide if he's worth it! He was going to shoot me in the
face!'

'It's an antique, he's always playing around with stuff like
that.'

The two children were staring at each other, Caspar long gone. Millie was trembling, but the joy of triumph was taking over. She had forgotten how invigorating a good fight could be, and she stood there drunk and dangerous.

'Honestly,' said Sanchez, trying to calm her. 'What he says is true. His grandmother owns the place – his parents are dead. She wants to close the school anyway, so you just give her more reasons to make trouble.'

'He got just what he deserved. I don't let anyone mess me around, Sanchez. Nobody.'

'Well, we spent all last term trying to ignore him,' said Sanchez. 'He does a few lessons with us – he's not worth worrying about. We don't fight him.'

'Sanchez, I don't need anyone telling me what I can and can't do.'

'Mum?' said a quiet voice. It was Sam.

'I don't want to tell you what to do,' said Sanchez, patiently. 'I don't want you or him getting hurt, and . . . what are you doing?'

'I'm having a cigarette.'

Millie had produced a slightly-crushed packet. She fiddled with the contents, one eye on Sanchez still.

'You shouldn't smoke. Let's just look after Sam.'

'Look,' said Millie. 'He's left his little gun.'

'Mum? Dad?' moaned Sam. Sanchez moved quickly to the boy's bedside. He sat beside him, and drew the blanket up to the child's chin.

'Sanchez,' said Millie, 'how am I supposed to sleep in a boys' dormitory?'

'I don't know. Ask the headmaster.'

'It's illegal for one thing. Who sleeps here, apart from you?'

'Look at him, man,' said Sanchez. 'He's yellow.' Sam's eyes were wide open. He was staring at the ceiling, licking his lips. 'Sam? Are you awake?'

'Where am I?' whispered Sam.

'You're at school, OK?' said Sanchez. 'You had an accident. Hey, Millie: he's hot. We need water or something. Do you want to go downstairs and get the captain?'

Millie sat down heavily on the nearest bed. She had a cigarette between her lips, but the lighter had disappeared. 'I'm not a nurse,' she said. 'The cook said he'd be fine – I'd leave him alone if I were you.' She put her feet up on the bed and found what she was looking for. From her breast pocket she extracted a thick silver lighter and lit up expertly. Lying back on the pillow, she inhaled and blew a smoke ring.

'Everything's . . . watery,' whispered Sam. 'I can't see properly, I don't . . .'

'*Millie!*' said Sanchez. He was torn between his patient and the strange, dangerous girl. He wiped Sam's forehead under the bandage, but his attention was caught by another plume of smoke. Then he saw the cigarette lighter. Millie had put it on the little chest of drawers next to the bed. 'That's my father's,' he said.

'What is?'

'That lighter.'

'Yes, he gave it to me.'

'He *gave* it to you? That's the one my mother had made for him.'

'Do you want a cigarette?'

'No, I don't. And I told you, we don't do this here.'

Millie blew a smoke ring. 'You don't do much, do you, Sanchez?'

'When did he give you his cigarette lighter? How come I didn't see?'

'Some time at the wine bar. You must have been kissing goodbye to your bodyguards.'

'I don't believe you. You're very insulting, and I don't think—'

'You're calling me a liar?'

Sanchez stood up and moved towards Millie. Sam moaned again, but he ignored it. 'I'm asking you if you stole my father's lighter. My mother gave him that; I think it's unlikely he gave it to you.'

'I think Sam needs you, Sanchez.'

'Yes or no, did you steal it?'

'Look at him – he's trying to get his bandage off.'

Sanchez turned and saw that it was true. Sam was sitting up now, in panic. His hands were fluttering around the dressing on his head. 'Where's Mum?' he said. His eyes were focusing now and he looked in terror from Sanchez to Millie.

'Not here,' said Millie. 'You're all alone.'

'Where am I?' said Sam. 'I want my dad!'

'Memory loss,' said Millie. 'He should be in hospital, he's going to die on us.'

'We need *help*,' said Sanchez. 'Go and get the headmaster.'

Millie came forward and leaned over the injured boy. 'You got hit,' she said, slowly and loudly. 'You got your skull cracked, all on your first day.'

Sam yelped, his right hand clutching his head.

Millie put the cigarette between her lips and forced him down. 'Don't touch your bandages, you twit!'

'Hey, be gentle! You're breathing smoke on him, Millie, leave him alone!'

Sanchez could stand it no more. He moved in swiftly and snatched Millie's wrists, yanking them away from Sam. Then he swung her away from the bed, towards the door. 'Go and get the headmaster,' he said.

'Sanchez, I told you not to touch me – get your hands off!'

'We need help, and you need to leave him alone . . .'

'Get off me, Sanchez, I'm warning you!'

Her hands were behind her back, her arms twisted. She could feel Sanchez's strength, and her instinct took over. She tried to pull away, but Sanchez was in control. 'I don't want you in here,'

58

said Sanchez. He was moving her to the door. 'He's sick, Millie! Please!'

Millie bent forwards slightly, aware that Sanchez was close behind her. She clamped the cigarette firmly in her lips, and smashed her head backwards, hoping to crunch it into Sanchez's face. The next moment, she stamped with her right foot, aiming at the boy's ankle. Sanchez was fast, though, and he just avoided both blows. Now she was twisting, and she knew he couldn't hold her for long. He put his arms right round her, but Millie was all elbows and kicking feet and in a second she had one arm free. She grabbed the cigarette from her own lips and plunged it forward. Sanchez ducked clear, so she pushed it into his shoulder, burning his shirt. He had to leap back, she'd caught the skin and he was gasping. He was better than she'd thought, though: he knew to come in under her arm, and she was in a headlock suddenly, bent backwards and round. Then she was on the floor, the cigarette gone. She thrashed with her legs and got one good, heavy kick in somewhere: then she was pinned down hard, both arms wrenched up again behind her back. Sam was wailing and Sanchez was panting furiously; Millie could hardly breathe. She could hear Sanchez at her ear, muttering in Spanish. Then his arms were under her again, and she was lifted and steered towards the door. She bent and writhed, but his hands had her wrists, folding her over. She tried to spin round but Sanchez pushed hard and her head cracked into the open door: a white light dazed her. She kicked out, but was thrown.

Suddenly it was all over: she was in the passageway. The door slammed shut and a bolt clicked into place. She sat down heavily on the floor, and waited for the world to stop spinning.

'Damn,' she said. Her nose was bleeding.

Chapter Eight

Downstairs, the headmaster was making a speech. He'd chosen the makeshift kitchen area in the central courtyard, as he considered it the heart of the school. This is where the children would eat, under the tarpaulins and the ruined roof. This is where the building would rise, and the grandeur of hall, chapel and library would all be restored.

He wanted the children to smell the history.

In the olden days, fine tapestries had covered these walls. Whole pigs had been roasted in a giant fireplace, and minstrels had piped and tooted in a gallery. According to history books, chandeliers with a thousand lights had cast their glitter over rows of elegant lords, ladies, dukes and duchesses – Henry the Something had visited, or promised to visit. Now, alas, it was mainly ash and soot.

It was eight o'clock, and the glorious sunlight had made way for a deep, purple night-time. A handful of stars were out already.

Candles stood in bottles and jars. The children perched where they could: there were a few plastic picnic stools, some chairs from a classroom and a deckchair. Three orphans balanced on a scaffolding plank, and two on the top of a stepladder. Dr Norcross-Webb, in Wellington boots and the long black gown of authority, stood on a pile of wooden pallets. He raised his hand for silence. The children were warm, full and happy.

'A vote of thanks, first of all, to our chef. Captain Routon: thank you.'

There was loud applause. The captain waved his spatula and took a bow.

'Please look at the lists on the notice board, as washing-up rotas start tonight. Note also who is on cooking duty tomorrow. Here at Ribblestrop, all burdens are shared. Every chore is a learning opportunity and tomorrow night I will be teaching the art of the vegetarian lasagne. Be aware, please, that we have an early start – lessons begin first thing, with Practical Geography. Let's hope for a dry day as you will be exploring and charting the grounds with our expedition leader. Our chef will transform himself and lead you on a ramble.'

The headmaster turned over his notes and moved nearer to a candle.

'Science lessons, yes . . . Science lessons will be underway in the very near future. We await the arrival of two new teachers, one of whom has already made her name in learned journals around the world. Professor Worthington is to be in charge of Science; she is currently gathering electrical equipment in Scandinavia and hopes to be with us directly.'

Captain Routon raised a finger. 'Might be worth mentioning the Brethren, sir.'

'Yes, indeed: the Brethren. What about them?'

'The vow, sir.'

'Good thinking. Children! We are privileged in having among us a small group of extremely devout monks, and they live in what was the old chapel and cloister, half a mile from here.'

'Underground, actually, sir. They moved.'

'I thought . . . Oh. Very well, it makes no odds. The thing to remember is that if you do see them, don't get scared. A "Good morning" will suffice, though please do not press them for a response as they have undertaken a vow of silence. I won't mention the cellars and tunnels, because they are strictly out of bounds, and locked – we did lock them, didn't we, Routon? . . . Can't read my own writing here.'

'The laboratory, sir?'

'I wonder if I should mention that? Yes, I think you ought to know. Every old house has its history, children, so you must understand that Lady Vyner has had various tenants, apart from our good selves. That includes, well . . . how would you describe those particular tenants, Routon?'

'It's out of bounds, sir – that's all I'd say.'

'Oh yes, absolutely, but I'm thinking it might be worth *alerting* the children to their presence. It's what we call a *research facility*, dating back to, ooh . . . Second World War and earlier. They ignored my letters, I'm afraid – I was hoping to fix up a tour, but they like to keep themselves to themselves. It's none of our business why, and the last thing we want is aimless wandering or exploring. In fact our new deputy has ordered some *no entry* signs, which are up in my room. And that, very neatly, brings me to the last item: Miss Hazlitt, who is actually on her way even now. I'm a little surprised she's not here already, some delay most likely. I ought to say just a few words about Miss Hazlitt because we are very lucky indeed to have her. She's going to be a very important member of this community and brings with her a wealth of experience and new ideas. She *had* retired, but agreed, after the events of last term—'

'Do you think it's time for rum-ration, sir? While you're talking?'

'Rum-ration? Oh, yes . . .'

One boy was snoozing – a high-pitched snore buzzed from a roll of plastic. And most of the orphans had glazed eyes.

'Just the one peg, sir?'

'No more than one. I should just say, boys, that rum is a tradition at the finest schools, and as the heating system here is . . .

primitive, well – a tot of rum keeps out the chill. Captain Scott served it on his way south, and it certainly kept me going in the Himalayas even after we lost the tents. Where was I? . . . Miss Hazlitt, yes. *On her way.* So! We'll sing the school song, which means I am required to teach it to you. I wrote it myself, last night. It is a *work in progress*, so to speak – so . . . stand up, everybody!'

The headmaster reached into the gloom by his feet and picked up an accordion. Its leather straps were awkward, and the stage he stood upon rocked a little if he moved too quickly.

'Anjoli . . . is that your name?'

One of the orphans smiled and jumped to his feet, shaking himself awake. Spiky hair refused to sit still under his cap. He smoothed his tie and stood rigidly to attention.

'Could you dish out that pile of papers, Anjoli? Watch out for the mud, it's a bit slippy. Now, the tune may be familiar . . . You'll soon pick it up. The only problem . . .' The headmaster tried to extend the accordion bellows; they groaned open lopsidedly. A rather mournful note blurted over the children. The sleeping orphan was laid on the oven; everybody else stood up straight. 'Can you sing that? Together . . .?'

It was surprising how loud fourteen voices could be when they all pitched in as one. They all hit roughly the same note, though Henry was a very deep bass in comparison to some of the shrill eight-year-olds. The headmaster was encouraged.

'First line, after me . . . Don't be shy! Ready?
Ribblestrop, Ribblestrop, precious unto me;
This is what I dream about and where I want to be.

'The words may change, but this is the first draft. One, two . . .'

The accordion bleated again and the choir sang, peering at the song-sheets, which were faint in the gloom. Perhaps the tune was indeed familiar? Whatever the case, the couplet was roared as if at a football match; it was more of a chant than a song.

'Very good!' shouted the headmaster. 'Stop! Stop. Now: there's only two more lines at present. More to come, so let's try what we have . . . Listen please:

Early in the morning, finally at night,
Ribblestrop, I'll die for thee, carrying the light.

'Or possibly, *fighting the good fight*, we'll see which one fits best. Can we try it together – ready?'

Before he had finished, someone tried to sing. There was laughter, and a small orphan clutched both hands over his mouth and danced with delight. He was pulled back by the oldest. The headmaster whined out the note again and the choir piled into the last two lines. Without being asked, they swung back to the start and sang it through again.

'My word, that really is excellent. No more verses yet, so feel free to submit ideas. Shall we just try the chorus? Captain, we may need a little more rum, I see some children have finished – we'll need a tot for the toast. You must wait for the toast, children. After three. One, two . . . sorry.' The accordion was collapsing again and the headmaster had to hoist it up with his knee. It gave an injured gurgle, then its one, plaintive note. 'Ready? Three times through. One and two and one-two-three!'

Three times came and went: the song had a momentum of its own, and by the time Captain Routon had refilled the glasses, the verse had been sung a full fifteen times, the word 'Ribblestrop' howled like a war-cry.

'Oh my dears,' said the headmaster. He had tears in his eyes. The pallets had toppled him into the mud, and he stood ankle-deep. 'Sing like that,' he said, 'and the world is ours. I have been waiting so long for this day. We stand together as a school – enough at last for a football team! Enough to build a dream.'

It was almost dark. Candlelight was reflected in every child's eye.

'This is our first evening,' said the headmaster. He spoke quietly now, because the children had come closer. 'So we will drink to our school and to our hopes. Just a small sip, children: alcohol is a dangerous, addictive drug, but it will help us mark this important moment. Nelson dished it out at sea and it kept spirits high in the trenches.'

They raised their glasses, and pursed their lips.

'Never look at our school and say, "Why?" Look to your dreams, and say, "Why not?" To Ribblestrop Towers!'

'Ribblestrop Towers,' said the children.

'We are a family now. A band of brothers. Look around you and look up.'

Every head looked up.

'Can you see through the plastic sheeting? Can you see through to the stars?'

'Big,' said an orphan, softly.

'Can we raise this roof again and make our school strong?'

'Yes!' again rippled through the children. A gust of wind lifted one of the tarpaulins, exposing a whole shovelful of peppery white constellations.

'Then let us drink to hope and vision . . . You are the arrows, children. A teacher simply holds the bow. How high will you soar? Ruskin, what's the matter, boy?'

Ruskin had let out a mournful sob and was sitting on a stool, his head in his hands.

'Sam, sir. I'm just thinking how he's missing this.'

'He's in capable hands, lad, there's no need to worry . . .'

'It's his first day, though. He's missed the song.'

'We'll go to him. Where's Sanchez? Ah, perfectly timed, right on cue!'

Sanchez had appeared through one of the tarpaulins, a relieved smile lighting up his face.

'Sam's better, sir, so much better! He was calling out for his father . . .'

'And Millie's nursing him, presumably? Pulling together, you see . . .'

'No, sir – he was calling for his father, but then he heard the singing. Didn't she come down here?'

'He heard the song, Ruskin, and was revived!'

'Yes, but I told him to rest, sir.'

'It's the restorative power of music, boys. We will go to him and we will embrace him. We need medals, Routon – warrior-hero of Ribblestrop, courage under fire.'

The headmaster staggered forward, tripping on a plank but staying upright. Boys bolted forward and steadied him, and Ruskin grabbed the door open. In a moment, the whole company were piling forward, stumbling on the darkened stairs, unsteady as they climbed with candles guttering. Boys laughed and squealed as they pushed each other.

'He received blows,' cried the headmaster. 'He was cut down, but he rose again . . .'

Fifteen boys and the headmaster wound their way up a hundred steps and piled into the dormitory. Sam lay there dozing and thus experienced a scene he would later assume was an hallucination brought on by fever: a sea of faces, blurring above his bed. Voices, words he could not understand, and then a sigh of music from an old accordion and a song sung like a lullaby.

'Shh, boys. Shhh! Sing:

Ribblestrop, Ribblestrop, precious unto me;
This is what I dream about and where I want to be.'

A number of hands felt his forehead. He could see black with stripes of gold, and dark, kind eyes. He saw the face of Dr Norcross-Webb, smiling proudly, and Sam wondered if this was Heaven, and if so where his grandparents were.

'See not the broken halls, Sam,' said the headmaster. His voice was calm. 'See not the smoke-damaged walls. See the stars, and see yourself – as a rocket, *rising* to those stars. Welcome to Ribblestrop Towers!'

*

Caspar Vyner was in bed. His bruises were inky violet, but the pain had faded. Both he and his gran heard the school song, drifting from the west tower. Lady Vyner's hands trembled with fury as she carried another icepack to the bedroom.

Millie was wondering where she was, and heard nothing.

Down in their bunker, seven monks were holding a night-time vigil, praying for troubled souls. They heard music; closed their eyes and prayed harder.

And in a laboratory, way under the school, animals shifted in their straw, listening in darkness.

Chapter Nine

Sam was shaky the next day and his headache nagged. Nothing, however, would persuade him to stay in bed and he got up at half-past five, showered, dressed, and joined everybody else at six o'clock for Captain Routon's special first-day celebration fry up.

'Captain Routon!' cried the headmaster, holding a clock. 'What's the time?'

'Seven-thirty, sir, on the dot.'

'Do we have the equipment?'

'We have what we need, sir.'

'Are the children gathered?'

'I believe so.'

'Then the term has started. Map the landscape, boys – I want this to be a ramble to remember, and when you're back I want to see it with your eyes. Everyone's got pens – now, who's that with the easels?'

'Asilah, sir!' cried the tallest orphan. Asilah was a slim, handsome boy with an intense look about him. He was the obvious elder and took his responsibilities very seriously. He was softly spoken and seemed to communicate a vast amount simply by the movement of eyebrows. If he wanted the children in a line, or sitting down, capped or capless – Asilah's quiet voice appeared to be law. He stood now with a number of large wooden tripods on his shoulder, as the smaller orphans lined up behind him. Anjoli – the child with the wildest hair – carried a roll of paper and a basket of felt-tips.

'We've got a picnic at base camp,' said Captain Routon. 'We'll move off in single file to start with; I don't want anyone getting lost. Henry, at the rear!'

Blazers were buttoned, ties were straightened, and the column set off. Captain Routon led the way, striding over the grass. The boys leaped behind him and the headmaster watched them disappear, waving. Like birds, they were: a flock of ducklings, following their leader. Their chatter and laughter faded in the crisp autumn air, and he felt tears in his eyes. 'My school!' he whispered.

He wandered back inside and gathered up the breakfast things. He had a slightly tricky telephone call to make now, and it would need all his concentration. The new deputy, Miss Hazlitt – not the easiest of women, he had to admit – had been leaving messages all the previous evening, and he'd been hard pressed to make sense of them. A delay in Reading caused by children *on a line* – a phone line or railway line, he couldn't be sure. Someone had possibly or possibly not stolen a purse full of brand new credit cards . . . he wasn't sure what that had to do with him. One of the cards had been found on the floor in a wine bar, but he couldn't hear what followed, because the voice on his answer machine seemed to be barking, like a dog. He caught the words *strained wrist* and something about concussion, and then all he could hear was the sound of saucepans clashed together. The final message talked about a hotel and *full recovery*, climaxing in the worrying phrase, *I'll be sending the bill*, which cut through all interference, crystal clear. Dr Norcross-Webb needed leaders and decision-makers, and if the woman had been injured in some way he'd want to help, of course. But if a bill was sent to him at the present time, there was no way he could pay it. He would have to persuade her to come, without delay.

*

A kilometre to the east, Captain Routon's bald head was getting pinker in the sun. His muscles bulged in his forearms as he checked his map. He trotted forwards, about-turned and trotted back. He trotted to the rear, then he skipped round to the front again. They had come down the slope of the lawn and turned towards the wood. It was the most beautiful day, and the children were happy and excited.

'Look to the left there, boys. Deciduous trees. View of the lake.'

The children rigged the easels and there was the frantic scratching of pens.

'Through the gap there, see that, son? That's an imitation Greek temple, that is. Just by the water. As I understand it, that was built in honour of one of the many Greek deities, in 1786. The lake is actually an *artificial* lake – no, we're not going swimming, not yet. On the other side, that's Neptune. Let's keep moving, you'll get better views the higher we go.'

'Sanchez,' said Ruskin, as they climbed into the trees. 'Do you know what happened to the new girl?'

'No,' said Sanchez.

'She wasn't at breakfast. Do you think she's sick?'

'Sick in the head, maybe.'

'It's strange, because she missed supper too. This is confidential, but Sam was telling me she was expelled from her last school. I hope she hasn't run away.'

'She's bad news, Ruskin. I talked to her and I'm telling you, you want to stay well away.'

'Yes, but how many schools can you get booted out of? My father says that in the end, you have to stick at *something*. It's no life, is it – always running away. Maybe she's on supper duty, I didn't look at the lists. This is lovely, isn't it? Getting a bit warm . . .'

The track had got narrower and took the party steeply down to a brook and then up again. The younger orphans were racing ahead and their cries were parrot-like. Occasionally one would climb a tree and ambush his friends, leaping from dizzying heights. They spread into the undergrowth, and the forest was alive with Red Indian cries. By the time they emerged, most boys had stripped down to their shorts, and ties were worn bandana-style. It was a mercilessly-hot day and the sun was still rising. Soon, they were ascending steeply and they came to a grassy peak with one lonely fir tree at the top. Again, the easels were distributed and the view was recorded. There was Ribblestrop Towers, like a honey-coloured sandcastle on a mat of green grass. There was the distant town, with a church spire turning grey-blue in the haze. Sam's picture was largely red and purple, because he was unable to distinguish colour. He was also seeing double and his headache was returning.

'Oooh,' said Anjoli. 'I think we have problem.'

Captain Routon was staring at his map. It was actually a rather creased, limp envelope with a series of biro marks. He turned a hundred and eighty degrees and looked up thought-fully.

'Wrong turn, everybody,' he shouted. 'We missed base camp. This is what I called "Beacon Point", and we shouldn't be here till later. Pack up your stuff . . . Whose shoes are these?'

'Is there any water?' said Sam.

'Yes, but not here. I'd left a little stash of squash and sand-wiches at the base, knowing we'd be peckish. I think we ought to find it . . . Best thing to do is to head nor'-nor'-west, which means cutting a path down there. Through – that.' He pointed down the other side of the hill, which was a tangle of gorse and ferns. 'What we do in this situation, is make a path. Come on, lads, papers away. We'll call this path the *Sanchez Path*, Sanchez, because I want *you* to cut it.'

'Yes, sir. What with, sir?'

'With a good stout stick. Such as you might find in the wood we've just come out of. Let's just rest a moment while you and I go off to find a, er . . . suitable stick. Sorry, boys, when I get hot, I tend to lose track a bit.'

'I'll come,' said Caspar. 'I know every inch of this place.'

'Very well, that's good. At ease, everybody, loosen up. Carry on with your pictures.'

In twenty minutes or so Sanchez, Caspar and Captain Routon returned. They carried hefty sticks and looked hot.

'Charting as we go,' panted the captain. His right eye was twitching and one hand was clasped to his temple. 'You see, boys – in many ways this is undiscovered country, virgin soil. From today, the maps will have to be redrawn for the *Sanchez Path*, eh?'

'We could do a project,' said Sanchez. 'Couldn't we, sir? We could make a model of the whole park!'

'I think you'd better all follow Asilah and Sanchez. I'm going to run round the perimeter here and see if I can reconnoitre the old railway and find base camp. I'll meet you at two-thirty, over there, with the refreshments. Damn, I've only got the one whistle, which is an error on my part . . . if I give this whistle to *you*, Henry, then if you do take a wrong turn, you can alert me. Careful, boy, don't break it.'

'In which direction, sir?' said Sanchez.

'Straight. Absolutely straight. Keep the sun on your . . . right.'

'Are you sure you're OK, sir?'

'It's the sun, Sanchez. I've got a metal plate just here, above the eye. Should have worn a hat, this is my fault.' He pressed his temple hard. 'Heats up in the sun and I tend to lose my bearings. But you will join up with the Edge, I'm sure you will.'

'Sir,' said Asilah. 'Is there water anywhere? I think some of the little ones . . .'

'We should have brought supplies. If we'd been going further, I would have issued water bottles, but you see the whole point of a nature walk is to remain unencumbered. We were used to twenty miles of this before breakfast, you know, out in Cairo . . .

I'll find base camp and meet you by the railway. Follow this boy, everybody – follow Sanchez. I'm going to run round and find a short cut.'

Sanchez started hacking his path, and everyone followed. It was slow going, because the boys were now carrying discarded blazers and shirts, as well as their own papers and easels. After half an hour Sanchez was soaked in perspiration and had to stop. Henry and Caspar took over and they made quicker progress, moving down into a copse of trees. After some time they found a fox run, and even though it took them slightly off course into brambles that were higher than their heads, they followed it. This in turn led to a small stream, where every boy splashed and lapped. It was hard to get a sense of direction, but nonetheless – refreshed – the line set off again, the sun roughly on their right.

After two more hours, they came to a great slab of rock, projecting out like a lip, with a sheer drop beneath it. Creeping to the edge of this rock and daring to look down, every boy was thrilled to see a great mass of boulders below.

'Do you think you should blow that whistle, Henry?' said Sam.

'I think we are lost,' said Sanchez. 'Do you know where we are, Caspar?'

'Somewhere,' said Caspar. 'I've been here before, I expect.'

Anjoli smiled and pointed down the cliff. He made diving gestures and Sanchez waved his hands: 'No. Not yet. We have to wait.'

'It's that stupid man's fault,' said Caspar. 'I bet he's gone and lost us. I bet he's got no qualifications whatsoever.'

Henry blew the whistle.

The landscape returned only the flap of a bird and a very distant sound of wind in treetops. This was repeated – the blowing and the listening – three times. Again, each boy sat and sketched the view. The world was melting in the haze.

'Are you alright, Sam?'

'No,' said Sam.

'You're dizzy,' said Ruskin. 'We'll get you home soon.'

'Perhaps he shouldn't have come,' said Sanchez. 'He should have stayed with Millie. Wherever she is.'

'I'm hungry,' said Caspar. 'We've got no lunch, no water – nothing. This whole thing is a farce.'

'Do you think we could find our way back?' said Asilah. 'What if we just turn round?'

'You've all drawn maps!' said Caspar. 'I should damn well hope you can find the way back!' He was sounding tearful.

'Sanchez!' said Ruskin, after ten minutes or so. 'I've had a thought. Do you think Captain Routon has set us a test?'

'What do you mean?' said Sanchez.

'What if he's sent us off, in roughly the right direction, to see if we can find our way home?'

'But how?' said Asilah, who was listening closely. 'We don't know where we are going.'

'That's the test!' said Ruskin. 'To see if we can keep our heads. That's just like him, isn't it? He's one of those war veterans. I bet he's had to live in jungles and all sorts. So here we are, experiencing *survival* first hand. Maybe we're supposed to spend the night out here – maybe all this art-stuff is for firewood!'

Henry seemed upset when he heard that. The whistle drooped from his lip and he started to rock backwards and forwards. Asilah put his hand on his shoulder and the orphans all huddled closer.

'Look,' said Sanchez. 'This is the Edge, isn't it? This is what Captain Routon was talking about.'

Anjoli said, 'We can climb down, no problem.'

Ruskin peered over the lip again. 'You know, it must be. I mean we are on *an edge*, aren't we? It's a big – what do you call it? An *outcrop*.'

'Hey,' said a voice. 'Look.'

The speaker was a small, earnest-looking boy, who had so far been very quiet. He had a fine stubble of hair under a cap he'd turned backwards. He was staring into the distance, his eyes mere slits. Sanjay was his name, and he'd been a ship's boy for most of his life navigating container-vessels over the South China sea. 'Railway,' he said, pointing. As soon as he spoke, everybody saw it. Just beyond a great tilted slab of rock ran a shoulder of track.

'The old railway,' said Ruskin. 'I know where we are!'

'Yes,' said Sanchez. 'I think Captain Routon said we would come to the railway line. From the quarry . . .'

'Which is – yes!' cried Ruskin. 'That's where we've come to. Well spotted, Sanjay! That must be the railway that was built to move the stone to the mansion building, so all we do is follow the tracks back . . . through the rock. I'm sure.'

Anjoli had followed most of this and he had certainly picked up Ruskin's excitement. He translated quickly and smiles of relief spread down the line like lights coming on. He was on his feet, pushing back his hair and pulling on his shirt. 'Let's go!' he cried.

'Hang on!' said Sanchez. 'This is dangerous. Why don't we rope ourselves together, with our ties? Then, if we fall . . .'

As he spoke, Anjoli jumped. One second he was there, and the next he was falling. Sanjay was right behind him, and – one by one, like highly-trained paratroopers – the orphans dived into space. The joy of fallen rock is that there are always footholds and ledges, and in seconds they were virtually cart-wheeling downwards. Nobody had realised that these children had been born into a terrain far more rugged than this one, and that they'd learned to climb before they could toddle. They rolled, they skipped, they threw one another. As soon as they reached the bottom, they came back up for another go.

The difficulty was handling Sam, but that was soon overcome by the Sanjay-Anjoli partnership. Henry lowered him gently down and the orphans took over, passing him between them like a precious parcel. It wasn't long before everyone was on even ground, and stood looking up at the distance they'd travelled. Ruskin was astonished at how far they'd come, and did a drawing of the trail – a beautiful, highly-detailed sketch, which he sent to his parents. It became a minor exhibit later on, when the police brought their final prosecution.

At three-forty-three precisely, they got to the railway.

Sanchez did a head count, and led them on. The direction was obvious: to the left, the railway went into a copse. To the right, it shouldered around under the Edge, just as Ruskin had predicted, in the direction of the school. The only problem ahead now was the fact that a little way down the line was a tunnel. One can't get lost in a tunnel – but it was very, very dark. Torches, perhaps? In every schoolboy's blazer, surely, a pocket knife and a torch, along with conkers and pet mice? Alas, the Ribblestrop blazers were new and their owners had in them only crayons and a copy of the school rules. Had they stopped to study those rules they would have seen rule twelve: *No Ribblestrop student will ever put him or herself in danger, or endanger the life of any other Ribblestrop student*. A fatuously vague rule . . . so easy to break.

'Shall we hold hands?' said Ruskin, as they entered the tunnel.

The darkness drew them in and rule twelve was thus broken.

'Henry?' called Sanchez. 'You stay at the back, yes? You whistle, and that way everyone stays in front of you. OK?'

'How long is this tunnel?' said Henry, slowly.

'It's not that long, actually,' said Ruskin. 'We were told. Twenty miles rings a bell.'

'That's too long,' said Caspar. He was sounding tearful. 'I can't walk that far!'

'Walk between the rails,' said Ruskin. 'Then you really can't get lost. And the sleepers are firm, too, you can sort of . . . get into a rhythm. Lucky they didn't tear all this up when it went out of use. You'd think, really –' Ruskin's voice took on an echo as they went deeper, '– you'd think really that people would want to salvage all the old materials. Let's sing as we go: how about the school song? We can teach it to Sam again!'

Seventeen voices sang:

'Ribblestrop, Ribblestrop, precious unto me;
This is what I dream about and where I want to be.
Early in the morning, finally at night,
Ribblestrop, I'll die for thee, carrying the light.'

At the end of the verse, Henry blew the whistle. Again and again they sang, and this time it was a work song: the kind of song a chain gang would sing as it laboured. Thus the party moved into the depths of the rock.

Four miles away, had you been in the cab of the 13:06 Intercity Penzance-Paddington service, you would have heard the slamming of a connecting door and the following conversation:

'Hello, Arthur! You haven't checked all those tickets already?'

'I have, Darren. Not many punters today for some reason, just the one gets on at Par. They all join at Exeter, that's when my feet don't touch the ground.'

'Better sit down, then. Break out that tea.'

'In your bag here, is it?'

The cab is small, but comfortable. It can accommodate driver and guard easily, and there's always room for a trainee or inspector. The hydraulic driving seats command a marvellous view of the countryside whipping by and, as the glass is an inch thick and bullet-proof, very little sound gets in to disturb conversation.

'Any more news on that mess yesterday?' said Darren. He was a thin, wiry little man with a lot of woolly white hair. New dentures allowed him to smile happily: he was a gentle soul and had been driving trains for nearly forty years.

'Not yet. Young girl, apparently – she pulled the lever on the other train. Then she jumped.'

'I couldn't see if it was boys or girls. Black-and-yellow uniforms, I'm pretty sure about that.'

'They're checking the Reading schools, they might find 'em yet.'

'She had a *very* narrow escape.'

'Hopefully they got a scare, those kids. You won't find them on the railways for a while! Look at that view, Arthur.'

'Take your tea.'

'See that piece of rock to the right? That's Ribblestrop Edge. I've been up there. You can see clear over the county – see Wales on a clear day. And then we bend round to the west and go through the Ribblestrop Pass, which is one hundred and thirty metres – excavated in, oh . . .'

'Signal, Darren – put your lights on.'

'Thanks, Arthur.'

Darren flicked a switch and the main beam came up like a searchlight.

'Irish built it, I do know that. It cuts through Ribblestrop Towers, where old whatshisname lived, the murdered scientist. I'm supposed to whistle here, just in case some poor badger's got itself halfway up the tunnel.'

'I wouldn't like to be a badger up that tunnel. Can I blow the whistle, Darren?'

'Be my guest, Arthur – it's above you. I tell you, I can really get some speed up in this tunnel, it's straight as straight. We're touching eighty miles an hour, you wouldn't believe it though, would you?'

'What's that up ahead?'

'Where?'

'*Ribblestrop, Ribblestrop, precious unto me;*
   This is what I dream about and where I want to be.
   Early in the morning—'

'Shush!'

Sanchez stood still.

'Henry!' he shouted. 'Was that you whistling, man?'

Silence.

'Did someone whistle?' said Sanchez, again.

'Stand close, everyone,' said Ruskin. 'Gather round. This is interesting: can you feel a sort of vibration? It's like a little earthquake almost, can anyone else feel it?'

'I can,' said Sam. He was sitting on the rail, head in hands.

The children moved into a tight cluster.

'Maybe it's blasting from the quarry,' said Ruskin. 'You don't think it's a train, do you? I know there are two railways in the park, because one of them's the mainline between Cornwall and London. We used to go down to the fence and wave. I hope I haven't got the two lines confused, that would be a real gaffe . . .'

Ruskin stopped there, not because he'd run out of things to say, but because the tunnel was filling rapidly with the most monstrous scream. The sound was spiralling round the walls of the tunnel, echoing on itself until it became an electrifying howl. It was the sound sheet metal makes when it is being torn apart by circular saws. The sound gets so far into your ears the very eardrums can split and all those little bones, the smallest in the body, simply fragment. It's the sound of an express train with eighty iron wheels hurtling through a tunnel at eighty-two miles per hour.

Darren the driver's accident report was not a long document. The handwriting was more wobbly than young Sam Tack's, because the writer had temporarily lost all co-ordination. Arthur, the guard, was barely able to speak, let alone write. He told only a police inspector what he had seen at one minute past four in the Ribblestrop tunnel: he never spoke of it again. Some memories have to be suppressed.

We were proceeding through the tunnel and I had whistled and illuminated my headlight prior to entry. I remember increasing speed because the restrictions had changed. My colleague and I were looking down the track and we saw upwards of a dozen small children all dressed in distinctive black-and-yellow school uniforms. I remember there was one lad, closest to us, who seemed bigger than the rest. Some of the little ones, I remember, were (the handwriting breaks down here) *were holding hands . . . One little fellow waved his cap. I applied the emergency lever but there was no way we could stop in time. They never stood a chance.*

Chapter Ten

What had happened to Millie?

She had left Sam's bedside, if you remember, after two ugly fights. The first she'd won handsomely. The second had humiliated her and she'd been thrown out into the corridor. She had sat for ten minutes or so, waiting for the throbbing in her head to die down. She calmed herself. Clearly, Sanchez was quick and well trained: some kind of martial artist, she imagined. Next time she would find an appropriate weapon.

Comforting herself with this thought, Millie stood up. It was dinnertime after all, and time to find again the bomb-site that the strange cook had called a dining hall. She descended the main staircase and set off along one of the school's many long, poorly-lit corridors.

Everybody makes mistakes, particularly in new surroundings. Millie had never mastered her left and her right and she *should* have taken the first turning. That would have brought her to the steps down to the hall. A right turn would have brought her into the yard, and there she would have been in time for the headmaster's speech. Alas, Millie went straight on and turned left at the *end* of the passage. There was no right turn to be seen, so she continued, past a suit of armour without a head. Someone had lit a candle at the far end, which seemed promising – so she pressed on, knowing that soon she'd spot something familiar. At the end of the passage, she came to a landing of some kind, with another staircase down. This would lead to the kitchens, she thought: the place she'd first met Captain Routon when they repaired Sam.

Down she went.

'Hello?' she cried. She was a confident girl.

Left turn into what she thought would be the kitchen's preparation area. Something rang a bell: she could see a chair that looked familiar. Right turn, towards a glow of light – a couple of right-angle turns that didn't seem likely, but now she'd come so far she'd soon bump into someone. Left, then right through an unlocked grille she'd definitely never seen before. A staircase down: not the way, but she heard some footsteps, so that suggested a human presence. She hurried down them and found herself in a narrow passage. No carpet any more, no boards even: the floor was stone flags. She knew she must be well under the mansion, in deep cellars. They would – they should – link up with the kitchen . . .

'Hello?' she called, again. 'Can someone answer, please?'

A very dead sound; a rather damp sound. In the distance, she could hear singing. It was low and mournful, like the chanting of monks. Even as she listened it stopped.

In her mind she was thinking. *This school is a madhouse. Only in a place like this could you get so stupidly lost in a few minutes . . .*

'Is anyone there?' she yelled.

Then she listened to the silence. Somewhere far off she heard a key turning in a lock, then – possibly – the shooting of a bolt. They weren't comforting sounds.

Millie turned around nervously and tried to find her way back. But after a few minutes the ground sloped away downwards and she knew it was hopeless. She lit Mr Sanchez's silver cigarette lighter and inspected the sandy floor.

There were boot-prints pacing away downhill. She followed

them. An iron gate stood on the left, all bars and chain; through the gate she could see empty wine racks. Opposite was an archway, with a broken door that stood open. Either side, soaring up high into the gloom, were marble shelves. It was a cold and clammy place, and Millie inspected it with her lighter. True, it *felt* like a tomb – but it wasn't one. There were no headstones or bodies and the smell was only a little bit musty. She worked hard at logic, forcing herself to be calm: this was simply a larder, surely, where cold cheese and meat would be stored. Wine store, cheese store. Everything has its place, and she was simply in the kitchen-cellars of a huge house where years ago they'd had dinners for a hundred guests. They would have had food and booze to last half a year . . . and they would also have staircases to get you back to the kitchens quickly, so Millie walked on, confident that in a short time she'd find those stairs.

It was the white rabbit that alerted her to the possibility that things were not really in control any more. She only saw it for a few seconds, but it was definitely a white rabbit. It looked at her. It seemed about to smile or speak – but instead it turned and bobbed away.

When she saw the metal door, she knew the rabbit must have emerged from whatever room that door guarded. Her mouth was dry, but she tiptoed to the doorway and peered inside.

'Excuse me?' she whispered.

The hallway was small. The walls were lined with old wooden shelves, and the shelves were laden with jars and bottles; there was a smell of must mingled with bleach. There was one neon light and it flickered on and off. It was some kind of passage, used for storage, therefore it ought not to have been frightening. Chemistry-lab bottles with heavy glass stoppers. Fat jars, thin jars, sugars and powders, liquids and crystals. Some of the glass had been scribbled on, in what might have been chalk. Some were thick with dust and some were clean. She moved

83

past them and came to a metal sink into which a tap was dripping. The water dripped over what looked like a soup-bowl, and something slimy seemed to be curled up inside, stinking – Millie caught the odour and turned her face away fast.

She saw a mirror. Reflected in that mirror was a pair of double doors. She turned, licking her lips which had become painfully dry. Through the doors she could see bright yellow light, and there was a soft humming and an electronic bleep. She tiptoed forward, feeling unsteady. Something had dripped on the floor and it was sticky. She peered through the doors, and – convinced the room was empty – slipped between them, praying for a staircase. There were more shelves, everywhere, on every wall. There was a metal table and steel counters, and a small trolley, laden with bottles.

As she stared around, she realised she was being watched.

She gulped, then heard herself whimper. She was not alone! Around her were a hundred little eyes. From the bottles and jars helpless faces peered – were they animals, or fish? She went closer, and backed away again – did she want to know or not? Eyes and mouths were floating in murky liquids, and some had little hands or paws, and some of the faces looked so wise. Oh God, they were rats and rabbits and creatures curled up so tight she couldn't recognise them, and some had mouths that were yawning, with teeth bared. She could see teeth straining, she could see wide eyes! And, in one particular jar above the eyes, what had happened to the skull? She shied away but she couldn't not look: the sad little creature held her gaze, and Millie saw that the head had been cut clean through. Its brain was visible, soft and bulbous. Next to that, a creature without fur – a piglet perhaps – its limbs twisted round itself, its eyes tight shut and its snout lifted. Once again, side on, the head had been cut and the brain was . . . balancing there. It wasn't a dream, she was looking at broken heads.

As she snapped her eyes shut, something whirred behind her

and she spun round with a cry. It was an animal cage, she saw it in a moment, and something was racing on a metal wheel, racing suddenly as if for its life. There were wires and dials coming from it, coming from its head. An animal cried out behind her, parrot-like, monkey-like, and Millie spun round again, and there was a bigger cage, with something cat-sized, rocking backwards and forwards staring into her eyes . . . She felt vibrations in the floor. Its skull . . . the creature's head – there was something wrong, but she'd managed not to see, and now her hands were over her eyes and her mouth was full of bitter vomit. Was the whole room really shaking, or was it just her own sickness? Glass was rattling, the animals were screeching, and it was as if an underground train was coming, getting closer all the time. The sound became a hammering of metal and some of the glass started to rattle. The monkey-cries got louder and Millie was panicking. She turned to the doors, she turned back. The noise was all around her and as she staggered there was the smashing of glass – her hand had caught one of the flasks on the trolley, and a powder fine as salt spread over the floor and her shoes. She was on her knees in the broken glass, her hands in the powder.

Then, up – up at all costs, because she had to hide. She could see a concertina'd metal door at the far end of the room, and that was where the noise was coming from. It was the door to a lift and that was the noise; there was a row of lights flickering above it, and she knew the lift was coming down. The animals were frantic, as if they knew too.

She hunted for a corner – how lucky for her that years of hiding from teachers had given her the reflexes of a panther so, as the noise built to a crescendo, Millie leaped sideways and slid between a rack of shelves and some kind of fridge. She was in a corner where a couple of freezers stood, lids wide open. In seconds she had rolled into the first like a soldier trained for such manoeuvres: it was wet and stank of bleach, but there could be no better hiding place. She pulled the lid down over her head, careful to let it rest open by a few centimetres. Her fingers were burning, her heart was racing, and her mouth was achingly dry.

'To me!' said a voice.

She was safe. She could breathe easily and she could still see out. She crouched there, trying to calm down. Yes, the lift door was open now, and she heard the metal grille slam into itself. Two figures. At first, they were shapeless – one in green, one in black. They were bent over something, and wrestling with it. It was heavy and they were grunting.

'Careful!' said one. 'Get your end up!'

Deep, panting voices – Millie strained to see more. Whatever they held was dead weight. She fought to remain calm and silent – her fingers were burning, and she must have touched her lip because her mouth was hurting too. She heard the second voice, filled with impatience: 'It's stuck your end!' The men were irritable. 'It's caught on the wretched door,' said the first one. 'Your end down!'

'Lift it! Ow!'

'Shut the damn door! Shut the damn door!'

The animals were quiet. The men were unloading something, but Millie couldn't make out what it was, it was still wrapped in plastic. It was big and black, with what looked like a crane attachment bolted to its top, all rods and levers.

They were both panting, but calming down. They had dragged the thing into the middle of the floor and were leaning on it, getting their breath back. A radio crackled and Millie saw that the man in black was in uniform. He wore a cap, and the cap was trimmed in a line of all-too-familiar check. The man was a policeman and Millie went cold with fear and closed her eyes.

'Basement one,' he said, into his radio. 'Elevator's with us, just unloading, over.'

'Where's he want it?'

'Didn't say,' said the policeman. Millie was watching again. 'Just said leave it on one. But he did say plug it in . . . Hey.'

'What?'

'Where's the rabbit?'

'What d'you mean?'

The policeman was standing still, looking around him, hat in his hand. He wasn't young, and she could see big, fat, red hands. He went to one of the cages and lifted it. 'It's open,' he said. The voice had a northern twang.

'He said he's finished with all this anyway,' said the other man. 'Didn't he? He said clear all this. We should have come the other way.'

'We need the cylinders in as well. Look, he might not need any of this but rabbits don't open their own cages. Look at this poor soul . . .'

She was watching, mesmerised, wondering what on earth she'd stepped into. The man furthest away had a knife, and was cutting and stripping, ripping through the cord and plastic that swathed the delivery. Oh, she could see what the thing was now, and it made her even colder. How many times had she seen just that kind of object? It was a dentist's chair. It even had the tray that sits close to your chest, where they hang the little drills. There was a facemask on a hook, and tubes looped from it upwards, out of sight. There were stirrups where you put your feet, and – worst of all – on the arm-rests, where your wrists would go, there were straps. So it couldn't be a dentist's chair . . . nobody got *restrained* in a dentist's chair, strapped in for treatment – that just didn't happen.

As Millie stared, the lamp came on. The man had thrown a switch and the inspection lamp was shining, bright and brutal. The chair yawned backwards, waiting – hungry for a patient.

'Let's do the freezers and go.'

The policeman was beside her; she hadn't noticed his approach. He was millimetres from her nose and she ducked backwards instinctively. As she did so, the lid slammed above her head.

'Do what to the freezers?' The voice was muffled now.

'Turn them on. It's on his list.'

Millie was in darkness. The lid had shut with a deep, rubbery thud, as if there was a tight seal. She closed her eyes and it made no difference: darkness had never been so close, or so black.

Seconds passed. The pain of her burning skin was forgotten because she needed to think fast. She should hammer on the side. *Be quick!* she told herself. A motor came to life underneath her and the freezer started to shake.

She pushed at the roof and it didn't move. It *would* move, if she got her shoulder to it. She would lie on her back and kick it open – no freezer locked, they were built to be safe so accidents couldn't happen. They had emergency release levers on the inside; there was probably a law about it, especially in a school, if this *was* part of the school. Millie pushed again, and the lid moved not one millimetre.

Don't panic, she said to herself. *Keep calm*. Millie had been in many dangerous situations, and the worst thing you could ever do was panic. Every situation you walked into could be walked out of, if you held your nerve. Freezers *didn't* lock.

A film of sweat broke over her. There was another sound there, too, and it mixed into the engine underneath her. It might have been the lift departing, or it might have been more freezer mechanisms, Millie didn't know. What she did know was that the temperature was already dropping. Her little store of black air felt stale already, the walls felt closer. She rolled onto her back and got her knees up over her chest. She put her feet against the lid and pushed with every atom of her strength. She brought her feet down and kicked. Once, twice, three times – three heavy kicks.

She had exhausted herself. She was gulping air way too quickly. The freezer was shaking, but it was the motor only – the seals hadn't budged.

She strained until the tears came and all her strength was gone. Still the lid didn't move. Then she screamed and started to hammer on the walls. To be so helpless and to know with such certainty that there was no way out, and that you were trapped in darkness and airless cold – the knowledge was so monstrous she simply screamed and screamed. She drummed her fists. She writhed back onto her knees and tried to force her finger-tips into the little gap she could feel, where the rubber was compressed. It was too narrow, but she might get some leverage if she pressed – there might be that catch, the emergency catch for just this kind of accident . . . With all her strength she pressed, and then she gasped as her fingernails lifted from her flesh, though the lid itself refused to budge.

Too late, she realised she had used the air around her. Mouth open, unable to believe how things could end, unable to believe how unfair it all was, she suddenly understood that she was going to die.

She put her fists together and used them to beat hammer blows on the side of the freezer. She was sobbing now and howl-ing, and that was how the last of the oxygen was wasted.

A science teacher could have helped her with the equation: lung capacity – 4.5 litres, absorbing 25% of available oxygen; 20 breaths a minute in a 264-litre freezer. That becomes:

$$\frac{(264 \times 0.2 \times 60) \times 0.4}{(0.05 \times 20 \times 4)} = 5 \text{ minutes } 28 \text{ seconds}$$

Millie was unconscious in less than six minutes.

Chapter Eleven

But Millie didn't die.

She awoke some time later, possibly from thirst. Her mouth was sore and her gums dryer than they'd ever been before. Her head was on a duck-down pillow and she was wrapped in a duvet. Her eyes felt puffy, and blinking seemed only to let in a hazy, smoky light. As soon as she'd blinked five times the throbbing of her head kicked in; then she became aware of her broken fingernails.

She sat up with a cry and saw at once that whilst she could breathe and reach out – whilst she was definitely alive – the nightmare hadn't ended. The freezer was gone, but somehow she'd been capsized back into the long curving tunnels of the previous day, and she was stretched out on sheets laid over a sandy floor, under some kind of shaft that went up. There was a breeze, there was a little light, and there was a duvet round her. Somebody really had saved her. She had been carried outside, she'd been deposited – by one of the men in lab coats? She'd been left like a parcel and they'd moved on, without saying a word. Her fingers were bandaged.

Millie tried to sort her experiences.

She lay them out in her mind, step by step, like a set of hideous playing cards. A door in a rock. Animals in cages. A lift and two men with a chair. Before that, what had happened? She rewound frantically. Sanchez and that horrible little Vyner-child. Sam and the falling teapot. Names came back to her and here she was in her school clothes: her shoes were next to her, with her socks neatly tucked into them. There were two candles burning beside her, both in rather nice silver candlesticks. And not far off was a breakfast tray, as if this was some bizarre hotel and she'd placed an order with room service.

She stood up, very gingerly.

Things were clicking into place remarkably quickly. Worst of all was the realisation that she still had no idea how to get out of the maze, plus she now had a great stack of unanswered, unanswerable questions. So someone had saved her, yes. So – logically – that person would appear very soon to lead her back to school. She looked at her hands again, and felt her mouth. Had somebody *washed* her? She shuddered and held herself. 'Help,' she said, very softly.

Next to the breakfast tray was a jug full of water. Next to that, a shallow basin, and next to that, a little face cloth and a sliver of soap. Clearly, it was a good hotel: someone cared about the details. The water was deliciously cold, too, so she knelt down carefully and bathed her face. She soaked the towel and held it to her eyes and nose. 'Alright,' she said. 'You're alive.' Her voice was deeper than she remembered it. 'You're not dead, are you? You're not dreaming, are you?'

She slipped into her shoes, put her socks in her blazer pocket, and sat down cross-legged in front of the breakfast tray. The questions could wait a few minutes and it would be better if she just stopped thinking for a short while. Hunger took over, uncoiling from deep inside – when had she last eaten? She'd missed dinner, and now – as she lifted the little cloth and saw white crockery and silver cutlery – the most delicious smell floated up to her nose. A glass of orange juice, a grapefruit half with sugar soaking into it, a rack of toast with a doll's portion of butter and marmalade. Under a shallow, domed dish, scrambled egg and tomatoes, with two sausages set to one side. There was even a napkin rolled up in a silver ring.

'This is very nice,' she said, softly. She would try to normalise things. The food was still warm, so somebody . . .

Millie ate, fast and hard. Everything was cooked to perfection, and every single thing went down, despite the pain of swallowing. The juice was thick and gritty, as if someone had squeezed it for her and crushed in a little ice – there just wasn't enough of it. She had the most terrible thirst. She ate the sausages with her hands and crammed down the four triangles of bread.

'No,' she said. The questions were buzzing again. Then, still softly, she called down the tunnel: 'Excuse me. Is anyone there, please?'

She drank more water and her mouth felt better. Then she looked again at the breakfast tray; she studied the details. Every plate had a little crest, and a scroll of letters floated above each crest. On the linen napkin too, the same design was embroidered: *OU*, possibly, or *OV* – it was too floaty and fancy. On the silver knife and fork, like a metalworker's hallmark, the same inscription.

Millie looked up and down, positive that whoever it was must be close. But the tunnel simply curved off in both directions, reminding her that she had no idea which way to go, and that she'd made absolutely no progress since she left Sam Tack's bedside, hours, even days, ago. She still had to get out and she still had no idea how.

'I want to go home,' she whispered.

At least she was refreshed. She stood up, and set off. She was bound to find a way out soon. Was it day or night? She had no idea, and it didn't matter. She walked, and was comforted simply by the rhythm of walking. She carried one of the candlesticks, and it gave her just enough light. It wouldn't be long, and she would climb a set of ordinary stairs and find herself back in the insanely horrible school that she didn't want to go back to, but had to be better than this labyrinth. A school for freaks and weirdos, where people seemed to nearly get killed on a fairly routine basis: yes, she would be back there. The headmaster would smile and she would explain that she had to leave, immediately.

She quickened her pace, the decision giving her energy. Oh yes, she knew exactly what she would do. First, phone her father and describe the situation. She remembered a telephone kiosk, along the drive. If the smiling headmaster didn't want her to use his phone, she'd trek off to that. She imagined how it would be to heave open the door and lift that receiver. *'Dad,'* she would say. *'I'm on my way to London. I'm checking in to Claridge's, and I am never going back!'* Slam. She would slam the receiver down hard. She rehearsed the conversation again. She won the arguments. She heard her father's voice, *'Fine, Millie, you're right . . .'* And then she would walk up the drive and find the open road. She would stand on it, with her thumb out – she wouldn't even gather up her stuff, all the lovely things she'd bought with that woman's credit card – she'd stand there and wait for the first car or truck that stopped. Whoever it was, wherever it was going, she would climb inside and put the miles between her and Ribblestrop Mental Asylum.

Millie walked faster. As she walked, she tore off her ridiculous blazer and dropped it. She threw away her tie: she would not need it. Millie started to jog, following her nose and knowing in her heart that no network of tunnels could be without end.

Several hours later, she came upon a blazer and a tie.

They had been neatly folded. There was a silver tray next to them, covered in a white cloth. She staggered to it, knelt, and found a club sandwich, skewered with four tiny silver swords. Lettuce, bacon, fried egg, tomato. There was a little dish of tomato ketchup. A hand-knitted tea-cosy sat over a tiny teapot, and under the teapot was a hand-drawn map.

Millie discovered her hands were trembling again, but whether it was fear or sickness or simple frustration, she didn't know. The tea was hot. The map was like a child's puzzle: lots of lines with elbows and intersections. There was a little stick-figure, with long hair. Some way away from her, if you followed the lines and didn't miss the turning . . . there was a train. The creator of the map had drawn a little train, with a puff of smoke emerging from its funnel.

Millie was about to cry, but she made herself sit calmly, and again she ate every crumb of her lunch. She had two cups of tea. She wiped her lips with the napkin and put on her blazer.

'Oh please,' she said. 'Please help.'

Silence.

'I need help! Why won't you talk to me?'

She waited for the voice or footstep she knew wouldn't come. She had forgotten if she'd come upon the tray from the left or the right; she didn't know which way to go to follow the map. If it was left, then that meant quite a long trek before a Y-shaped fork. When she came to that, she should take the right-hand tunnel. But what if it was in the other direction?

She closed her eyes. 'Dip-dip-dip,' she said, quietly. 'My little ship. This is the way to get out of here . . . quick.' She opened her eyes and her finger was pointing left. She held the map out in front with both hands, as if it were a steering wheel: she must not get lost. Again, the promise of freedom kept her going: the open road, a fine hotel, her father's astonished apologies. She followed the map so carefully she was talking to herself without noticing, still deep-voiced with a throaty rasp: 'Second right, so that's the first. We don't take that, we go on to the next. Coming soon, here it comes. What's this? A circle. We're coming to a circle – no we're not.'

She walked on. There was a gleam of very soft light from above. Standing under it, she looked up and saw a tall chimney of brick shooting up above her. Was it daylight all the way up

94

there? There was light from somewhere, so Millie called: 'Hello?' and heard her voice spiral up in echoes and disappear. No ladder, no ropes, no way of getting up. But the chimney or air-vent must be the map-drawer's circle, which suggested she was moving in the right direction.

Millie found new energy and set off at a brisk walk. Up ahead was a T-junction, which was where she turned right, and that was where she came upon . . . train track.

She started to laugh. Yes, she was following the map correctly, something she'd never been able to do before. How many car journeys had ended in screaming rows because Millie couldn't see that the yellow B road didn't join the blue motorway but went underneath or over? Now she was map-reading for her life, and she wasn't going to end up a pile of bones wrapped in a stupid blazer. *I've learned one skill today*, she thought. *One useful skill at this horrific school.* She heard herself giggling.

The tunnel was going uphill: that was promising. She marched between the railway tracks – it was only a narrow gauge thing, long out of use. It had a gentle curve, and as she came round it she saw how the tunnel bulged and the tracks became two. Something huge lay up ahead. She grinned broadly, understanding the map-drawer's plan. Here was the train! Vast and brown and orange with rust, it sat there fast asleep, dreaming of the days it heaved carriages. She touched a wheel. Every valve must be seized-up and dead: had nobody wanted it? She marched on, smiling, not really noticing that the tunnel was getting darker. Not noticing that it was getting clammier, as if the air could not circulate. She had to light the precious cigarette lighter then, because it was very dark indeed.

When she came to a solid wall of rock, she had to stop. She was precisely where the map told her to be, but it was a very, very dead end. A cliff, in fact. A great blockage of tombstone granite. Someone had lit a little oil lamp, on a tiny stone shelf.

Next to it was a glass of water, and it sat on a piece of paper with a large X filling the white space.

It occurred to Millie that possibly, just possibly, she was the victim of an appalling joke. Why had she assumed her map-drawer was on her side? Because he'd provided food. But he hadn't made himself known to her. And had there been any other dead ends? No: this was the first. All the tunnels had looped and forked, there had always been a sense of progress, even if the progress was insane. Millie leaned against the stone. She screwed the map up and beat her head gently on the rock. She looked up and around, thinking maybe there could be steps cut in, maybe a way . . .

She saw nothing. Her lips were dry again, so she drank the water. As if the water went straight up into her eyes, she found she was in real danger of crying. She could feel it coming in a great tide of despair: she could not walk any more, she could not retrace her steps.

She looked to where freedom might be, above all this tonnage of rock: and that was when she saw the lever.

It was just above head height. It blended into the rock, but on close inspection was of steel, emerging from a socket in the stone. The lever had a handle shaped to take human fingers, so Millie did the obvious thing. She would not allow herself to hope, because she had been hoping for so many hours. Weak and tired as she was, she reached up to take a firm hold.

'Oh God,' she said, very quietly. 'I don't believe in you. I have never believed in you. So I don't expect you to be listening, and if you are I certainly don't expect you to help, there's no reason why you should. But if you are, if you could just possibly, please, let this be an exit. If this gets me out, I will believe in you for ever.'

She pulled, and nothing happened.

'I will sacrifice goats to you,' she whispered.

She pulled again. Nothing gave, no movement – but over-head, maybe a distant vibration?

She began to curse, closer than ever to hysteria. The vibration was real, and reminded her of trains. She put both hands round the lever and pulled with all her strength and all her skinny weight. She lifted her feet from the ground and braced them on the wall: she could hear a roaring. She hauled again, crying out with the pain and frustration. And, *slam!* – the lever shifted violently down, trapping her little finger and making her gasp. Then, immediately, gears and pulleys sprang into action.

At first Millie thought she'd caused an earthquake – the world seemed to be ending right over her head. The roof slipped and there was dust and dirt cascading. Worse than that, there was a sound of thunder, and it was booming into her tunnel. She'd woken up a monster and it was roaring down on top of her. She cowered on the ground, the ceiling above her swinging away: the whole roof of the tunnel was lowering like a drawbridge and impossibly, there were bodies tumbling down towards her. Children, crying out and slipping, screaming, down into the tunnel. The roof had become a set of steps: and the bodies were falling down them. Above it all there was a shriek of screaming metal passing overhead with the frantic rhythm you'd recognise anywhere as a hurtling express. In the dim light, she could see that these human forms wore blazers: black and gold. Some of them were sitting up, on the newly-formed staircase and the floor of the tunnel. One of them was groping for something, on its knees, hands exploring the soil. A smallish, fattish form: it found a pair of glasses, and the blinking, mole-like face of Jacob Ruskin stared down at her.

'Millie!' he said.

'Ruskin!'

'Where have you been? We thought you'd gone home.'

Then Sanchez was in front of her, on his knees. His hands found her shoulders. He was peering into her face, grinning broadly, panting with joy. 'Millie!' he said. He shook her, gently.

He shook her harder. He embraced her. 'You save our life. You save everyone's life!' Then she was hugged harder than she'd ever been hugged. A whole scrum of boys formed around her, and everyone was hugging her, laughing and cheering, clapping and dancing.

Chapter Twelve

Dear Mother and Father . . .

. . . imagine our astonishment when, just as we thought death was certain, the ground seemed to open up and the friend I told you about - Millie, who is a very brave girl - was there in person, having opened some kind of magic cellar or passageway. We found out later that smugglers used it in the old days! Amazing that the mechanism still worked after all those years - actually, a bit suspicious!!! Anyway, I spoke to Sanchez, who is helping me write this letter, and he agreed with me that we ought to call it after her: I haven't had a chance to chat it over with the girl herself as she is in a bit of a state, talking about hospitals and sweets that give you visions, which nobody understands! Sounds to me like she had a nightmare - and not surprising either as she had been lost for nearly twenty-four hours. Anyway: my own idea is to call it Millie's Chasm of Death, even though, of course, nobody died. It is halfway along what my new best friend Sam wants to call The Tunnel of Fear.

Near thing, though, eh? So long for now - please don't forget to send postal-order. I am totally penniless due to some very unforeseen circumstances. And dead keen to be first with a school bank account. The headmaster says he needs cash, urgently - rates of interest very good. (Joke!) TTFN! Love to Gran. Yours ever, Jake.

This letter was item 9b in the ultimate Police Prosecution. A legible version is reproduced here with the permission of the Ruskin Estate.

Chapter Thirteen

You entered the headmaster's study through a thick, black door.

Millie had been asked to wait outside it, so she stood with her ear pressed to the woodwork trying to make sense of the muffled voices within. She'd seen the policeman arrive, driving over the park in a big white car, brilliant with fluorescent markings. She'd noticed a chrome searchlight on the driver's side and tinted windows. She had been warned that she might have to give a statement, though her instinct was to say nothing at this stage. She had no idea who to trust, and knew from years of experience that the moment you commit lies to paper, you're at a major disadvantage. In any case, how deep would they dig? One of Millie's fears was that someday, someone would start gathering together all the little crimes that she'd so far concealed – and that might include her recent spending spree in Selfridges, and several like it. She never kept the credit cards, of course, so in theory they had no proof . . . but it was always a worry.

She thrust her hands into her pockets and paced up and down. She could not make sense of the recent past, and had found it difficult to describe the horrors she'd been through. Sanchez, Sam, Ruskin, big Henry, the orphans – they'd looked at her as if she was mad. It wasn't that they didn't believe her, exactly. It was simply that they didn't know what to say. The bottles and jars, the caged animals, the little paws and faces and the creature that rocked and chattered – she'd described it all as vividly as she could, and everyone had been suitably horrified. She'd talked about the chair, the freezers and her blackout. Then the food on the fancy tray left by someone invisible; then, as if that wasn't enough, the long trek in a maze designed to send you insane . . . Everyone listened, but what could anyone say? Millie ached with frustration. Yes, she wanted sympathy and a fair bit of admiration – both would be useful. But most of all she wanted a chorus of furious outrage followed by a full investigation. She knew that what she'd seen was sinister and dangerous – and certainly secret. Talking about it to the wrong person would be even more dangerous, so she kicked the wall, and put her ear back to the panelling.

On the other side of the door sat Percy Cuthbertson. He was sprawled on the sofa, smiling broadly. Percy Cuthbertson – Chief Inspector of Police to the district of Ribblestrop – was in a very good mood. He was a meaty man, with iron-grey hair combed thin across his skull. His teeth were on full display, as if someone had asked to see them. There was something shark-like about the smile, as if the little beady eyes had spotted prey. He'd been in this room twice before, and always profited. He was a man who made a profit most of the time.

'Little terrors, all of them,' he chuckled. A northern accent: Percy Cuthbertson was a Yorkshireman by birth, but had moved in on Ribblestrop fifteen years ago. He'd brought two brothers and a nephew down, over the years, and now had a nice little network operating. 'You don't need to tell me, sir,' he laughed. 'I've had three of the wretches myself. Two boys and a girl and they drove us to distraction – specially the girls, eh! Children are children, y'see. They get into scrapes, they go where they're told not to, and they put grey hairs on your head!'

'Well, I'm relieved to hear you say that,' said the headmaster. 'Understanding is what we need at the moment.'

'If a door's locked,' said the inspector, 'a child wants to see inside.'

'Yes.'

'When a child finds a tunnel . . .'

'Yes.'

'. . . it wants to explore. That's the natural way with children, and you can't change *natural* law. What a good job they're right as rain, eh? What a good job no one was hurt.'

'Yes, they seem to have passed it all off as an adventure. Which is marvellous.'

'The natural resilience of youth, sir. Moments from death, and they pass it off as a bit of a lark. Have you sacked that man, whatshisname – *Routon*? He must be feeling pretty sick.'

'Well, it was an honest mistake. He has a war-wound, and—'

'A dozen or so kids lost up a tunnel . . . honest mistake?' Inspector Cuthbertson paused, and sipped his tea. 'A little girl rummaging round underground . . . an honest mistake? She's poking her nose into who knows what, and they're all seconds away from a very nasty death, and it's all because of a war-wound? It's the *timing*, sir, that's what bothers me. The bad luck. Just as you thought you were turning the corner – just as we thought everything had been . . . straightened out – lightning strikes twice.'

'Yes,' said the headmaster. There was a new edge to the inspector's voice and the headmaster felt it was wise to be silent.

The policeman was staring hard. He had a gingernut between fat fingers. He spoke softly and quickly, the smile well and truly gone. 'Lightning does strike twice sometimes, doesn't it? And it's never convenient. Not when everyone's hoping for improvement. The new deputy on her way, eh? Past mistakes behind us. New children, looking forward to the term, and even a bit of cash for new projects. Out of the blue – *crack!* – a disaster that could close you down.'

'Nobody was hurt, Inspector.'

'Yes, but an enquiry, sir. A full-scale public enquiry looking at all your certificates and insurances, just when you don't want one.'

'I'm sure the children will get over it—'

'Awkward questions. Requests to see licences! "Duty of care", they'll say. "*In loco parentis.*" Journalists sniffing around and – oh my word! – prosecution for gross negligence. All because *an honest mistake* lets the little terrors up the wrong railway line. Headmaster, I did not expect to be sitting in this office quite so soon. This is incompetence way beyond anything I've ever seen. You say no one was hurt, but have you talked to the train driver? *Psychological damage*, sir, that's what we're dealing with. Seems a very similar thing happened to him just the other day, in Reading. *Passenger delay*, sir. Claims for compensation. Questions about trespass, access, maintenance: are you covered against this sort of thing, sir? How many millions of pounds of public liability do you have?'

The headmaster found his voice was shaking. 'Well, it's not something one can plan for,' he said. He tried to find a deeper register, but his voice insisted on rising high.

'Is it not?' said the inspector.

'Well, no.'

'Some would say it's your job to plan.'

'Ah.'

'Some would say it's your job to play safe rather than sorry, especially after the disappearance of little whatshisname last term, our little orphan boy. No, don't say anything, sir – I know that's all been dealt with. You're dealing with a man who doesn't like the past to be raked up, what's behind us is behind us. But I said to you at the time, *learn your lesson!* Those tunnels are private. We're in the same place we thought we'd left, and it looks to me like it's the same lesson all over again. How much money have you got in that safe?'

The headmaster felt the room tilting under his chair and he

realised he was cornered. He felt handcuffed and helpless, as if the big man was sitting on him.

'What we've got to do,' continued the policeman, hauling himself to his feet, 'is act fast. You understand? Ten thousand, I'd say. Ten thousand, and we might stand a chance. If we spread a little goodwill now, and make a few offers in advance of a prosecution, well . . . I think the red tape could be cut. Have you got it, though, that's the question?'

'Well . . .'

'You've got new pupils. You must have fees.'

'I do, but—'

'What about those foreigners, don't they pay? How much have you got, man?'

'It's just that the money is . . . allocated.'

'*Un*-allocate it, sir.'

The headmaster's muscles had gone soft and he wondered if he could stand. Ten thousand pounds represented Sam's fees, Ruskin's insignificant little top-up, the cheque from social services for Millie, and the first orphan down-payment. Lady Vyner was chasing ten times that amount! He found he was looking at the wall safe. He found he was on his feet, with the key in his hand. The inspector was moving towards him and the silence was throbbing; he fitted the key and the safe was open. He stared at the piles of notes. They took up such a little space, and the only other item on the shelf was a conker he'd promised to look after for Ruskin. He pulled the money together and counted it onto the desk, his hands shaking, notes fluttering.

'This is all the . . . cash I have at present.'

For a big man, Inspector Cuthbertson could move quickly. He was at the desk in a moment, and his meaty hands took over, flicking the notes like a cashier. In seconds they were folded up and tucked away and the pile was gone. He patted his jacket pocket and put his shoulders back. 'Good man,' he said. The headmaster could smell gingernut. 'I like to keep things simple, and I'll say it again: trust is the key to this town. It's the oil that greases the wheels and we all speak the same language. So I'll tell you something else.' The inspector lowered his voice. 'I did you a favour last night. Now you've got eleven, I mentioned you to my brother.'

'Oh?'

'Harry Cuthbertson, you've still not met him. Director of Sport at the High School. Yes, sir – we were at a council dinner, we were sorting out a few bits and pieces and your name was mentioned. I said, "They're up to eleven now – he'll be up for a game!"'

'In what . . . why? I don't understand. Eleven what?'

'Boys, sir!' The inspector was putting on his coat. 'Eleven men – a football team! That's another reason we don't want you closing down, it's the football season and our Harry's looking for fixtures. I said to him, "Get in touch with Ribblestrop". His boys are mustard, though – you won't stand a chance, but a game's a game. There's a lad named Darren – seriously, best centre-forward I've ever seen, and there's a scout coming down from a London club, keeping an eye.' He was putting on his hat. 'Keep out of trouble, sir, and give me a ring if you need to – you've got my private number.' He touched the peak respectfully, and opened the door.

Millie fell into the room and sprawled on the carpet. She was up at once and stood neatly to attention.

'You wanted to see me,' she said.

'Millie!' said the headmaster. 'Well . . . yes, we did. The inspector here was—'

'I'm sorry, I was leaning against the door. Hello.'

'I forgot about you,' said Inspector Cuthbertson. 'You're the little explorer.'

He stared at Millie and Millie stared back. She knew him instantly, from the checked band around his hat, to the quarryman's hands. She knew his voice and shoulders and his bright eyes, which – close up – had a hint of madness.

'You're the one who got herself lost,' he was saying. He'd put on a slow voice, as if Millie might have problems following language. 'I was saying to the headmaster here, my own kids were just the same.' He took the lapel of Millie's blazer between finger and thumb, and went down on his haunches.

'Millie was a bit of a hero,' said the headmaster. 'All things considered.'

'A very lucky girl. Does she realise that?'

'Why am I lucky?' said Millie.

'Brave, as well,' he said. He showed Millie his teeth and locked his eyes onto hers. 'I'll tell you why you're lucky, my dear. You got yourself lost in a very dangerous place. Catacombs and labyrinths, you can wander down there for days. I've heard all sorts of things about those tunnels.'

'Yes. I expect they're quite famous.'

'What's your name again, lovey? It's gone clean out of my head.'

Millie swallowed her irritation and smiled: 'Millie Roads, sir. Pleased to meet you.'

The inspector had his head on one side. 'You don't call me "sir", my dear.' He wagged his head like a clown. 'You call me Percy. All the boys and girls round here call me that. I help with the youth club, do the Christmas disco. I do Santa Claus up at the hospital.' Millie was trying not to blink. They were staring each other out. 'I've always had a soft spot for kids.' The inspector bent forward and pushed a strand of Millie's hair away from her eye. 'Your headmaster and me work together, keeping everybody safe. Now, what did you see down those tunnels?' he whispered. 'Buried treasure?'

'No. Not a lot really,' she said.

'Secret rooms?' he chuckled. 'Ghosts and ghoulies?'

'No.'

'Anything strange, lovey? Anything a policeman should know about? Like I said, there's a lot of gossip about those tunnels and who's down there.'

'I just got very tired. What might I have seen?'

'That's what I'm asking, lovey. You'd be wise to tell me.'

'Haven't you been down there?'

Inspector Cuthbertson stared at her in silence for a moment and his lips gradually closed. 'You'd better listen to me, chicken,' he said. He pushed at another strand of her hair, both hands close to her head. 'What's out of bounds is out of bounds for good reason. We're going to get new locks fitted and you need to tell your little friends to stay above ground.'

Millie said nothing. She drew back her lips, itching to bite the fat fingers or the chubby wrist. She remembered a friend of hers at a previous school. One of the Maths teachers had attempted to straighten her tie. She'd bit hard, clamping her jaws shut tight. Oh, the screaming and the jet of bright red blood. He'd lost the movement of three fingers; the teeth had cut clean through the sinews. After all, the jaw muscle is one of the strongest in the body. And all for the sake of a straightened tie.

The telephone was ringing on the headmaster's desk. 'I hope we meet again,' she said. 'I'll pass everything you've said on to my friends, so thanks for the advice.'

'Ribblestrop Towers, good afternoon.'

Millie and the inspector continued to look at one another.

'How did you hurt your fingers?' he said.

Millie still had her hands behind her back. He must have noticed the bandages as she fell through the door.

Over at the desk, the headmaster's face was turning pink. 'Clarissa!' he cried. 'You're here already – that's wonderful!'

'I fell down,' said Millie.

The inspector lowered his voice. 'I like to know who's on my patch, Millie Roads. I gather you like lighting fires, like another little boy we had here.'

'Oh, that's excellent news!' said the headmaster.

'If you light fires round me, it's you who'll get burned,' whispered the policeman.

The headmaster was chuckling. 'Yes, of course! I'll pull the children together, they'd be delighted. Just a moment – Millie?'

'Sir?'

'If you've finished, inspector, we've just had some wonderful news. Our new head of Science – just arrived! She's parking up on the terrace and it's all hands to the pumps. Millie, could you round up the others, we need to unload some equipment. Clarissa,' said the headmaster into the telephone, 'the police are just leaving: we're on our way. Stay exactly where you are.'

Chapter Fourteen

Professor Worthington, MA(Hons.), BSc., FWIW, CCS (Ottawa) made a dramatic first impression. The sound of the screaming engine had drawn the boys already: they were there before the headmaster. As he emerged from the main gate, gown fluttering, he was in time to see a large hire-truck make another violent effort to get its backside up the stone steps to the terrace by the fountain. It had made the first five and now appeared to be stuck, motor howling. He sprinted to the scene, as the driver's door flapped open. An elderly lady was at the wheel, craning her head round the shoulder of her vehicle. The engine roared yet louder and the back wheels shot gravel in all directions: there was a crunch as another step was mounted, wedging the chassis on old stone.

'Stop!' cried the headmaster. 'Stop, Clarissa!'

'Giles! Is that you?'

The driver swung herself down from the cab and tottered on the balustrade. She let herself be helped to safety by the head-master and they clasped each other's hands. Sam, Ruskin, Millie and Sanchez were now gathered, watching the spectacle – the couple kissed lightly on both cheeks, then the driver let the headmaster help her to firmer ground. She had the look of an elderly movie-star: her grasshopper skinniness was wrapped in furs and feathers, as if she'd dressed for the premiere of her own film. She smiled broadly.

'And these are the children!' she gushed. 'Here they are, all four of them! Oh my word, this is your dream, Giles!'

'Just part of it, Clarissa – this is a mere fraction!'

'There're more? That's wonderful . . . you always said you wanted your own school, and here you are!'

Dr Norcross-Webb was rocking with pleasure, his hands still clasping those of the professor. He was blinking back tears. 'This is an emotional moment for me,' he said. 'And something of a landmark. Boys, listen. Only a few of you will remember just how painful Science lessons were last year. Remember, Ruskin?'

'Yes, sir, they were very difficult.'

'And why were they difficult? You will be too polite to say, so I will answer my own question. Because *I* was teaching them and science is not my strong point.'

'And, sir,' said Sanchez. 'As you said, sir, we had no facilities.'

'Apart from the saucepan,' said Ruskin.

'Which is precisely why I have invited a very old friend to join us. "Begged", would be a better word. I wrote letters, I made calls – for this is Professor Worthington: Zoologist, Astrologist and Meta-physicist. How have we persuaded her to bring us her skills?'

'A question he's *not* going to answer . . .' muttered Millie to herself.

'Because here at Ribblestrop, we're at the cutting edge! Considerable investment has been made. Am I right, Professor Worthington?'

'Very considerable, Headmaster, but worth every penny!' She had a fluting voice. The notes lifted and streamed upwards. 'I've brought everything we need, I've just rolled off the ferry from Norway. So, the first job – which is the most exciting always, like Christmas and birthdays all rolled into one – is getting all the boxes into the lab and unwrapping them. When do we start?'

'Right away. No lessons, children. Today's a day of prepara-tion! Now, the orphans are upstairs—'

'There *is* a lab, isn't there, Giles? You said there'd be a lab?'

'You have your own *tower*, Clarissa – north tower, I sent you a sketch! Routon and I were working all through August and the orphans are up there now.'

'Just a few jars and bottles, then, boys. It won't take strong men like you more than a moment.'

Jars, thought Millie. She remembered the underground room and the rows of little faces. She felt her stomach turn over and she went cold. Somebody had saved her life. There was a whole stretch of time blanked out, but that room was etched in her mind . . . Were they going down there, now?

'Come on, Millie!' said Sam. 'Aren't you coming?'

'Something's not right,' she said. 'I'm telling you, Sam. Listen.'

But Sam was scampering off with the others, and she was left to plod wearily after them.

It actually took all day to unload the truck, and they didn't go down any stairs. Professor Worthington's laboratory appeared to be at the top of the north tower, which meant climbing one hun-dred and thirty steps, countless times. The truck was piled high, and box after box emerged, followed by bag after bag. The names on the sides were unpronounceable, but two words became very familiar. *Fragile* screamed in red. *Danger* shouted in black. Here and there the skull and crossbones was painted, as if the goods had been supplied by pirates. Often the language was that of a distant country, the letters making no sense at all.

Conversation was not easy, but Millie persisted. Sanchez was the one she picked, and she tried to make him listen. 'You think I was dreaming, don't you?' she said.

'You weren't well,' said Sanchez. 'You admitted that.'

'I saw what I saw. I was not having hallucinations. We are

moving stuff, and I think it's the stuff I saw – jars, bottles. Bottles with animals in!'

'Oh, come on. You were frightened, Millie, you were exhausted . . .'

'That doesn't mean you see things that aren't there!'

'Don't shout at me!'

'Then stop calling me a liar!'

Sanchez stepped back in frustration. The girl opposite him was like no girl he had ever met, and yet again she seemed ready to do him violence.

Ruskin stepped in: 'Millie, nobody is calling you a liar.'

They paused on one of the landings, sweating and panting.

'How much else did I make up?' whispered Millie, furiously. 'What is all this? Am I just trying to get attention?'

'I did not call anybody a liar,' said Sanchez, bitterly. 'Come on, keep moving.'

'Look, Sanchez, I saw something dangerous. You said yourself strange things were going on last term. Children ran away. One boy disappeared completely.'

'That was Tomaz and he went home. All I'm asking, Millie, is what we can do. Can you find this place again?'

'Possibly not, but I can try.'

'You have the map? The one you found.'

'I didn't just find it – it was given to me, with my food.'

'Where is it now?'

'I dropped it. It's somewhere under that staircase. Look, what you're saying, Sanchez, is forget all about it. That is your solution. But I'm telling you, that lab is really very weird . . . laboratory. I nearly died down there, I still don't know why I didn't! That policeman was down there too – and he was asking me about what I saw.'

'Did you tell him?' said Sam. 'If it's against the law—'

'Of course I didn't tell him! I don't talk to policemen or head-masters – I don't trust any of them. Look at this place!'

'Millie,' said Ruskin. 'Your box is coming undone, you're spilling stuff.'

'Shut up. Look at this place. There is no way this is a proper school – it's the most dangerous place I've ever been. He lets you go wandering onto railway lines. He lets Sam get his skull broken. And then, just when we all need a rest, we're made to unload a lorry.'

Sanchez took Millie's box and set it on the steps. The children looked at each other and Millie wondered if she should try again or simply hit someone. The frustration of not being believed was hurting even more, and her skin was fizzing as if she'd been sunburned. She'd had two hot baths. She'd eaten well and slept on a camp-bed the captain had rigged up for her, having smothered her fury that there were clearly no facilities for girls. Still, the urge to set off down the drive and make that phone call – the urge to leave all this nonsense behind her – rose up again. 'It's slave labour,' she muttered. 'Slaves to a bunch of crooks and weirdos.'

'Millie,' said Sanchez, gently. He sat down on the steps and the others did the same. 'We are simply helping move equipment. You can't expect the new teacher to do it by herself.'

'What about the lift?' said Millie. 'Why aren't we using the lift?'

'Because there isn't one.'

'I saw one! They don't want us to know about it, but—'

'But you don't know where you were!'

'I was under the school, I know I was. Damn this, what's her name, this woman? Professor Something?'

'Professor Worthington,' said Sam. 'I thought she looked rather strict.'

'I thought she looked nice,' said Ruskin.

'You're not listening to me! What about the invisible person who saved my life? God give me strength, why won't you—!'

'God should give you manners,' said Sanchez, and Millie stepped forward with fists clenched.

'I'll show you manners,' she hissed. 'Do you want round two, Sanchez? Any time you want, I'm ready!'

'Ah!' said a voice. 'Having a rest?'

The four children looked around, guiltily. A woman was beaming at them from the landing above. She'd changed into a filthy white coat and her hair was wild. She peered through large safety-goggles. She had coils of thick cable over her arms and shoulders. One was looped round her neck.

'Not much more,' she cried. 'We're on the last leg! Put the boxes outside, we'll ferry them in – it's pandemonium in here! Keep going!'

After dark the headmaster emerged on the terrace with a trolley of soup and rolls. They sat on the steps under the first glimmering of stars, chewing happily.

'Where are the orphans?' said Sam.

'Inside the lab,' said Sanchez. 'Didn't you see?'

'I didn't go in.'

'At the top of the tower. The orphans are doing the plumbing.'

Millie said, 'How can they do plumbing?'

'Talk to Asilah,' said Sanchez. 'He's telling me, that was their job, some of them. They work in a factory as slaves, and the headmaster paid for them to leave.'

'Oh, right,' said Millie. 'I am getting the whole picture. Slaves in Bogga-Bogga Land, slaves now at Ribblestrop Towers.'

'Yes, you ask if they are unhappy,' said Sanchez. 'Unlike you, they are prepared to work.'

'It's called exploitation, Sanchez. This whole place is wrong.'

'Where's Bogga-Bogga Land?' said Sam.

'Sam,' said Sanchez. 'It's a place she makes up because she knows nothing about them and is also racist.'

'You think I'm a racist?'

'Have you spoken to them? Do you know anything about them? They *want* to be here!'

'They don't know any better, do they?'

'Millie,' said Sanchez. 'We are all so tired.'

'Listen. What if a group of people have been doing animal experiments? It's possible, isn't it? And now, a crack-pot scientist arrives with a whole load of orphans at her disposal. How can you tell me all this is in my imagination? Last term they lost a boy! Is that suspicious, or is that suspicious?'

'OK,' said Sanchez. He was gritting his teeth. His hands were fists. He spoke quietly. 'We'll go down, Millie. We will go down and see.'

'When?'

'Soon!'

'You promise?'

Sanchez closed his eyes. 'Anything, Millie. I just want you to stop talking for a bit and running our school down. And by the way, I'm not being personal, but you've got a nasty sore on your lip and it's bleeding.'

Chapter Fifteen

'When I was at school,' said Dr Norcross-Webb, hours later, 'you had to keep your hands off.' He was sitting by the fountain, stirring coffee. The star-studded night had given way to the first pink strand of dawn. The children sat beside him. 'I vowed that if ever I was in charge, the children would put their hands *on*. You can only learn by doing.'

'I've certainly learned how to move boxes,' muttered Millie.

'How much do you know about electricity, Sam? Ever wondered what it really is? Ever seen the lightning land between your feet or felt a blast of volts right across your heart?'

'No.'

'That woman . . . Look at her.'

They peered upwards and saw a thin frame leaning out of a window over some winching gear.

'She waits for a thunderstorm,' continued the headmaster. He wiped a crumb from his chin. 'She waits for the thunder, then she goes outside, and flies a kite on a metal cord. Why? Why would she do that, Millie?'

'Because she's insane?'

'Yes!'

The headmaster fixed Millie with a devilish smile. 'Exactly right: she has the insanity and the madness of genius. She wants to harness the elements. Under her command, I have seen dead things stand up on their hind legs and dance. And I'm not talking about putting a charge through a frog, Sanchez. I'm not talking about experiments that were done two hundred years ago: I'm talking about new science – science that hasn't even reached the journals yet. We're in the frontline here, boys, Millie. Planting the flag, leaping onto sands that haven't seen a footprint.'

'Why is she teaching us if she's so high-powered?'

'Ah, what a good question. She is to be our Scientist in Residence. This lady has her research facility here and will teach in the mornings.'

'And what exactly is she researching?' said Millie.

'New energy,' said the headmaster. 'Lightning.'

'Hello-oo!' A high voice was yodelling from the tower top. The headmaster leaped to his feet.

'Everything alright?' he called.

'Giles, it's fantastic – come on up. We're ready for take-off!'

'How much can we cram into one day, Sam? Sanchez? Are you needing your beds?'

'No, sir,' said Sanchez.

'Discovery doesn't wait for the sleepy-headed. I tell you something: when I was your age I got two hours a night.'

The first thing Sam noticed as he pushed open the laboratory door was a large pair of hairy knees sticking out from under a bench. He noticed them because in his exhausted state he tripped over them and, as he was carrying a box full of testtubes, the result was noisy.

'Sam!' said the owner of the knees. It was Captain Routon.

'Hello,' said Sam. 'What are you doing?'

'Finishing off, lad. Finishing off. Been at this for weeks; it's nice to see you up so early. Meet the team!'

Sam looked around and noticed the room was full of

orphans. The light had a blue tinge, because their hands were nursing blue jets of flame. The lab was completely round and high-ceilinged: the children were dangling from rafters, cables and shelves. The air was that of a firework-factory: if there was any oxygen, it was fighting amongst clouds of acrid smoke. Sam peered into it as one of the smallest orphans curled upside down on a spike just under the tall cone of the roof. His tie dangled in his face and he used his shirt-tail as a rag, polishing a thin coil of wire to a dazzling shine. His blow-torch muttered in the back pocket of his shorts, the flame soft and green. As Sam watched, the boy reached behind him, coaxed the flame into a powerful, shrieking jet, and hoisted it round to his knees. He played it expertly over the coil. Suddenly a new fountain of sparks was foaming onto the backs of his friends. They didn't notice it. An even smaller boy was ripping open a sheet of solid metal, dragging some kind of power tool down its centre: another shower of sparks and that same, dreadful sound of express train. Sam closed his eyes.

'Is that the last?' called Professor Worthington. She was wearing large gauntlets now, and a filthy white lab-coat. Her make-up was running in little sweaty channels down her nose and in front of her ears. She gave the impression of someone melting: she had big front teeth and she trembled like a nervous horse. She was smiling and shaking. 'Are we ready?'

'OK, OK!' shouted Asilah. 'Henry, get back.'

The orphans lifted their thumbs and Henry was eased gingerly away from the winch.

Professor Worthington pressed a fat red switch on the wall and the room exploded in light. Fluorescent tubes popped and flashed and the tower room was suddenly luminous. But what was the hissing? Sam's eyes hunted for snakes: there were enough glass tanks to house something terrifying. Then Sam saw the gas taps, set into the stone wall: they were open and pumping gas. Anjoli was grinning, moving from nozzle to nozzle with a flaming taper, and everyone gasped at the jets of flame. Ruskin's eyebrows were burned from his face and he cowered backwards. Millie leaped into the centre of the room, holding singed hair. The orphans were capering joyfully: not one had a tie that wasn't singed or a shirt that wasn't stained with soot.

'This is mad!' cried Millie – but her voice was lost. Above her the ceiling was opening, folded back by invisible wires, powered by hydraulics that whispered as calmly as the gas-jets. Sam rubbed his eyes, but a whole section of roof really was opening in petals, and the dark blue of the starlit dawn seemed close enough to touch.

'Hey, careful,' said Sanjay. 'You're on the gantry.'

Millie allowed little hands to draw her back to safety. The floor on which she'd stood was now opening too, and a long piece of Meccano, like the struts of a crane, was pushing upwards. Telescopically it extended and extended, cogs whirring and tiny cables straining: up to the ceiling that wasn't there, beyond the tip of the roof-cone and still extending. Then the orphan with the blow-torch – his name was Israel – stepped confidently from his beam, out onto it. Still it unfolded, so the child rose with it out into the breezy night. He scampered higher, his grey shirt billowing off his shoulders, a sailor in the rigging of a tall ship. Millie just about heard his voice singing something. The notes fell about her.

'Acha, yes,' said Asilah. 'Everything's OK. My brother says is OK.'

Yet again, thought Millie, for the hundredth time, *I'm in a dream, I'm in some kind of lunatic asylum. And the maddest thing is I haven't yet left.* She was caught by a snatch of freezing air. *I should be dead . . .*

'We'll find out how the world works!' shouted Professor Worthington. 'We'll ask a few questions!'

This isn't right, thought Millie. *This isn't a school . . .*

Explosions ripped across the sky.

*

Lady Vyner was jolted into a sitting position and her breath came in quick gasps. She heard Caspar scream and then she heard him wail. Utterly disorientated, she fumbled for her glasses. More explosions, quick as gunfire. Lights blazing. It was the north tower, opposite: they were blowing up her home, with her inside it *and* her grandson, heir to the Vyner dynasty.

She blundered to the window, slipping dangerously on rat-eaten rugs. An empty bottle skittered across the floor and an ashtray clattered. She pushed the curtain up and stared out. Someone was letting off fireworks.

'What a lovely idea,' said the headmaster, gazing upwards.

Israel had a pocketful of rockets. He climbed to the very top of the needle and stuck the fireworks one by one into the metal-work. The rockets soared up and burst, and great handfuls of red stars blew gently off in the breeze.

'Why fireworks?' said Millie.

Asilah was sitting close by. 'Just a blessing,' he said softly.

'To thank God,' said Sanjay.

Someone started to sing – it was Israel, who was descending now. All at once the tower was full of the most beautiful music. More fireworks were crackling, the gunshots battering back and forth over the park.

Millie left the laboratory quietly.

A hundred and thirty-something steps: she wasn't sure if she could get down them. She wasn't sure she could remember where she'd rolled her sleeping bag or where the landing off the boys' dormitory might be. She would sleep anywhere. All she wanted was a corner and to have no more strange experiences. She touched her throbbing lip and stumbled.

'Millie,' said a voice. She leaned against the wall, feeling a little faint. The headmaster was above her. He spoke softly: 'You're not well, are you?'

'What?'

'Do you know where you're going?'

'No.'

'My dear, we're working you too hard, I could see how tired you were. And you haven't seen the girls' boarding house. All this excitement, the most basic things sometimes get forgotten, I am so sorry. Where did we put you last night?'

'It's fine. I was fine.'

'You're in a whirl, aren't you? And you have been neglected. I'll show you the way and you can sleep for as long as you like. We retrieved your trunk, by the way, so it's all unpacked. You've pretty much got your own facilities, until more girls come, of course.'

Millie blinked through her fatigue: 'Are there going to be more girls?'

'You won't be alone for long, that's for sure.' The headmaster looked at his watch. 'I've got people signing up all the time, and the deputy head is very keen to develop the girls' side of things. Oh, drat: we're going to cancel morning assembly, aren't we? I think we all need a bit of rest and relaxation. Nearly there, keep going.'

'How many girls will there be?'

'Hard to say. The dormitory can't cope with too many, but that being said, expanding it is top of the agenda. Careful, there: mind the step.'

The headmaster took Millie gently by the arm and led her out of the tower. They walked slowly, following the outer wall of the mansion. 'Millie, you know that policeman chap, Inspector Cuthbertson? He's our local man. He asked me one or two questions about you and I was a bit thrown.'

Millie prepared herself.

'Can I ask you – were you on a train at any point, coming down to school?'

'No.'

'You weren't? And yet your luggage, and Ruskin's and Sam's – it all ended up in Penzance. Unclaimed, at the station.'

'Yes, we put it on the train in London. Then we met Sanchez and his father offered to fly us in the helicopter.'

'Right.'

The headmaster was trying to frame his next question, delicately. Millie was thinking hard and fast. 'You didn't go shopping in Reading, did you? About lunchtime?'

'I haven't any money. No.'

'Actually a credit card was used. That's all part of the mystery, you see. Our new deputy headmistress, Miss Hazlitt . . . Funny story in a way. She was on the train, the same one as your luggage. And she had her purse stolen. She was actually injured quite badly, not when she lost her purse, but later, when the . . . when the train did an emergency stop because there were three children on the tracks. Or something like that, I have to confess I got quite confused. Anyway, a number of witnesses say that the children were wearing black-and-gold blazers, rather like . . . ours.'

Millie went to speak, but the headmaster carried on quickly. 'Now I know that many schools have a similar uniform to ours. So no conclusions will be jumped to.'

'Is she alright?' said Millie.

'Still in London. Health comes first, doesn't it, and she's not the most robust . . . No: the train was delayed and her wrist was sprained. So she, er . . . checked into a rather expensive hotel. But she hopes to be down tomorrow.'

Millie said nothing. 'Bit of an all-rounder, this Miss Hazlitt. She's been asked to take us in hand, trying to sort out some of our problems.'

'Where am I sleeping?' said Millie.

'Nearly there. So. Ha. You don't have a credit card?'

'I'm thirteen.'

'Yes indeed.'

'I'm really tired.'

The headmaster tried again. 'Millie,' he said, as gently as he could. 'What exactly did you see in the cellars? Will you tell me?'

'Nothing.'

'We should have sealed them last term. I was looking at the map last night and they are an absolute maze: the sooner we have that stairway bricked up the better. I was told they'd all been closed, after the suicide, but there was a boy last term who found a way down.'

'What suicide? Who?'

'Lord Vyner. Cyril Vyner, the late husband of our landlady. You met her, didn't you?'

'Yes, she threw crockery at us.'

'Her husband killed himself down there, years ago. She refuses to believe it, thinks he was murdered. Caspar's grandfather. He did a lot of work for the government in the Second World War, some kind of experimental science. They do say there's a tunnel that takes you all the way to London, though again, it should have been bricked up by now.'

'Why did he commit suicide?'

The headmaster paused. 'Nobody knows. Life just got too much, maybe? They say the experiments were getting more and more bizarre – top secret, he and his partner virtually lived down there. He cooked for himself, hardly saw a soul.' The headmaster had stopped, and was looking hard into her eyes. 'Is there anything you want to tell me?'

'No.'

'You're looking anxious, dear.'

'I'm tired. I suppose . . . The idea of suicide . . .'

'People do say he's sometimes seen. On the lawns. Coming down the stairs. Always carrying his supper on a silver tray – he was a very fine cook, apparently. I was just wondering if maybe you had seen something? Something that had upset you.'

'No.'

'We had a little boy last term, by the name of Miles. He saw the ghost. Do you believe that?'

'No.'

123

'You're a rationalist. So am I.'

'Was Miles the boy who ran away?'

'No. Tomaz was the boy who ran away. Miles was a casualty of a different kind. He had to leave us – against my wishes, but that was one of the conditions of staying open, I'm afraid. He was very upset when Tomaz left, and . . . he did something very foolish.' They stood in silence for a moment. Then the headmaster said, softly: 'I've tried to be honest with you, Millie.'

'Yes.'

'What I also wanted to say is that this school needs people like you. We could all learn a lot from you, and Ribblestrop will be a better place with you *in* it. Do you understand me? I want you to stay here. So if there's anything on your mind, let me help. I know what you did at your last school, of course I do. We can all do destructive things, they're very easy. It's building things that's hard.'

Millie met the gaze of the headmaster, trying to work out if he was as daft as she had first thought. She had the alarming notion that he was playing a rather clever game.

'I really am tired,' she said. 'Could we talk in the morning?'

'Yes. Absolutely . . . I'm babbling on, and you need some sleep, of course you do. Just round here, we're very nearly there . . .'

They set off, turning into a small yard. They crossed it and came to an archway. Broken stone littered their path and the smell of burnt wood was strong.

'Follow your nose, eh? It's round the back of what was the library, through here. Now, if you do get lost for goodness' sake don't start going down any staircases. Here we are . . .'

'Where?'

'Just here.'

There was no dormitory. There was only a small shed, the type her grandad had kept spades and pitchforks in on his seedy little allotment. The headmaster opened the door.

124

'Don't see it as it is. See it as it will be.'

'It's a shed.'

'Your very own.'

Among the spades and pitchforks, beside a large lawnmower and under a shelf full of paint-pots stood a small bed. It was fully made up with sheets and duvet. A familiar trunk with the words *Millie Roads* stood at the foot.

'There's an outside tap round the corner,' said the headmaster. 'I put your toothbrush in a glass, just next to it. And your bags, from Selfridges – I put them in the corner. Everything OK?'

'Yes,' said Millie.

'I know it's a bit Spartan . . .'

'No . . .'

'Not too primitive?'

'No.'

She felt a gentle hand on her shoulder.

'Look up, eh? See the stars.'

'Yes. Sir . . .'

The headmaster waited, but Millie said nothing.

'What is it?'

Just for a moment, an inexplicable moment, Millie wanted to confide in him. It was like a chink in her armour, she felt the need to pour everything out about what she had seen, what she feared, what she wanted, and why she couldn't work out if she should stay or go. It unnerved her, almost as if she had been hypnotised for a second. He had very piercing eyes and the temptation to talk into them was almost overwhelming.

'Nothing,' she said.

The headmaster nodded.

'Goodnight,' he said.

Chapter Sixteen

This hectic speed of life could not, of course, be sustained. The headmaster realised it and allowed the children two full days off timetable. They wandered here and there until they became familiar with the layout of the school. There were piles of rubble in the corridors, as well as in the courtyard. There were doorless rooms with sagging ceilings; there were holes in the floor, and queer staircases that led to chained gates and bricked-up archways. There were whole corridors barricaded with the word *Private* and *No Children* – some of them scrawled rather frantically as if the writers were frightened.

There was a crumbling chapel set in an abandoned graveyard. Sam saw a monk, and gave chase. Alas, the old man fled and disappeared before the boy could say hello.

There were wild patches full of nettles and thorns and sudden lawns that sloped off to the woods by the lake. The children explored the lake, of course. None of them had trunks, so they had to swim in their shorts.

It was smooth and beautiful, deep and dangerous, black and silver – huge, it seemed, but in fact you could walk all the way round it in an evening. The Greek temple at the end – so promising at a distance – was a disappointment. The plaster was crumbling and green algae was reclaiming it. It tilted into the water and was full of old rubbish from tramps or tourists. There was even fire damage up one wall. But if you sat inside it and looked between the pillars, you got the best view of the Neptune statue. Neptune was pearl-white, and he gleamed in the water that ran down his enormous shoulders, chest and thighs. He was sprawled out, up to his knees in water, majestic and lazy, his trident high. Just beyond him, two little humpback bridges took you onto a small island. On the island was a plinth, and rising up from that was a column. A bronze Lord Vyner stood on the top, staring at the house, hand on hip: the Vyner monument.

Caspar had declared that his family went all the way back to 1066. He told the children that it was his ancestor who had shot King Harold in the eye at the Battle of Hastings, and as a result William the Conqueror had given half of England to the Vyner family. Millie disputed this. She looked hard at the statue on the column and decided that it was far too camp to be heroic.

But as the children explored, Millie kept her eye out for an air-vent. She recalled the chimney-like shaft that had funnelled oxygen to her underground labyrinth, she remembered the glimmer of daylight she'd seen – and knew it had to be in the grounds somewhere. Of course, her journey through that maze was beginning to seem as bizarre as the thought of seventeen children lost up a railway tunnel. The sun was out and the leaves were turning coppery gold. Freezers and ghosts seemed more and more ridiculous; no crockery dropped from high battlements, so . . . the school seemed peaceful and rather beautiful.

Millie's real complaint – and it was a major distraction – was the sore on her lip.

Everyone had noticed it twenty-four hours after her adventure, and several people pointed it out. She had to admit that, days later, it was not healing. She didn't want anyone to know, but the one sore had been joined by others. She used the boys' showers for bathing, having made a large cardboard sign which read: *Girl Warning – Stay Clear.* She would hang this on the bathroom door and know she had her privacy.

But taking off her clothes had become a frightening experience.

She'd had reasonable skin all her life. Now, however, it was blotchy and unpleasant. Her neck, her shoulders, her ankles and, most horribly, her face – all were affected. A pimple would appear and then break into a sore. No amount of cream or subtle make-up hid them, and she had to work hard not to scratch. One Maths lesson Lord Caspar announced she had leprosy and gave her a small bell to ring. Once again, physical violence was prevented by the intervention of Sanchez.

Otherwise, a sort of normality took hold.

The Mapping Project continued, and pictures and charts spread along the main corridor. Captain Routon started fitness classes in the morning, and everyone went for long runs around the grounds. Ruskin's model roof – the one he'd shown Sam on the train – won first prize in the Model Roof Competition. There were no other entries, since Sanchez had forgotten all about it and Henry had never understood the requirements. Ruskin was awarded a certificate and a hand-made rosette (in black and gold). The model was put on display in the dining hall, and used by one and all to work out timber-sizes and angles. A planning application was submitted and, if all went well, construction would begin towards the end of the term.

The next Monday, the first Science lesson took place.

The plumbing was complete and most of the equipment was stowed. Professor Worthington gave a lecture on safety in the laboratory, which seemed very ordinary and dull. The homework involved sketching things like goggles and gloves, but you were allowed to draw pictures of what might happen to people if they didn't wear them. Some children spent hours on this, filling their margins with gory illustrations.

But it was Captain Routon's special announcement that

caused most excitement. It was the end of the third week. Sam would never forget the moment. His bandages were off, and he was now totally bald. He had been working on a new letter to his parents, as he tried to write one a day, and had just completed the word 'Dear' when the captain appeared with a tray full of doughnuts. It was early evening.

'Big day coming up,' he said, with exaggerated calmness.

'Why?' said Millie.

'Haven't you heard? Oh, I thought he'd break the news himself.'

'What news?' said Sam.

'What news? We've got a match.'

'What sort of match?' said Ruskin. 'What do you mean?'

'A football match!' said the captain.

Sam nearly fell off his chair. 'I was only saying!' he cried. 'Just last week, I was saying! I was writing! I said to my dad . . .'

'It's all coming together,' continued Captain Routon. 'This headmaster, I don't know how he does it. A fixture: just like that. Against a cracking good team, too.'

Sanchez said, 'But how? We've never played football, so I don't understand how we can get a side together so soon.'

'The pressure's on, boys,' said Captain Routon. 'We need a side for next month, so the pressure is on. We're up against the High School – home game – to be followed by a return fixture at their place. I'm in charge of training. It's a tough side, but I think the home advantage is very, very important.'

'Hang on,' said Millie. 'Hang on a second. How can we play another school here? We don't have a team. We don't even have a pitch.'

'There was a tennis court,' said Ruskin. 'They used it in the old days. But the donkeys live on it now.'

'Do we have a ball?' said Millie. Captain Routon was studying some paperwork. 'Do we have goalposts? Kit, boots . . . corner-flags? White lines marking out the penalty area? How do we get any of this together for next month?'

'We work hard,' said Sanchez. 'And by the way, you can play football without a kit and without a flag. In fact, where I come from you play without a ball.'

Millie snorted.

'I am serious, listen. On the beach where I come from, the boys play with a plastic bottle and you see magic. There's a friend of mine, his name's Imagio. If he was here, they'd be making him professional, and he plays with a tin can, Millie – so you don't know everything.'

Millie said: 'What about your own skills?'

Sanchez stared at her. Ruskin said quietly, 'Millie . . . didn't I mention what happened?'

'With a limp like yours,' said Millie, 'I would have thought your footballing days are over. You can cut up the half-time oranges if you want.'

'I can play.'

'Well, that's heroic, isn't it? The problem is I have to think about the team. We must play to our *strengths*—'

'Listen, Millie—!'

'We'll try you out as soon as we can! I'm just saying, don't get your hopes up.'

'I can play!' shouted Sanchez. He was standing and his fists were clenched. He was completely red in the face.

'You seem upset,' said Millie. 'Are you losing your cool?'

'He's a jolly good goalie,' said Ruskin. 'Nobody gets past Sanchez.'

'What I'm worried about is the ball,' said Sam, quickly. 'I mean, do we have one? It would be nice to have as much training as possible. I'm still seeing things a bit fuzzy, especially in the sun. But I did play for my last school.'

Captain Routon looked up. 'I suggested to the headmaster that we should cancel all these lessons for a while and get cracking. Once again, you see, it's about working together and putting the group shoulder to the wheel. We did the same in

Algeria when I was prisoner-of-war: the lads wanted a football pitch. We said to the commandant, if we knock down the wash-room and rebuild it there, we'd have the space. He said, "You've got till midnight." You've never seen so many men work together so fast, so hard. No tools, of course – just our bare hands, shifting stone, digging the foundation. We did it.'

'Do you think the orphans play football?' said Ruskin. 'I don't know what they do in the Himalayas.'

'I imagine they play more on horses,' said Sam. 'I was speaking to Israel and Sanjay, and I think they were talking about the sea and horses. Maybe it's a kind of water-polo.'

'They'll learn to play,' said Ruskin. 'They're a plucky lot.'

'Seven o'clock, soon as it's light,' said Captain Routon. 'I'll meet you on the pitch.'

'But there isn't a pitch!' said Millie.

'Oh, Millie!' said Sam, in a rare show of impatience. 'We're going to make one – that's the point!'

Chapter Seventeen

At seven o'clock the trees were still holding the early-morning mist in their arms. The sun poured thick gold light, horizontal over the ground. Two donkeys did a slow circuit of the old tennis courts, nibbling.

Captain Routon had removed the mower from Millie's dorm. At two minutes past seven everyone was swirling through the mists, bouncing over the turf. The donkeys wobbled away to cover; the children cheered and moved off in work parties to attack weeds and nettle-patches. At nine-thirty Dr Norcross-Webb appeared with lemonade and two buckets of white-wash. There was no machine available, so he and Captain Routon laid out lines of rope.

Pythagoras's Theorem was invoked and suddenly the antique words *hypotenuse, perimeter, circumference* transformed themselves to boundaries, centre-spots and penalty areas. Anjoli became a human chalk mark on the end of a radius, sprinting and laughing, tied at the waist. Thus was the pitch painted. Just before lunch a flat-bed lorry delivered a dozen strips of planed-up three-by-two, and hammer blows ricocheted over the school, the orphans balancing on one another's shoulders. The goalposts went up square and true, dug into firm earth. Hooks were screwed in strategically and some old tennis nets were tailored into shape. By the early afternoon, Henry had successfully removed two trees from one of the penalty areas, and – hot and sweaty, but feverishly proud – the children surveyed their work. The pitch tilted, no doubt about it: but that would advantage nobody. One of the touchlines bulged outwards where Ruskin had fled a wasp: such things would be corrected.

'Police,' said Sanjay.

'What?'

The child had the eyes of a buzzard. He was stripped to the waist as usual, his tie bound round his temples again to keep the sweat from his eyes. Sure enough, an engine got closer and after several minutes, a large white car came into view. The children waited, slightly nervous. They weren't aware of laws preventing the creation of football pitches in the grounds of old stately homes, but a police car is never a comforting sight, unless you've been mugged. The driver's window slid down and a grinning, grey face peered at the children.

'Ribblestrop Towers' first eleven!' said Inspector Cuthbertson. 'Am I right? I'll be rooting for you, boys – wish I could be there at the match. Now, look: I was in town yesterday, and I thought of your penniless headmaster. A little gift – tell him it's from me.' There was a football on the passenger seat. He picked it up and made as if to throw it. 'Anyone been down in the dungeons again?' he whispered. The whisper turned to a giggle, and his gaze moved from orphan to orphan, from Sanchez to Sam. He found Millie and his smile seemed to get stuck. 'What about you, my dear? Ooo, my word . . . what happened to your face?'

Millie said nothing.

She looked past the policeman's eye, taking in as much detail as she could. There were fish-and-chip wrappers stuffed into the door-pockets. There was a clutter of loose change, sweets and paper cups. The policeman had twinkling eyes and at the back, again, she saw a hint of madness – she'd seen it in a dog once, just before it went for her. Millie had never liked policemen, largely because they'd never liked her. He had bad skin too and there was a dressing taped over the knuckles of one hand.

'I'm not going down there again,' she said. 'You made it sound so scary.'

'Very wise,' said the inspector. 'I'm talking to a sensible girl, aren't I?'

'Did you find your rabbit?'

'What?' The smile disappeared. 'What did you say?'

'I said thank you for buying us a football, it's a very nice gesture.'

Inspector Cuthbertson blinked. One of the orphans was reaching to grab the ball and there was a twittering of excitement. 'That's not what you said,' he cried, but Millie was letting herself be jostled out of the way; the policeman was shouting, but he couldn't make himself heard. All at once the ball was flung high in the air and then booted hard. Everyone was running and the whole crowd flew to the other end of the pitch. When Millie looked back at the car, she saw the inspector sitting at the wheel, motionless.

'He seems nice,' said Sam.

'Did you look at his face?' said Millie, to Sanchez. 'He's got the same sores as me. Just by his lips. Would you trust him, Sanchez?'

'Where I come from you don't talk to policemen, ever.'

'He's up to something. They're working together, all of them.'

There was a shifting of gears and the police car drove off, windows closing.

'Up to what, Millie?'

'Something that stinks. The headmaster said he had a map of the cellars – we've got to go back down. I haven't forgotten your promise, you know. You're hoping I have, but I haven't.'

'Kick!' shouted Captain Routon. It was evening. He was bowling the ball towards the line of orphans, who were decked out in school shoes, grey school shorts and vests. Millie, Sam, Henry, Ruskin and Sanchez were all watching: they did not need the basic practice the orphans did.

'They're coming on,' said Ruskin. He said this just as one of the smaller boys – his name appeared to be Eric, but that seemed unlikely – kicked hard and high. Having missed the ball completely, he ended up on his backside, his face split in half by a delighted smile.

'There's no shortage of guts.'

'Stickability,' said Sam. 'My father told me that you should always stick at things. They're definitely sticking at it. Are they really all brothers? Whenever I forget a name, someone says, "This is my brother, Ajay," or whatever.'

'I think,' said Sanchez, 'they use brother to mean *close friend*. They call Asilah "uncle".'

'They lived in the same village,' said Sam. 'I think they must be sort of related, they behave like they are.'

'They'd be good in a crisis,' said Ruskin. 'Have you seen how they work together – when they're getting food, for example?'

'No.'

'Everything's divided fairly – the big ones check the little ones eat first. Where do they sleep, d'you think?'

'They have the east tower,' said Sanchez. 'Henry visits them sometimes – they had to rebuild part of it. Look, they can't see the ball any more.'

'I wonder if Captain Routon ought to postpone his tactics lecture,' said Ruskin. 'Save it for when we're all fresh. By the way, I thought you were excellent, Sam. First class.'

'Oh. Thank you.'

'I'd make you captain. You said you played for your last school?'

'I did, actually. It was only a small school, but we—'

'I'm captain,' said Millie. 'I've already said.'

'Why?' said Sanchez.

135

'Because I'm experienced. I understand the word *strategy*, which no one else here could even spell.'

'Captain Routon's in charge,' said Sanchez. 'He'll select.'

'As long as he selects me, that will be fine. The High School won't know what's hit it.'

'You know,' said Ruskin, 'I try not to take these games too seriously. As far as I'm concerned it's going to be nice to meet some boys from a local school. Dr Norcross-Webb thinks it could be the start of all sorts of interesting projects – stamp swapping, Scrabble tournaments. I've never been one for inter-school rivalry. Life's far too short.'

'Is it a mixed school?' said Sanchez.

'Oh yes.'

'Good,' he said, looking at Millie. 'Maybe we'll meet a few proper girls.'

Chapter Eighteen

The homework that night was to write an account in symbols and words of the process of laying out bisected rectangles and inserting radii of different lengths. It was to be accomplished with pencils, string and a drawing pin – and every child scored full marks.

The headmaster beamed as he served the night-time cocoa. They had moved to the dining hall and two bright braziers flamed away to take the chill off the air. The wind tugged at a tarpaulin and there was the feeling of an army gathered. Sugar had run out as rations were low, so he distributed boiled sweets which were dunked for a few minutes in the scalding china cups. Millie had been made hot-water-urn monitor and had taken great care in filling them, especially as so many of her customers were almost too tired to hold the handles. The orphans had a knack of using each other as furniture: before nine o'clock the smaller ones were leaning fast asleep on the older ones.

'Another fabulous day,' whispered the headmaster. 'Just time for an evening prayer.'

Millie looked up. 'I thought this wasn't a religious school.'

'Well, it isn't, Millie, you're right.'

'You said,' said Millie, challengingly, 'that you didn't believe in God. You said you were a rationalist.'

Sanchez looked down and put a hand over his eyes. 'Millie,' he said, 'must you always be the one to embarrass everybody?'

'I'm asking about religion, why is that so embarrassing?'

'Man, because maybe it's personal?'

'You're not religious, are you?'

'Yes.'

'Really? Hindu?'

'Just how ignorant are you?' snapped Sanchez. 'I come from a Catholic country, don't you even know that?'

'I've been asked to say a prayer by Captain Routon,' said the headmaster. 'He was a little dismayed by football practice this afternoon. Not dismayed at the effort or the . . . *enthusiasm*. But he does feel we might appeal to a higher power, and out of plain courtesy I think we should assist him.'

'Do you need a prayer-mat?' said Millie, to Sanchez.

'Shh!' said Asilah.

The headmaster stood up and leaned on the table. 'You can keep your eyes open if you want to. I'll ask everyone to bow their heads.' He was thoughtful a moment; then he looked up and said to the ceiling: 'Thank you, God, for what makes us different and thank you for what makes us the same. Thank you for all the awkward questions in the world and the honesty in asking them. God . . .' The headmaster paused. 'Please look down on us all in your mercy and if you can consider assisting us, that is . . . offering us some *guidance* in the rather everyday matter of ball control . . . we would be most eternally grateful. We ask for no unfair advantage, nor do we ask for miracles. Just a sense of direction.'

Amens rattled out among the snores.

Then, in the peace and quiet – that lovely moment of meditation – a voice creaked out from the darkness. 'Headmaster?'

Those who were awake turned, abruptly. The voice came again, urgent and impatient: 'Where is the headmaster, please? I'm looking for the head—'

'Oh, my word – Miss . . . this must be Miss Hazlitt!' The headmaster's voice was full of warmth, and he leaped to his feet. 'Is that really you?'

'Nine-thirty, you said. It's nine-forty.' The figure emerged from the doorway, clutching the wall for balance. Now the light caught the black fabric of its dress and the whiteness of its face. Tall and thin, so easy to overbalance, the figure rocked from side to side, unsteady on a plank. Little arms and legs jutted from the long body as if a child had sketched them; a high collar supported a face that was all sharp angles. Millie recognised her immediately: the woman from the train, complete with metal briefcase. She managed to step down to one of the duck-boards on the mud. Yes, it was the same sharp discus of a hat, throwing the woman's face into shadow as she looked down. When she looked up, her lipstick was red as a wound. 'I'm very keen to meet the pupils,' she said. Miss Hazlitt brought her voice down to a whisper and there was a soft growl to it. 'Could you bring them to the office, perhaps – one by one? It's the uneven ground, I'm not finding it easy.'

'You can meet them here, my dear! Come on in!'

There was an urgent chirruping sound from a bag or a pocket. Like a gunfighter, the cellphone was drawn in a blur of long, slim fingers, and was at her ear. 'What?' she said. 'No, no, not right now, no . . .' She was bent over like a hook and the voice rasped with impatience. There was a gust of sweat and cigarette. She looked even more bug-like than Millie remembered – elbows out, head forward on a surprisingly long neck. 'Try again,' she said, angrily. 'Contact him, get an estimate and run it past the major; keep me in the loop . . .' She cut the line and came further still into the wreckage of the hall, picking her way, holding walls then tables for balance, the briefcase now under her arm. She licked her lips eagerly, keying a number into the phone. 'Item for agenda,' she said quietly. 'Health and safety in eating area; request survey of facilities and double-check all insurances.' She looked up, and tilted her head to one side, trying hard to smile, stretching her lips. She put out a hand and took an orphan by the tie. It was Anjoli. 'Uniform, headmaster? We agreed on a dress-code, I thought. What's your name, little one?'

'Anjoli,' said Anjoli.

'Miss Hazlitt, we were just relaxing, we were—'

'We can't call this a uniform, can we? Not according to the diagrams we exchanged. A little street urchin perhaps, but oh – look at this . . .' She ran her hands around the boy's head, her thumbs exploring and pressing. 'Does this child not have a comb? What kind of hairstyle is this?'

'Well, it's the evening,' said the headmaster, moving towards her. 'After a day of sport, things get a little casual, and we've all been running around! Anjoli, for example, plays midfield.' He drew Anjoli out of the woman's grip.

'Sport?' she said. 'Today's Friday. I could have sworn . . .' She'd found a pair of spectacles and was looping them over her ears. They flashed as she turned her head this way and that. She had a paper in her fingers and peered through thick lenses. '*Tuesday* is sport,' she said, trying to chuckle. 'Tuesday!'

'Yes, but there's been a bit of good news—'

'You see,' she cried. 'Exercise must never be random. I drew up the timetable weeks ago and it distinctly says – I have it here – sport on a *Tuesday*. A structured programme, children – that is the key.'

'I think I need to update you on a few developments, Miss Hazlitt,' said the headmaster. He clapped his hands. 'Children! Can I have your attention?' The orphans were sitting up uneasily. Anjoli had moved well back, towards Millie. She put an arm round him, and was surprised to feel his heart beating rapidly: the boy was terrified. 'Miss Hazlitt has come all the way from London,' said the headmaster. 'She used to work with a number of very important people and she even did work for the government. So, we are very lucky, and very glad to have her here until . . . well, Christmas at least!'

'Stand up, all of you,' said Miss Hazlitt. She had at last managed to stretch her lips into something resembling a smile: at least, you could now see her teeth. Millie saw at once that they were false. The make-up was thick and the hair couldn't be her own – was it attached to the hat?

'Do you want the names?' asked the headmaster. Everyone was standing, so Millie got to her feet as well.

'No, no, I have the list,' said the woman. 'Why don't I go down it? It won't take a moment. I've been dying to put faces to names. Tack, Sam Arthur. Which one's he?' Sam raised his hand. 'Ah, now you're a newcomer, aren't you?' said Miss Hazlitt. 'Put your hand down, child. Roads, Millicent . . . also new, special arrangements according to my list. Which one is the Roads girl?'

'That's me,' said Millie. 'Hello.'

Miss Hazlitt's head swivelled and her neck seemed to get yet longer. She locked onto Millie's eyes, her spectacles two little discs of light. Millie's adrenaline was pumping and she knew enough about situations like these to steal immediate advantage.

'Welcome to Ribblestrop,' she said, in her friendliest voice. 'We heard your train was delayed; that must have been so tiresome.'

'Ha!' barked the headmaster. 'She's with us now, aren't you, Miss Hazlitt? That's what matters.'

'My train was delayed,' said Miss Hazlitt. Her voice had fallen to a rasping hiss and Millie thought of rattlesnakes. 'It was most extremely delayed, due to criminal behaviour and theft, which is being investigated. Massive inconvenience, massive delay, and a potentially dangerous injury. Ah . . . You appear to

141

be wearing make-up, my dear.' The woman came closer, tilting her head and peering into Millie's eyes. Her cellphone chirruped again.

'So do you,' said Millie.

'Hello, Hazlitt? Jewellery too, I see you're wearing . . . earrings. Are they new?' Her hand reached out to touch one of them and Millie drew back. She had long, fine fingers and the nails were carefully trimmed.

'Yes,' said Millie. 'My mother gave me the bracelet, whereas—'

'No, no, no. Ask them to revise the schedule and send it to me, we can't assume anything. Good.' She looked from Millie to the headmaster, her fingers poised. She was so close to Millie, Millie could smell her. The clothes were old; they had a jumble-sale, stored-away-for-decades odour. The scent she wore would not cover it. 'I wear make-up,' she whispered, staring hard at Millie, 'because I'm an adult. You, my dear, are a child and you're breaking an important school rule.' Her cellphone rang again.

'Ah . . .' said the headmaster.

'Give them to me, please. The earrings. No, no, no – he's got to be involved – we'll have to set up a video link. Talk to my secretary, call me back.'

'You know, I haven't read that rule,' said Millie. Her heart was beating faster, just like Anjoli's, but she managed to keep her friendliest voice. The woman's hand was so close to her cheek, and Millie fought the urge to bite. 'I've been trying to get hold of a new rule book for some time,' she said. 'I lost my copy and I feel rather at sea without it.'

'Oh, I'll find you a rule book,' said Miss Hazlitt. Her voice had dropped still further. It was a poisonous whisper. 'Don't you worry about a rule book, child. We'll be looking at the rule book, line by line. We shall learn it by rote if necessary, because routine and regulation are the cornerstones – the pillars – of any great construction, which this school will be. A school to change history.'

The headmaster laughed softly. 'Ah, yes, construction is the word. Though, as you know, Miss Hazlitt – hah! – we have a very relaxed approach here. Now, why don't you meet the orphans? Children, Miss Hazlitt was instrumental in smoothing the way for you boys, so I know you'll want to make her welcome. Come along, now, out of the shadows!'

Miss Hazlitt's eyes left Millie's. She turned away, her gaze shifting from child to child. She moved from cluster to cluster, peering hard. Now and then she touched a chin or a shoulder, or turned a head to see the child in profile.

'Sit,' she said, at length.

'Some of you may wonder,' said the headmaster, 'why Miss Hazlitt is here. Well. It's for many reasons. Administration and finance are two of them.'

'Health,' said Miss Hazlitt. 'Safety and discipline.'

'Yes, indeed. So? A round of applause, I think, to welcome a most important member of staff.'

Everybody clapped and the cellphone chirped again under it. The woman's thumb was a blur as she dealt with the call. 'I'll start tomorrow with the one-to-one interviews,' she said to the headmaster. 'I need to cross-reference my own notes with your filing system and I need to conduct medical examinations, as a priority. There seems to be very little information about any of them, so that will have to change . . . I will also be teaching, children. So I will have the opportunity of getting to know you *intimately*. Think of me, if you will, as both teacher and friend.'

'Yes,' said the headmaster. 'I suppose—'

'Note to self,' said Miss Hazlitt, into her cellphone. 'Address timetabling issue re: personal-conduct classes and ensure exercise is part of an appropriate programme – double-check timetable. A lot of red meat, headmaster. I don't see any balance in this diet.' Miss Hazlitt's eyes flicked over the ranks one last time. 'I'll see you all tomorrow,' she said. 'Ties properly worn. Shirts buttoned at the neck and tucked in smartly. Blazers done up.' She held Millie's eye a little longer. 'Doctor, I think you and I need to talk.' She tried to turn and a plank shifted under her. She grabbed a bench for stability – nearly dropped her brief-case – and righted herself. She tried once again to smile. Everyone saw her dentures shift. She picked her way across the hall to the corridor, the headmaster following.

'Wow,' said Millie. 'What a cow.'

The hall emptied. Millie was on washing-up duty and she worked at it slowly. Her mind was buzzing. There were two bags full of stolen goods she had to conceal, and she wondered how long she had. The woman had recognised her, and cross-referencing the credit-card records with the goods in her shed would be all too easy. There was a very conspicuous fur coat that had been ridiculously expensive and the earrings had nearly been taken. Everything would have to go, she knew it. She could wrap it in plastic and hide it in the woods, maybe. Reclaim it before Christmas? How infuriating . . . Millie was so engrossed in her plans that she didn't hear Captain Routon behind her; didn't notice him even as he leaned in next to her.

'Millie,' he said, softly. Millie started, and swung round. 'I know why you're wearing make-up.'

'What?'

He had a torch in his hand, but it wasn't switched on. He was looking at Millie hard, in the candlelight. 'I've seen those sores before,' he said.

'What sores?'

'The ones you're trying to hide. The sores on your face.'

He spoke gently and sympathetically. There was no threat.

'I'm not trying to embarrass you, Millie. The fact is I know

144

they're not cold sores – that's what the headmaster thinks they are. That's what we told him.'

'What *are* they?' said Millie. Her mouth had gone dry.

'You've been near acid.' Captain Routon paused. 'You've been near something with ammonia, and quite a dose. I was speaking to Professor Worthington and we think you've had a blast of something nasty, unless you're allergic to bleach.'

'Are they on your feet?' said another voice. Millie saw a shape in the shadows of rubble and timber. It was Professor Worthington, cocoa in hand. 'You often get them where the skin is stretched,' continued Professor Worthington. 'Ankles, scalp. They don't clear up with a bit of moisturiser, Millie. The captain's right.'

Millie discovered her hands were shaking. Her fingers were up at her mouth, hovering over the little pustules.

'Captain Routon said bleach, but it's not, is it? I think it's something more serious. I'd like to know where you've been, Millie.'

'Nowhere. It's just eczema, I always get it. It's fine.'

'Millie. I need to look at your skin.'

Both adults came towards her. She was desperately aware of the darkness all around and the fact that every other child in the school was high up in a tower, a long way from where she stood now. Captain Routon switched his torch on and the powerful beam flicked madly over the makeshift kitchen. There was a knife block close to the taps. Six knives stood ready: she could reach them if she needed to. They knew she'd been in the cellar, they must do. Was it *their* laboratory she'd found?

'Can I see?' said Professor Worthington.

Millie's mind was racing faster. She knew what was causing her sores, she had no doubt at all. It was the white powder from the bottle she'd broken, the stuff she'd so stupidly touched. Professor Worthington had recognised it and wanted to be sure. That meant . . . That must mean it was her laboratory. If it was her laboratory, she now knew Millie had been inside. The child closed her eyes. What choice was there? The teacher held the bright light centimetres from her; she felt the breath of Professor Worthington on her cheek.

As if the woman could sense her fear she said, gently: 'I'm not going to touch you, Millie. I don't need to touch you. The captain's here because he's seen this before and I wanted a second opinion. Don't be frightened.'

Millie flipped an eye open and the light was merciless. She closed it again. For a split second she imagined herself in a dentist's chair, tilted to the light.

'Where have you seen them before?' she asked the captain. Her voice was a strange, grating squeak.

'Pakistan,' said Captain Routon. 'Some of the local boys used a thing called myelin.'

'Heard of that, Millie?' asked Professor Worthington.

Millie shook her head.

'It's a nerve agent,' said Captain Routon. 'Developed in the Second World War, liquid form. They'd put drums of it in a car and get some madman to drive it into the barracks. Grenade goes off, you've got a blast that takes the skin off your bones. Now the gas . . .'

'Hold your collar open, Millie. I'm not going to touch you. They're all over your gums as well, aren't they?'

Millie nodded.

'The gas is different,' said the captain. 'Anyone sniffing the gas knows about it. The sores they get are just like what you've got.'

'I would say,' said Professor Worthington, 'that you've been exposed to a sulphur-based acid compound. It could contain myelin. It's not been a severe dose, or you wouldn't have any skin left. It's stored in powder form, to keep it stable. If it touches water, you get the vapour. You've been somewhere dangerous.'

'I haven't been anywhere,' said Millie.

'Millie,' said the captain. 'Why don't you tell us, love?'

He waited with patience. He turned off his flashlight. All three stood in the candlelight, and the silence went on, and on. Someone had to speak, or it would be midnight.

'Nowhere,' said Millie.

Professor Worthington sniffed. She felt in her pocket and brought out a squat bottle. There was a paste inside, like mayonnaise. She said: 'Rub this on tonight. And tomorrow morning, lunchtime and night. If you run out, come and see me. I'll give the treatment three days to work and if your skin hasn't cleared up we'll take you to hospital. And I'll need to tell the police, because that stuff is illegal unless you're licensed. You may have to tell them something, Millie.'

'The police?'

'Chemicals like that are controlled, you need a police certificate just to store them. Now rub this onto the skin, right into the sore. I'm not going to press you, because that's not my nature. But I'll say this: if you are getting into places where somebody's playing with myelin, you must have a death wish. There is no more painful way to die.'

'Are you listening?' said Captain Routon. Millie nodded.

'It destroys brain cells. It was developed as a nerve agent, to destroy memory. It attacks the brain and leaves you without a mind.'

'I understand,' whispered Millie.

'Good.'

'We'll see you in the morning,' said Captain Routon.

Chapter Nineteen

'Are you awake, Ruskin?' said Sam, just after lights-out.

Sanchez was breathing evenly. The night was peaceful, though Henry was just starting to snore. He barely fitted in the bed, and it creaked under the rise and fall of his massive chest. Of all the children, Henry had worked hardest. He had exhausted himself removing the trees from one of the penalty areas, a task that had kept him occupied for most of the day. He'd only had ten minutes for training, but his huge kicks had impressed everyone. He had also eaten the most and had dozed through Miss Hazlitt's maiden speech at Ribblestrop.

'I'm awake,' said Ruskin.

Sam said, 'Have you played football much before? You seemed ever so good.'

'I enjoy it,' said Ruskin. 'I thought Sanchez did some cracking saves. You know, I think Henry should be centre-forward. That's pole-position really: he can sweep the ball up the pitch and get it up to you and me.'

'And Millie,' said Sam.

'She's fast,' said Ruskin. 'She'll be dangerous in the penalty area. You see, I'm not sure the orphans will have much grasp of strategy. Yet. I mean, don't misunderstand me – I think they're doing frightfully well. But it is all a bit "kick and rush" as my father says. They'll be at the opposition like a flock of birds, we'll see some real skirmishing. But in terms of a controlled attack . . . Well, I have a feeling that's for us more experienced players. I think you and Henry ought to practise together tomorrow.'

'OK.'

Silence fell. Sam stared into it with wide-open eyes. How he wished his vision would clear. As he stared, he noticed the light change. The door was opening slowly; a ghostly beam entered. It was torchlight. A small figure padded across the flagstones.

'Anyone awake?' whispered Millie. Her voice was low and rasping.

'Hey!' said Sanchez. He sat up angrily.

'Millie?' hissed Ruskin.

'This room is for boys!' said Sanchez.

'I know, I can smell that. I'm only visiting.' She crept in and sat at the end of Sanchez's bed.

'Aii! Jesus! You sat on my blasted foot! Oh my sweet . . .'

'Sorry,' said Millie, rearranging herself at the end of the bed. 'That was an accident, Sanchez. Look, this is urgent. We've got to get down to that basement room. I know you want me to forget all about it, but I can't. I've been contaminated. I was rescued by some weirdo who didn't want to be seen and we can't ignore it any more.' She paused, to let it sink in. Then she said, simply, 'I'm going back down.'

'When?' said Ruskin.

'Soon. The headmaster said he had a map. I'm going to find it. I'm going to break into his study.'

'You're crazy,' said Sanchez.

'And you're a coward,' said Millie. 'You're stubborn and you're frightened and you think saying "You're crazy" over and over again will make the whole thing go away. But it won't. Without your bodyguards, Sanchez, you're just a scared little boy. Caspar Vyner would be more use than you.'

'You can't break into places, certainly not the headmaster's—'

'And you can't ignore something that you know is totally wrong and puts the fear of God into you!'

'Look, there are places down there rented out quite legally to other people.'

'That's true,' said Ruskin. 'We were told that on the first day, we mustn't interfere with the other tenants.'

'A boy went missing, Sanchez! A friend of yours!'

'What has that got to do with anything?'

'He was never seen again! I've been thinking and thinking: what if there's a connection?'

'He ran away! Tomaz went home!'

'They're playing with dangerous drugs and chemicals down there, it's happening right under our noses. How can we pretend it's not happening?' There was a silence. Millie spoke again, this time in her bitterest voice. 'OK, boys, I just popped in hoping someone might have the guts to help me. I thought I'd give you the chance. You don't want to: no problem, I'll go alone.'

'It's kind of you, Millie,' said Ruskin. 'But this football training has really done me in.'

'I don't mind—' said Sam. But he was interrupted by a sudden flurry of sheets and duvet as Sanchez leaped angrily out of his bed.

'OK, fine!' he said, in a savage whisper. 'Yes, you are crazy. Second, also, I am not a coward. I will come, if that's what you want: and I will prove you're crazy. We'll go downstairs together; we will find a map, except we probably won't find a map. If we do, we will go underground, and we will find out what's going on, which is nothing, and then we get some sleep. OK?'

'Fine,' said Millie.

'Turn round.'

'Why?'

'Because I'm going to get dressed and I don't want you looking.'

Minutes later, two small figures crept down the tower stairs.

'You really think I'm mad?' said Millie.

'Yes.'

She laughed suddenly. 'Here. If we get caught by the Cockroach, she's going to think we're sweethearts.'

'Who's the Cockroach?'

'Who do you think? Miss Hazlitt. What kind of name's that? The human-insect. Listen, if we get caught she'll assume we're off in the night for a secret snog. Can you think of anything worse?'

'I would rather cut my throat,' said Sanchez. 'You know that?'

'You know where the headmaster's room is?'

'No. My sense of direction's non-existent.'

'Then you're lucky I came. Follow me.'

They came to the main corridor, and then the smaller staircase that led to the corridor with the headless suit of armour. Sanchez led the way: up a short flight of steps to another corridor. Left, then right. Soon they were at the imposing black panelled door of the study, which – not surprisingly – was shut.

'You think it's unlocked?' said Sanchez.

'I doubt it. But I have a way with doors. I have a little tool kit with me. Try it.'

'OK ...' So, gently, as if fearing for alarms and guards, Sanchez tried the door handle. The door was locked. 'No luck,' he whispered.

'OK ... Shine the torch. We can try this a few times.' She searched a pocket and produced a toothbrush. The end had been melted flat. 'Here's one I prepared earlier,' she said.

'Your toothbrush?'

'Sam's actually. I thought he'd like to do his bit. Now: hold the torch, nice and steady. This is how schools get burned down.

151

Oh – hold on. Oil the lock.' She produced an oilcan. 'Found this in my dorm. Bit of luck they gave me the shed, eh?'

'I don't understand.'

'I oil the lock. It's easy only if the lock is smooth. Now: I'm going to warm up the toothbrush. One lighter . . .'

'You thief!' said Sanchez. 'You've still got it! That's my father's bloody lighter!'

'Stop swearing. Your language really deteriorates when you're cross. I'll give it back to you, I just couldn't resist it. He's a rich man.'

Sanchez muttered in Spanish. Millie held the lighter up and flipped out a strong flame. She then rolled the end of the plastic toothbrush into the hottest part and kept it there. She played the flame on both sides.

'I needed a good lighter. This is perfect, you see: you have to get it just right, nice and wet. But not too wet.'

'Wet?'

'Molten. Melted.'

'Why?'

'I'm going to put this end into the lock. The molten plastic will form itself into the shape of the key. Once it's cool, we turn the key. Are you ready?'

'Yes.'

'Two, three . . . go.' Millie pushed the plastic firmly into the keyhole and felt the soft end squirm round the metal. She pushed further, seeing in her mind the plastic stretch and bulge. Then, she waited. 'Now it cools.'

'I blow on it, yes?'

'Yes. And give it five minutes.'

Sanchez blew into the keyhole. Millie pocketed the lighter and they sat, backs to the door, legs outstretched.

'You do this before?' said Sanchez.

'Once or twice.'

'Does it work?'

'Only if you let the toothbrush cool and harden. If it's stuck to the lock casing, no chance. We must take our time: the plastic contracts.'

They sat in silence again.

Then Millie said, 'Sanchez . . . what was it like, being kidnapped?'

'Look, Millie, please don't wind me up about that.'

'I'm not. I'm serious; I'm interested.'

'I'm sure you are interested. You want to know, so you can laugh? Make fun? OK, I tell you: it was a very happy time for me, like a holiday. I meet interesting people, I—'

'What was it *like*, Sanchez? I want to know.'

'It was . . .' He paused, hunting for the words. He said quietly: 'OK, I'll tell you. You ever have nightmares?'

'No.'

'Never? Not when you're sick?'

'Not that I can remember.'

'So you never get scared?'

'I'm not trying to show off, but, no . . . I don't get scared.'

'You're lucky. I got taken away, OK? By someone I thought was a friend; it was our driver. I thought I could trust him and all he wants is money. You realise then, that your life is nothing. Just some money. We had been in a restaurant and he said he had to take me home.'

'What did he do?'

'You want to see?'

'Yes.'

'You sure?'

'Yes.'

'Hold the torch. If you want to see, I'll show you.'

Sanchez had pulled on his school shirt. He undid the cuff of his right arm and rolled the sleeve. Millie shone the light and watched as he revealed his forearm. Just below the elbow was a patch of mutilated flesh: it was scar tissue, not unlike the remains of his father's hand.

Millie touched it gently. She whispered: 'Oh my, what did they do to you?'

'You want to know? I'll tell you. There were three of them. One man, he telephones my mother. The other two are holding me and they put me on the phone, talking to her. One man takes a cigarette and puts it out on me, here. On the skin. So I am screaming. OK? They do this five, six times: they make my father listen also. The police . . . Everyone gets to hear me screaming.'

'That's horrible.'

'Then they say, "We are very serious, Mr Sanchez," and they hold me and one man – he cuts off my toe.' Sanchez paused. 'My father says . . . Ah, but you don't need to know.'

'What?'

'You don't need to know, I don't need to tell you.'

'Yes you do. What did your father say?'

'My father says it's what killed my mother. That's what he says.'

'Oh.'

The children sat in silence. Millie tried to think of something to say, but it was Sanchez who continued, very quietly.

'So I'm not a coward,' said Sanchez, 'but my father says never to take risks. It's why he sends me here, he doesn't want me to die. I'm the only son.'

'I'm sorry, I—'

'You don't have to be sorry, it's fine. Let's try the door.'

They got up onto their knees. The toothbrush looked ridiculous sticking out of the keyhole: it was stripy purple and green. Sanchez knelt beside Millie and trained the torch up close; Millie – carefully, and oh so slowly – gripped the brush, and twisted it.

Nothing.

She counted to five. Once the weakened plastic had snapped. Once it had jammed. She twisted, just a little harder . . . 'Go on,' she whispered. And with a rolling click, the mechanism turned.

'Wow,' said Sanchez.

'Thought I was crazy, didn't you?'

'I think you're very crazy. Truly amazingly crazy.'

'I'll go first,' she said, pushing the door open. 'Welcome to my office, Mr Sanchez. Come and sit down.'

They crept inside. They closed the door. Moonlight flooded in through high windows and soon they could make out the desk, the chairs, the sofa.

'The tricky bit now,' said Millie, 'is where on earth do we start to look for a map? Let's try his desk.'

Chapter Twenty

The desk was a mass of paper. Sanchez held the torch, Millie did the sorting. She was brisk and efficient. She moved to some trays and pulled out plastic wallets. 'Bills . . . bills.' She read quickly. 'Look at this, the bank manager seems a bit upset. Ooh, a solicitor here, getting involved. More bills: final demands, look.'

'Be quick, OK? This is not our business.'

'Letters . . .' she muttered. 'Oh.'

'What?'

'Look. Who's Miles Seyton-Shandy? I've heard that name. Letter for Mrs Seyton-Shandy, about a *Miles* Seyton-Shandy.'

'Yeah, he's very bad news. He was kicked out. He's the one who set fire to the library last term.'

'Bad boy. Oh, listen to this though: poor Mrs Seyton-Shandy. Listen. "Dear Mrs. After lengthy consultation . . . blah-de-blah . . . I'm afraid it will not be possible to accept Miles back at Ribblestrop. We have considered our position most carefully, and feel that in Miles's own interests . . ." That is such nonsense!'

'What?'

'They kick you out and then say they're doing you a favour. Poor boy, passed on to some dogs' home somewhere.'

'He was trouble; he was dangerous.'

'I like the name Miles. Look, this is his file. Look at the photo!'

Millie was staring at the passport-size photo of a young, blond boy. He was grinning happily; his eyes were wide and luminous. His hair was tangled over his forehead, his tie was off centre. He was blazing with energy and laughter.

'I'm in love,' said Millie. 'He's beautiful!'

'For Chrissake, Millie, I tell you, if he ever came back here, I would leave. I swear to God I wanted to kill that boy.'

'You do have a temper, don't you?'

'What are you doing?'

'Changing the letter, Sanchez. Shine the torch.' There was a pen in a jam-jar. 'I know it'll look a bit strange, but a good lawyer could say it's a contract. Here we go, we cross out the "not". There we are: "in Miles's own interests" he should "return immediately".' Millie scratched and wrote, and laughed. She held up the letter and waved it, to dry the ink.

Sanchez snatched at the letter and the torch beam spun crazily.

'Hey!' Millie held it away from him. 'Give him a chance!'

'He is totally psychotic!'

'He sounds interesting and this is a school for freaks, so let's have a handsome one. I'll post this tomorrow.'

She stuffed the letter and its envelope into her pocket. And that was the moment they heard a jangle of keys.

Freezing involves the heart turning to ice and fear spreading over the entire body, toes to brain, in one split second.

Both children froze.

'Good Lord, it's a toothbrush,' said a voice.

'What?'

'Oh, this is so silly, it's jammed as well. What possesses them? Why would anyone . . .?'

'Let me see, stand back.'

The children recognised the voices immediately: the head-master and the new deputy. They were fiddling with the toothbrush, trying to remove it. It took a full minute, and that's what saved Millie and Sanchez. Torch off, papers hurriedly stuffed back into trays, they hid in the only place they could see: the cubbyhole under the desk. This meant easing limbs together and, by the time they were hidden, their noses were nearly touching.

The headmaster said: 'Oh Lord, and I didn't even lock the door!'

The light clicked on. 'You didn't lock the door?' said the other, more penetrating voice. Definitely Miss Hazlitt – they could hear the queer blend of grinding gravel, and the hyena-like bray at the end of the question. 'Security, Headmaster . . . is anything more important in a well-run school?'

'Well . . .'

'That's two lapses and the term has barely started. Video surveillance in due course, I think; one would like to have all the central areas covered and a camera over the main gate. One needs to know where the children are, and believe me . . .' There was a chuckle. It sounded like a flurry of stones breaking glass. 'It's what today's children respect. How do you turn this . . . device *on*, Headmaster?'

'I trust all the children here, but I was foolish mentioning the map to Millie. I bit my tongue when I said it.'

'*Foolish* isn't the word – you've opened a can of worms. I've met characters like that one before, you know. A doctor would say medicate, but parents are always reluctant. She'll be challenging everything we do and say, it's her nature . . . Where's the map?'

'Right here.'

'The only cost-effective thing now is opening the door and waving goodbye; she'll infect the others. Influence is what she has, and—'

'I think we may have different views of young Millie. I was chatting to her the other night and I think she's got a lot to offer.'

'Attention is what she feeds on. It's all documented, the ego fighting for dominance because the amygdala is in constant stimulation—'

'What on earth is the amy—?'

'It's a part of the pre-frontal cortex, the brain. Like I say, ritalin, methahydroxane – it would have some effect, it was all road-tested in the fifties. We could put her in for a scan but you'd be throwing good money after bad: you have to work on these children at an earlier stage. It was her on the train, I'm sure of it. She's a very accomplished liar – you look at her eyes, and watch the pupils. Eighteen hundred pounds in less than two hours – a rather desperate spending spree, I'd say. Perfume – she wants attention. Earrings, fur coat – she knows she's unattractive, that's a desperate insecurity. You could try a course of methotaxadil, that's another possibility, just to get some of the adrenaline down. Otherwise you'd have to be a little more drastic – cut and remove.'

'Well, that's not my field at all, and I'm reluctant to assume anything about the credit-card episode. If the police come back to us—'

'I've had a word with our local man, Cuthbertson. He's on our side, we can count on him. He suggested I search her room, which I should have done as soon as I arrived, or *you* should have done. Soon as she's off at breakfast, I'll turn that little shed upside down. I'm tempted to wake her up now, that's when interrogations work, you know. You shake a lot more out at midnight.'

'No, I honestly think we have to respect privacy.'

'I don't. I have to show that I mean business, and this country will thank you in the end. Children like the Roads girl – they're a kind of *viral infection* and we're losing our resistance. Where are the parents?'

'London, though the mother no longer shares the family home.'

'It was a rhetorical question, I've read her file. I'll tell you about the parents: the mother refuses to see the child. The father's remarried and his new wife won't have her in the house. She spends half her life in hotels because the family's imploded. It's a social problem, this legion of unwanted, unloved *pyschomaniacs* and – like I said – it's sinking the country. I want a school that offers solutions.'

'When will you be able to restore our licence, do you think?'

'How long does this thing take to warm up? Not yet. Rules and uniform – it's an old combination, but my goodness it works.' The cellphone bleeped. 'Diet, with appropriate medication – I'll introduce that sparingly at first. Hello, Hazlitt? And plenty of sleep. I'm with him now, down at Ribblestrop, I'll call you back. Yes, it's logged.' Her thumb danced over the keypad. 'You get the basics into place and everything else follows. If I do my job we'll have it sorted by Christmas. You're going ahead with the building programme, aren't you?'

'Oh yes, but—'

'Good. I'll ask for an inspection next year, my people will insist upon new buildings. We can't show stinking ruins, not if we're to attract proper funding. Third note to self: update and cross-reference building programme, revisit schedule.'

'The roofing is important, yes. I firmly believe if these boys help *rebuild* the school, there'll be a real sense of ownership.'

'Till the little girl burns it down again. I liked the brochure, I have to say that. You're undercutting everyone at the moment and the pictures look good. What we need is a stall at some of the international fairs, and a few charities on-side. One or two children to smile: proper, smart uniform, night and day. That's what sells a school. I'll need to run a course on basic manners, so I'll need a couple of classrooms and this office, as well. Ah, we're in business . . .'

From under the desk, Millie and Sanchez heard the photocopier come to life. It buzzed and hummed for a little while. Then the headmaster said, 'That's that. Oh, I'd better lock the door this time.'

'We need a proper isolation block. Did you get my fax about a removal-system? It's been trialled in some very difficult American schools on the basis of rat behaviour. If you surround one child with a limited set of stimuli and bombard it with selected messages—'

'After you, Miss Hazlitt.'

'The results as published are breathtaking – I'll find you the journal. I think the first job is to weed out the dead wood. Turn the light off . . .' The voice faded into darkness.

The door was shut and locked, firmly. The children remained utterly still.

'Count to a hundred,' whispered Sanchez.

They did, slowly. Then Sanchez turned the torch on. Still they remained crushed and hidden.

'You OK?' said Sanchez.

'Yes.'

Sanchez could feel Millie trembling. He squeezed out of the recess and stood. 'That was close,' he said, awkwardly.

Millie said nothing.

'Funny, eh? He hides the map away from you; you come looking. He's not so dumb.'

Millie still said nothing. She remained under the desk.

'Come on,' said Sanchez. 'She's got a big mouth, that woman. She said stupid things. Millie?'

'She's dead,' whispered Millie.

'What do you mean? Stand up.'

'What she said about my mother . . . I'm going to kill her.'

'Hey . . .'

'I'll do it slowly. I'll make sure she suffers. She has just made the biggest mistake of her life. I hate her.'

'Look,' said Sanchez. He knelt down close to her. 'Hang on. She jumps to conclusions. She loses a credit card, she thinks she saw your face on a train—'

'Oh, she did,' said Millie. She stood up slowly. 'She's right about that. She left her purse on the seat, she was bending down looking for something. I robbed her blind, she was asking for it. I just wish I'd spent more. I wish I'd bankrupted her!'

161

'Look, she's upset you.'

'No she has not!' Millie wiped her eyes savagely and crossed the room. 'She's just made me angry. Oh, this school! An inspection coming up and she's been brought in to sort it all out. She's the boss, isn't she? She was bossing him around and he doesn't have the spine to stand up to her. Right, I'm staying. I'll help her make a few changes, I'll show her manners – I'll show her a *viral infection*. Me *and* Miles when he comes back . . . Hey.'

'What?'

Millie's hands had needed to hold something. They were trembling and, in her wandering, she had settled them on the lid of the photocopier. For no reason, she had opened it. She didn't need torchlight to see that there was a paper on the glass.

'Sanchez.'

'What? What have you got?'

'They've left the original,' she said. She started to laugh quietly.

'What do you mean?'

'So thick. Look: when they copied the map. They left it on the glass.'

'Millie,' whispered Sanchez. 'They may realise. They may come back any minute.'

Millie was laughing still, quietly and bitterly. 'We've got what we came for,' she said, sniffing heavily. 'And I know I'm about to be searched. And I know what she's doing, so I can plan. I think this has been a successful mission.'

'We're locked in,' said Sanchez.

'Big deal. We climb out of the window. Down the drainpipe.'

'We're on the third floor, Millie.'

'Yes?'

Sanchez said, quietly, 'I can't climb any more. You may have to help me.'

They eased the window closed after them, and climbed down the drainpipe together, Millie leading. She took Sanchez's weight and helped him to the ground. Sanchez took her hand and shook it. 'I think you're very brave,' he said. 'I think you're very strong.'

'When do we go down?' said Millie.

Sanchez closed his eyes.

'You promised, Sanchez. We've got a map, there's no excuse now!'

'Friday night. After football training.'

Chapter Twenty-one

The changes to the school were immediate. There were new rules, a new timetable, and a new sense of scrutiny. The medicals were prioritised, just as Miss Hazlitt had promised. The very next night, every orphan was ordered to a dusty, charmless classroom where two neon tubes had been strung from the crumbling ceiling.

The orphans had heard rumours that they were to be examined and they were quivering with excitement. Not one of them had ever been weighed in his life. They hadn't been timed, probed, listened to or even poked – the thought of anyone paying careful attention to their chests and their tongues filled them with such joy that they couldn't keep still.

Once they'd been through the first series of checks, they simply went to the back of the line and, inventing new names for themselves, managed to go through the whole procedure again. This led to confusion, of course, as Miss Hazlitt couldn't yet put faces to names and had to keep changing her glasses. Her briefcase contained folders full of complex-looking grids that folded out over the table, some of them three metres long; soon the papers were utterly confused. She had been told there were twelve orphans when there appeared to be twenty-one. The roll-calls she attempted were chaotic as she couldn't get the children to stay in one place, and Asilah – being as excited as the rest – exerted no control. Miss Hazlitt abandoned the first medical at three o'clock in the morning, looking haggard, and Anjoli boasted that he had been examined four times with four different hairstyles.

The next night, she started again.

She was clever enough to take photographs and clip them to the orphans' files. She had more equipment this time, including an exciting little torch that could shine right into the centre of an eyeball. She wheeled in a machine that buzzed and bleeped and was wired to a kind of hair-dryer on a tripod. This sat on an orphan's head, and was then connected to what might have been a telephone exchange or a very old computer. Soon she was producing charts that rivalled the children's maps of the school. Nobody knew their function, but they spread importantly across the classroom walls, surrounded by numbers, arrows, pins and cascades of tiny handwriting. She would take pulse rates in the morning, afternoon and evening. She took blood-pressure and heart-rates. She measured chests, necks, wrists, waists, kneecaps, nostrils and earholes, and an orphan discovered he could be weighed and measured several times as he moved from one lesson to the next. The sight of Miss Hazlitt with some new measuring device became as common as the chirp of her cellphone.

One lunchtime, a new rumour circulated that Miss Hazlitt was getting ready to distribute medicine.

Now the orphans lived in a part of the world where a family might save for months to buy half a dozen pills. The idea that such things were to be given out free turned them into a squabbling mob. They bolted their food and soon a pushing, scrambling queue had formed by the classroom door. When the door opened, the orphans gasped: there were capsules and powders, pellets and liquids . . . It was a paradise of psychedelic medication, and the orphans were open-mouthed.

'What exactly are these things for?' said Professor Worthington. She had heard the excitement and had pushed to the front of the queue.

'It's all in my report,' said Miss Hazlitt.

'I haven't seen a report. I don't know where to get it – what report are you writing?'

'We've got problems, Worthington. I've discovered that most of these children are completely without resistance; we need to get them properly vaccinated.'

'They seem pretty hardy to me.'

'That's the self-serving instinct of the physicist, my dear. If you think I'm going to stand around waiting for measles, or chickenpox, or worse – then you underestimate my sense of duty. If we act now, we can avoid a lot of very messy illnesses, if not the closure of the entire school . . . Israel! Don't you dare touch that! Who are you?'

'Sanjay,' said Sanjay.

'But there's no name on this bottle,' said Professor Worthington. 'What's in this?'

'It's all in my report: *Legal Responsibilities to Children of Foreign Origin*. Please put that back, Eric – did you swallow that pill? Where's it gone? Professor, you're distracting me. I have a duty of care, because we have admitted children from the other side of the world, and we have to ensure they are properly inoculated.'

'I don't doubt that, but are you qualified to administer drugs like this?'

'It is part of my duty and yes, I am. Anjoli, get your hands off! I saw you take it and that was for whatshisname!' The cellphone was ringing, and Miss Hazlitt's temper was beginning to break. 'Put it back where you found it and get to the back!'

Workmen arrived.

One of Miss Hazlitt's obsessions was punctuality, and she had bells and clocks installed over almost every door. The timetable

166

had been rewritten, so lessons were no longer able to start and finish according to interest and enthusiasm. A long bell meant change of lesson; a short bell meant break-time. The three quick rings meant stand by for end of break-time, and two meant the lesson should have started. A continuous bell meant fire-drill, but continuous short rings meant emergency roll-call. If you forgot which bell meant what, it was printed on the new bulletin board that had been hung in the main corridor: you passed it several times a day.

There were diagrams on how to wear your uniform smartly, and these were further illustrated by a life-size model. He appeared one morning and was chained to the wall. He was child-sized, and he wore his uniform as neatly as a shop-dummy, standing proud with both cap and briefcase, and a little smile on his fibre-glass face. He was an instant hit, partly because he had moving arms and legs, and a rather feminine wig. It was Millie who christened him George, and the poor dummy suffered end-less indignities. Someone stole the wig on the first day, so he suddenly aged sixty years. Hours later, his shorts were round his ankles and he was wearing make-up. The children would come downstairs and George would be doing press-ups or sucking his toes – his positions and activities got more and more bizarre. Of course, nobody was ever *caught* vandalising George, but everyone knew it was Anjoli and Millie. Since the break-in to the headmaster's study, Millie had cultivated little Anjoli, recognising in him a sense of humour as evil as her own. They'd formed a partnership, and spent hours together planning their moves. They managed to deface notices, silence bells, and on one famous occasion glue Miss Hazlitt's hand to a thermometer.

In response to these outrages, more cameras appeared, including one in the main corridor ceiling. It revolved and zoomed, and the orphans liked to dance in front of it. New rules were created every day and appeared on the board as special bulletins in big black letters. For example, one morning you might be reminded that running inside school was forbidden. The next, you were told that someone had been seen walking on the left rather than the right of the corridor, causing congestion and confusion. Miss Hazlitt pinned the notices up and kept the camera trained upon them.

'It's all she does,' said Sanchez. It was ten-thirty five on a Thursday, which meant lesson three should have started five minutes ago. 'She makes up new rules and then when someone breaks them, she makes up more to stop us breaking them!'

'I don't think there were any rules last term,' said Ruskin. 'We seemed to get on alright.'

'What lesson is it now?' said Sam. Of all the children, Sam seemed to be the most confused. He had copied out the new timetable with great care, and Ruskin had helped him colour-code it so he'd never be in the wrong place at the wrong time. It was pasted into his personal copy of the rule book – every child had been issued with two copies – and it was always on-hand in his blazer pocket. Sadly, Sam's vision was still obstinately black and white, and the paper had become such a confused mess of letters and numerals that he could no longer remember what was the top and what was the bottom.

'Manners,' said Anjoli. 'Lesson three – Manners!'

Sam was turning his book this way and that, squinting. 'I thought it was reading . . .'

'We just had Science,' said Sanjay. 'So now it's Manners – same every day, man. Practising your handshake.'

'It's not called "Manners",' said Millie, putting on a grating Miss Hazlitt voice. 'Use the correct title, please! "Manners and Civilisation: an Introduction to . . ." Oh no, it's Caspar – what are *you* doing here?'

'What?'

'I said what are you doing here, deaf-boy?'

'I can come to whatever lesson I like, leper-girl. There's nothing you can do about it. And by the way, you've still got my gun! I don't forget!'

Caspar's fists were clenched and his mouth had formed a venomous pout. Millie stepped forward, ready for action, when the classroom door was yanked open and Miss Hazlitt stood there, glowering. Children were still wandering down the corridor, despite the fact that the two short rings had rung.

'Late again!' she said. 'Anjoli, your shirt is a disgrace and so is your hair! Sort yourself out! Podma! Are you Podma? Put your shoes on, and get in line!'

'Miss, are we going to do door-opening?' said Ruskin. 'The reason I ask is that I had an idea last night that might make it easier for Henry—'

'Be quiet and line up. The first rule of manners is that we don't shout out – how many times must I say that?'

'That's rule forty-one, miss,' said Sam, who had memorised the rule book.

Miss Hazlitt had been true to her word and despite her other responsibilities, she had insisted on teaching the ten-thirty lesson every day. She took this particular slot because she believed it was when the children's concentration was at its peak. After all, manners and social conduct were fundamental to the discipline she longed for.

She gave the lessons all her energy. She patrolled the line now, immaculate in her darkest funeral suit, the collar of her blouse high round the neck. She licked her thin lips and the children gradually stood to attention, their hands by their sides.

'Good,' she said, dabbing at her brow. 'I want everyone standing quietly behind their desks; I don't want a whisper. Lead in, Sanchez.'

The children filed in and there was a tremor of excitement. Standing in the middle of the room was an artificial door in a freestanding frame. This meant that, just as Ruskin had anticipated, the class was revising door-opening, a process few had grasped to Miss Hazlitt's satisfaction. Everyone enjoyed Science with Professor Worthington – you never knew what would happen or how many times you'd be electrocuted. The headmaster's lessons in reading and writing were also popular, particularly since he had taken to teaching punctuation through dance. Captain Routon's classes in roof-building were adored, and often overran as the children wrestled with timber and tools. But Miss Hazlitt's lessons in manners and civilisation were like no others, and the children had come to live for these mid-morning encounters. They had an atmosphere that was little short of thrilling. Even little Caspar had noticed it, and made the effort to get out of bed in time.

Why were they so popular? The reason was very simple. The war between Millie, Anjoli and Miss Hazlitt used this classroom as the principal battleground. The duo had devised a strategy for wrecking each and every class, and that strategy seemed so innocent that it was always successful. With the help of all the others, they simply bombarded the teacher with questions. The enthusiasm was like an ever-rising wave, and before ten minutes had gone by Miss Hazlitt found that she was being interrupted in the middle of every sentence and sometimes before she could speak. The requests were so earnest: 'Why?' 'What for?' 'How?' 'When?' They came from every side of the room, and often she wouldn't see the questioner in time, and would spin round to identify him. As she spun, someone else was calling out. Periodically the cellphone would ring, distracting her further. How could you teach when so many people needed your attention? How could you teach when you still weren't sure of the names?

Today was Thursday and all Miss Hazlitt wanted to do was revise. Last time she had used the door to the classroom, and this had been a mistake because children had repeatedly wandered through it and away. This time she had the model, knocked up by Captain Routon. She would be able to keep her eye on everyone. She would start with a demonstration, then move to role-play in pairs. She would work in some basic conversation, and the homework would be to write a simple door-opening playscript.

'Listen carefully,' said Miss Hazlitt.

'Miss?' said Millie. Her hand was straining. 'What are we going to do today?'

'Do we need our notebooks?' said Anjoli. 'I got a pen.'

'Shh!' said Ruskin. 'Miss, do you want the blackboard cleaned while you're—'

'Quiet!' yelled Miss Hazlitt, and everyone saw her dentures slip. She was gasping already. One day, the teeth would fall – everybody knew that – and every child was hoping it would be in response to his question.

'Miss?' said Sanjay.

'No! Be quiet, and listen. I will explain everything . . .' The cellphone rang, but she ignored it. She had their attention; they were staring at her with eager eyes. Miss Hazlitt licked her lips and mopped her brow again. 'The opening of the door for the guest touring the school,' she said. 'We practised last week, so I am hoping that you'll all remember the basics.'

'Miss?'

'There will be a time, soon, when guests *are* touring the school. Prospective parents. Inspectors, perhaps, who—'

'Excuse me, miss?'

'. . . want to see our school at its best!' she shouted. 'Visitors from overseas, keen to see how polite we are! *That* is why our appearance is so important – will you please sit down, Anjoli!'

'I can't find my ruler, miss, Asilah took my ruler—'

'Sit!'

'Miss?' said Millie, with intensity. 'I'm curious: when you open the door, would you actually *talk* to the guest, or would you pause, in order—'

'I will explain if you'll let me explain!' cried Miss Hazlitt. Her hands had turned to fists, and she could feel the sweat all over her scalp. The children could see it too, glinting on her forehead; they knew that soon the make-up would be running. 'It is very, very simple and once we've practised it I shall put diagrams on the board, so just wait. I need a volunteer . . .'

The class erupted into a fever of leaping boys and straining hands. Why she chose Anjoli she would never know. Perhaps it was simply that he leaped the highest, or maybe he was simply at the front of the class before she could stop him. *She* played the guest; *he* played the pupil. She walked towards the door. Anjoli, positioned some distance away, prepared to open it. He was in a fever of excitement and anticipation, and it was obvious that things were going to go wrong. He bounded to the door, laughing; he yanked it almost from its hinges, giggling. Standing to attention, he could not resist saluting, and his 'Good morning!' was yelled as if he were welcoming troops.

'No!' hissed Miss Hazlitt. Her face was getting grey under the make-up and she could feel tears of frustration pricking her eyes. 'We went through this last time. You don't run. You don't shout. Shirt, Anjoli – will you please . . .' Her cellphone bleeped again, and she pressed her fingers to her eyes. 'Show him, Sanchez – it really isn't that hard.'

'Miss?' said Henry. He had been formulating his question for several minutes. 'When Anjoli opened the door—'

'Put your hand up, Henry. *Please* put your hand up.'

'Should he have moved behind the guest or in front?' shouted Millie. 'I'm sure last time you said—'

'I go in front,' said Anjoli. 'She said, go in front!'

'But is it ever right to open the door from the left side? You know, if you didn't have time to get into the right position?'

'No, I don't—'

'Yes, I go from the right!'

'Which is the right? Which is right?'

'I think a lot of this is instinctive, according to distance,' cried Ruskin over the baying of orphans. 'If I was on the left, I would probably stay on the left. Likewise, if—'

'Again, miss!' shouted Anjoli. He spun on one foot, leaped in the air and slammed the door closed with both hands.

There was a cry of both fury and agony. Miss Hazlitt fell against the doorframe, clutching her hand. Anjoli had not seen that she had been leaning on the woodwork, and he had dealt her a heavy blow across the knuckles. The woman sank to her knees.

'Bullseye,' said Millie.

'That's the . . .' Miss Hazlitt could barely speak. 'Oh, what have you done?'

Sanchez stood at her shoulder wondering what he should do, or who he should call. Asilah had his arms round Anjoli, who was standing in shock, his hands over his mouth.

'That's my right hand . . . You don't know what you've done!'

'Is it broken, miss?' said Ruskin. 'Can you move your fingers?'

'Oh no. No. End of the . . .'

'Shall I get Captain Routon?'

'Leave me alone,' whispered Miss Hazlitt. She made no attempt to stand. 'It's not broken.' She took the dentures from her mouth and the children looked with dismay at how old and sick she suddenly looked. 'End of today's . . . lesson,' she said.

173

Chapter Twenty-two

Miss Hazlitt was not seen for the next fortnight. Whilst her hand wasn't broken, she had to visit London for what the headmaster called *specialist physiotherapy*, and for a few precious days a more relaxed atmosphere pervaded the corridors. George the model was put in a deckchair with three empty rum bottles and a cigarette, and the bells were silenced. Best of all, a letter arrived from the local council, announcing that planning permission for the new roof had been approved, and an impromptu party went on for most of the weekend.

The children were thrilled to discover they would be doing all the construction work, and that the roofing classes were therefore doubled. Professor Worthington teamed up with Captain Routon, and they led them together. Maths now took on an urgent aspect as the children calculated quantities of slate, nails, lead, timber, insulation, and felt. They had to consider the different timber sections and practise the different joints that would be necessary. Everyone worked on scale models and studied the trigonometry involved. They worked in the Tower of Science late into the night; Professor Worthington would start the generators and plumes of sparks illuminated the children's exercise books, burning tiny holes in their shirts as they slaved over their calculations.

In fact, the pressure on the school day was becoming intolerable: there was simply too much to do. Clubs and activities started. There was Stone Dressing Club, which met on the ruined walls, from six-thirty to eight-thirty. There was Timber Reclamation and Site-Clearing Society, which started in the dining hall before dawn. The headmaster continued with his reading and writing sessions, and he also ran a very popular Music Appreciation Society, just after midnight, with cocoa and biscuits. Homework was slotted in wherever you could slot it, and there were occasional rambles, so that the map of the school could be extended.

Most importantly of all, Captain Routon was demanding more and more football practices, and this provided Sanchez with an excuse *not* to explore underground. Millie was furious, but as she had been unable to locate an access point to the cellars, there was little she could do. She studied the map daily. She walked the grounds, hunting unsuccessfully for the shaft she'd seen from underneath. The door she'd accidentally wandered through all those weeks ago seemed to have disappeared, and her quarrels with Sanchez ended in frustration: without knowing *how* to get down, how could they proceed?

Football dominated. The High School had confirmed the game in writing, and Ribblestrop Towers had been formally entered into the league. The captain did not find it easy to discipline his side, because – as in Miss Hazlitt's classes – wild enthusiasm was getting in the way. The frenzied kicking had to be tamed. He hated to see some of the boys' looks of boredom, but with one ball, he felt he had to concentrate on simple passing. True, the orphans no longer handled the ball, but they seemed to hate the idea of sides: it was so much more fun to tackle anyone and everyone.

It was Wednesday night, six weeks into term: sunset. Captain Routon had split the group into two teams and watched in despair as the game flowed off the pitch, down to the lake. The ball was soon in the water, but as the orphans were all excellent swimmers, water-polo seemed to come very naturally.

By dusk, not a child was dry. Heads bobbed way out into the lake and somewhere in the reeds a rowing boat was found. The ball was booted onto the island and forgotten: the two teams fought for control of the vessel. Shrieks and splashes were trilling over the lake. There seemed to be a diving contest taking place.

When Captain Routon blew the final whistle, nobody heard. He had to blow it several times, before the boat turned and nosed back towards the bank. Ruskin and Asilah were at the oars, and the children were singing. Laced with weed, slimy with mud, the boat moved gently to the bank, the mariners singing their hearts out:

'Ribblestrop, Ribblestrop, precious unto me;
This is what I dream about and where I want to be.
Early in the morning, finally at night,
Ribblestrop I'll die for thee, carrying the light.'

Millie and Sanchez were dispatched with flashlights to find the ball, while everyone else trooped home for showers.

Dr Norcross-Webb had managed to hold on to a corner of his office, much to Miss Hazlitt's irritation. The rest of the children were passing under his window and he smiled as he heard them singing. Asilah was leading, his strong treble voice calling, and the rest of the boys chanting a lilting, lyrical response. They had moved on from the songs he'd taught them; this time they were singing one of their own. It was a sort of lullaby the Himalayan nomads sang when they were thanking the Creator for the mountains, and the headmaster had heard it years ago on a climbing expedition. It was the sweetest of songs, with a simple refrain that he now started to hum. Laughter was drifting up over the singing.

It was interrupted by the sound of a window clattering open. Then a voice: 'Sam Tack!'

The song stopped. Miss Hazlitt, who had returned to Ribblestrop that very day, was leaning over the window sill, her bandaged hand a claw over her chest. The headmaster had forgotten she'd been working at the big desk, and he stood up, wondering what could be wrong.

'Yes, you!' she shouted. 'Tack!' The voice ricocheted off the courtyard and walls: it surrounded Sam like the voice of a vengeful God. He couldn't see where it was coming from; it was all around him.

'Hello?' he said.

'*Yes, sir*, is what you say!'

'Yes, sir? I mean, *miss* – can I help you?'

The team clustered around Sam, looking up. All were dripping; all tried to make out who could be leaning out under the gargoyles, screaming.

'I want to see you in my office!' boomed the voice. 'Immediately. In full school uniform: is that clear?'

'Er, yes, miss. Ah . . .'

'What's the problem?'

Sam's heart sank. He had never mentioned it. He had tried to forget it. Nobody had ever said anything to him despite the fact that every orphan had one and wore it with pride. The loss of his cap had always been there, nagging at his mind. Even Millie had one, though hers was nailed to the outside of her shed as a toilet-roll holder. He braced himself for fury, and decided to deal with the matter then and there.

'Miss, do you mean with my cap?'

'Are you trying to be clever, Tack?'

'No, miss. It's just that when I was getting on the train – you know, before we got off it again and got in the helicopter—'

'What in Heaven's name are you talking about?'

'I had a fall. My father was going to send it on, but he couldn't get down from the platform.'

'They're not really part of the uniform, are they?' said Ruskin.

'Aren't they optional?'

'Don't interrupt!' howled Miss Hazlitt. 'I've had quite enough of your irrelevant nonsense, I'm not putting up with any more. I am talking to Tack, and I want him up here in five minutes! In my office.'

She slammed the window so hard a pane of glass fell and shattered at Sam's feet.

'Is everything alright, Miss Hazlitt?' said the headmaster.

'We've got him,' she said. She turned, and there was a curious gleam in her eyes. She wore just the same black, funeral skirt and jacket, shiny with age. Her hair was drawn back, and her face looked dangerously sharp in profile. In her working hand, she held a toothbrush. 'I've got him,' she whispered. 'I'm going to get to the bottom of it now, once and for all – it's been Tack all along.'

'Bottom of what? I'm not sure what you mean.'

'Aren't you? That surprises me, Headmaster, a man like you, with such a firm grip. I've been doing a little *investigating*. I put a camera in the boys' bathroom, since they chose not to answer my questions. I thought a little surveillance would do them good, and I'm pretty close to a breakthrough.'

'Miss Hazlitt, I don't follow—'

'They think they can away with anything, that's the problem with this school. They all think it's forgotten and that's why they get confident. It's a war, and they think they're winning.' She laughed. 'This toothbrush – you don't know what it is, do you? It was in the door, but you never stopped to think. I'll tell you: it's a key. I had it examined by a locksmith in London, and it belongs to Sam Tack. He was using it to pick the lock to this office. I've filmed them cleaning their teeth and he's the only boy without a toothbrush! What do you make of that?'

'You filmed the boys in their bathroom?'

'I'll shake the truth out of them yet. I'll find out what they're up to . . . You know the map's gone missing?'

178

'What map?'

'For goodness' sake, the map to the cellars – the one you left in the photocopier! I told you, somebody must have broken in and removed it.'

'But we photocopied it, we must have copies . . .'

Miss Hazlitt covered her eyes.

'You'll have to excuse me,' said the headmaster. 'I need to chat with Routon about the roof-trusses, the deliveries are going to be very tricky. But, you know, I can't imagine Sam stealing *anything* – he's just not that kind of boy.'

Sam was shaking. He was a brave, resilient child, but he had a horror of being in trouble. He was racking his brains for some crime he'd committed, and the cap seemed the only one. He had the fastest shower he could decently have and emerged in his towel.

'Ruskin, do you have a cap?'

'I do, but I don't know where it is.'

'I wonder if Sanchez has one. I can't just go through his things . . . Where is he?'

'They went back to the island, him and Millie.'

'What shall I do?'

'Sam, get dressed and see what she wants. It's probably something nice, like a food parcel.'

Sam knocked so timidly on the headmaster's door that Miss Hazlitt didn't hear him. He stood there, sweating, too nervous to knock again in case she was deliberately ignoring him. Fifteen minutes passed, and Miss Hazlitt decided to storm the boys' dormitory. She ripped open the door, and there was Sam, shrinking in the blast of sweaty perfume. She nearly fell over him, but grabbed the doorframe with her injured hand. 'Where have you been?' she hissed. The pain brought the usual beads of sweat to her brow and her face changed colour.

'Here,' said Sam.

'Where?'

'Here. I knocked, but—'

'Don't lie. Don't lie to me, you're in quite enough trouble as it is!'

'What?'

'And don't say *what*, say *pardon*. *Pardon, miss*. How does it take a boy twenty-five minutes to come from outside there to here?'

'I had to take a shower.'

'Why?'

'I, er . . . We . . . We were in the lake, and—'

'What on earth were you doing in the lake? Out of bounds! Seriously dangerous: do you know what would happen if one of you drowned in that lake? We'd be closed, just as we're getting somewhere. You don't think, do you? Get inside!'

Sam had been rocked onto his heels. His mouth could barely close. The noise, the sheer volume, was aching in his ears. He entered the headmaster's office. There was no headmaster, and Sam's heart fluttered with fear. He watched with alarm as the woman slid out her cellphone and turned it off. On the desk was a glass of water and a selection of brightly-coloured pills.

'Stand up straight,' she said. 'We've got all the time in the world.'

The voice had softened. It was now more unpleasant. It reminded Sam of his dentist back at home: an elderly man who didn't believe in anaesthetic. When he said, 'Open wide, Samuel,' it had just the same, soft menace as Miss Hazlitt.

'Straighten your tie, please, Sam. I want you to take these pills.'

Sam looked at the desk again and felt his mouth go dry. Off to his left, he heard a soft, metallic purring, but he couldn't take his eyes off the dish and the multicoloured sweets.

'Miss. What are they?'

'What are they? You want the chemical formula? Why?' Miss

Hazlitt was behind him now, and it was even more unsettling than when she'd been in front. She was fiddling with something at the wall, and he could hear some kind of lock mechanism.

'I don't know, I was told never to take sweets from ... from ...'

'Be a good boy, Sam, and swallow them. Everything's going to be easy if you co-operate. Here we are, Inspector: you've arrived at just the right time. Samuel here is being very helpful and I'm quite sure we'll get to the bottom of everything. I'm sure he has nothing to conceal. In fact, I think he's covering for someone, and will feel *better* when he's got it all off his chest.'

She was still behind him. Sam could hear heavy footsteps and the sound of a door squealing on unoiled hinges. Then a deep, northern voice, slightly breathless: 'This is Sam, is it?'

Sam managed to turn, just his head. For a moment he couldn't get his bearings; one of the walls seemed to have shifted. Part of the panelling had swung open, and there was a metal grille, like a tiny prison cell. In front of it was the police inspector – the one from the car, huge in a cape-like raincoat. Miss Hazlitt was at his side, folding the panelling back as he watched. It closed with the softest of clicks and Sam realised he had glimpsed a lift, and that's what the purring had been. A lift to where, though? To the police station? He felt his knees beginning to tremble.

'Inspector Cuthbertson's here,' said Miss Hazlitt, 'because things are getting a little bit serious. Luckily, there's still time to straighten everything out, but only if you're ready to tell us the truth and help us. Now what I want you to do is swallow your medicine, like a good boy. Can you do that?'

'I don't know.'

'Perfectly harmless, son,' said the inspector. 'We use them all the time – they help people relax and tell the truth.'

Sam felt a hand on his shoulder. It was Miss Hazlitt's. The glass of water was in front of his nose suddenly, and he had no choice but to take it. One by one, he swallowed the pills. They immediately lodged in his throat and he was retching; the glass was at his lips, and he was gulping it until it ran down his chin and his shirt.

'Stand up straight,' said Miss Hazlitt. 'Hands by your sides.'

She was perched on the desk, her good hand holding her chin. Sam adjusted his uniform, put his arms down by his sides and stood to attention. He was breathing heavily and he knew the policeman was behind him. He closed his eyes and offered up a silent prayer, clinging to the fact that he had nothing to hide. Honesty, he thought: always the best policy, and the railway authority was looking for the cap, his father had told him as much in a recent letter and would be bringing it down personally the moment it was found. *Tell the truth, Sam* – his father, his mother, the Sunday School woman, they had all said the same thing. In any case, there were truth drugs in his system now and he had nothing to hide. 'I'm sorry,' he said. 'It went under the train.'

'What did? What train?' It was the inspector.

'It's why I'm not wearing it.'

'The train in the tunnel? What went under it?'

'My cap.'

Miss Hazlitt stood up. She moved in and put her face closer and closer to Sam's. Sam could see the make-up. He could see the little hairs you normally don't notice. The pores. The blood vessels. She'd been eating peppermints, but he could smell the meat she'd had for lunch. Why was the make-up so thick? You could pick it with your fingernail and lift the whole thing off like a mask. Sam took a step back, but the policeman was right there, with a hand on his shoulder, gripping his blazer.

'Listen to me, Sam,' said Miss Hazlitt.

'Stand up, son,' said the inspector. 'Stand up straight.'

'We've had experience with your sort. The inspector sees people like you every day – in the cells, in the courts, and finally in prison. So, listen.' She shouted suddenly, like a dog barking: '*Nobody is interested in your wretched cap!*'

182

Sam was so shocked by the noise that he put his hands over his face. He tried to turn but his arms were gripped and then, before he could flinch, they were twisted up behind him and he was forced back to attention, the tendons straining. Miss Hazlitt was still close enough to bite him and he knew he would be sick. The policeman was horribly strong, and Sam was on his toes.

'When did you last clean your teeth?' she said. There was a hand on his neck. She sounded even more like his dentist! He couldn't speak: he had no oxygen.

'Answer the question,' said the policeman, squeezing the boy's arms higher.

'Answer the question, Tack, answer a simple question!'

Sam managed to squeak, but no words came. 'Alright! Alright!' said Miss Hazlitt. Now he could feel her spit on his face. 'Put him over the desk! Where. Is. Your. Toothbrush?'

'I don't know, miss!' he squeaked. The policeman had bent him in half, he was jack-knifed over the desk. He cried out, 'Ow! Stop!' – but who was there to hear him?

'Whose toothbrush are you using when you do clean them?'

'I don't know! Please! I lost it, I lost it!'

'You lost it, did you?' said the inspector. 'I'm not sure that's the truth!' The voice was a whisper, but right in Sam's ear; he could feel the air and smell the sourness of the man's breath. 'I think you've been picking locks and stealing. Did she make you do it? Shall we beat it out of him?'

'You want to take all the blame, Sam?' said Miss Hazlitt. 'We're getting to the bottom of this tonight! Did you lend it to her?' She took hold of the boy's tie and wrapped it round her fist. 'Or are you in it together?'

'Where's the rabbit, Tack! Where did you put him?'

'I don't know!'

'Oh yes you do, and what we really want to know is *how much* you know!'

183

Sam could only endure. He'd been on the summit of Mount Snowdon with his father, in a hurricane as fierce as this. True, he'd had his father's arms round him: but he could survive this, he had to. The hands on his wrists felt like iron and his arms were being dislocated. Miss Hazlitt was yelling, but the words had become inaudible to Sam. He waited for the thunder to roll past and, as it did, magically a green-and-purple toothbrush appeared by his nose. The policeman had leaned in from behind and was holding it between finger and thumb. He was jerked upwards, onto his toes again. 'I've had enough,' the policeman was saying. 'If this one thinks he's going to wreck years of planning with a wretched toothbrush, he's wrong. Now where's the map?'

'I d . . . d . . . don't know! Please!'

He was spun round and there was a hand under his chin. All he could see, in monstrous monochrome, were the inspector's nostrils and one of his eyes. 'I'm going to ask you one more time.' His feet weren't touching the floor and the policeman held the toothbrush like a knife. Sam squeaked, and tried to kick. The words cracked him over his skull. 'Where. Is. The. Map?'

'Sam!' said a voice. 'Good Lord . . . Inspector! What on earth is going on?'

There was a flurry of footsteps and Sam was falling. His throat was free and he was on his knees, gasping. There was a flurry of scraping furniture and more footsteps. Voices competed, braying against each other, and Miss Hazlitt appeared to be grunting and stumbling. The policeman's voice was repeating the same line: 'Steady on, sir – just a moment, just a moment!'

'Mind my hand!' cried Miss Hazlitt, and she cried out.

Then Sam was lifted, and the study floor was moving under him. There was a voice speaking over him and the voice was kind. '. . . not sensible, Sam . . . playing games with something so important, eh? Miss Hazlitt is quite right to bring it up, but here we go, now . . . on your way, and let's hope that's the end of it!'

'Headmaster!' The woman was turning and her voice was a low crackle of hatred. Sam had never seen a face look more angry. The skin was raw, the eyes were bulging. Her hair was lopsided on her head. Sam noticed his own hands were both on the headmaster's, holding it firmly, clutching it as if it could pull him from the sea. He was being led to the door, and the inspector was backing away, red-faced, breathing heavily, a truncheon in his hand.

'Always clean your teeth, that's my motto! Now you'd better get moving – really, he should, Miss Hazlitt. This chap's our striker, you see, and he needs an early night for tomorrow's game.' He had the toothbrush in his hand. He popped it into Sam's blazer pocket. 'Off you go, Sam. Hurry. Run, please.'

The door was closed after him and there was an immediate flurry of furious voices – three adults all yelling and another squeal of furniture. Sam was tottering along a corridor that appeared to have no end. He felt he was falling down the long lens of a telescope and that he might disappear, or drop out of the end. The voices rose behind him, like clamouring birds. Miss Hazlitt was the loudest, but Sam couldn't make out what she was shrieking because it seemed to go on and on, like a high-pitched drill. He reached the stairs, tripped and clung to the banister. Taking deep breaths, he started to descend and the dreadful row faded behind him.

Ruskin was at the bottom. 'You alright, Sam?' he was saying. 'How did it go?'

Chapter Twenty-three

'I posted the letter to Miles,' said Millie.

Sanchez said nothing.

'I'd forgotten all about it, but it was in my blazer pocket. A bit mangled, but intact. I hope he hasn't found somewhere else.'

'I hope he has.'

'What didn't you like about him?'

'He was mean. Selfish. Dangerous. Foul-mouthed. Destructive. Crazy.'

'Ah, this is the difference between us, Sanchez. You see the worst in people; I see the best. You see, if it was me, I'd try to work out what was troubling him.'

Millie's hand had snaked through Sanchez's arm. They were both cold, so they were walking briskly. The night had come down, and their flashlights bobbed ahead of them.

'I don't think we're going to find that ball,' said Millie.

'I know where it is,' said Sanchez. 'Israel booted it onto the island, I saw it.'

They walked in silence.

Then Sanchez said: 'Actually, Millie, you are totally, completely wrong. You always jump to conclusions. I really tried to help him.'

'By making speeches about rules?'

'By trying to be nice! It was me, Miles, Ruskin, Henry and Tomaz. We got on fine, we were good friends. Except – we play a game, Miles has to win. We go swimming, Miles has to try and drown someone.'

'He had a sense of fun!'

'Yes. Conjuring spirits in a Black Mass. You think that's fun, do you? You think that's funny?'

'He was into Black Magic?'

Inevitably, as if on cue, an owl decided to hoot. Millie stopped. They'd come to the first humpbacked bridge, and the lapping water and the wind in the trees took on a more ominous sound.

'He was bad news, Millie. He had a death wish. He took something of mine and he scared Tomaz. He scared everyone.'

'Slow down. How? Tell me.'

She found herself hugging Sanchez's arm closer. Sanchez let her: they were both getting colder. He spoke quietly now. 'You heard about the man who was killed? Lord Vyner?'

'Yes. Suicide.'

'He was shot in the head and Caspar said he saw the ghost. This makes everyone scared. Then Miles decides he's going to talk to him, properly. You know – talk to his spirit.'

'I heard about this. Go on.'

'We go down to the chapel, late one evening. I don't know why I said I'd do it, but I did. Tomaz too. Miles just kept on and on – he had a way of persuading you. So Miles is in charge, and we take a couple of torches, and it's very scary – the chapel's a ruin, the monks don't use it. He draws a big circle on the floor, with letters and symbols and all the stuff he gets from some book. And we're sitting there, with candles all around us – there's Ruskin, Henry, Tomaz, Caspar. All of us. We have this glass and we have our hands on the glass.'

'A *ouija board*, that's what it's called.'

'That's right, a ouija board. And we start trying to raise the ghost of Lord Vyner.'

'This is amazing! I didn't know you got up to this kind of stuff, Sanchez. I thought you were just a boring prefect. What happened?'

'Miles starts to ask questions. He does all the stuff: "Is there anybody there? Do you have a message for us?" – all that stuff. It's really freaky.'

'Is the glass moving?'

'Yes.'

'So he's getting answers? What does it say?'

'Millie, I never saw anything like it. I thought it was Miles pushing the glass, but it's going so fast I realised it couldn't be. It starts spelling out words, real words and sentences. I just sat there . . . I could not interrupt, or say anything. Miles keeps asking questions, "What do you want from us?" *Help.* "Are you at peace?" *No I am not.* So Miles starts reading the answers out – we're all reading them, but Tomaz couldn't read so we're saying them out loud. Then the glass starts moving, and it spells out: *one of you is in danger.*'

'It said that? The glass spelled out that?'

'Yes.'

'The ghost of Lord Vyner, *warning* you! So who was in danger? Wait, Sanchez – stop a minute.'

'What?'

'Look up.'

They had arrived on the island and, by eerie coincidence, they were standing directly under the monument to Lord Vyner. It was silver in the moon. The statue gazed back to the house. Its eyes seemed to be fixed; it seemed hungry for something. The two children stared up, shivering.

'There's the ball,' said Sanchez. 'I'll get it.'

'I'm coming with you. Who was in danger? Did Miles ask who it was?'

'Oh yes. I saw the name get spelled out – T.O.M.A.Z. Tomaz. The spelling was perfect. Miles told him, and Tomaz didn't believe him for a second. Then he just went crazy – he completely flipped. He got up and he ran out the chapel. I tried to talk with him, Miles tried. But two days later, Tomaz is gone.'

'Because he thought he was in danger. He must have known it – that's completely logical. Maybe he was being warned, Sanchez! And he ran straight into the trap – they kidnapped him!'

Sanchez grabbed Millie's arm. 'Shh!'

'What?'

They both stood absolutely still. There was a sound, but they couldn't tell what it was or where it was coming from. They listened harder, and it seemed to rise from beneath them: it was a groaning noise.

'Holy Mother of God, Holy Mary . . .' Sanchez was crossing himself. He was backing away, poised to run, but Millie held him back.

'It's singing!' hissed Millie. 'Is it the ghost? Sanchez, he was following me underground, it must have been him! He blew his brains out and now he's haunting the place!'

'Shhh!'

'He was cooking me food! This is so horrible!'

They listened harder than ever, rooted to the spot. The noise rose, then fell. It seemed to get closer, and both children realised at the same time: it was the chanting of monks.

'It's inside the monument,' said Sanchez. He shone his flashlight at the stone base.

'Underneath,' said Millie. 'It's coming from underneath.'

Sanchez swung his torch slowly. There was a plaque, which bore a lengthy inscription in Latin. The plaque was set into a low stone archway and, looking hard, they could see how the plinth was constructed. They hadn't been this close before because of the brambles, but now they were beside it, they could see that the monument base was a kind of cube, built as a set of arches. Long grass had grown, and a rather forlorn wire fence ran round the whole thing, as if to deter you from exploring further. But the sound, which rose now in a wave of mournful voices, was definitely rising beneath those arches.

'It's the monks,' said Millie. 'I heard them when I was down there. It's the monks, singing.'

'I thought they were on a vow of silence.'

'Maybe singing doesn't count.'

They approached the shaft slowly, as if the monks might leap out at them. Sanchez stepped over the fence. He shone his torch down and, as Millie came up beside him, she could see a deep vertical shaft disappearing into the dark ground.

'It's the air-vent,' she said.

'What air-vent?'

'Look. You can't fall down. There are bars. Oh wow, this is what I've been looking for. It's the air-vent down to the labyrinth. That's where I was – I was standing down there, looking up!'

She moved closer and knelt. It was like looking down a chimney: the brickwork was meticulous, and a tiny disc of sand was visible at the very bottom.

'Sanchez, I walked along that tunnel. I must have been so close to an exit. How can the monks get down there? This is fantastic! When do we go down?'

'We don't.'

'Oh yes we do. We'll come back tomorrow, with tools. We've got to go down!'

'No way, Millie, this is too much.'

'Sanchez, we have the entrance point, we have the map! We need to find out what's going on down there. You tell me Tomaz disappeared. He was warned he was in danger, so maybe that's exactly what he was in. We have to go down! Don't we?'

'Shut up! Yes.'

'You'll come down with me?'

Sanchez had his hands on his head. He thought hard. 'Yes,' he said.

Millie smiled. 'Good. Now let's get the wretched ball and get some food.'

They were both in time for supper.

'Alright, Sam?' said Sanchez.

Sam seemed to be sitting in a strange, stiff position, and was surrounded by the other boys. The food was a pre-match carbo-hydrate special: shepherd's pie with jacket potatoes. Sam had a portion on his plate, but couldn't seem to open his mouth. Anjoli stood behind him, massaging his shoulders. Asilah had a forkful of food, and was holding it close to Sam's lips.

'What happened?' said Millie. 'You haven't seen a ghost, surely!'

Sam swivelled his eyes. His whole neck had seized up.

They sat down next to him.

'Thief,' whispered Sam.

'What?'

'I'm a thief.' Sam's voice was high-pitched: it was a mouse, squeaking. 'I'm going to prison, that's what they said!'

Asilah patted Sam's shoulder. 'You're not a thief, Sam. Eat your food.'

'She's crazy, man!' – that was Sanjay, on his other side.

'What have you stolen?' said Sanchez. 'What are you talking about?'

'I can't make this out at all,' said Ruskin. 'The whole thing seems jolly unfair. If I understand it correctly, Sam's been accused of breaking into the headmaster's office with a toothbrush. He's just been interviewed by that policeman, and by all accounts they got pretty rough!'

Millie stared and noticed the familiar purple-and-green plas-tic handle sticking out of Sam's blazer pocket.

'He thinks he's going to be expelled,' said Ruskin. 'He thinks they're going to call his parents! He's been sick and everything, and she made him take pills. Look at this, everyone's got more pills – what is going on?'

'What pills?' said Millie. 'What are you talking about?'

Millie and Sanchez looked about them. Beside every orphan there was a small glass dish with the child's name taped to it. Inside lay a cluster of bright little pills and capsules, and next to that, a glass of water.

Millie sighed with frustration. 'What has this got to do with Sam?' she said.

'I don't know,' said Ruskin. 'Something about a truth drug. They made Sam take a load of pills and then they were asking him questions about going underground with you and a tooth-brush.'

'Sam,' said Millie. 'Look at me. What exactly were they asking you?'

'They wanted to know,' sniffed Sam, 'if I knew what you saw . . . when . . . If I knew what you saw when you went under-ground.'

'Underground? They were asking you about me?'

Sam nodded. 'They think I stole a rabbit!' Tears were drip-ping down his cheeks.

'How do you break in,' said Ruskin, 'with a toothbrush? I vote we go and see this policeman and put in a formal com-plaint. They have procedures, and I don't believe they would allow Sam to be . . . *terrorised* like this.'

'Shut up, Ruskin.'

'No, I won't shut up. Apparently, the headmaster came back and broke the whole thing up, otherwise goodness knows what could have happened. All over a wretched toothbrush!'

'Look,' said Sanchez. 'The toothbrush is a key. Millie made it when we went looking for that map – she used Sam's toothbrush.'

'And now they think it was him!' said Millie. She put her hands over her face for a moment, trying to conceal a smile. 'Sam,' she said. 'Were they seriously trying to blame you? Did they threaten to *arrest* you, for breaking and entering? For being part of my gang?'

Sam managed to nod and his tears plopped into his dinner.

Millie was silent for a moment and then she started to laugh. It was just a quiet chuckle, but then it took hold of her, and in seconds she was giggling with delight. The laughter rose until she was howling. 'Oh my, they thought it was him!' she gurgled. 'Look at him! Sanchez, look at him! As if Sam's going to break in anywhere! What did you say?'

Sam couldn't speak. He put his hands over his face and wept.

Millie's laughter got louder and louder. Meanwhile, Sanchez could only stare. He didn't trust himself to speak. He looked from Sam to Millie and back again. The orphans were all watching, totally confused. Sanchez looked at his hands, and wondered if now was the time to break one of his father's golden rules: *You never hit a girl . . . Smash her!*

'I don't get this at all,' said Ruskin. 'But I tell you something – it's not right.'

Sanchez put down his knife and fork. He stood up and found that his fists were clenched. He said to Millie, quietly: 'You are disgusting. How can you laugh? Look at him! You are disgusting. You are not human.'

Millie brought herself under control, and looked at him through moist, laughing eyes. 'Sanchez, it's *funny*. This place is so weird, and they give themselves away! They're frightened!'

'You . . . are not a girl,' said Sanchez. He picked up his plate and cutlery, very carefully. He was bright red. There was an unoccupied table and he started to walk towards it.

Millie was looking at him, smiling; she seemed bewildered. Sanchez turned on her hotly. He said, 'You are . . . a maggot. I don't want anything to do with you. I am not helping you, I don't even want to speak with you. You go exploring by your-self and leave me alone!'

Chapter Twenty-four

The next day was the big match, which made further argument impossible. Football came first, and everyone accepted that.

The dining hall had been swept and dusted. The tarpaulins were stretched tighter and new planks were laid over the mud. An extra trestle table had been found, and jugs of juice were arranged on doilies. Captain Routon had been up long before dawn preparing ham, chicken and roast beef with a number of attractive-looking salads. There was a cheese board, fruit and various yoghurts, and Professor Worthington – with the head-master – had been up in the Tower of Science most of the night sculpting a sugar-and-meringue model of the school. This was, after all, the first time Ribblestrop was hosting visitors.

Over the main table hung a banner, which read: *Welcome to our High School friends*. Ruskin and Sam had designed it, but everyone had contributed to the bright border of handprints and smiling faces.

The visitors were staring, square-jawed and mean.

They wore emerald-green blazers. Some of the larger boys hadn't been able to find jackets big enough, and looked rather uncomfortable. A tall, lean man stood among them, noticeable partly because he was completely bald. This was Harry

Cuthbertson, brother to the inspector. He was a younger, fitter man, and he had the same searching eyes, with that hint of madness.

'. . . so welcome, warriors-all!' finished the headmaster.

There was a smattering of applause from the home side. He'd been speaking for ten minutes or so, and it was clear his speech wasn't working. He hadn't expected whistles or cheers, but he had hoped for the occasional titter or smile. Homer's *Iliad* had been his text, and he'd made a number of interesting references to the changing profile of sport in Western civilisation. Sadly, his guests weren't listening. Their eyes were locked onto the eyes of his own children: they seemed to be fixated. Ruskin was smiling, and so was Sam. The orphans never stopped. The guests, however, *weren't* smiling. They had the look of boxers just before round one, when the referee has brought the contestants together.

The applause died quickly and Harry Cuthbertson shouldered his way to the front. He had a strong nasal accent and spoke quickly.

'Oh, thank you very much, thank you very much indeed, Headmaster, boys . . . Thank you. It is really very nice to be made a fuss of like this, not what we're used to at all, is it, boys? Very kind indeed of you to lay on a lunch like this . . .'

He was immaculately dressed and his forehead was polished almost to metal. 'Hope that nobody takes it amiss if we eat a very light lunch,' he went on. 'Nought to do with the hospitality, needless to say, but we do like a *light* lunch before a game – tend to eat up a bit after, eh lads? Eh?'

'There is a hot meal planned for six o'clock,' smiled the headmaster. 'And we thought we might even serve beer, if that's permissible, and show some slides on our new projector.'

'Have to be off by four, Headmaster, we train extra on a Friday, but another time we'd make special arrangements for that, wouldn't we, lads? Don't say no to a glass of beer or three, do we, Darren?' There was a little ripple of amusement from the visiting team. 'Do we, Darren – eh?'

Darren was a slim boy with a small slit of a mouth. His jet-black hair was greased back till it looked like a layer of creosote. His lips stretched into a knife-cut of a smile; then it was gone, and he was adjusting his shoulders in his blazer. Clearly Darren liked beer.

'Where do we get changed then, sir?' said Harry.

'Here,' said the headmaster.

Silence.

'We don't have changing rooms,' he continued. 'Thinking ahead, you see: we got so involved in the pitch . . . Could you use these benches, once we've had lunch?'

'Get changed here, like, in the . . .' He looked at the blackened timbers above his head. 'Is it safe?'

'Oh yes. It's our hall. Do you have much stuff?'

'Well, aye, yes we do. We have our kit and our bits and pieces; I mean we can change here, course we can, it's just . . . What about your lot?'

'We'll be outside.'

'Where's the showers?'

'Ah, we can't offer you showers, I'm afraid,' said the head-master, smiling. 'But we've fixed up a hosepipe just behind you. By the sink.'

'Right-o, boys, last few words of wisdom!'

Captain Routon was jogging round the group, trying to corral the orphans into one area. There had been angry scenes as he tried to count the team down to eleven, and for the first time Millie had seen real tempers and tears. A cluster of three boys had at last been separated, including one of the oldest children: the concept of 'reserve' had finally been understood.

'Our strength,' said Captain Routon, in his final address, 'is speed and passing. Henry? Passing. Everyone clear?' He could feel

196

the excitement and the tension. Anjoli was simply bouncing, and a number of the orphans seemed electrically charged. 'Sanchez,' he shouted. 'Don't come out too far, I don't want any unnecessary contact between you and some of those tough ones.'

'Who's referee?' said Millie.

'Their man, Cuthbertson. He's a bit more up on the regs than me and, I told you, I'm no good in the sun.'

There was a shout from the other end of the pitch. 'Get that donkey out the goal!' It was Harry Cuthbertson, transformed. He was in black shorts and a lightly striped black T-shirt, the breast-pocket neatly buttoned over cards and papers. Whistle and watch flashed in the sunlight as he doubled on the centre-spot, knees as high as his chin. His own team were stretching, running and passing the dozen footballs they'd brought with them. They'd scored so many practice goals that the net they'd been warming up in was torn from its hooks. The headmaster and Professor Worthington were hastily putting it back up.

The whistle blew: it was two o'clock.

'Captains?'

'You go,' said Sam, to Ruskin.

Millie was already on her way, moving confidently to the centre-spot. Her shorts were roped in tightly with a black-and-gold tie, which drew attention to the pencil-thinness of her waist and torso. 'Heads,' she said, loudly.

'Alright, alright,' said Harry. 'We want a clean game, alright? This isn't World War Three, this is a game of *football* – play hard as you like, but play *fair*. Twenty minutes each way.' He looked at his own captain, who had tattoos up his neck. 'We've got extra training tonight, so treat this as shooting practice. I don't want to see no holding—'

'Heads,' said Millie, loudly.

'You what?'

'Heads. That means your team's tails. Can we get on with it?'

Harry Cuthbertson stared at Millie, shocked into silence. His short speech had been interrupted. He discovered he was panting slightly. His own captain didn't seem to have noticed the insult. He put his face close to Millie's. 'I've heard about you,' he said.

'Who's been talking?'

'My brother. He said this was a school for weirdos. Are you a boy or a girl?'

'I'm both,' said Millie. 'And you should see a dentist. Your breath stinks.'

Harry Cuthbertson felt blood rushing to his skull. It was slooshing up the big vein in the neck and painting his whole forehead red. He stood up and bounced the ball hard. He trapped it neatly under his boot and rolled it to the spot. The coin in his hand was twirling as he did so; he snapped it, hand on wrist: 'Heads it is,' he snarled.

'We'll kick off,' said Millie.

'Downhill first half,' said the High School captain.

'Yes!' hooted Ruskin, waving his arms and dancing. 'We won the toss. Always a good omen. Come on, Ribblestrop: take no prisoners!'

A minute or so passed as the teams organised themselves. The High School jogged confidently into their positions; Ribblestrop Towers needed a little longer, partly because Henry was still pushing at one of the donkeys and partly because nobody could keep still. Was it nerves? The orphans were running on the spot, flapping their arms. Sam was turning in circles, clapping his hands.

The whistle blew, and Millie knocked the ball to Ruskin. Everyone was astonished at the immediate ferocity of the High School side. The players weren't fast, but they were powerful and their tactics were simple. Like dogs off leads, they bounded at their opponents: they only needed short-swords and shields and they would have been gladiators, trained in the art of death. So in the first seconds of the game, Ruskin played by instinct. Seeing a giant hurtling towards him, he smashed at the ball, hard as he could. His right foot missed and he tripped, allowing his left foot by sheer good luck to trickle the ball neatly between his opponent's legs and into the path of Sam Tack. It looked like the most amazing dummy and pass, and Sam tricked the ball forward on his left, then got it on to his more confident right. Two High School giants came at him, and Sam dribbled skilfully, just the way he'd been trained years ago by a favourite uncle. He had two exquisitely good tricks, and he used them both: the hesitation with the right that dodges forward on the left, followed by the leap to the right coupled with the lightest flick with the left heel: to watch Sam play you'd have thought you were at a dance class, a celebration of the Highland Fling.

But Sam was never selfish.

He hunted for Millie and he hunted for Ruskin, hoping that both would keep up: alas, he was ahead of himself. He was coming to the penalty area and a Roman armadillo of defenders had formed between him and the goal. He spun back on himself, preparing to boot the ball backwards: a sliding tackle just in front ploughed a long deep flowerbed into the pitch. He leaped the High School player responsible, and dribbled the ball to the right.

'*Shoot!*' someone cried.

'Go on, Sam!' came a joyful voice: it was the headmaster.

Shooting was unthinkable because Sam was not the finisher. At his last school, his job was to get to here, just outside the box, and loop the ball in for a trio of sharp-shooters. But there were no grey shirts: only the green armour of the opposition, swinging round in bomber formation. The thoughts came impossibly fast: back to Millie, move inside; hesitate and wait for Asilah on the wing; alternatively, curl the ball – risk a wasted shot – but let one and all see that Ribblestrop Towers meant business. The goalie was blind, the defenders had built a virtual wall. He blasted it. The ball whisked the goal-net clear of its hooks and settled in the nettles.

One-nil.

Sam remembered running, then his feet were treading air. He was on someone's shoulders, arms out. Millie had simply lifted him up and he was being carried towards the Ribblestrop Towers' goalmouth, half boy, half trophy. Orphans were flocking round him, screaming. Henry was waving his arms, and Sanchez was there, hands up ready to clasp him by the cheeks and plant a kiss of religious intensity firmly on his hairless head. When he turned and the noise quieted, he was aware of eleven High School boys rolling up their sleeves. There was an eerie silence now and the ref had the ball on the centre-spot.

The High School looked like demolition men, itching to get a job started.

There were thirty-nine minutes left.

The High School captain kicked off – this was the tattooed boy. There was a quick bit of rudimentary passing. Ruskin nearly intercepted, but tripped over the ball. This was fortunate, as the tactics had changed: the High School forward pounced on the spot where Ruskin would have been, and those watching had the strong sense that the smaller boy would have been mashed into the soil. As it was, the ball trickled away and a herd of High School players advanced steadily. The first hint of murder was when one of the wilder orphans rushed in to tackle. Without fear, he crashed in to sweep the ball away. The opposition leaped forward, knee dangerously high: and Sanjay was spread-eagled on the grass. He lay there, panting, unable to get his breath.

Free kick to Ribblestrop Towers. First reserve on.

Millie came forward and booted the ball high. Sam got to it, but a High School boy got there first. Punted it back, down on the wing. Three orphans chased the ball, but the green shirt cut through all of them: a fine cross, with three attackers there in the goal-mouth. Sanchez jumped and caught the ball safely: he also caught a cruel headbutt, firmly in the face. He went down, the ball safe to his chest: the knees of his attacker came down hard on his shoulder, crunching him against the goalpost.

No foul given.

For Sanchez, it was a shocking moment. He said something in Spanish and smiled, wondering if his opponent would recognise the unusual combination of the words *mother* and *skunk*. He appeared not to, so Sanchez kicked the ball into play. The referee turned his back; tattoo-boy looked at Sanchez and stepped towards him. 'I'm Ken,' he said, 'and you're dead.' He threw a punch at Sanchez so hard it would have cracked the goalpost, and it was sheer instinct that saved the goalie. Sanchez ducked and curled all in one movement, bringing his right knee over the top. It was a move he'd learned from his senior bodyguard: a move reserved for close combat, when you'd lost your weapon. Sanchez scored a full-on strike: Ken caught the knee full in the jaw and lost two molars. The lad crawled from the pitch.

'What the hell happened?' said Millie.

Ken was spitting teeth on the touchline, gargling and weeping. Play had stopped: the ref had him staked out in the recovery position.

'Sanchez – what happened?'

'I'm not talking to you, Millie.'

'Don't be so stupid! You almost killed him, what did he do?'

'Alright, he tried to kill me!' said Sanchez.

'Look at your face!'

'Get lost, Millie, I'm—'

'Come here . . .' She had a handkerchief in her hand and simply grabbed Sanchez by the hair. 'He's cut you to pieces, you stupid idiot. Keep still.'

Harry Cuthbertson spoke to the headmaster and there was much gesturing. In the end, the ball was back on the centre-spot, and the High School started.

201

But something was wrong. It may have been the sense of fear in the air, but it was clear that the orphans were no longer enjoying themselves. Their usual joy in the chase was disappearing and they rushed at the ball hoping to kick it anywhere. When they did get close to the action, they were inevitably swept from their feet. Several knees were now caked in blood, and only their instinct for leaping and diving kept them from more serious injuries. Millie and Sam were everywhere and Anjoli was working hard. They yelled and encouraged, running the length of the field – defence and attack – but it was clear that things were slipping away for Ribblestrop.

Henry was the next actual casualty.

He had had only one convincing attempt at a tackle. He wasn't fast, but the High School boys were wary of his size: like Sanchez, he was a marked man. He was standing still when the incident happened. True, the ball was rolling towards him, and true he was preparing for a major kick. As he did so, two High School players rushed him together; a knee went up, concealed from the referee . . . Henry was flat on his back, gasping, and had to be helped from the pitch.

Second reserve on.

After ten minutes of the game Ribblestrop Towers had used up its full quota, replacing injured boys. The score still stood at one-nil, but it didn't look like holding. Sanchez had made three excellent saves, and tried to get the ball out fast, knowing he'd be dead meat in another goal-mouth skirmish.

Despite his isolation, Sam glowed. Ruskin was a fumbler and Millie was getting nervous. Anjoli too had a skittish look, and so nobody could get a manoeuvre together. Sam yelled for the ball, ran for the ball, jumped for the ball – he was faster than he'd ever been, and played with a fearlessness nobody had seen in him before. Alas, the High School boys had him covered. Again and again, the ball was driven back down the pitch, left wing or right, crosses to midfield, and Sanchez was called upon again to save constant shots. The lead could not be sustained; the pressure was impossible. The green shirts piled it on, abandoning defence. They hungered for the equaliser; their mouths were speckled with foam.

It was two minutes before the end of the first half. The High School had barraged the Towers' goal-mouth. Sanchez could barely stand. His head was throbbing and nobody could believe he'd kept the ball out. Player after player was virtually camping in the Towers' penalty area, determined to even the score. Sanchez looked up through his own sweat, and saw Sam with his arm up, jumping up and down. He wasn't marked. Sanchez was crying for half-time, but he sent the ball up hard and long, just over the centre-line.

Sam was on it, trapping it neatly and putting it straight back to an orphan. The High School defender didn't read the signs, didn't realise the orphan could barely kick: he ran at him. The child booted the ball as hard and as far as he could, which sent it rolling ten feet over to Millie. The sliding tackler rushed at her, and Millie, also exhausted, leaped out of the way . . . the ball bobbling feebly in Sam's direction.

He was there, he took it up. He toed it ahead and beat another defender, saving it just from the touchline. Again, that cry, 'Go on, Sam! Shoot!' – a woman's voice, he saw the flashing teeth of Professor Worthington, arms above her head, baying for all she was worth. She had a black-and-gold scarf, she'd knitted it for the occasion. He was down, he was up again: the penalty area was under him. The High School boys were running back, but they were also tired: could he pass to Ruskin? The boy was yelling and jumping, but even Sam knew a ball to Ruskin was a wasted ball. Why not use him as a distraction? He made to pass, the defender leaped: Sam kept possession, dummying neatly and using again the old right heel. The last player should have closed him down, should have predicted the trick, but Sam was in luck. He was round, with only the goalie to beat and the goal was wide.

Top right, said a voice in Sam's head. *No, no, round him and go for the bottom left.*

The goalie was hovering, trying to cover all the ground: their eyes met, minds trying to read each other. Sam hated to shoot; he knew his first goal had been a fluke. *Stay in control*; he was small and quick. He slewed to the right, and darted left – the goalie came out and Sam was ready for the shot, a whole flank of the goal-mouth open wide, unmissable.

Everyone saw what happened. The incident had the slow motion of a car crash. Sam had skipped like a ballerina. He was easily clear, in total, beautiful control. So the goalie played the man. No doubt about it; no attempt at the ball. As he spun, he kicked out at the child, recklessly. A vicious, scissoring right came at Sam's groin, studs up. It was later discovered that the studs were illegal, the metal pins worn through the plastic. Sam was caught as he jumped and the studs opened a gash all down the thigh. Worse than that, he was flipped like a coin and went down hard, head first, onto the mud. The ball settled in the back of the net, but Sam was unconscious.

Not a cheer. Not a clap. The ref blew for half-time, the score standing at two-nil.

Chapter Twenty-five

The survivors gathered that evening in the dining hall. Captain Routon had cooked another handsome meal and the rum bottles were out, everyone allowed a tot to keep spirits up. But the cold wind of failure blew and stripped the building back to what it was: a semi-derelict stone box, smelling of ash.

Eleven-two, the final score.

Amazingly, there were no broken bones. There were cuts, bruises and sprains. There were black eyes. And there was Sam, deep in a coma, with a tube down his nose. He was breathing, but only just. Captain Routon had set up a primitive ventilator using a desk-fan and one of Professor Worthington's electric timers, but everyone knew it was a dangerous situation. He was under blankets in the west tower, and the headmaster was with him.

The rest of the children sat at their tables like an army, routed and cheated. An army that had been trodden underfoot: rabbits in a stampede of buffalo.

'There's always the return game,' said Professor Worthington. She was on the little stage of crates, balancing as best she could. Her hair was wild; her scarf looked ridiculous. 'We'll show them next time,' she whispered.

It was not the thing to say. Nobody wanted another meeting

with the High School unless it was with crow-bars and shot-guns. The sense of fair-play had been snuffed out like a night-light.

'It could have been worse,' continued the doctor. 'There were some cracking saves, weren't there, Miss Hazlitt?'

'Sanchez can hardly walk,' said Millie. 'Ruskin can't talk.'

'Oh, Millie. Don't despair!'

'We need wheelchairs and morphine. Not fantasy. And by the way, our loyal deputy headmistress wasn't even watching.'

'What you need,' said Miss Hazlitt, 'is a little bit of discipline.' She rarely ate with the children, but had chosen to do so tonight. Her black dress gleamed and she hunched over her food, long and thin. Her face was startlingly white. 'I *was* watching, as a matter of fact. The reason you lost was because you don't work together.' She allowed herself a rare smile. 'Every man for himself. I've seen it in class; I see it round the school – the dominant ego seeking gratification.'

'Where have you seen that?' said Sanchez.

Her voice took on a strange chuckle. 'In your lessons,' she said. 'You can't take orders. Rebellion has become—' Her cell-phone shrieked and she snatched it to her ear. 'As I predicted, *instinctive*. You're an interesting case study, Millie. Look at the way you dress and speak to your elders. Hello?'

Ruskin tried to protest, but his jaw was locked in distress.

Asilah stood up. 'We practised hard! Sam was . . . amazing!'

'Wait a minute,' said Miss Hazlitt into her phone. 'Don't shout out, Asilah, you can see I'm talking . . .'

'We worked together,' cried Sanchez. 'We always work together!'

'Yes!' said Israel. 'So what you said is not fair.'

There were murmurs of support and one of the littlest orphans leaped to his feet. 'Ha!' he shouted.

'I'll call you back, run it past my secretary.' Miss Hazlitt snapped the phone away, and let herself smile again. The light caught her glasses and she seemed to be examining the crowd through two, luminous discs. 'What you need,' she said, 'is a new start, and that is just what I've been trying to give you. You chose Millie as a leader, and that was foolish. If ever there was a child driven by selfish desire—'

'No!' cried Anjoli, also leaping to his feet. 'Millie is . . . our hero!'

'You're proud of yourself, are you, Millie? Where's your tie, by the way?'

'Holding Sam's leg together,' said Millie. 'The one useful job it's ever done.'

'Yes, you're out of control,' said Miss Hazlitt, calmly. 'You really are. These sugars and carbohydrates don't help, particularly when you're on medication. As for alcohol, well . . . it's a lethal combination and it's why my predictions are being thrown off course. *Swallow* your pills, boys – don't play with them!'

Once again, there was a little plastic dish by each orphan. Once again, it contained an assortment of pills and capsules. The orphans hoarded and traded them, but very rarely swallowed.

'What exactly are you predicting?' said Millie. 'Nobody here understands what you're doing or what you want.'

Miss Hazlitt spoke loudly and firmly. 'I'm here to sort the school out; that's what you were *told*, at the start of the term. We need to change our approach here. We need a new attitude to dress. We need to comb our hair, Anjoli!' There was a rising grumble, like a murmur of distant thunder. 'You can protest and complain, you can resist and resent it – but I'm telling you, discipline binds a community. I'm sick to death of it, my notice has been up there in black and white for days.' She had to raise her voice to a shout. 'A special feature on tidiness – with pictures! Look at you, Sanchez! Where's your blazer?'

'OK, listen,' said Millie, standing. 'I read the new rules. It's the third time since you got back – the third rule book you've given us. That's pretty much all you do, make up rules, change the old ones, and – I don't know – pretend to be some kind of doctor.'

'Children need regulation! They need to understand—'

'Walk on the right!' cried Sanjay. 'Who knows which is right? I don't!'

'No running,' said Israel. 'What if we are late?'

'Yes!'

'What if you are being chased?' whispered Eric. 'What if a monster—'

'No hands in pockets,' said Millie. 'That is so stupid. There's hardly any heating in the school and we don't have gloves. You're making up rules because you've got nothing better to do. Your lessons are boring, you pick on kids who can't fight back – like Sam! – and you seem to think you're in charge, when you're not!'

There was a burst of applause. Miss Hazlitt was changing colour under her make-up.

'Look at you!' shouted Millie. 'You take notes, you spy on us, you film us! What for?'

The woman's cellphone was squealing, but she ignored it. 'Sit down, Millie! I *am* in charge here, I have special authorisation – and it's about time you and a few other people understood that.' There was a tremor of fury breaking in her voice, and the voice dipped an octave. 'You're the principal reason my life has been made so difficult! You should have been expelled weeks ago!'

'Expel me now if you want. You'll need that policeman though.'

Miss Hazlitt was standing up as well now, shouting over Millie. 'I'm not surprised the High School ran rings round you. You're lazy and slack and you've been getting away with too much for too long. Leave the room, please, Millie, and pack your bags: I'm suspending you for gross rudeness.'

'I'm not going anywhere; you can leave if you want to.'

Every child burst into more sustained applause and Millie sat down. She helped herself to trifle.

Miss Hazlitt, sadly, had gone too far to back down.

'I'm suspending you, Millie. I won't say it again: go to your shed.' Her voice was deep, husky and dangerous. 'The headmaster has put me in charge of discipline, and you've had too many chances. Pack your bags.'

'Pack your own. I'm hungry.'

Had Miss Hazlitt experienced similar showdowns? She must have done, but possibly not with someone as single-minded as Millie. If the headmaster had been there, he could have intervened. Professor Worthington was too involved to speak. She was feeling the electricity in the room and wondering again how it could be harnessed. It was too late to dash for her anometer, so she simply stared. Her eyes leaped from adult to child, her chin in her hands: the voltages were critical and she could see the connections.

'Stand up,' cried Miss Hazlitt.

'No!' shouted Anjoli. There was a sudden crash of cutlery as the boy smashed his knife on the table, this time deliberately.

Miss Hazlitt swung round and stared at him. Sanchez had his blazer in his hands. He threw it gently into the mud at his feet and pulled the front of his shirt out. Israel, one of the smallest orphans, lifted up a spoon and slammed it onto his plate. Sanjay had a knife in one hand, a fork in the other: he raised them slowly, staring through wild eyes. A number of children did the same, and – *slam!* – Anjoli led the beat. The noise made the trestles shake.

'I will count to three,' hissed Miss Hazlitt. 'One. I'm warning *all* of you!'

The last word was obliterated in another crunch of steel on wood. Anjoli pulled off his shirt and leaped onto a table. He jumped in the air and slammed both feet hard on the timber. A rhythm developed immediately, getting faster.

Miss Hazlitt tried to speak, but the volume was increasing and there were cries now. She was shouting at Anjoli, then at Millie. She was turning, struggling to balance. Anjoli leaped across to

209

the sink area and picked up the bucket of slops. Someone whistled in a shrill, common way and she spun round hunting for the culprit. She turned again, and saw that Millie had a forkful of custard with cream, poised like a catapult. She pointed a long finger, but whatever she said was lost in the din.

Millie was smiling. Anjoli was smiling too, staring at Millie. The smiles suggested pure, vengeful joy. It was wrong, they both knew that. It was insulting, and it was a waste of good food. But the deputy headmistress's blouse had frills, and the deep V of her jacket made her chest the most attractive target. From above, Anjoli could see the tight curls of grey hair and a forest of pins.

'Two!' yelled Miss Hazlitt.

Millie flicked, and a line of gunk sprayed over the woman's chest all the way up to her cheek. Anjoli up-ended the bucket and the woman was drenched. A cheer went up, and the hammering of feet and cutlery became a roll of thunder.

Only then did Miss Hazlitt realise just how terrible was the danger. Something hit her back: a bread roll. Podma had a handful of rice in his hand. He threw it hard and the spray caught the woman's cheek, even as she ducked. Ruskin was standing, a slice of courgette at the ready, which he skimmed like a stone so that it glanced off a shoulder. That seemed to be the signal: every child grabbed whatever was available.

Miss Hazlitt backed away in a hail of food, splattering and smearing on her head and clothes. Custard, jelly, cream, sauce and vegetables: the children hurled it at her. She slipped, and it was Professor Worthington who caught her wrist.

A bench went over. A table was lifted. Anjoli and four of his brothers were building a defensive shelter, barricading the door. A fifth lifted a tray of fried tomatoes and started to fling them, one by one. There was water from jugs and handfuls of mud.

Miss Hazlitt and Professor Worthington were both clambering through the debris, hunting for the exit.

The rain of food and drink continued, plates smashing, cutlery flying. Asilah had moved back to the sink, and had the hosepipe out – he was refilling the jugs. In seconds, it seemed, every child was soaked and the cheering had become howls of ecstasy. Miss Hazlitt was cowering under a table as Professor Worthington cleared an escape route.

The children danced among the remains of supper, trampling blazers and ties, then wrestling in the mud. In their ecstasy, they didn't even notice their teachers' flight.

Chapter Twenty-six

In the west tower, the headmaster sat with Sam.

The child's skin was clammy. They'd rigged up two electric fires but the dormitory still felt cold.

Captain Routon stood with a thermos flask. The bedside table was covered in dressings, gauzes and ointment tubes. Sam's breathing was even, but fast. The fan fed him oxygen, but it was as if he couldn't breathe deeply enough.

'He's in a bad way,' said the headmaster.

'I think he's stable though, sir,' said the captain.

'What if it's concussion, Routon? Internal bleeding.'

'There's nothing a hospital can do that we haven't done.'

'Unless his pulse starts going down again . . . We just can't risk it, Routon! We can't play God with this little fellow, and in any case, his parents should know. I should call them this minute.'

'If they see him like this, sir. I dread to think—'

'I know, dammit, I know. And I'm a hopeless coward. We've got Miss Hazlitt watching every move and taking notes. Have you seen her report on Health and Safety?'

'No, she doesn't talk to me.'

'It was on my desk late last night. She wants me out, Routon! We had the most terrible row after that incident with Sam, and she said as much.'

'She's all bluff, sir, I've met pen-pushers before.'

'You're wrong, Routon. I wish you were right, but she's got government authority: she wants the school! It was the one thing I never imagined when I agreed to her wretched contract. When she sees Sam like this, she'll bring that wretched policeman back and file her report. We're up to our ears in debt, no way of paying Lady Vyner—'

'You've got to hold to your nerve, sir! Trust me. Look at the boy – is it so much worse than his first day? He's got another scar up top, stitches in his leg. He'll come through this, and look! He's smiling in his sleep!'

'He might not wake up. He might be smiling like that for years to come!'

'No, no, no – he's cleaned up nicely. His pulse is good. Sleep is all he needs, you've got to trust me on this one. I saw just the same thing in Sri Lanka after a grenade attack.'

'What's he smiling *about*?'

The captain had done the stitches, with the same purple twine he'd used weeks ago after the teapot attack. The blanket was rolled up to Sam's chin. The smile, if anything, was getting wider.

'I'll stay with him,' said the captain. 'Soon as the shock passes, his breathing will slow and I'll whip the tube out. Heart of a lion, this one. Look at those eyes . . .' The captain lifted Sam's lids: first the left, then the right. 'Don't call his parents yet.'

'Very well. But stay with him, Routon. I think I ought to be downstairs, I'm worried something's wrong. I feel it in my bones: something's dreadfully wrong. I just don't know what that woman wants!'

'She wants to be important, sir – I've seen it a hundred times. Now your place is with the troops. They need you.'

'Call me if anything happens, yes?'

'It's our bleakest hour. We must hold our nerve.'

*

Down in the dining hall, the children were having the de-brief they needed. The floor was a mess of mud and food and the children themselves were drenched and dripping, as if they'd been hauled through a stew. But the mood was joyous.

'Where we went wrong,' shouted Sanchez, fighting over the noise of Asilah and Eric, 'where we went wrong was defence!'

'Rubbish!'

'The defence was good!'

'The defence was you, Sanchez – the best goalie . . .'

'We didn't use Henry,' said Ruskin. 'That was our big mistake.'

'When we play again,' said Millie, 'we have to work out the attack strategy. Sam was brilliant, but he needs more support. We need Anjoli further forward.'

'Henry should be forward!' yelled Israel. 'Henry is the secret weapon!'

There was cheering and Henry stood, bewildered and beaming.

'But that's what I said, weeks ago!' said Ruskin. 'Sam and I were reading this – listen!' He was holding up a piece of newspaper, which was turning to pulp in his hand. 'It's all about tactics and there's some seriously good information here, listen!'

Anjoli leaped back onto a table. 'Let's face it,' he shouted. 'They were dirty, filthy pigs and Sanchez smashed one!'

The hall rang with cheering and clapping.

Sanchez joined Anjoli, riding the noise. He put his arms round the boy and shouted: 'Train harder – that's what we have to do! And put Henry here.' Henry was wheeled into the centre of the hall. Sanchez and Anjoli jumped down and hauled the benches into goalpost formation. 'If I'm in goal, OK, I need him eight metres out.'

'He's a full-back,' said Millie. 'That's what he is. Asilah, back left; Israel right.'

'Where's a ball?' shouted Ruskin. 'Let's practise.'

The ball was found and Sanchez kicked it into play. Nobody heard the headmaster enter the room. The door was already open and he appeared suddenly, through a plastic sheet. He looked around the devastated room in astonishment and was about to call out, when something held him back. He watched for a full five minutes as a whole series of tactical manoeuvres were worked out and practised. He watched the ball passed back and forth; he saw the attacks tried and adapted, the quarrels rising and falling into high-fives and handshakes.

It was Millie who saw him first, and silence fell.

'Hello, boys,' he said, quietly. 'Millie.'

Sanchez saw immediately that the headmaster had aged. He was wearing his gown, but it was muddy. It looked heavy on his thin shoulders and his hair was wild.

'Good evening, sir,' Sanchez said.

'Good evening,' said the orphans, one after another.

Professor Worthington came in behind him. Israel and Sanjay grabbed chairs, and placed them behind the adults, adjusting the planks and pallets to ensure they were safe. Everyone was sitting down, one by one. The headmaster squeezed the bridge of his nose, and closed his eyes.

'I'm sorry I couldn't join you for dinner,' he said. 'I'm glad you went ahead without me. Here's your tie back, Millie. We washed it as best we could.'

'Thank you, sir.'

He sat down. 'Well, well, well.'

'How is Sam, sir?' said Sanchez.

'Yes. He's . . . comfortable. You will be pleased to know that Sam has fallen into an easy sleep and though he's not out of danger, he has an excellent nurse and the love of his friends. I will not lead a prayer, because I know every one of you, whatever your faith, will want to pray in your own way tonight.'

There was a silence again, and one or two voices murmured, 'Yes, sir.'

215

'Let me say something. About the match.'

The children looked at each other nervously. The headmaster stood up.

'Something needs to be said, and I think the words, "well done", would be useful. Well done, boys – and Millie. It was a cracking game and Sam's goals were joyous. Will goals ever be better scored? Possibly not. A fool would dwell on the fact we lost, eleven-two. An idiot would suggest our performance was some kind of failure. For me, it was a very proud day because I saw bravery and teamwork and . . . power. Was it a proud day for you?'

Sixteen heads nodded and there were earnest mutterings.

'We lost the battle. We did not lose the war. I hate to use military metaphors for something as wonderful as sport, but you know what I mean. The High School were tough; we met them with fire. Even Mr Cuthbertson, their . . . leader, was impressed. Let's face it: the enemy did not go home without a bloody nose.'

There was applause.

'Part of winning is learning how to lose. Part of playing any game is knowing when to fight back and *how* to fight back.'

'We need more balls, sir,' said Anjoli. 'If we're to train. We want to train!'

'Balls will be provided,' said the headmaster. 'We cannot build without bricks.' He looked up. 'But of course – listen, please – a cathedral is far more than stone. A cathedral is *of* stone, but first it needs builders. Am I right about that, Millie?'

'Yes, sir.'

'We shall take the game to them and I shall phone Harry Cuthbertson and ask him for a return match immediately, on his territory. I shall tell him we are longing to meet again: do I have your support in that?'

There was a long burst of applause, like the rattle of guns.

'There was no photographer at the match, so I want sketches

of the game. Pen and ink, so I can publish them in the first edition of our school magazine – of which you, Ruskin, shall be editor. Drawings of Sanchez's extraordinary saves shall be welcome. Sanjay, you shall be in charge of artwork. A team photo will be taken tomorrow, in Sam's dormitory as we don't want to move him. Tomorrow I declare a holiday, which is a small, perhaps inadequate token of my respect and admiration for all of you. Tomorrow, then, will be a proper celebration of the distance we have travelled, children. Never, in my life, have I seen such courage! I applaud you all!'

There was another burst of applause, this time like hail on a tin roof. Sanchez found himself standing up; Asilah stood next to him. Ruskin got up too. In a moment every pupil was on his or her feet, and the clapping became rhythmical. Who started the singing wasn't clear. It was a high-pitched voice – possibly Ruskin's – like a choirboy finding his choir. It soared suddenly, like a violin let fly by an orchestra of drums, into the first line of the school song. The children picked up knives, forks and cups and beat time. The song did well as a chant, and it gathered momentum as they sang: *'Ribblestrop! Ribblestrop! Precious unto me!'*

Twice through, three times. Some children were linking arms. And then, just as suddenly, it died. It was killed, as it were, by a thin, cracked voice, which somehow penetrated the din with two words, sung out high-pitched and long: 'Excuse me . . .'

Every head turned. The smaller orphans moved towards older brothers.

'My, my, my, what a mess you people make. Good evening one and all, don't stand up for me, please. Sit down.'

Lady Vyner had entered as silently as the headmaster.

'Lady Vyner.' His nervousness had returned. He stared, a little wild-eyed. 'Ah, can I introduce you to the children? You haven't met them all, despite—'

'I haven't, but don't bother now, it seems hardly worth it. The light is dying, and soon it will be dark. The sun goes down; the stars don't always come out and children, well . . . they find other schools.'

'Light some candles,' said Professor Worthington.

Candles were produced and the hall was warm again. More than ever, there was a sense of an army encamped, and this was an army that now knew it was under siege. The gaunt creature in a nightgown and Wellington boots stood in its midst like a dangerous angel.

'Defeated . . . but he offers you a half-holiday or whatever it was. Eleven goals to two, and the ashes of failure are no doubt thick and bitter in your mouths. Swallow them fast, there's more where that lot came from. Aren't you ready to give up, Headmaster?'

'Lady Vyner, is it me you want to see? If so, we can—'

'No, no: I was keen to see you all. Exploited orphans, arsonists, lunatics. Victims of the farce that is your school: good evening indeed. I'm not here to make speeches; I'm simply here for the rent. I was chatting to your deputy headmistress today, and she let it slip that . . . things were going badly. I feel I have to press for payment, having been burned in the past. End of the second month, you said; you're now in breach of contract, and I have eviction papers ready. Crippen?'

'Could we settle this privately, Lady Vyner?'

'Crippen, I don't think he's got my rent. He may need to be flung out onto the steps. Caspar's watching from the window, hopeful as ever.' The elderly servant had appeared behind her, panting. He held a fat document under his arm, and leaned on a chair.

'I most certainly do have . . . *some* of the rent, Lady Vyner, but now isn't the time to be transferring cash across the table.'

Lady Vyner brought her right hand up. Crippen staggered forward and passed his bundle into it: it was a thick, cream-coloured thing that suggested seals, lawyers and signatures. 'A contract is a contract,' she cried. 'I had this one checked and double-checked, I don't make the same mistake twice. I also have your latest Health and Safety report attached – Miss Hazlitt was most helpful, pointing out just how many rules you're breaking.' Lady Vyner smiled and shook her head, sadly. Then her voice rose to a crescendo: 'If you don't have the money, the contract's clear: get out of my home!'

'Lady Vyner, please! I will have a significant proportion of your money by the end of term, trust me.'

'Trust you?' Lady Vyner laughed. It was the sound of knives sharpening.

'We've just finished our first football match!'

'Trust!' she cried. 'It's contracts I trust, and this one says, what? *You're out of time, you're out of luck. No second chance without cash deposits*, that's what it says. And you owe me one hundred thousand pounds, Doctor! That is what you promised me, that's what you signed up to deliver. And I don't take cheques, not from you. Not after your little stint in jail.'

All eyes travelled to the headmaster. He was on his feet still and he met his landlady's icy stare. The silence grew intense.

'You have another three and a half hours, till midnight. And then I'll call our friend the inspector and have you thrown out on your ear. He owes me several favours and does just about anything for a little *baksheesh*, as you probably know. Now where's that lovely little girlie, the one in mid-field?'

In the subsequent silence, it suddenly occurred to Millie that Lady Vyner was referring to her. She stood up. 'Here.'

'And what's your name, my dear?'

'Millie Roads.'

'Handsome. Pretty girl. Amazonian, I wouldn't wonder, once she gets a bit of flesh on her bones. What are you doing here, child? Why on earth did you pick Ribblestrop Towers?'

'I got thrown out of my last school, miss. No one else would have me.'

Lady Vyner snorted. 'Ask a good question, get a good answer. If it's not too personal, why did your last school expel you?'

'I bombed it.'

Lady Vyner snorted again. 'Excellent. Quite excellent – I have to say, unexpectedly, this is all putting me in a better humour. You bombed your school, I'm sure you had your reasons. When will you put this one to the same flaming torch? Once we've rebuilt it? I suppose there's not much to bomb at the moment.'

'I don't want to . . . burn this one, ma'am.'

'No?'

'No.'

'Why not?'

Millie was silent.

'Come on, don't lie . . .'

Millie had no intention of lying; but she couldn't think of the reason. The ghostly figure of Lady Vyner stood before her, almost transparent in what happened to be a spectacular moon gazing through the tarpaulins.

Millie said: 'I've made some friends here.'

'Really? No other reason?'

'I'm having fun. Some of the time. I think it's a good school.'

The sound that followed reminded Millie of an angry wasp when you've caught one in a glass. It rose, though, from a whine to the rasping of a hacksaw on sheet tin: it was Lady Vyner's laughter, and it had moved up a register so it veered into sobbing.

'Oh, I do love the innocence of youth; I love to observe its brief life. Friendship, you said. She has discovered it, here in Ribblestrop, at the feet of our jailbird headmaster. Caught up in a confidence trick, little whatshername discovers the joys of loyalty. Oh my, there is a God and His divine sense of humour is twisted indeed! I'll teach you a lesson, girlie: don't rely on anyone. They'll say "Here we are, working together . . ." and they shoot you like a dog, in your own laboratory! In the back of the head!'

Lady Vyner sat down on a bench. She banged her fist on the table.

'Your headmaster owes me money, and I'm not moving till he pays me. Sell your worthless degree, sell it back to the crack-pot college you bought it from. Write a prison diary, that can make a fortune these days. By midnight, Headmaster – cash payment, in full. That's your deadline, so let's wait for the clock to strike.'

The children stared, terrified. Dr Norcross-Webb said, simply and quietly: 'To bed, everybody. We have an exciting day tomorrow. A nice holiday.'

The hall emptied quickly.

Chapter Twenty-seven

'So he's not even a real headmaster, Sanchez. You heard what she said.'

'I do not want to hear.'

'He has a police record, he's done time in jail. We've got to go down to the cellars and see what he's up to. Tonight.'

'No. You're listening to a crazy woman.'

'Is she making it up? What if she isn't? And why would she? It was noticeable that he didn't say anything.'

'Keep it down, Millie!' hissed Ruskin. 'Sam's sleeping.'

They sat in the boys' dormitory. Nobody even thought of going to bed. 'Perhaps he has a little dignity,' said Sanchez. 'People go to prison, that happens all over the world. My father spent time in prison: it does not mean you're a crook. For me, he's the headmaster. I like the school, and you said you do also. So where is the problem?'

'Problem one: he's stealing the money. My fees are being paid, so how come he's not paying his rent? Problem two: a boy disappeared last term and there are strange things happening in the cellars, so I think we ought to find out what. Problem three—'

'OK!'

'It's not OK. Problem three is lying in that bed. In his first term, Sam has been mutilated. That's hardly childcare at its finest, is it? Problem four—'

'I don't want to hear about any more problems! And for another thing, your problem one is not a problem, I have all the money here. OK? Under my bed.'

'What?'

'My father sent it. To the headmaster.'

'How much?'

'I don't know. More than *she* wants.'

'Your school fees are under the bed? When did this happen?' Sanchez looked embarrassed. 'The first day, I just kept forgetting. I've hardly unpacked, alright! One minute we're in a tunnel running from a train, the next it's training for the football. We have homework, I'm writing letters, I'm looking for your blasted map. I forgot the money, OK? Is it a problem for you?'

'Don't you pay by cheque?'

'No. Always cash, it's the way my father does business.'

'Oh.' Millie stared at Sanchez. She said, quietly: 'I'm glad you still have faith in him. But listen to me: you can get as cross as you like, but you're not going to shut me up or make me feel bad about saying what needs to be said. I saw a laboratory. I saw something like a dentist's chair and they are getting very scared about what we know. We have a map; we found the access point. I think we should go down and see what they did to Tomaz.'

'Oh my God, all I want to do is sleep! Tomaz went home!'

'You're getting angry because you know something's wrong. You know as well as I do, Tomaz never got home!'

'Nobody knows that!'

'We should be doing something about it, but you're too scared! We have an incompetent headmaster, an insane deputy headmistress, a so-called Head of Science who thinks we have batteries in our heads—'

'Shhhh!'

The door opened. 'Sanchez?'

223

'Headmaster. Sir.'

Sanchez leaped to his feet, almost to attention. Millie rose as well.

'I'm sorry, my dears, I can sense I'm interrupting. I wanted to check up on Sam . . .'

'Sorry, sir, of course. Please come in, you are very welcome, sir.'

'Little chap's on my mind, I can't settle.'

'Sir.'

'Did I interrupt something important?'

'Certainly not, sir. Will you have a glass of water? Refreshment?'

'No, no, no. There was another matter, too, Sanchez. Millie as well, but that can wait. How is the little chap, any improvement?'

'He was speaking in his sleep, sir.'

'Really? He may have fever again.'

'No, sir – I could not hear his words, but they were quiet. He's not running a temperature.'

At that moment, Sam rolled over and let out a groan.

Millie said: 'Shouldn't we get a real doctor? He might be dying.'

'Yes. I think maybe you're right, Millie. The time has come to end this, hasn't it?'

'To end what, sir?' said Sanchez.

'I think we have to face the facts. This is the end of the road. I've just been looking at the eviction papers, there's no room for appeal. I promised, you see, and—'

'No . . .' said Sam.

'Promises must be kept. And Miss Hazlitt has asked for my resignation.'

Sam's voice was faint. It was a groan of pain. His eyes were closed and his face twitched. As they stared, the eyelids opened. *'Where are you, Ruskin?'*

'What did he say?' said Ruskin.

Sanchez sat beside Sam. 'I think he wants you. Sir, I have something for you, I managed to forget it.'

The headmaster pulled up a second chair and sat on Sam's left. 'Ruskin's right here, Sam. Right beside you – do you want to talk to him?'

'No!' The boy's voice was stronger. 'Into the centre. I can't do all the work. Millie, play the wing, stay out of the way and I can push it to you. You can cross, you can cross! Oh, go on! Anjoli!'

'Sir, he's out on the pitch, sir.'

'I think you're right, Sanchez. He's reliving the game. His breathing's better as well. Routon took out the tube – he said he'd come round.'

Sam's eyes closed again. 'To me, to me. I can't pass, there's no one to pass to. OK, alright, *but don't blame me* – on the left, he's through, it's up to Tack. Oh! Incredible play, he's out on his own . . .'

'He's going to score, sir!'

'Astonishing, where did he learn to do that?' Sam's voice had deepened; he spoke confidently. The voice was a TV commentator's: 'The crowd are on their feet now, they rise as one: it's Tack. All the way! The opposition doesn't know what to do, they didn't expect humiliation like this. Oh! Oh! On he goes, this is poetry – through the legs, over the shoulder, this is football, the goalie's dithering . . . Yes! Yes! Ah!'

Sam sat up in bed, bolt upright.

'He's delirious,' said Millie.

His eyes were wide, his arms were flung open wide. 'Three-nil!' he shouted. 'Hat trick! Yes!'

'Sam!' shouted Sanchez. He held him gently, by the shoulders.

'What?'

'The game's over.'

'What? Where am I? Oh. Am I late? My cap . . .'

'Sam, you're in bed,' said Ruskin. 'You've been hurt again.'

'The game finished hours ago,' said Sanchez. 'You've been unconscious, man. Do you recognise me?'

'Of course I do. Did we win?'

'No, we lost.'

'Oh. Was it my fault?'

'For goodness' sake, Sam,' said Millie. She sat down on the next bed. 'Get a grip. You were the hero, alright? You were scoring number two and their gorilla of a goalie kicked your head in. You were stretchered off and we went down eleven-two.'

'When's the next game?'

'The next game! Sam, *look at yourself*! Look at your leg!'

'Why?'

Sanchez put a hand on Sam's arm. The headmaster stood up and moved back, simply watching. There was a movement in the doorway – the orphans had come, unable to sleep themselves. They pressed silently into the room.

'Sam,' said Sanchez. 'I think you are in for a big shock, yes? When the goalkeeper came at you, he messed up your leg, pretty bad.'

'Oh.'

Sam lifted the sheets and peered down at his legs. 'Where?'

'You lost a lot of blood, man.'

Sam pulled the sheet off completely: his left leg was swathed in bandages. He moved his hands down his thigh, to his knee. He moved the joint; he flexed his toes.

'It's not broken.'

'Keep it still,' said Asilah. The room was now full of children. Every orphan was carrying a sweet, as tribute to Sam.

'My dad says you can always tell a break,' said Ruskin. 'You can't move anything.'

Millie said, 'You lost about ten pints of blood. You've been in a coma.'

'Oh no.' Sam laid back on the pillow. He closed his eyes and

226

seemed to go pale. 'Oh no, just imagine. He did me with his studs?'

'Yes.'

'Ruskin! Millie!'

'It's alright,' said Sanchez. 'You're OK. We're here.'

'Oh thank you!'

'What?'

'It's my left leg, isn't it? Oh thank Heaven! I lead with my right: if he'd done me on the right leg, I might never shoot again. You see, Millie? It's just like my dad says. I'm so lucky. I'm so lucky . . .'

And with that the boy's eyes closed and he fell fast asleep and snored.

'He was raving,' said Millie. 'He's off his head.'

There was suddenly the loud blowing of a nose. 'I'll leave you to it now, children,' said the headmaster. 'I'm afraid the school must close . . . We can't go on, boys. Rent has to be paid, and . . . she's right. The contract is watertight – I ignored it. Lady Vyner is victorious.'

He made for the door, slightly unsteadily. Anjoli opened the door for him, and saluted.

'Oh, sir,' said Sanchez.

'Yes?'

'Sir, I am very sorry. I have something for you which I should have given you weeks ago. From my father, sir.' Sanchez stood and moved to his own bed. Then he was bending low, leaning in under it. He had to lie down full length, and even then stretch. After some time, he re-emerged, clutching a shoebox. 'I don't know why I forget, sir: my father will be angry. He said make sure this is given straight away, but with all the things that happen . . . I forgot.'

Dr Norcross-Webb took the box. You could see him caught between excitement and fear. You could almost read his thoughts: *What if this is some well-meant gift? . . . A handful of*

227

cigars, perhaps. A Colombian doll in national dress . . . It was heavy. He didn't dare open it.

'No problem at all, Sanchez. Thank you.'

'Aren't you going to open it?' said Ruskin.

'No, no . . . I'll look at it tomorrow.'

'Is just some money, sir,' said Sanchez. 'My father says not to use the bank, I don't know why. Oh, but sir.'

'What?'

'Sorry, I think I left my gun inside. Can I just . . .'

Sanchez lifted the box-lid gently and reached in. He took out a handgun and, as he did so, the headmaster glimpsed whole bricks of banknotes, tightly packed. The notes were fifties, and even the swiftest glance confirmed that this was more than enough for the rent, the new roof, and other projects besides.

Sanchez replaced the lid. 'I think it's everything for the year,' he said. 'And he told me to say thank you very much.' Then he tossed the gun onto his duvet and smiled. 'Good night, sir.'

The headmaster stood rigid, unable to move. Very slowly – as if needing support – he put out his hand.

Sanchez took it and shook, firmly.

Chapter Twenty-eight

Millie decided that she had wasted far too much time already. The following day, she made her plans. The whole school was distracted by frenzied preparations for the roofing, which, after Sanchez's cash-injection, was now full steam ahead. The materials had been ordered and delivery was set for dawn the following day. Captain Routon wanted everyone on site at six o'clock sharp, ready to finish clearing the ruins. This gave Millie the excuse she needed to disappear early. She was in bed by eight-thirty and she set her alarm for one.

Flashlight, gloves, crowbar, wire. She had everything ready, stuffed into a sports-bag. The other essential tools she'd have to steal, under the cover of darkness. She dozed fitfully and rose before the alarm went off. Checking for the loathsome Miss Hazlitt, who'd been known to do a little midnight prowling, she got dressed and slipped out of her shed.

The first thing she needed was a vehicle, so she crept round to the school's parking area, at the back of the mansion building. She'd broken into cars before, of course, and knew that beaten-up old wrecks were the easiest. There were two candidates: the school bus – which was an old builder's van owned by Captain Routon – and the headmaster's battered little heap of rust. It looked sorry for itself next to Miss Hazlitt's recently-purchased four-wheel-drive.

Millie slid between the two and went to work. It was a fiddly process, but the wire bent through the old seals of the car door, lifted the locking pillar, and Millie was inside. How nice it was to be working without boys. You could do just what you wanted at the pace you preferred . . . She flashed her torch around and then jerked backwards with fright. Across the park there was a pair of headlights, bumping down the drive.

She clambered into the rear of the vehicle and turned off the torch. The headmaster kept his back seat flat for some reason and the car was littered with old tools and rubbish. She peeped through the window, her heart thumping. Incredibly, the vehicle approaching was a police car – she could see its fluorescent stripes. She swore softly, unable to believe her bad luck. It crawled closer and closer, into the car park and alongside her. She could see the craggy profile of Cuthbertson. Why would he be patrolling at this hour? She swore again. Like a shark in deep water, the police car paused for ten heart-stopping seconds . . . and rolled forward again, in search of other prey.

Millie breathed out. She thanked her stars she hadn't left the car door open, or been caught as she crossed the yard. Somebody was looking after her, maybe. All she needed was gear for a wheel-change, so she turned the torch back on and kept the beam low. There were tools and rags jumbled under a bit of old blanket. She searched and found a heavy hammer and a towing rope. Both could be useful. After more rummaging, she located the precious wheel-jack, resting against a very bald spare tyre. It was well-oiled, compact and ready to go – never been used, obviously. She put everything in her bag, and clambered out of the car. Her load was heavy now and it chafed her leg.

She lit a cigarette and got her nerve back. She closed the door gently and set off, eyes peeled for headlamps. Nothing, so she dared herself into the open, over the lawns. Where the driveway curved, she could see the telephone box, with its light always on. She wondered for the fiftieth time if anyone ever used it and why the telephone company bothered maintaining it. She set her sights on the lake and tried to feel brave. Just then, as she crossed the lawn, two figures appeared on the first humpback bridge.

Millie stood stock still, unable to believe her bad luck.

There was no way she could conceal herself, she was on wide-open ground. She would have no explanation. As she stared, the smaller person waved, and she saw that it was Ruskin.

'We thought we'd missed you,' he said as she joined them.

'I thought you were teachers,' said Millie. 'What made you change your mind? Or do you still want to prove I'm crazy?'

Sanchez wouldn't look at her. 'We all know you're crazy,' he said.

'Ha!' cried Millie. 'So why are you here?'

'The only reason I'm here,' said Sanchez, 'is because we thought it wasn't fair to let you go on your own.'

'Look, the police are around,' said Ruskin, quickly. 'I think we should get out of sight as soon as possible. And, Millie: we have a plan. Sanchez and I have been talking, and we think this is *far* too dangerous, so I'm going to stand guard while you two go down together. Then, if anything happens, I can alert the appropriate authorities.'

'No,' said Millie. 'I've actually planned this down to the last detail.'

'You want to go alone?' said Sanchez. 'You can if you want! I thought—'

'All I'm saying,' said Millie, loudly, 'is don't tell me what to do. I have a strategy.'

'Fine.'

*

The Vyner monument was black against a deep blue night-time sky. There was a strong moon still, hovering low, and a strange, metallic light. Millie squeezed under the fence to the shaft and laid out the tools.

'Hold the torch, Ruskin. We're going to prise the bars apart and go down on the rope. There's no way of lifting the grille.'

'How far down is it?'

They shone their torches down into the black. Ten metres below was a sandy-looking disc of floor.

'You could almost jump,' said Millie.

'I brought a rope,' said Sanchez.

'So did I,' said Millie.

Sanchez moved in and together they positioned the jack. Working as one, they spun the wheel and within a minute there was a gap between the central bars, a good thirty centimetres wide. They attached both ropes.

'I hope you brought the map,' said Sanchez.

'I did bring the map. I do have a brain cell.'

'After you, then. Ruskin: are you going to be alright, here on your own?'

'Oh, don't worry about me. I'm not sure I'll be able to pull you back up, though.'

'We'll climb,' said Millie. 'All you need to do is help us through the bars. I want you to give us two hours, alright? And if we're not back by then, go to the phone box and raise the alarm.'

'And tell the headmaster?'

'No, Ruskin. No. You go to the phone box. You ring my father.' She took a pen from her blazer pocket and scribbled a number onto Ruskin's left hand.

'Here,' said Sanchez. He wrote a number on the boy's right. 'Phone my father too.'

'You do not tell the headmaster anything,' said Millie. 'You don't phone the police. You get through to these numbers and explain that we're lost underground and need a search party.

Tell them the headmaster is chief suspect, along with Professor Worthington and Hazlitt and the inspector. And probably Captain War-hero.'

'OK.'

Sanchez had a bottle of rum in his hand. He took a quick nip and handed it to Millie. 'Keeps out the cold,' he said.

Millie stared and then she smiled. 'Sanchez, you little hero! You're turning into a thief, bad as me!' She took a sip too and smiled a little more broadly. 'You're scared, aren't you?'

'Very.'

'Did you bring your gun?'

'No.'

'That, my friend, might have been a big mistake. Why do you keep a gun if it stays under your bed?' She handed the bottle to Ruskin. 'Don't get drunk,' she said. And with that, she squeezed through the grille, expertly transferred her weight to the ropes, and descended.

Sanchez held the torch, then followed her.

Ruskin dropped the flashlights down to them. 'Good luck,' he called, softly. 'Send me a postcard.'

He sat back then and wished he'd put on a coat. The school blazers were warm, but there was a chilly breeze. The lake was generating a mist, so the clammy air surrounded him. He rubbed his hands vigorously. Some creature of the night squawked and there was a rustling nearby. Ruskin gritted his teeth and prepared for a long, cold vigil. He wished he had never heard about the ghost of Lord Vyner, and he wished he'd never been part of that circle in the chapel conjuring him up. Sitting under the family monument in the darkness seemed to be asking for trouble, and Ruskin wanted no further contact with the spirit world. There were a few lights on in the distant school building and he fixed his eyes on them. He hummed the school song, and took a mouthful of rum.

*

233

'That way's north,' said Millie. 'Towards the house. I say we go towards the house and we should come to this intersection *here*.'

'And then we go left,' said Sanchez.

'I've marked it in red. I'm sure that is the laboratory. I've been thinking and thinking: when I went down, there was Cuthbertson and someone else setting something up. Animals, things in jars . . . it's research, Sanchez. And I bet you it's *illegal* research. And I didn't ever tell you, did I? Professor Worthington recognised the sores I was getting, the ones on my mouth. She knew it was from some chemical, and she knew the antidote. Now the only chemical I was ever exposed to was in that room – it was a sort of white powder, when I broke a jar. I think the school is a front for something very, very wrong.'

They walked in silence for some time. The tunnel was smooth and straight, and their flashlights bounced. After five minutes they came to the first turning.

'By the way, you didn't finish your story,' said Millie.

'What story?'

'You told me all about Miles. You told me Tomaz ran away. But you never got to the end: you never told me what happened.'

Sanchez hesitated: 'Maybe we should just concentrate on not getting lost,' he said.

'Sanchez, tell me the story!'

'Alright! Alright. Tomaz left, yes? But there was a big problem.' He paused. 'Nobody knew where he lived, so . . . how could anyone be sure if he'd got home or not? All we knew was that he'd gone. So when—'

'How do you know he wasn't kidnapped? This is what I'm saying!'

'Millie, listen. You want the story, I'll tell it, OK? OK. He told me he was leaving. He liked the school, but he was scared of Miles, and the Black Magic thing freaked him out completely. We all saw his name, it was written out, two or three times. He wanted to get out, but he didn't know anyone and he couldn't get his passport back, because the policeman had it.'

'Why would Cuthbertson have Tomaz's passport?'

'I don't know, I'm just telling you what happened. Tomaz came to me and asked for money, so I gave him what I had. He was staying in the grounds, living rough. So he came back one night, up the outside of the tower, and he said he needed more cash for tickets. I didn't even know where his country was, I hadn't heard of it. Uzbeki-something.'

'How old was he?'

'Thirteen, nearly fourteen. Very small, but so strong. Like a little buffalo!'

'He sounds brave.'

'He was amazing. He told me somebody in the town was getting him papers. They were smuggling him out in a lorry. I got more money from somewhere, and Ruskin had a bit. We were trying to get more, so we put food out for him, every night, while we were—'

'Like he's a dog? What's the school doing?'

'What do you mean?'

'Sanchez, a boy's gone missing, yes? Turn left here – I mean right.' Millie checked the map again.

'The school's going crazy,' said Sanchez. 'We have the policeman round, asking everyone questions. We have searches. The headmaster was up all night, he was making himself ill. Miles was going crazy, he loved Tomaz! And I didn't know *what* to do! I was taking Tomaz his dinner every evening. We had a special, hollow tree and I always leave food. This goes on for a week or more and then suddenly, I don't know . . . nothing. The food isn't touched, it's just where I left it. He got his ticket home, he must have done.'

'Without the money?'

'He must have found some. He had what we gave him, Millie: he *must* have gone home.'

'What about his family? Surely there was someone . . .'

'No. He was a street kid . . .'

'Why is this school so interested in orphans?'

'He couldn't read or write, he was here on some . . . special arrangement.'

'So Tomaz was the first. You're starting a school and you take kids who can't pay fees. What kind of logic is that?'

'Charity, I don't know.'

'An orphan disappears and there's no one to ask too many questions, no inquest. It all dies down—'

'It didn't die down, the school nearly closed! That's why this woman is here, we lost our licence! It's why Miles set the place on fire.'

'I don't believe Tomaz ever got home. I think he was the first victim and I think they're doing some kind of Frankenstein thing. Why do they need freezers? Why the rats and rabbits? And what on earth do they need a chair with straps for?'

'Shh.'

'What if they kept him alive? What if they're—'

'Shut up!' Sanchez was still. 'Did you hear something? There's someone behind us.'

The children flashed their torches behind them. Millie turned hers off; Sanchez did the same. There was a glow from dim electric lamps above: nothing else.

'I can hear a machine,' said Millie.

'So can I.'

'We're closer than I thought. It's a generator, I bet.'

Millie set off again. She went slowly now, and very quietly. The tunnel curved and led to another intersection. Turning right, without the torches, they could see a soft glow of light in the passageway ahead. Sure enough, there was a light bulb emerging from the rock.

'Bingo,' said Millie. 'We've done it.'

'What do you mean?'

'This is exactly where I was. Millie Roads, A-star map-reading scholar: that's the door.'

'It's closed.'

The door was a plate of grey steel in a wall of granite. The two children stared at it and then at each other.

Millie said: 'I've always felt that one mustn't be put off by a closed door. One has to think round it, over it, and under it. And I always carry this.'

'What?'

She took out a small penknife.

Chapter Twenty-nine

Millie was standing on Sanchez's shoulders and he braced himself against the metal. Around him, short, squat screws fell in the sand. After a few minutes, a large wire grille rattled open, swinging on its hinges.

'You coming?' said Millie.

He looked up and she was forcing the thing upwards. She had her tie in her hand and had lashed one end round the frame. The other end was over the light-cable. The flap rose inch by inch, and suddenly Millie's torso was disappearing, and her weight was gone. She squirmed back around and let down a hand, grinning in triumph.

There wasn't much room in the air-vent, and Sanchez was an awkward climber. They lay there together, wet with sweat, getting their breath back. Then Millie led the way, spreading her weight like a lizard, inching through the metal trunking. She dreaded something giving. It was built for air, not for children and was thick with dust and dirt – nobody had ever cleaned it. She imagined falling in a cloud of filth and landing at the feet of angry teachers. What would actually happen to her if they really *were* about to interrupt some horrible experiment? If Professor Worthington was there, knife in hand? Millie hadn't thought about this before; for Millie, consequences only suggested themselves seconds before they occurred.

She gritted her teeth and inched forwards.

The air-vent had started square: it now converted to a tube the width of a large rabbit hole. The children wormed through, flashlights between their teeth. Mercifully, there were no right-angles. A gentle curve took them about six paces in, and then the metal under them turned into a perforated grille, where the air was either pumped in or extracted out. There were lights below, but Millie couldn't get her bearings. She whispered back to Sanchez: 'Somebody must be down there, the lights are bright.'

'Yes.'

'They work late. When they think we're in bed, they come down here. I bet it's her, our trusted Professor Worthington. Her tower is a complete red-herring: this is where she works. And I bet the lift goes straight to her room.'

'How do we get down, Millie? This is painful.'

'It's wider here, give me your hand. We can unscrew a section and drop.'

She helped Sanchez out of the tube and turned to the bolts. The whole venting system was simply built and it wasn't long before a section was opening upwards, like a hatch.

Sanchez was muttering a prayer. Millie hesitated too. 'Maybe I should have just called my father. Or maybe we should have called yours.'

'Shall we go back? We can phone him, but I don't know what he can do . . .'

'I don't know what *anyone* can do,' said Millie. 'I don't know what we'd say without any proof.' She started work on the last bolt. 'Let's do it,' she said. 'We'll get some evidence, then leave.'

The panel tilted, and it wasn't hard to slide it to one side. Millie peered downwards into the quiet. It looked like that first room, the storage area, but she wasn't sure. She tested the supporting rods and started to lower herself. Her feet found some kind of work surface and she was steady enough to help Sanchez. They jumped down onto a tiled floor. Millie wondered why Sanchez was clutching her. Then she realised she was clutching him too and they were both breathing fast.

'Was I telling the truth?' she whispered. 'About this place?'

'Yes.'

'Am I crazy?'

'Oh yes.'

'This is where I started and those are the doors into the lab. They could be in there, Sanchez, there's lights on everywhere! Keep to the wall, OK? Don't say a word.'

'What's that smell?'

'Shh!'

'It's like a hospital. Disinfectant, or something. It's so damp, it's horrible!'

The children huddled themselves together and crept forwards, keeping low. Sanchez looked at the doors and shuddered. They reminded him of operating theatres – the thought made his heart lurch. He'd seen doors like that when they'd wheeled him down the corridor after the kidnapping, hoping to save his toe. Doors that flipped open so the trolley could be raced inside.

He was aware of a humming and a ticking: the sound of fridges and their motors. Millie was beside him; he felt a hand on his arm, and her voice was high-pitched, right in his ear. She said, 'You know I told you I never got frightened?'

He nodded; he couldn't speak.

'I was lying,' she said. 'I've never been more scared.'

They were at the doors now, squatting. Sanchez felt for Millie's hand. He swallowed. 'If it matters,' he said, and his voice was shaking too, 'I think you're the bravest person I know. And I'm very frightened, also.'

They started to rise, inch by inch. 'Are you ready?' whispered Millie.

'No.'

Their hands were clasped. He had a vision of the doors crashing open. She had a vision of a room full of people, turning to stare – but they forced themselves up and their heads came level with the windows.

'*There's someone in the chair,*' whispered Millie.

She was staring at the monstrous black thing, which sat there just as she remembered it. It was tilted back and drenched in light. 'Look, Sanchez – *look!*'

'I can see . . . but—'

'Someone's in it. Someone is sitting in the chair. Oh no, what if it's him? It's Tomaz.'

'It can't be, how can you tell?'

'I can see feet. Use your eyes, you can see a pair of feet! It's a boy, and his feet can't touch the ground, he's small. I can see his *hand*. Stand here, you can see his hand. It's Tomaz, it must be.'

'It *can't* be . . .'

'We're going in.'

'No. Call the police.'

'How? One of them is probably down here!'

'This is so dangerous, Millie!'

'He's on his own! We're going inside!'

Chapter Thirty

Above ground, Ruskin's night was getting worse as well.

His imagination would not stop working. The cold had crept up from his feet and met the cold coming down from his hair. He didn't know whether to keep still or move, and the time was ticking by, ticking by. He drank more rum and the injection of warmth was the most welcome feeling he had ever felt. More welcome even than the black-and-gold rosette, first prize for the Best Roof Model. More wonderful than the time he'd taught his little brother to whistle, or last Christmas with Gran when she'd sung a carol with him, after about half a year of silence . . . His mind was rambling and he discovered his eyes were full of tears and mist. He so wanted to be home in bed, he stood up and flapped his arms.

Ribblestrop Towers still had a few lights on. As he looked, he saw them switch off, which gave him a lonely feeling. He sang the first line of the school song again, then lapsed into silence. The problem with silence and stillness was that the two things combined to make him feel he was being watched. He could not stop thinking about Lord Vyner and the awful story of his suicide or murder. If he managed to blot that out, he'd start to think about Sanchez and Millie disappearing underground, down into that black, black hole. Oh . . . there the statue was, up above, staring at nothing.

Ruskin knew that if he ever returned as a ghost he would certainly want to settle close to his birthplace. He was fond of his semi-detached home in outer London, and he knew that once he'd made a few trips and seen a few sights, he'd happily settle down to haunt it. Inevitable then, that Lord Vyner would be nearby, watching over the estate with half his head missing. Miles had spoken to him. They'd met on the lawn, if you could believe Miles, and Miles had described his speech impediment and the supper-tray that he carried.

Suicide or murder? The thought of an old man with the top of his head blown off wandering through the woods made Ruskin feel physically weak. He sat down again and stuffed his hands in his pockets. He kept his eyes down and tried not to listen to the wind rising in the trees. He put his hands over his ears and went through the whole school song as loud as he could. As a result, he never heard the footsteps behind him, nor the soft rattle of glassware and crockery.

Back in the basement, the floor seemed to be tilting sideways for Sanchez, as if he'd stepped on board a ship. The chair had its back to them still. There were legs and feet visible and now he could see the shape of a head, and he didn't want to look. Around him stood shelf after shelf of jars and bottles, rising to the ceiling, and he didn't want to look at them either – they had things in them that were looking at him. He took a deep breath and moved on towards the chair.

Whoever was in it was Tomaz-size. Yes, he could see a little white hand emerging from a grey shirt-cuff and a black-and-gold blazer. There was a leather strap over the wrist, tight enough to hold it firm.

'Tomaz?' said Millie. Her voice was hoarse.

Sanchez tried to speak, but nothing came.

The child in the chair didn't answer. They were both behind him still; they couldn't bring themselves to move in front – to the face. The prisoner remained silent and motionless.

'Tomaz?' she said again, all moisture gone from her mouth. 'Sanchez is here, it's OK. You're safe now.' She looked at Sanchez with tears in her eyes. 'Speak to him.'

'Tomaz?' he said. His voice was a husk.

'We're friends,' said Millie. 'We're going to help you . . .'

She forced herself to move. The face was coming into view, the whole profile. An eye, wide open, staring forwards. Not a blink or a twitch. Sanchez was beside Millie, swaying and holding her shoulder; he was dragging himself forward. He took a step and stared. How quickly sight imprints horror on your brain.

You cannot un-see what you've seen; it's there, photographed into you. They were both looking at him, immaculate in his Ribblestrop uniform. A chalk-white face, with staring eyes that had no life. The lips were apart, as if the boy had died speaking, and he was bolt upright. But worse, much worse than this – was the sight neither Sanchez nor Millie could look at . . . the top of the skull had been removed and, sitting there ripe and raw, like a brightly-coloured dessert, was the child's brain.

Millie realised she was making a noise, just trying to breathe. It was a horrible, guttural moan and Sanchez, who had backed away, was getting ready to scream. He took another huge pace back and fell onto his behind, overturning a stool.

Millie cried out and backed away too. '*It's not real!*' she shouted. 'It's not real, it's not him!'

Sanchez was still on the floor. Millie forced life into her hand, her arm, and stretched it out. She touched the boy's shoulder, and he wasn't real. She moved to the neck and it was hard as stone. She touched the cheek. She traced the smoothness up to the too-long eyelashes. Plastic or fibreglass. Not flesh.

'Sanchez,' she said. She swallowed hard; back in control. 'It's a dummy, it's the same as George. There's another one!'

'Where?'

'Stand up. Come here.'

'I don't think I can. What *is* this, Millie?'

'Keep calm. There's another one behind you. They're just models, Sanchez. Like the one by the notice board. It's George.'

Sanchez had managed to turn his head and, sure enough, standing over him but staring past into nothingness – was a second child. The same uniform, the same face. The skull was intact on this one, though the thing was bald. It carried a tray as if it might be waiting for a food-order.

'What are they?' said Sanchez. 'Millie, there's one in the corner, over there!'

'They're just models. Look at this! Come here. It's a medical model, isn't it? They had something like this at my last school; you could take them apart and see all the bits.'

'Why are they dressed up? Why are they *here*?'

'I don't know. Look at this, it's beautiful . . .'

Sanchez came slowly and stared with Millie at the one in the chair. Under the drenching light, the brain was shiny. It was also lit from within and, up close, you could see transparent panels which allowed you to look deep inside, where pin-pricks of light illuminated different shafts and channels. The children looked and looked: the colours of the brain were gently changing.

'Millie!' said Sanchez.

But Millie was lost. She was staring deeper, hypnotised by the wonder of the thing.

'Millie! I can hear something! We should go.'

Sanchez was listening hard, trying to work out where the noise was coming from. Even as he spoke, soft vibrations had turned into a hammering. He grabbed Millie and she was jerked back to reality; she felt and heard it too. The noise was in the floor and the walls; it felt as if someone was shaking the whole, hideous laboratory; the glassware rattled, and trickles of dust fell from the brick arches.

'Let's go! It's the lift.'

Louder and louder, the sound of metal sheets clashing together, the squeal of an engine. The noise was way too huge for a lift, Millie knew that now, and there was a screech of brakes. All at once she made the connection. It was a train, not a lift. The rumours must be true – there was an underground line, and it still ran.

She looked around wildly; she would not be caught twice. Sanchez was turning, like a deep-sea diver, unable to decide on a direction. Millie made a grab for him, and they were in each other's arms as if they'd decided to dance. Cabinets and shelving surrounded them, and there were the freezers – but Millie knew she would never go willingly into that kind of darkness again. She span around and around, desperate for an exit – the doors were no good, they'd be cornered in the storeroom.

'Up!' said Sanchez.

He was looking above the chair, at the ceiling. The venting system came into this room too and let air in through a large, perforated grille. Direct centre was a maintenance hatch. Millie leaped onto the back of the chair; she got a foot on the inspection lamp and Sanchez helped her balance. Then she was rising, pushing at the hatch with outstretched finger-tips. It flipped open and she was hauling herself back into the roof-space, elbows in, waist disappearing.

The noise around them made speech impossible, but Sanchez was shouting something. He was following her, teetering crazily, stretching up as high as he could. He felt a hand on his hair and another on his shirt collar. He jumped and slipped; he kicked; and with superhuman strength Millie lifted him to where he could grab the ceiling rods.

They lay together panting; they heard the dreadful ratcheting noise of an iron gate opening, and they rolled over. They pressed their noses to the grille and scrambled the hatch back into place.

And now they couldn't tear their eyes away, because, oh . . . it was impossible: the noise they could hear was that of a whole wall opening, concertinaing back to reveal a narrow concrete platform and the side of a silver tube-train.

Chapter Thirty-one

Who was opening the door? A big man was straining till he was pink in the face, and pinker through the sharply-combed grey hair. He wore a uniform that was too tight and, as he shifted around to drag the gate further back, both children gulped. It was Inspector Cuthbertson.

They tried to back away, but the ceiling flexed under them as if it might collapse. A cluster of men were entering the surgery. They were dressed in dark clothes – funeral suits and raincoats – no, one man wore a white coat, and he was ushering the others in. They carried briefcases and one was talking into a cellphone or radio-set, mumbling quietly. The man in the white coat was moving from wall to wall, pressing switches. Here and there monitors flashed into life, at first black and white, then panels of static. There was a flurry of squeals and chirps.

'Who are they?' whispered Millie. She was holding Sanchez's arm, and she all but crushed the bone. 'That was Cuthbertson. Can you see Worthington?'

'Shh! I've no idea!'

'He was opening the door. Who's that? I can't see . . .' The man in the white coat had moved to the model's head, talking quietly. Everyone else gathered around him, just under the children. He had a bird's nest of white hair dragged over a skull that seemed too big for the shoulders. He was thin and leaned forward, rubbing his hands thoughtfully, playing with his fingers – a surgeon's elegant hands, pale and slender.

Everyone was staring at the model.

'We'll see a result,' he said. 'If we hold our nerve, I guarantee it. I want to show you the results of the serotonin, you'll be—'

'We've heard this before,' said somebody.

'And I still don't think we'll ever get past its reputation,' said somebody else.

The white-coated man put a hand on the model's shoulder and picked up a long needle. 'You've asked me to demonstrate,' he said. He sounded just a little nervous. 'And this is the best I can do at present. You have to inject deep. In a rabbit, for example, you've got the possibility of twelve different reactions. I will be in a position to demonstrate if you give me time.'

He peered up at one of the monitors, and the children could see his eyes. Such a wrinkled face, the skin of old fruit. Little black eyes, sharp as stones. His voice was rasping, as if he'd been talking all day and all night.

'People are dubious – and for the right reasons,' said a man in grey. 'It's never been properly tested, and that's why your work was so important. You've documented the dangers frankly and faithfully, and I feel we've had value for money.'

'Mr Jarman,' said another voice. The children couldn't see his face, but the man's tone was sharp. He stood close to the model with his hands clasped behind his back. He wore a bowler hat and black gloves. 'How much longer do you actually need? The school seems to be in chaos. You don't seem to be getting anywhere . . .'

'I'm nearly there. Christmas, at the outside. The end of the term.'

Inspector Cuthbertson said, 'There's been a lot of interference, sir. Some of the English kids have made things complicated.'

There was a woman's voice: 'Talk me through the process again. I'm impatient, like everyone else. But assuming you do

249

have an opportunity, let's say before Christmas – talk us through the procedure. You're still with myelin?'

'I'm still with the myelin, ma'am, yes. It's dangerous, I acknowledge that. But parts of the brain have to be neutralised first and that's what we developed it for. It's a far sharper tool than serotonin, for example, and we still have a great deal stockpiled here.'

Millie and Sanchez could see perfectly: as he spoke, he was feeding the needle into the doll's brain. A screen above the chair lit up. Everyone gazed at it and colours appeared, composing themselves into spheres and hemispheres. A whole galaxy of what looked like transparent planets started to break open. The man in the white coat inserted a second needle and more images scrolled quickly. 'The myelin neutralises and the surgery removes. Drugs *and* surgery – you can't have one without the other, because I'm killing parts of the brain that the knife won't reach. This is the uniqueness – this is the art. I've said all along, you won't get what you want by drugs alone; you have to intervene, boldly, with corrosives. I'm referring not just to the amygdala, which you can see just there.'

Millie counted the needles. There were five in all, deep in the brain, and the surgeon's voice had taken on a strange confidence and passion.

'It's a *shorthand*, of course it is – we're penetrating the interdependent cortexes, because it's in this part of the brain that we find *desire*. The need – if you will – the *instinct*, to challenge and question.'

'It's late, Jarman – keep it simple.'

'I'm talking about the very thing you asked me to investigate: *ego*, if you will. The desire to rebel. The chemistry used to unpick and eradicate that sense of self – well, it's going to vary from child to child, of course it is. Heavy doses of stimulants are required alongside every injection.'

'Let's go,' whispered Sanchez. He was inching backwards. 'I've got to get out, Millie!'

The bowler hat spoke. 'We're actually no further forward. We've all seen the paperwork but what we need is the demonstration, and I think Christmas is unreasonable. The money's run out and there's still nothing to show – my chairman's going to laugh at me.'

'Can I ask a question, old boy?'

The voice was new and it was followed by total silence. Millie and Sanchez went rigid again. They hadn't noticed him at first. He had remained at the end of the laboratory. His raincoat was buttoned up and belted tightly. He carried an umbrella and a briefcase, and he had the worst moustache Millie had ever seen. It was thick and dark, and made her think of caterpillars. His voice was refined and friendly – even apologetic. 'My committee feels – unreasonable as it may seem – that it pulled a few strings on this. Considerable risks were taken, some would say. Against the advice of several officers!'

'I understand that, Sir Peter.'

'Some of us feel it's now or never, and the delays we've had—'

'The delay was caused simply by a small injury I sustained . . .'

'Well, we seem to have had one delay after another, don't we? Not pointing a finger, old boy, not a bit of it. But we have to move to phase two, or the whole project founders and leaves egg on our faces. There's similar stuff being trialled in Thailand at half the price – you know that. You've got access. You've had the green light. Let's do it.'

Everyone started talking at once. A cellphone was ringing and there was a squeal of hydraulics. Over it all, the man in the white coat was calling. 'Listen!' he cried. He plucked the needles from the brain, one by one. The chair was tilting under his hands and now it was rising; the model was leaning backwards in the chair, its empty eyes fixed on Millie and Sanchez. Its head was opening. The brain was rising and unfolding like a flower, revealing honeycombs of purple, orange and red. 'Everything is ready!' said the man in the white coat. 'We're ready to try! We drill the skull in five places. There, and there – those are the first points, that's the nerve centre. The marks will be invisible, it will take eight hours and we'll have him back in his bed before dawn. He's ready, and you're right – we can't keep putting it off.'

'Please . . .' whispered Sanchez. 'I'm going to be sick, really.'

Sanchez had seen a gap a few metres to his left and was pulling at Millie, pointing. The air-conditioning opened up to a funnel, and from the top of the funnel ran a shaft, at least the width of his shoulders. There was a narrow ladder bolted to the side and he moved towards it. Millie squirmed after him, as the voices below got louder, arguments flaring. It took the children a few minutes only. The disk of light shrank below them; the sound finally faded. They climbed steadily, hoping for daylight. Hand over hand in darkness.

After some time, they found themselves on a narrow maintenance platform. In front of them was a deep shaft, and in the shaft a cluster of cables. Millie recognised it at once: it was a lift, and the lift car sat just a few metres below them. She went first and helped Sanchez onto its roof.

Millie spoke softly, with absolute conviction. 'They were talking about Tomaz. "*Back in bed before dawn . . . invisible marks.*" They're talking about Tomaz! – they've got him, haven't they?'

'No,' said Sanchez. 'He got home.'

'He's their prisoner! They're going to do something—'

'No, Millie! Don't say it.'

Chapter Thirty-two

Back at school, the headmaster hadn't gone to bed.

He and the captain had meant to have an early night, because of the big day ahead. However, as had happened so often, the two men had got side-tracked into redesigning tiny details of the roof interior. Not a week went by without some idea occurring, and right now the two men were sitting in the office, staring at Ruskin's model, trying to devise new supports to the hip-rafters. Routon had realised that if the vertical struts of the current design were replaced with diagonals, the hips would still be supported but a lot of extra attic space would be made available. Both men were repositioning the doll-furniture, excited by the versatility of the new area.

'You could put a sofa there,' said Captain Routon.

'Yes you could. Move the table back a bit – is there room?'

'Bit of a squeeze, but it could be done.'

'What about a stove?' said the headmaster.

'Why not? A nice woodburner – we had one of them in Al-Houti, kept us warm during the coup. Imagine that in the evenings, eh? All the boys, curled up with a bit of Kipling. Just a case of ordering a flue.'

'When I was a boy, Routon, we used to have two hours' reading every night. It was one of the few good rules. A reading club.'

'Call it the Reading Room, sir.'

'Excellent. Make it part of the library – you could link it with a staircase, just there. Imagine that! You could have discussions, Routon. Lectures, seminars . . . We could have visiting speakers and the boys could question them over a glass of port. It was like that at my old school, you know. We'd retire upstairs, serve a few snacks . . . *What the hell was that?*'

Routon had leaped to his feet. His hand had sprung to his hip for the revolver he no longer carried. An explosion had come from the very roots of the building and, as both men stood horrified, it came again and then a third time. It was the most furious knocking, as if Death had come to claim a victim.

'My goodness, Routon – it sounds like cannon fire.'

'It's the door, sir! Someone's at the door!'

'Whatever's the time? It can't be!'

'Oh my word, it's nearly five o'clock. It must be the deliveries, that's all it can be. They said dawn, but—'

'Lady Vyner's not going to be happy about this. Quickly, we—'

But his voice was silenced again by another volley of thunderous knocks and the two men made for the stairs. They had to go carefully, because the moon threw long, strange shadows through the narrow windows and it was so easy to miss your step. As they descended the stairs, they ran straight into Professor Worthington, whose eyes were wide with panic.

'Headmaster, someone's outside,' she cried. 'I can't get the door open, someone's bolted it.'

'Oh Lord, we don't need this!'

'Why is everything locked and bolted? Who's doing this?'

'Miss Hazlitt.'

'Why?'

'It's part of this wretched drive for security. She's convinced that some of the children are getting into the grounds at night, so—'

The knocking came again and, now they were in the lower corridor, the vibrations seemed to set them stumbling. Routon knelt down and attacked one of the bolts, whilst Professor Worthington turned away helplessly. 'I don't like it!' she cried.

'What's going on?' said a voice. Miss Hazlitt stood at the end of the corridor. She was leaning against the wall and she looked unsteady. They watched as she limped towards them. She was only half dressed – a disturbing combination of long skirts and a man's dressing gown. She hadn't had time to fix her wig properly and without make-up there was something hungry and cadaverous in her face. 'Who's been out?' she said. She was having trouble getting her breath. 'Someone's stolen my briefcase – there are children in the grounds, it's intolerable—'

As she spoke, there were three more stone-breaking knocks. 'Alright!' she roared, and her voice echoed in the hallway. The volume seemed to use up the little strength she had left. She turned to the headmaster; her eyes were mad and staring, as if she hadn't slept – as if she'd been searching the school all night. 'Somebody has stolen my briefcase,' she whispered. 'Some of the most confidential papers I own. There are thieves in the school, Headmaster, and they're out of control. We've known that since day one, when my credit card . . .' Her cellphone bleeped, but she ignored it. She bent down awkwardly, fell to one knee and shot the lower bolt. Routon wrestled with the top one, and at last the door was unlocked. 'I've had just about enough,' she said, gasping for air. 'My report . . . I can tell you, my report! It will be that girl, I'm positive . . .'

They heaved the door open together and, in the thin light of the approaching dawn, everyone saw – not a crane driver with a clipboard of papers to sign, nor a delivery man of any sort. The figure staggering back from the doorway appeared – at first glance, with the moon over its shoulder – to be a small silver bear, wearing glasses. As everyone stared, the bear clutched wildly at the doorframe, and then took a big step backwards.

'Ruskin,' said the headmaster.

'I got so cold,' said the bear. Then it pirouetted twice and sprawled backwards, paws in the air.

Ruskin's world had gone violently out of control.

He had been getting colder and more frightened. There are only so many times you can sing the school song and only so many shots of rum you can swallow. By the time Millie and Sanchez were staring at the brain of the plastic child, Ruskin had got through half the bottle and the world was beginning to swirl.

He'd taken off his glasses again and jogged on the spot to coax some feeling back into his feet. Then, when he staggered round to look for his spectacles, he couldn't find them. This struck him as funny rather than frightening, and he laughed.

He drank more rum and felt better, so – forgetting his glasses – he decided to go for a short, brisk stroll. His vision was now doubly blurred and he noticed that he was far from steady on his feet. He set off bravely and found the night air bracing. When he tried to retrace his steps, however, everything had moved around and changed. Still, he didn't panic. He giggled and squinted into the night. Sure enough, there was the Vyner Monument, but if he was correct, the man now had his back to him. More worryingly, there seemed to be two columns, which meant two Lord Vyners – so Ruskin made for the ground between them. He wove his way round the front, stumbling in undergrowth that was thick and wet. There was the sports-bag and the line of tools, exactly as he'd left them. Ruskin found he was talking aloud, telling the tools how pleased he was to see them.

There was something else though.

Impossibly and ridiculously, there was a tray of food laid out just where he'd been sitting. He racked his brains. Had he brought a complete dinner-for-one with him and simply forgotten? Had his friends returned, having stopped at a restaurant? It was a silver tray and the white cloth over it was immaculate. Just beside it – as if it might serve for a seat – there was a large, furry object. It had been folded neatly, and laid on a Selfridges shopping bag.

Ruskin knelt down, unsteadily, and unfolded it. It was a rich, silver-coloured fur coat, and as he shook it out he was reminded how cold he was. He put it on and buttoned it up. Then he attended to the tea-tray, drawing the cloth to one side. There was a slice of meat pie with roast vegetables in thick gravy. There was a half-bottle of red wine, complete with a crystal glass. The food was piping hot and the smell sent saliva squirting round his mouth. It was all on fine-quality china too, and there, best of all, on a serviette, were the glasses he'd forgotten he'd lost. Some thoughtful soul had even put a coffee pot and an after-dinner chocolate next to them.

Ruskin had no answers to the questions that buzzed in his head, so he ignored them. He sat down and ate. He drank the wine and had another nip of rum. Needless to say, by the time he'd finished this, he had only the vaguest memories of his duties. They had become so muddled that places and names were merging into one. A telephone and a policeman . . . but what the message was and when it was to be delivered was all simply gone from his mind. He couldn't even recall why he was out, alone, at night, sitting under some monument.

It was at this point that Ruskin decided to go home and see his good friend Sam. So, he set off for the bridges amazed to see four of them swirling round in front and behind. Laughing again, he aimed for one and hauled himself along the rails. It swung madly under him and suddenly tipped him forward onto the path. He kept his balance and started for one of the schools in front of him. Now and then he fell, but he was so padded and furry that he didn't notice. The mansions seemed to be avoiding him, so he had to keep changing direction: in the end, he reached the front door. Of course, he had no key, but luckily, there was a heavy knocker. He was giggling more and more. He was singing the first verse of the school song again, loud as he could. He grabbed the knocker and held himself upright. Oh, it was so cold to the touch, the frost was freezing . . . He hammered it down three times. The noise reverberated in his head and all at once he felt rather ill. Nobody came, so, despite the fact that the knocker now felt heavy in his hands, despite the need to sleep, he crashed it down three more times, then four. That was when the whole world tipped backwards and he found himself on his back in the gravel.

Miss Hazlitt was outside first, and in seconds she was standing over him. 'Ruskin . . .' she snarled. 'Where are the others?'

'My goodness, this is terrible!' said the headmaster.

'Where's he been?' said Professor Worthington. 'It's freezing! Get the boy inside!'

Miss Hazlitt was leaning over him. 'Red-handed,' she said. 'A thief, caught in the very act! Out of bounds, stealing about, and look at this, just look at it . . . It's the coat. It's the coat that I paid for, I'll bet money on it! Get on your feet, child! I want my briefcase!'

She hauled Ruskin to his knees, and Ruskin felt the world spin under him. It was like being on a roundabout that the bigger boys had set going too fast; he was getting giddier and giddier and wishing he'd never got on. Miss Hazlitt's face was coming closer too, and was getting huge and fat as if he was looking into a spoon. He put an arm over his face and tried to curl up. 'No!' he cried. He felt hands under his arms, and caught a whiff of the woman's sweat. 'Please!' he said.

'Get yourself up!' she was shouting. The words were echoing in his ears. 'Where's the girl, Ruskin? You're in it together, aren't you?'

'Miss Hazlitt! Please!'

The headmaster's voice crashed in from a great distance, clashing like cymbals. The woman was ignoring it. Ruskin felt himself hauled up into a standing position, but his legs just wouldn't work. The world was a whirlpool. He felt more hands under his arms and he knew suddenly that he was going to be sick. He looked up into the deputy headmistress's angry, straining face. He looked around in panic and tried to warn those carrying him. Too late, the drive bucked him forward onto his elbows. He breathed deep and swallowed, but it was no good at all. It came from deep inside, a whole bucketful of rum, pie, vegetables and red wine. Ruskin vomited noisily and the geyser emptied itself over the deputy headmistress's sensible shoes. She danced backwards, slipped in the muck, and ended on her backside. Ruskin vomited again, rolled onto his side and was unconscious.

Of course, the Ruskin distraction was the piece of lifesaving luck Millie and Sanchez so desperately needed. As their lookout was weaving his way to the school gate, they were swinging down the thick, oily cables of the lift-car, hoping there would be an emergency hatch. They knelt on the roof together, torches back in their teeth, and fumbled in the dirt. Millie scratched with her penknife and at last located some kind of channel and handle. They twisted and pulled and at last the hatchway gave. It took ten seconds to swing themselves into the lift-car, and five more to negotiate the 'up' button. All at once there was a surge of power and they were rising.

'Where's it go?' said Sanchez.

'Up – that's the main thing.'

'Sam said there was a lift. Do you remember? In the head-master's study. He said the policeman came that way. Stop,

Millie! What if the head's working late? What if Miss Hazlitt's there?'

'I don't care. I want to get out.'

'What did we see?'

'I don't know. We've got to do something, though, and do it fast.'

'They can't have Tomaz! He must have got home!'

'Sanchez, face the facts! They're getting him ready! They're mucking about with kids' brains, and we'll be next if we're not careful.'

'There was a train down there! I don't get it!'

'It was a research centre – you knew that! During the war. We were told that. Listen. The government is paying the head-master for all these orphans to come here. There's a lift from his office to the lab: what does that say?'

'But he wasn't there.'

'What was the name of the old man? The one in the white coat?'

'Jarman. Shh!'

'And the bent policeman was down there too.'

'We're stopping.' Sanchez's voice was a whisper. 'I think we should go to the phone box and phone my father. You think this is the headmaster's study?'

Millie inched the grille back. 'Let's get back to your dormi-tory. I tell you one thing, you should carry your gun. And we should all stay together.'

There was a brass catch in the woodwork and, as Millie touched it, the door sprang gently open on oiled hinges. Both children stood poised and ready to run. Early-dawn light fell through the elegant windows; there was a familiar desk, a sofa they'd sat in, and the usual snowfall of paper. It was the headmaster's study and it was empty. Breathing quick, shallow breaths, they closed the grille and swung the pan-elling back into place. Millie tiptoed across the rug to the study door.

'It'll be locked,' whispered Sanchez. He went to the window. 'Oh, no – Millie! Come here.'

'What?'

'They've got Ruskin! And there's people coming! Look – it's too late!'

Millie could hear a siren wailing and ran to Sanchez. They gazed across the park and found that once again they were holding each other in fear. The drive was clear in the moonlight and swimming down it there seemed to be a whole river of revolving lights. There were amber lights, red lights, and the fierce halogen lamps of what looked like motorway-maintenance vehicles. There was a police car in there somewhere, but it seemed to be moving in the opposite direction and there was a great blaring of angry horns. The vehicles were fanning out over the grass and moving in like artillery. One after another they paused in a burst of air-brakes, and there was a flurry of door-slamming. The figures in the courtyard were lit by a hundred headlights and stood shielding their eyes. Big men in gloves were leaping from cabs. There were boots on gravel and voices shouting.

'Come on,' said Millie. 'Let's get out.'

'How?'

Millie pulled Sam's toothbrush from her pocket. 'Don't you remember?' she said. 'They gave it back.'

In seconds they were standing in the corridor. They would have to go downstairs, past the front door and up again, so Sanchez led the way, Millie keeping one eye behind. They hadn't reached the top step before they heard urgent footsteps racing towards them and there was nowhere to hide. Someone snapped on the lights and the children were caught like rabbits in the road, wide-eyed and open-mouthed.

'Millie. Where have you been?'

It was the headmaster and he was almost running.

'Nowhere,' said Millie.

'Are the orphans up?'

'I don't know,' said Sanchez.

'We need Henry, urgently. This is all a bit of a mess, quite frankly.' He was moving past them, towards his office. 'I really did not want to start the day this way. Ruskin's chosen this night of all nights, it's such a shame – Miss Hazlitt's furious. He's drunk as a sailor. Can you help me, please? I want to get everyone assembled in the courtyard so we can unload, and Captain Routon wants to get the crane into the construction area first. They're early, which is wonderful, but we've been caught totally on the hop.' He was opening the door; he didn't notice it was unlocked. 'The trusses can be carried in,' he called, over his shoulder. 'But tell Asilah there's a fork-lift for everything else. Oh, and Millie – will you get everyone to put overalls on? I don't want your blazers getting mucky.'

He was through the door. He didn't notice two sets of filthy footprints over his rug. Nor had he noticed the grime and oil on the children's faces and clothes, or their zombie-like expressions. He needed his lists.

How many hours had been spent working out quantities of ironmongery, timber and tools? So many lists, so many orders, all cross-referenced and ready to be checked, item by item. The headmaster was trembling with excitement: the roofing was about to begin.

Chapter Thirty-three

Lady Vyner looked down at the scene with disgust.

There was a crane, two flat-beds, and too many support vehicles to count. It was a military assault, and the world was rolling in diesel smoke. They'd laid heavy ramps, and one truck was reversing round the fountain; a high-pitched alarm was wailing over the park. There were two articulated lorries carrying giant triangles, and orphans capered about, their cries floating upwards as they leaped on and off the trucks.

'Pray for an accident,' she muttered. 'Fall under a wheel, someone.'

Every ornament on Lady Vyner's sideboard was dancing as the crane moved through. When the old woman went to the other side of the room and peered down, there it was in the centre of the courtyard. Seconds later its long arm was extending higher and higher, the greased steel flashing in the floodlights.

'Who is that?' she shouted. 'There's a child on the crane!'

Caspar looked up in time to see a boy level with the window, waving.

'Anjoli,' said Caspar. 'He's a show-off, Gran.'

The boy wore a bright yellow hard-hat, and his grey shirt flapped in the breeze. He seemed to skip up the metalwork and then he jumped down to a giant hook that was now swinging over the walls. It lifted him higher.

Lord Caspar had no interest in the construction project. The only reason he wasn't in bed was that a very special parcel had arrived the previous day and he'd been working on his own obsession all through the night. He'd ordered a length of high-tension cat-gut from an archery specialist in London and it had finally arrived. There it was, on the table in front of him, long and rubbery. Next to it were the components of an ancient crossbow. He'd been restoring it for eleven weeks, ever since he'd lost his flintlock pistol to Millie. Bolts, pins, washers, timber-sections and metal rings: he'd cleaned and greased them all. He'd assembled and disassembled them; he'd rebored holes and re-grooved channels. He'd fashioned a new trigger from an old coffee-pot, and he'd sharpened three beautiful arrows that he'd found his gran using as back-scratchers. He trimmed the cat-gut with a razor and now he stretched it across the arms of the bow. He didn't notice the walls and floor shaking around him, not even when glasses smashed in the kitchen.

Caspar was ready for Millie; round two was approaching.

It took fifteen minutes to get the trusses in, then an hour to move the pallets of slate. With sixteen willing helpers, every piece of kit was in position by breakfast time. The drivers got their papers signed and piled into their trucks. They'd never seen a team like it; the children had terrified them and they were pleased to speed off out of the park. As day broke, the line of children worked, singing. Arc-lights went up. A storage hut was hauled onto an earth platform and hooked up to power. Henry dragged in a cart laden with scaffolding boards, and soon the flat earth was duck-boarded and a couple of narrow towers were tied into the walls. Everyone was hard-hatted and over-alled, and all wore boots.

'Clarissa, are you down there?'

The children looked up and saw the headmaster at his study window. 'We need to get the first truss up right away, so we need everyone on scaffolding. Routon suggests bracing it from about where you're standing. I've got to have a little chat with Miss Hazlitt about this briefcase business, so I wonder if you could supervise the block-and-tackle. Millie? Can you and Sanjay sink a tent-peg, just where you're standing. Then we'll throw a line down to you and use that as a cantilever. The first truss is the hardest!'

The tent-peg he had in mind turned out to be a five-foot iron stanchion. It was so heavy the two children could hardly lift it. If it really was a tent-peg it would have also anchored a trawler. Several orphans assisted and Israel got to work with the sledge-hammer. He sat up on Sanjay's shoulders as he swung it, smashing the top of the peg with such force sparks were struck from the metal. When it was in, Henry attached a rope and the end was flung up to little Anjoli who was still on the crane-hook. He wore a headset and gave instructions to Professor Worthington, who was back at the controls.

Around her, the scaffolding was going up. This was bamboo, and the orphans had had enormous fun practising their pole-vaulting skills. Several bundles had been lying ready for days, and the long poles were so bendy they could send a child up as high as the headmaster's study window. Under Asilah's super-vision, the poles were now lashed together into quadrilaterals. Captain Routon took a ten-minute Geometry class, making vari-ous observations about angles, and there was a short delay because one of the smallest orphans had trouble understanding the concept of congruence. After that, the scaffolding rose quickly.

'Sanchez, we need to talk,' said Millie.

'I know,' said Sanchez. 'But I don't know what to say. I'm thinking and thinking, and the plain fact is I don't know what to do. We didn't get any evidence.'

'I know.'

'We need to go down again, don't we? We need to photograph the place, or film them in action.'

'We need to look for Tomaz!'

'I know, and we need a meeting. We need to tell everyone what we've seen. If we get everyone together, tonight—'

There was an enormous cheer as she spoke and a howl of engine noise. Both children swung round and saw the crane juddering into life, its wheels spinning. The air seemed to go hot in waves, and then the gearbox burst in a series of gunshots. Professor Worthington was at the controls, reversing into position.

'Sanchez, I've just had an idea!' shouted Millie. The great hook swayed over them all and Israel directed it down. 'Why don't we find out who rents that place? Surely we can find out who's in charge.'

'How?' yelled Sanchez.

'Lady Vyner!' cried Millie. She put her mouth close to Sanchez's ear. 'I should have thought of it before. She must know her own tenants, so she must know who Jarman is! We'll find out the *background*!'

'OK,' shouted Sanchez. It was his turn to yell into Millie's ear. 'But she's not going to tell us anything. She might be in on the whole thing.'

'Send Sam,' cried Millie.

'What?'

'Send. Sam. I'm serious! It's a brilliant idea. He looks harmless. Send him in with a bottle of booze. Get her drunk. Get him to ask a load of questions. We'll talk later, my voice is hurting!'

They stepped back out of the fumes in time to see Anjoli lean down from the crane's hook. Smaller boys were passing him a canvas sling on bamboos, which he attached and pushed on to Henry, who supported the first roof-truss. Knots were tied and Anjoli put his thumbs up. Asilah radioed Professor Worthington and suddenly the gigantic triangle was floating upwards, rising to the mansion walls.

To see the great beam bridging what had been, for so long, an open, burnt-out space, was an emotional moment for all. The timber peak soared upwards like a spire and traced the line the roof would take. The headmaster found his eyes were blurred with tears. He saw Anjoli run up to the top, like a bare-chested angel. He received the bracing rod, tied it off quickly with a black-and-gold tie, and saluted again. Israel lit good-luck crackers and there was a volley of triumphant explosions.

So the trusses rose; timbers braced and connected them and before lunchtime all eighteen were in position. The carpentry team started work on windows. The masonry squad, under the personal supervision of Captain Routon, were sealing the beams in place. Four hip-rafters were slotted in, fitting perfectly, and there was the ribcage of the roof ready for batons and slates. The cathedral was rising.

Chapter Thirty-four

What was Miss Hazlitt doing?

She was sitting at her desk staring at her hands. Her briefcase had not reappeared and that was making her sweat. The incessant hammering was making her head ache and she was starting to twitch. She had closed the window on the headmaster and now she looked hard at the telephone, getting her thoughts and her plans in careful order. She hadn't slept for three nights. It was Ruskin and Sanchez who'd been out in the grounds – she'd watched the surveillance footage. There had been a third figure too, moving in the darkness, and that had to be Millie. She'd called Selfridges and described the fur coat. They had positively identified it, priced it, and the price coincided with one of her credit-card bills. It was evidence and it proved what she'd known all along. Now, when she thought about what was at stake, the pressure felt physical. The eradication of Millie was urgent.

It was mid-morning when she took the inspector's call.

'We've got problems,' he said.

'I know we've got problems. I've been trying to reach you.'

'Did you find your briefcase?'

'No. There were three children out last night. I have been trying to discuss it with our headmaster and I'm getting nowhere. I don't know where they went, it may have been a drunken—'

'Wait a moment, listen.'

'What?'

The inspector paused. 'Are you ready for this? We found a tie. First thing this morning when we were tidying up. A school tie, black and gold.'

'*Where* did you find it?'

'Traces of blood, chewed at the end. It was holding up the cover to an extractor fan, out in the tunnel. It wasn't there yesterday.'

Miss Hazlitt said nothing, but her heartbeat increased. 'Have you looked at the tie? You should find that every school tie has a name tag.'

'Well, I'm ahead of you there, sir. My training as a police officer stood me in good stead, because that was just what I looked for first.'

'And? Millie Roads?'

'Our investigator-cum-thief. She took the rabbit, and I think she took your briefcase. Sanchez and Ruskin were probably the watchmen. We looked at the venting system and there're nuts and bolts strewn all over the place. It's a confident entry: second visit, no doubt about it. What do you want to do?'

Miss Hazlitt thought hard. 'Right now,' she said, 'I'm not sure I want to do anything. She's outside, working, and she's not going anywhere. She's not trying to make telephone calls and I doubt if she knows what to do herself.'

'She must have told someone by now. We can't turn a blind eye to two mistakes, can we? We're going to have to do something, specially if the boy's ready. What was in the briefcase, dare I ask?'

'I'll deal with her. I'll sort it out.'

'How? What was in the briefcase, was it important?'

Miss Hazlitt dropped her voice to a whisper. 'The boy's medical records – all his scans and an outline of phase two. If she's the intelligence to understand it, and if she's had time to read it, then—'

'She's a bright girl. She'll get there.'

'Who's going to believe her, Cuthbertson? She's known to be a liar and an attention-seeker, what on earth is she likely to say? If she phones the police, she'll end up talking to you.'

'If she's got the medical records, she's got evidence.'

'I realise that—'

'If we postpone again, they'll drop you. You could see how twitchy some of them were – where the hell did you leave the damn thing?'

'I was getting changed—'

'We promised Sir Peter total – *total* – security, that was what we guaranteed. I am so on the line on this one.'

'Shut up, Cuthbertson! You're very rich on this one, as well, and likely to get richer. We won't need to postpone and we *are* secure. I'll sort the girl and I'll find the wretched briefcase. You've got the boy to think about.'

'Listen,' said the inspector. He spoke in an even lower voice. 'If the kids are building a roof, why don't you organise a little accident? If she had a fall—'

'I've thought of that! I am not a fool, and the last thing I need—'

'If she had a fall, we could bring another prosecution. For negligence, and . . . listen – that would tie in with everything you've been documenting. The man's on borrowed time already; a fatal accident would destroy him, and Routon would be out on his ear as well.'

Miss Hazlitt thought hard, gritting her teeth. The line remained silent as the two adults breathed at each other. Then Miss Hazlitt said: 'I've got a better idea. She's a smoker and she sleeps in a shed. I think we wait until lights out. I think she might have a little fire.'

'I warned her about fires . . .'

'She does like lighting them. How awful if the door to the shed was jammed shut. If she just couldn't get out in time.'

'We can still bring the prosecution. It's still criminal negligence, so he's out; you're in. You'll also call the police, which gives me a very nice excuse to be on the premises just when I need to be. What *time* for the boy, is that double-checked?'

'Half-past eight, Routon doesn't change his schedules.'

'Kitchens, yes? He'll be alone?'

'I just told you. I've put his name in the rota – they don't miss their turns, it's a point of honour for them.'

'I don't know their names, what if there's two?'

'Relax, man, there won't be! He's got long hair and he'll be on his own. It takes about thirty minutes and his name's Anjoli – he'll be just where I showed you. One sniff, alright?'

'Alright!'

'That's all he'll need, he's tiny. I need him conscious, you understand that?'

Miss Hazlitt put down the receiver, breathing hard. She stood and walked to the window. There was Millie, tieless in her overalls. She was talking earnestly with the little bald boy, Sam – innocent after all. She could see the precious Anjoli too, up on a roof-truss, wearing only his shorts. His tool belt looked heavier than he did and his hair was fluttering like a flag. The headmaster had a hammer and was bashing away at something; Routon and Worthington were stretching a chalk-line between them, inching up the trusses. Everyone distracted, everyone at work . . . how easy it would be, if the team kept its nerve.

Timing was important – she ought to double-check that. They'd eat at about eight, and she knew it was a pizza night. Anjoli would be clearing up from, what? Eight-forty . . . nine o'clock at the latest? So having worked for eighteen hours they'd be asleep by ten. She had a spare can of petrol in her Landcruiser, and nobody would be surprised if there turned out to be a bottle in the girl's shed. Once the fire was going, it would spill – the place would go like a bomb. The crucial thing was to wedge the door shut and get good burnable rubbish, with an

271

air-flow, underneath – she could do that now. Then if *she* raised the alarm, it would make the headmaster seem even more incompetent. There'd be fire-crews, ambulances, the rush to casualty . . . Little Anjoli might not even be missed. Allowing for new scans, and recalculations, she would need six hours in the chair. The injections took twenty minutes each, but you had to leave time for the skull to cool. She could have him back in his bed by seven in the morning, if there were no complications.

The first boy, reconfigured. A loathsome child, reborn.

There he was, saluting again! Millie's little helper. She was longing to see that smile removed from his face.

How steady were her hands? She stretched out her fingers and noted they were absolutely still.

Chapter Thirty-five

Sam had not welcomed his mission. He had wanted to join the carpentry team which, after lunch, had fanned out over the roof like an army. The hammering was like machine-gun fire. Sam longed to be involved, but with a bandaged leg, concussion, and double-vision, his balance was less than perfect. He had been forced to agree with Millie that so far, he had done very little to make a name for himself at Ribblestrop Towers. Two goals in the football game, but his team had lost. He'd lent his tooth-brush, but he couldn't claim any glory for that as he hadn't known it was being borrowed. Ruskin had acted as watchman while Sam slept, and seemed to be staying mute under interrogation. Sam's life at the school so far had really been one long list of injuries sustained. Surely, said Millie, it was time he took the initiative and did something brave.

'I'll try,' he said. 'But I bet I don't get through the door – she won't even talk to me!'

'You take her some rum. You smile.'

'I haven't got a bottle of rum!'

'Oh, Sam, don't be wet! You know where we get them.'

'I know where we get them, but it's stealing, Millie. I want to do my bit, but I've been in enough trouble over that toothbrush, which you said you'd give back . . .'

'You are *borrowing* a bottle, not stealing. It's for a very important reason. Now straighten your tie . . .'

'I need a cap.'

'You don't need a cap. You look geeky enough if you tuck your shirt in; come here . . .'

Millie spat on a piece of rag and wiped Sam's face. A tuft of hair was growing back, so she flattened it over his scalp. She buttoned up his blazer and Sam stood up straight, hands behind his back.

'Are you scared?' said Millie.

'Yes.'

'You can do it, Sam. Think of this as a mission. We want to know everything you can find out about the basement.'

'I'll do my best.'

Captain Routon's rum-store was under the flight of stairs that led to the headmaster's office. Sam pushed a bottle into his pocket and moved quickly down the corridor to the south tower. One hundred and fifty-two steps later, he was putting on his nicest smile, and knocking.

'What do you want?' snarled Caspar, yanking the door open.

'Hello, Caspar. I was hoping to see your granny. Is it a bad time?'

'She's been hoping never to see any of you lot ever again, especially you. She's watching you lot work, hoping someone's going to break their neck. What do you want to see her about?'

'Actually, Caspar,' said Sam, 'I wanted to see you as well, because none of us see as much of you as we'd like any more, and we wondered if everything was OK.' Sam realised he was improvising. He felt a little spurt of confidence. 'Yes, I was hoping to see you both, and I bought a present for your gran to say sorry for all the noise and disturbance. A few of us clubbed together and bought *this*. Can I come in and give it to her in person?'

'Caspar! Who's at the door, there's a freezing cold draught!'

'It's a boy, Granny. He's brought you some booze.'

Sam hadn't seen Lady Vyner for some time and her spectral form appearing in the hallway made him nearly drop the bottle. Her nightgown was a soft green with little pink roses sewn around the collar. Her cardigan was blue. The gentle colours made her blotched face all the more horrible.

'Who sent you?' she said, bending down and pushing her nose through the crack in the door. The cigarette smoke nearly made him cough.

'Nobody sent me, but a group of us ... some of the orphans ... we thought you might be a bit fed up with the banging, so we—'

'*Fed up with the banging?* What are you talking about? Fed up with all of you, that's what I am!'

'My name's Sam. You saw me play football.'

'A bottle of booze. Poisoned, is it? Filled it with something foul, I bet – oh no, I stand corrected. The top appears to be sealed.' Skinny hands reached out and took it from him. Sam could think only of a praying mantis from an old biology book. 'Football, eh? Oh ... you're the little *goal-scorer*! I won a bet because of you.'

'Shall I push him down the stairs, Granny?'

'Leave him alone, Caspar –'

'I could try out the crossbow! You wait, Sam – you won't believe what I've got! Can I show him, Gran?'

'Darling, let him be. You can practise on the foreigners.'

Sam saw that he had the advantage. 'Actually,' he said, 'I do need to talk to you, Lady Vyner, I really do need to talk to you.'

'Talk about what?'

'The house and the war.'

Lady Vyner stopped and sniffed. 'We're doing a project,' continued Sam, 'and some of the boys said that the prime minister used to stay here. Sanchez says he was a friend of your husband,

275

but then Millie had a bet that it couldn't be true, because . . . well, you know the way people make up stories.'

The door opened wider. 'Is it true?' said Sam. He found inspiration: 'The headmaster said it was a lie.'

'He said *what*?'

'He said it was very unlikely. He said there's no proof Churchill was ever here. And he says that now all the tunnels have been closed, there's no way anyone—'

'*Stop right where you are,*' cried Lady Vyner. 'Stop, before you say something you'll regret for ever!' Her face was a rictus of fury, but she managed to bring her voice under control.

'What does that man know? Eh? What does he, or you, or anyone else in this *hell-hole* that used to be my home *know* about my husband and Winston Churchill? I bet you don't know who Winston Churchill was, nobody teaches history any more!'

'Well,' said Sam. 'I know—'

'He won the war! He was the best prime minister this country ever had, that's who he was! And he was loyal! He wouldn't have . . . *betrayed* Cyril, not Winston. I tell you something, child – I danced with Winston Churchill. I *ate* with Winston Churchill – and that second-rate clown of a headmaster wouldn't be fit to light his cigars! Get inside, you're cluttering up my stairs! Churchill, I'll have you know, begged my daughter to marry his nephew's friend . . . Wipe your feet, boy – these rugs are worth a fortune!' The woman laughed like a power tool. 'Oh, this is rich! Your headmaster pretends he knows about this house – Crippen! Get me a glass! I tell you, the Vyner family had the pick of them all. I could tell you stories. Caspar? Get me a glass, or find Crippen!'

'I don't know where he is,' said Caspar.

'Then get me a glass! Get some ice and some juice, grate a little nutmeg if you can find one and see if there's any crisps, those cheesy ones. What's your name? Sam . . .'

Sam found there was a claw on his shoulder. He was being

276

pushed down a corridor, into a fog of old smells. He had not realised that people could live in carnival ghost-trains, and here he was, entering one with the controller. No wonder Caspar was strange. 'I'd love to know about the house,' he said in a small voice. He was trying to take shallow breaths. The house stank.

Nobody cleaned this part of it, that was for sure. The elderly servant was snoring, slumped in a dark, undertaker's suit that was messy with drool. The wallpaper – where you could see it behind the mass of pictures and mirrors – had a damp, yellow tinge. Hallway and lounge were cluttered with the sort of furniture that was so dark and heavy it probably wouldn't burn. There were rusty-framed photographs, statues and statuettes, ridiculous pots and vases of dead or dry flowers. Part of the ceiling had collapsed under the weight of a chandelier, and Sam wondered what creatures lived up in the velvet dark above: bats, surely, and whole plaguefuls of rats. All down one wall was a rusty stain that meant either the rain was getting in, or some captive in the attic had no toilet.

'Some of the boys,' he said, 'say there are secret tunnels and that people still work down there doing secret things, but nobody . . .'

He couldn't concentrate on his mission, the apartment was so cluttered. There was a statue standing against the wall, holding a tray. It made him think of George, the model, but this one looked sad and had a cracked head. You could see gears and metal struts, and one of the hands was missing so the tray was lopsided.

'You need a bit of background, don't you?' said Lady Vyner. 'Right: this house was the wartime base for Military Science – do you know what that is? Course you don't. It's part of the war office, and ran nearly two hundred scientists who were trying to come up with new ways of annihilating the Germans. Why was Military Science based here?'

'Well,' said Sam, 'I would imagine—'

'I'm *telling* you, child, I'm not asking you! Listen if you want to learn something – and sit down. Military Science needed *rural security*. This house had a whole labyrinth of tunnels and bunkers – all excavated in the eighteenth century for smuggling purposes – that is why it was declared the perfect base. Are you with me so far? That was Mr Churchill's first visit, you see: to check for security. And he liked it, child. He liked it so much he had his own office built, just under my husband's lab: the Churchill Room it's known as. And it was he who had the underground train installed, so he could shoot back to Downing Street when he wanted to. So don't tell me he never came here!'

'Yes,' said Sam. 'No.'

'Caspar!'

'I'm doing it, Gran!'

'Just a glass,' whispered the old woman. 'It can't take even him this long. *Look in the kitchen! Forget the blasted* . . . What's your name?'

'Sam.'

She fished an empty bottle from a bloated, drowned-looking sofa, and lowered herself onto the cushions. Then she turned her attention to Sam's rum. 'I don't drink in the daytime,' she said. 'Not normally. But when I get a bit of good news, I allow myself a snifter.' She was panting with the effort of breaking the seals. 'Ha! Rent increases, that's my bit of good news . . . this new woman, this deputy, she's keen to sign a new lease. Seems pretty sure Norcross-Whateverhisnameis has had his day. Stop looking at the toys, boy!'

'What?'

'You're looking at the robots, you're not listening to a word I'm saying.'

'Oh, I am! I was!'

'*Churchill's little army*, we called them. We had a dozen at one point, and that's another link you won't find in the history books.'

'I think there's one by our notice board,' said Sam.

'My husband knew more about automata than anyone in the world.'

'Auto . . .? I don't know what that is.'

'Mechanics, child – that's what you're looking at. An automaton: a machine that contains its own power source. The prototypes were clockwork – the ones up here are pretty simple. But down in the basement, that's where the real work went on. They were loading in computer systems. Cameras, voice-boxes. Jarman loved it! You see, the War Office had *imagination* then, because it had a war to win. Winston and my husband used to sit for hours, drunk as lords, plotting and planning. This little fellow still does a few tricks . . .'

As she spoke, her old hands had reached to the neck of a model Sam hadn't even noticed. It was a curious, bent little thing, half hidden by the chair. Lady Vyner drew it close and Sam saw that the poor creature's lips had come off, so it wore an expression of horrified shock. A section of the forehead was missing as well, revealing a spaghetti of wires. It wore evening dress, and its arm was raised, like the other one, balancing a tea-tray. On the tea-tray stood a small china vase.

'064 Gerald,' said Lady Vyner. 'Caspar used him for target practice, but he's a robust little chap – he'll outlive me. He could cross the ballroom with a martini, and serve it un-spilt. Then he'd come back with the ice. We had one could cook an omelette. That little girl there . . .' She pointed to another one that Sam hadn't seen. It was a child, and it was hunched over a piano in the corner. It wore a silk dress so worn that, once again, Sam could see the metal struts of her back and shoulders. 'That's Lucy 027. She could play a Mozart piano concerto, note perfect. Can you imagine the engineering behind that, Sam? – the memory?'

'No . . .'

She pressed a switch on Gerald's neck and the toy straightened up. 'Can I help you, sir?' it said. 'Can I help you, sir?' The voice was refined and respectful and the words came crackling from the lipless hole that was his mouth.

Lady Vyner winced; she took a slug of rum direct from the bottle. 'My husband's voice,' she said, quietly.

The tape was clearly a loop; it paused, and came again. Then: 'Thank you, sir. Thank you.'

Sam watched as it started to move. Its hips rotated. It glanced up at Sam and then at the ceiling, and it veered off to the left, as if it was searching for the door. It moved on hidden wheels and seemed to know the steps of its own dance. It twirled; it checked itself and stepped forward again, the voice repeating: 'Can I help you, sir? Thank you, sir!'

Caspar appeared with a glass and pushed the little butler out of his way. 'Can I show Sam my crossbow?' he said.

Lady Vyner looked at him with dislike. 'Go and have your bath,' she said. 'You can show him afterwards.'

Sam was still riveted by the robot, which had stopped moving, its nose to the wall. 'I wish Ruskin was here!' he whispered. 'He loves this kind of thing! Did your husband make them?'

'He did the engineering, yes. Jarman did the heads and the eyes. They'd worked together since university, you see. Churchill's little army.'

'But if they were toys, how—'

'They were *prototypes*, Sam! Don't be so literal. We called them toys, but they were experiments in robot-science, they weren't toys at all. They were going to be used in weapons manufacture, then mine-clearance. It was the time of mad, wonderful ideas. An assassination squad, I remember. Stick one in a Hitler Youth uniform and send it into the bunker.'

'But if—'

'Hush.' Lady Vyner poured a good three fingers of rum into the glass and paused to take a huge sniff of it. 'If you listen, I'll tell you. If you interrupt, you can clear out. Nuclear weapons was to be one application. You'd need robotics to handle plutonium, wouldn't you? That made sense. You'd need robotics to position a device and detonate it – we're talking wartime, still. They were dreaming, Sam – so many plans. And my husband dreamed until the war ended, and he made plans for a little while longer . . . and then what happened? How good is your history? Churchill was out, and suddenly the government lost interest.'

'What happened?' said Sam. His eyes were wide.

'Jarman happened. Jarman saw the future.'

'Who was Mr Jarman?' asked Sam.

'He's not in the past tense, child. You need to say, "Who *is* Mr Jarman?" Ha!' Lady Vyner closed her eyes for a moment. 'All dead and buried. Forgotten by one and all – except for me, and him. Crippen remembers. Sometimes.' She seemed to be searching for words. She hunched forward and looked into Sam's eyes. 'I'll tell you if you want, boy, if you're old enough to understand. My friend Mr Jarman saw the future, science-wise, and you know – looking back – I think he saw it before the war even started. He just didn't let on. He stayed close, learning everything he could from Cyril, because Cyril was the engineer. Jarman, you see, was the neurologist – that was his passion. He devised the minds and the eyes. Robotics was in its early days.' Lady Vyner drank again, thinking hard. She smiled. 'What makes us human, Sam? Do you think about that? What's the difference between you and those little robots?'

'Well, I play football, and I—'

'The capacity for thought. You *think*, don't you?'

'Yes.'

'That's the magic – inside your brain. No robot is ever going to be human, and Jarman saw this when Cyril didn't. I can remember it, still: Cyril coming home, blood on his apron. The look on his face. I don't think he believed it himself.'

'I don't understand,' said Sam.

'His hands were bloody. He hadn't even washed. I said, "What are you doing down there? What's he made you do?" because I was in no doubt – Jarman was in control.' She drank again, nose in the glass, and slopped out more rum. 'They'd been working on pigs. Jarman had ordered piglets, and he was wiring in their brains. He kept the creatures alive, wide awake – and he was cutting into the brain. And you know what? – that night my husband howled in his sleep, he woke up weeping. It went on for a week, then on again for a whole, long month. I said "You can't carry on like this". It was killing him, Sam – Cyril wasn't a butcher! They had a monkey down there. Oh! I couldn't listen and he could hardly speak. It was a Friday night, I remember . . . and he came home shaking. And he said to me: "No more".

'What had happened?'

'"I'm closing the lab," he said. I think he'd seen the future too.'

Sam was open-mouthed. He'd drawn his knees up to his chin and had both arms tight round them. He managed to whisper the obvious question: 'What did he see?'

'You want nightmares too, do you, Sam?'

Sam shook his head, but Lady Vyner's eyes were misted over with tears. 'I told the police; they didn't care.' She looked hard at Sam. 'Cyril had an assistant,' she said. She spoke slowly. 'He was a boy, really, and he lived down there. They needed a porter to ferry things in and clean things up. Boys started work at thirteen or fourteen, and he'd worked for Cyril for some time – didn't have a family; he'd been grateful for a job with a bed. Cyril had found him, wandering the streets round Paddington station.'

Sam saw two tears slide down the woman's cheeks.

'Jarman took this boy and gave him a mild sedative – just enough to keep him under. All alone he was, that night – Jarman could go for days without sleep.' She paused. 'He got the boy onto the table and he drilled a hole in the back of his head, just here. Injected something, some chemical they'd been using – I think the Nazis were working on it, too. And it was the break-through moment, for Mr Jarman. He'd realised it, and this was his chance: you can't make robots *human*, Sam. But you can make humans into robots.' She sipped her drink and wiped her eyes hard. 'Ha! The next morning he told Cyril what he'd done, and he made the boy – who was slow, but up on his feet . . . He made him carry some boxes. He could still do it, of course, very effectively. He expected my husband to be excited – to be awe-struck with admiration. Pig-brains, human brains . . . he was changing the world as he'd always planned, you see. He talked and talked, and the boy kept on carrying boxes from one side of the lab to the other, hard at work. He could make an army of them, he said. Men, women, children – all with their brains changed. He'd worked out how to destroy the inconvenient. So you'd have workers who would never stop working. Soldiers who would never stop fighting – keep going, whatever the odds. Children who would be only obedient – who'd do anything you programmed them to do.'

Lady Vyner took a mouthful of rum. Sam saw that she was struggling not to sob. 'Cyril said it was the most disgusting thing he had ever heard of. He said he'd report Jarman, and he wrote the letter. He showed it to me. He rang the police. He rang who-ever was in charge, in the war office – I heard him on the phone. He went down that night – Saturday night – to throw Jarman out, once and for all. He was going to seal the lab.' She paused and swallowed. The words wouldn't come. 'And Jarman was waiting for him,' she whispered. 'Jarman shot my husband dead. Crippen saw it all.'

'Crippen?'

'My manservant. The gentleman behind you.' Lady Vyner realised Sam was slow. 'He was the boy, Sam. Crippen was the young lad who had his brain drilled, I can show you the scar.'

Sam turned and saw that the manservant – perhaps he'd

heard his name – was standing to attention, with a tray under his arm. He was licking his lips thoughtfully, as if he had something important to say. There was a line of drool down his chin and he had his eyes closed.

Lady Vyner, meanwhile, had started to sob in earnest. It was the sound of a nail being scraped across tin in a slow zig-zag. 'Do you know why I let Caspar play with weapons? It's because one of these days we're going to *find* Mr Jarman and Caspar's going to kill him for me. He's still down there. Still working . . .'

'But the tunnels are sealed. The headmaster said they were all locked—'

'Why does he tell you lies?' she cried. 'Sam, how do you seal tunnels that are still in use? The train still runs, you fool! Jarman gets his supplies. The lease was for ninety-nine years, I can't get him out! He has police protection. I used to have a map but that disappeared. Neptune's an exit. The chapel goes down, and there's a lift in one of the towers. Oh, and the telephone box, of course. Ever tried to dial from there? Don't, Sam – stay away from the phone box! Dial 1939 and ask for Mr Winston . . .'

'I think I ought to go now,' said Sam. He had managed to uncurl and was standing.

Crippen was still trying to remember whatever it was he wanted to say; Sam stared about him, wildly.

'Don't go, Sam. Caspar needs a friend, stay the night.'

'That's very kind, but—'

'I've scared you, haven't I?'

'No!'

'I don't know how to talk to children . . .' She reached for Sam's wrist and he backed away.

'Your glass, ma'am,' said Crippen, in a deep, slow, aching voice.

'I have to go,' said Sam. 'Millie's waiting!'

As he spoke, there came the most terrible scream from the bathroom.

Chapter Thirty-six

Millie had never been able to resist temptation and, as we have discovered, she had no real conception of consequences. She would reflect later on whether things would have turned out for better or for worse if she'd resisted this one.

The children had been working in freezing temperatures all afternoon and as the sun went down it was getting even colder. By five o'clock the flashings were on and the slate was nearing completion. It was a production line: fourteen boys, one girl and three adults moved over the roof until dusk; the last tile was pressed into position as the rim of the sun touched the lake.

They had their roof. Lots to be done still – but a watertight roof.

Now, the children perched upon the ridge like birds on a wire: exhausted, but unwilling to descend. The towers around them were turning from yellow to pink, and the weathercock that sat high above had been caught in one, last, honey-coloured sunbeam: it appeared to be made of solid, fairy-tale gold. Eric had a bag of sweets; Ruskin had struggled up with two flasks of hot chocolate. He had been declared sober, so this was his first appearance off the ground, and it was met with a small round of applause. They all sat together passing the cups and the sweets: they were so happy they didn't want to speak.

'I wonder how Sam got on,' said Millie, at last. Darkness was falling.

'I wonder if he got in,' said Sanchez.

'He should have finished by now. We'll meet tonight in the orphans' room, after I've had a chat with him. They want to have a party, Sanchez.'

'I know; Sanjay's cooking.'

'We ought to stop them. You know what their parties are like – if we've got serious business, we'll never get it done.'

'What time do you want to meet?'

Millie thought. 'I'll pretend to be tired and go straight to my shed. If we try and meet by nine-thirty, we can explain what we saw and go down again.'

'All of us? Tonight?'

'Yes. I think the more witnesses the better. And by the way, Ruskin's got a camera.'

'Has it got film?'

'He says it has. We'll go down and we'll do a proper search, checking the freezers and looking in those jars. Once we have evidence, we can do something.'

'Right.'

'And if Tomaz . . .?'

'If he's down there, we'll find him. We've got to.'

'Yes.'

'You agree?'

'Yes.'

'Sanchez. This is the first time ever you have agreed with anything I've said. You're becoming reasonable.'

Sanchez closed his eyes and kept silent. The orphans' chatter died away too and a nightingale started to sing. Lights came on round the school and in the cold of the evening ice started to form on the new slates. It was then that Millie's eyes wandered to the south tower and she saw something strange.

'I'm confused,' she said, after another long silence. 'The head-master doesn't live in the south tower, does he?'

'No. He lives above his study, in the attic.'

'I'm just getting my bearings. That's Professor Worthington's tower, yes? The one with the big metal thing. So that's Lady Vyner's place? South.'

'Yes.'

'Can you see that window – the little one, under the bird's nest? Sanjay! Come here!'

'What about it?'

'I can see little Lord Caspar, in the bath.'

Sanchez followed her gaze and Sanjay skipped across to join them. They peered hard, and, sure enough, through one of the leaded windows, a figure could be seen.

'That's private,' said Sanchez. 'Don't look. He should draw the curtains.'

'I can see his bum,' said Millie.

She stood up carefully and crossed the ridge. Sanjay was gig-gling and helped her slide gently down the hip so she could stand in the sloping gutter. This brought her to the halfway point of the south tower, which shot up far above her head. Her nose came level with the sill of the lowest leaded window. Some of the orphans were standing too, intrigued. Soon, there was a little crowd.

Sanchez followed, slowly and carefully. 'What are you doing, Millie?'

'There is a God,' said Millie. 'Did I ever say there wasn't? From now on I will say my prayers with you, every night. Come here.'

Sanchez was not at all confident in high places, so he gripped Millie's arm when he reached her. He looked through the glass and found that, just as his friend had said, he was right outside the Vyner bathroom. The lights were on; the room was just a little steamy, condensation moist on the window. But you

287

could still see someone standing in a small bathtub, and that person was definitely Lord Caspar.

'Don't say a word,' whispered Millie.

Sanchez was about to. He felt strongly about intruding on anyone's privacy and was about to state his outrage. But he hesitated and found that a grin had grown across his face. He found himself squeezing closer to the wall and window; Ruskin was there too, right at Millie's elbow.

'Steady me,' said Millie.

'What do you mean?'

'I need both hands.'

Like all the children, Millie was wearing a tool-belt. Such things are essential when you need your hands free. You can slip your hammer into it and there's a sizeable pouch for nails and other odds and ends. Millie delved and pulled out an old, but clean, flintlock pistol.

'What are you carrying that around for?' whispered Sanchez. He gripped Millie by the back of her shirt, keeping her upright as she rummaged. Anjoli had crawled in front of her. He put his shoulder against her chest, giggling with anticipation. She snaked her arms around him and steadied the pistol with two hands.

'I've been carrying this since day one. You're the one who leaves his gun at home – I've got more sense.'

'It doesn't work!'

'You don't know everything, Mr Colombia. My friend Anjoli found some flint. I know a little bit about gunpowder. We've been a pretty successful team.'

'Millie, this is dangerous . . .'

'All I'm doing is returning Caspar's property. I've been waiting for the chance all term, but I don't see as much of little Caspar as I'd like.'

'You can see a lot of him now,' said Ruskin.

Millie had found a short roofing nail without a head. It was a little shard of metal about as long as a pin, with a tiny barb at the tip. She loaded, cocked, and raised the pistol so that the muzzle was against the glass. Anjoli saw that the window seals were coming apart and, with delicate fingers, he managed to slide the tiny pane out completely. He was rocking with silent laughter.

'Keep still!' hissed Millie. Lord Caspar was rinsing his hair with a jug and had no idea what a target his buttocks presented. He was a skinny, pale-skinned little boy, and the two orbs of his backside seemed to glow.

Millie aimed carefully and Sanchez steadied her. The boy bent down to refill the jug and his bottom seemed to expand. It was now or never, so she closed one eye and pulled the trigger.

The scream that interrupted Sam was wonderful. There were three distinct parts to it. There was the shriek as the gunpowder exploded. Then there was the gasp as a sizzling pain seared into the buttock: that feeling of acid injected deep into muscle. The gasp turned into a moan and it got louder. But the richest part of the trilogy came when Caspar turned and saw Millie, Sanchez and too many faces to count grinning at him. That produced a high-volume, full-throated shriek, which cannoned the child backwards out of the bath altogether. Caspar sat hard on the bathroom rug, and the dart was pressed deeper still. The scream was cut off into a series of agonised gargles.

Sam leaped to his feet and Lady Vyner struggled onto hers. Unfortunately, she was so drunk that she immediately lost her balance and fell heavily onto the coffee-table, which folded like matchwood under her. Crippen was still stuck in mid-sentence, so offered no help. Lady Vyner grabbed at the standard lamp, hauled herself upright, and cannoned into the piano, knocking Lucy 027 aside and producing a symphony of chaos. Her shot-gun was leaning in the hall. Grabbing it, she made for the bathroom, ricocheting from wall to wall.

Sam ran for it.

In seconds he was down the tower steps, in time to hear Lady Vyner's cries of rage echoing over the school. The other children were leaping and scuttling to their dormitories, and Sam followed them. What was the garbled mess of information he had worth? It had to be worth something. He had never felt so intrepid or important in his life, and a new career was presenting itself, to be pursued alongside professional football. Sam Tack, double-agent. DI Tack, first on the crime-scene: *'Not so fast, let me take a look at that!'* He threw himself into his dormitory and did a cartwheel over Ruskin's bed. Sam Tack, private investigator: he landed flat on his back, panting, and heard the door slam.

Millie leaned over him, her hands on his shoulders. She was grinning with glee. 'What have you got, Sammy boy?' she said.

'Everything,' said Sam. 'And it's terrifying.'

Chapter Thirty-seven

Captain Routon had excelled himself once more with a fabulous array of pizzas. The school song was sung again and again, and the mood under the new roof was triumphant. Anjoli was frantically washing the plates and pans, desperate to finish and join his friends in the east tower, the orphans' dormitory. The kitchen was dark and nobody liked being alone in it. More importantly, though, he knew that Eric – who just a few months before had been a pot-boy in a roadside restaurant – would be cooking more of his unique party-sweets, and the first-day-of-roofing celebration party would be kicking off. Despite Millie and Sanchez's pleas, the party was going ahead, and it was going to be a wild one. The orphans practised their partying skills hard, trying to get several in each week. Usually, it was a birthday party. None of them knew when their real birthdays fell, so every boy was allowed five possibles. There were parties on Fridays to mark the weekends, and parties on all holy days, and every full moon. There were parties to mark feats of courage or cleverness: for example, there had been a three-night party when Anjoli slammed the door on Miss Hazlitt's hand. There were actually parties in the orphans' dormitory most nights.

Tonight, however, was special even by their standards. By

nine o'clock the air was thick with cinnamon and coconut; milk was boiling over a camping stove and a twenty-pound bag of sugar was standing by. The rest of the orphans were soaking wet, but that too was a regular thing, as their showers usually turned into water-fights. This was the east tower and it was semi-derelict; the orphans had spent considerable time making it home. They'd reconstructed the fireplace, so the room could be made deliciously warm. They'd done away with the collapsing ceiling and built shelves in a rising-step formation up into the witch's hat of the turret: these shelves served as beds, and you looked up into a high grotto of hammocks and drying laundry. Tonight, candles stood on every rafter. Candles hung in jars and candles lined the windowsills.

Nobody was going to bed.

They had a wind-up gramophone, so the jazz had started already, and whilst Eric nursed his sugar-and-rum truffles, the bigger boys were preparing for Battleships. Sanjay had invented Battleships, and it was the current favourite game. The rules were simple and everything depended on two large sets of bunk-beds, where the littlest boys slept. You hauled these beds to the centre of the room, so they were parallel; you then attached ropes, made from twisted sheets. These went way up to the rafters and the light fittings. You then got all the rest of the furniture: chairs, desks, lockers, boxes, spare mattresses – in fact, anything you could carry – and you piled it on. When you stepped back you could convince yourself that you had constructed *not* dangerous piles of junk that could collapse at any moment, but a couple of rigged galleons ready to do battle on the high seas. Asilah would take over at this point and decide the teams for the night. Dressed only in pyjama bottoms and black-and-gold bandanas (for piratical authenticity), the two crews would assemble on their craft. When Asilah said 'Go' you simply had to take possession of the other ship, whilst defending your own. This meant jumping, swinging, pushing, wrestling and punching until you had knocked every one of the opposing team to the floor. Aerial assaults were allowed and it was entirely legal to overturn the whole bunk if you had the manpower.

By ten o'clock, it was just getting brutal. Sam, Henry, Sanchez and Ruskin appeared, but nobody heard them. The noise was tremendous and the acrobatics terrifying.

Millie, meanwhile, was stuck in her shed.

Things were getting increasingly complicated and she was sitting on her lawnmower in silent despair. For one thing, she could hear the noise and knew a party had started. More worryingly, she knew she was being watched again and she wasn't sure she'd be able to get out: there had been rummaging round the shed for the last half-hour and the sound of footsteps. Her brain was melting from the information Sam had given her and she was desperate to act. She had no interest in the past and no interest in clockwork toys – she didn't even care about whether or not Lord Vyner had been murdered. She recognised the name 'Jarman' and the stuff about pigs' brains obviously tied in with the creatures in those ancient jars – but she was no nearer knowing how Professor Worthington or the headmaster fitted in, and Sam had forgotten to ask anything about what was going on *now*. The sense of urgency and helplessness was like physical pain: they had to go down again and find evidence! And what about Tomaz – why was she the only one convinced he'd never made it home?

She made her decision and stood up. She stuffed a few clothes under the duvet and put a small pail on the pillow, which she covered with the sheet. She lit her candle and, yes, in candlelight the body looked semi-convincing. She had a torch, she had a knife, she had the map – it was now or never. She pressed gently at the door, intending to crawl silently: the door was jammed.

She pressed again, and felt the resistance. Somebody had

293

wedged the door shut and it wasn't giving an inch. How lucky she always followed the double-exit strategy – a survival mechanism handed down by every villain Millie had ever worked with. Always have a secret exit: never get cornered. The shed window was fixed shut, but Millie had loosened the glass in her first week, knowing there'd be a point someone would try to contain her. She removed it now and rolled out over the sill. Then, cat-like, she made for the east tower.

When she opened the orphans' door the noise was like a physical force. The room was hot as a sauna and Israel was swinging like Tarzan, a rope round his ankles, trying to swat children off a bunk-bed with a pillow. She clutched her brows in despair and shouted. She jumped and grabbed, but she couldn't make herself heard – even Sanchez, Henry, Sam and Ruskin were all intent on the game. At one point she was picked up bodily by someone she never even saw and hurled to the ground. She managed to stagger to the side, where a warm ball of rum-soaked sugar was pressed into her hands. She shouted louder, but there was no point. If the party continued like this, surely Miss Hazlitt would come barging in – but what could a mob like this do anyway?

'Listen!' she screamed for the tenth time. She searched for Sanchez, but he was hanging from the top of a wardrobe by his fingertips as Podma clung to his knees and pulled. Sam was on Henry's shoulders involved in a tug-of-war with a bedsheet, and Ruskin was on hands and knees hunting for his glasses. In despair she marched up to Sanjay, snatched an empty bottle from his hands, and hurled it against the far wall.

'We need to talk,' she said in the sudden silence.

'Why?' said Israel.

'We've got to go down. All of us.'

Everyone stared. Everyone was panting. One by one, the

children dropped from their perches and came closer. Millie was surrounded.

'Sanchez, have you told them what we saw?'

'No,' said Sanchez. He looked a little ashamed of himself, though he was smiling. One of his shirt-sleeves had been ripped clean from his arm and was in Eric's hand.

'Have you told them what Sam found out?'

'Not yet. I was waiting—'

'Can we finish the game?' said Ruskin. 'You could be on our side, as they've got Henry.'

'No,' said Millie. 'We've got a job to do, and you're behaving like a crowd of kids! Where's Anjoli?'

'Look!' said someone.

'Ah!' said one of the smaller orphans. Everyone turned and saw that a little orphan had opened a window and was trying to catch sparks that were dancing past in little flurries. He was transfixed.

'Last term,' said Millie, 'there was a boy called Tomaz . . .'

But the orphans were moving to the windows, where the sparks were now rolling in little billows of smoke. The boys were talking in their own language and suddenly they moved back as one, as a sheet of redness lit the glass.

'What is that?' said Ruskin. 'It looks like fire.'

The word had been said – that dangerous word. It was whispered again now and it caught and crackled between them all. 'Fire . . .' they said. 'It's fire!'

'It can't be,' said Sanchez. He elbowed his way to the front and pressed his face against the windowpane. 'I don't believe it,' he said. 'It's the roof!'

Just at that moment, as Henry let out a great sob of horror, a column of light shot upwards and nobody was in doubt. As if to confirm the nightmare, a bell began to clang wildly. There were distant cries and a woman's voice started to scream. It was unmistakable then, because the voice was thin and desperate, sailing over the rooftops – she was crying for help and the bell became frantic and constant. Like a flock of birds, they moved together. Some managed to grab shoes and blazers, others just ran barefoot. They piled out of the door and were leaping the stairs, three, four at a time.

Sam said, 'It can't be, can it?' but there was no one to answer him. Asilah was in the lead, but when he cannoned out into the corridor and raced to the doors, he found them locked. Children were piling down the stairs still as those at the bottom tried to fight their way back up. The door had never been locked before.

Somehow the tide turned and Sanchez led everyone back to the left, then a right. It was the back way and they were wasting precious time. They now had to go through the herb garden and round the front of the building.

The main doors were locked as well and the glow was fiercer. They could hear a roaring, and everyone knew that awful, furnace sound. They saw a tower of flame licking upwards and they ran even faster. The bell was louder too – the type you ring by hand – and Miss Hazlitt's voice was screeching over and over again, 'Help! Help us here!'

Israel shouted, 'Follow me, I know another way!'

He led the way to where the school van was parked and the children flooded through a narrow arch into the courtyard. Millie had lost her bearings for a moment and she couldn't see at first. She couldn't understand, because looking up, the new roof seemed to be intact and safe. The fire was coming from somewhere else – her little yard, separate from the kitchen and the hall. Another plume of sparks rose over the dividing wall and something detonated like a bomb, the air around them suddenly charged with the stink of petrol. Somebody was screaming and there were adult voices yelling orders. But most terrifying of all was the unending, rising roar of the flames as they devoured Millie's little wooden shed.

'She's in there, she's in there!' yelled a voice.

Henry was cowering backwards from the heat; Professor Worthington was there, so was the headmaster. Sanchez tried to force everyone back, but Millie fought her way to the front, ducking under his arm. She knew, somewhere she had known, and she'd been a fool not to anticipate this. Her shed was the furnace.

Someone's arms enclosed her and dragged her back. The wooden walls were simply sheets of flame and something else exploded inside. She could feel her eyebrows singeing, and there was a clamour of voices shouting about water and a hosepipe, and the fire bell kept on ringing like madness.

Then, above the whole cacophony was Captain Routon's voice. He'd just arrived on the scene; he was in his pyjamas and he was roaring like a madman, 'Millie! Millie!' He was pounding on the burning door, standing in the flames. He crashed at it with his shoulder, dragged it backwards, but the door wouldn't give. He was beaten back by the heat; he turned away smouldering. His jacket was blackening.

The shed roof was ablaze now; a hosepipe began playing a stream of water, uselessly, over the inferno. Then Captain Routon, with no heed to his own safety, sprang at the flames and began to hack the timbers away with his bare hands. The door was down. He found something, some burning timber or tool and started to swing it wildly. Bits of flaming wood and cloth flew left and right as he struck. Then he moved into the fireball – at least he had boots on – and the walls disintegrated about him.

Millie couldn't speak. She saw inside. She saw her own bed and it was rolling in fire. The flames were over it like a fluid and there was an awful sighing as the mattress was consumed. She could see bedsprings and the whole black chassis with a burning pail turning to liquid. Captain Routon was on fire too. He'd dropped his weapon and was searching madly, moving like a drunk man. He kicked the bed over, he turned in the blaze, searching and searching. The headmaster appeared beside him. He'd grabbed the hose and was trying to drench the captain. And then, suddenly, as if someone had pulled a lever, because the shed was so small the flames began to die. The inferno divided itself into a few ragged curtains and fell to the floor. The flames were extinguished in the gravel.

Captain Routon dropped to his knees, panting and moaning.

Then Professor Worthington was shouting, 'She's there, Routon! She's there!' and every head was swinging round. A gap formed around her and Millie stood with her mouth open. It was dawning on her what the captain had been doing. He could barely lift his head and he certainly couldn't stand. His face and head were a mass of dirt and stubble, and Millie realised the new smell, the barbecue smell, was cooked human flesh. He was lifting his hands, and they were cumbersome as claws: they'd been roasted. His dry lips were moving and over and over again he was blubbering, 'Oh Lord, thank you . . . Oh my sweet, sweet . . . thank you . . .' but the words were indistinct because his tongue wouldn't work and he was weeping.

Millie was embraced by Professor Worthington. She had never been held so tight.

'I'll get my car,' said the headmaster. 'He needs a hospital.'

'How did it start?' said Millie.

Routon was mumbling and moaning, and it was Sanchez who got under his arm and tried to lift. That was when the big man howled in pain.

Millie was feeling very sick and very cold. She was trembling all over: shock was kicking in as the adrenaline reduced. She had survived; she was alive; she should be dead. She should have been burned to a crisp inside that shed, stretched out on the metal of that bed . . . She saw herself for a split second, naked on the springs. Charcoal-black, teeth bright white between charred lips. She had survived.

And there was a new terror as well, which fought against any relief. *Sheds don't catch fire. Fires are started. If fires are started, somebody started this one. That means somebody wants me dead* . . . As the thought solidified, as the lump of certainty formed, there was a sharp whistling sound and the crack of a whip. Something flew past in the night air, close to her face.

She looked to her left. One or two of the orphans had heard the noise, but there was still too much going on. Captain Routon was being helped back towards the kitchen by Sanchez, Asilah and Sanjay. The noise came again, and this time Millie felt a rush of air pass her ear. There was a buzzing mosquito noise and a sharp snap. Sanjay had heard it too and now he pointed to the ground some three metres behind.

An arrow was sticking out of the earth: only a few centimetres of the shaft were visible. Sanjay looked up, followed the trajectory, and pointed at the south tower. The top window was in clear view, and there was a figure leaning out, something huge in his arms.

'Caspar,' said Sanjay.

Millie was to think later how slow reflexes could be. She was standing still, looking at Caspar and Caspar's new crossbow. She was a stationary target, offering herself; the child was leaning out as far as he could, lining up his third, lethal shot. It was only when that third arrow smacked into a nearby door, millimetres from her head, that Millie really understood.

She threw herself to the side and never found out if a fourth shot came. She rolled and was on her feet again, cowering to the wall. There was another door and she backed through it into the corridor. To one side was the wide staircase to the headmaster's study and she felt safer under cover.

Miss Hazlitt was standing there, with a bell in her hand. She wore an expression of both rage and astonishment; it left her mouth twisted half open. 'Stay where you are!' she said.

Then, from off to the right, another voice – one word she didn't understand at first.

'Assassin!'

The voice was behind and above her; it came from the stairs. People wanted her dead; they were trying to kill her. Two attempts, and now?

'Assassin!' screamed the voice again.

Something mechanical ratcheted hard and fast, and even Millie recognised the sound of a shotgun.

'You shot him in the bath!' yelled the voice, and Millie turned, stepping wildly. She was off balance; she swung drunkenly into a large clock she'd never noticed before – where could she run? It was Lady Vyner, pale as a ghost, moving down the stairs towards her. She had a shotgun in her hands, and was raising it. 'I know what you are!' she was shouting. 'I know what you did!'

Millie threw herself at the door of the school. Locked, of course. She huddled against it, tearing at the bolts. She was crying and panting now, the hysteria taking hold.

'Millie, wait!'

Sanchez had appeared and was calling her. He hadn't seen Lady Vyner. The door wouldn't budge. She could hear Israel and perhaps somebody else, their feet on the stairs. The bolts of the door were so stiff Millie's hands were bleeding. She smashed at the metal, waiting to die.

Miss Hazlitt's voice cut through the mayhem: 'Millie Roads! Stay where you are!'

Then there was an explosion so loud it seemed to turn the world over and a rain of plaster was falling on her head.

The last bolt slid to the side; the door opened and Millie fell out of it. Someone fell on top of her – it was Sanchez, but she disentangled herself and tried to run. The boy had her by the arm and was pulling her back. He got his arms round her.

'Wait, Millie – wait!'

Millie swore and kicked. She got a knee up and felt Sanchez double up in pain, but he would not let go. She glimpsed his face, pleading, panic-stricken now but still hanging on in an

300

effort to restrain her. She punched as hard as she could and she was free. She ran faster than she'd ever run, losing both shoes, slipping in the gravel and tearing her elbows and knees. Then she was on her feet again, sprinting over the grass.

There was a second gunshot behind her and she managed to run even faster, clearing the lawn then blundering on. Her chest was heaving; she aimed for the lake, with no plan in her head any more. All she wanted was to get away from fire, from crossbows, from shotguns and from people . . .

Chapter Thirty-eight

'You're in charge, Sanchez,' said the headmaster. 'You're senior boy; I'm counting on you one hundred per cent. We're going to the hospital, I want you—'

'I've got Routon,' said Professor Worthington. 'Let's go.'

'Millie's gone,' said Sanchez. 'Anjoli, too – he was washing up, and Israel says he hasn't been seen—'

'Find Miss Hazlitt, she was here a second ago.'

'The car's right here, Headmaster. Hurry, every second is crucial.'

'What about Millie, sir? Please! She's out there—'

'Phone the police and find Miss Hazlitt. If you can't find her, use the phone in my office.'

Captain Routon was groaning. Asilah and Sanjay had found towels in the kitchen and were wrapping them, wet and sodden, round the man's blistered hands. But the blisters seemed to go up his arms and on to his shoulder. He was grinding his teeth and shaking his head. They'd sat him down, but he had to stand up again and Professor Worthington could barely support him.

'Tell the police we've got serious problems here, we need a search party out looking for Millie. Was Anjoli with her?'

'Nobody knows, but probably. We can start looking, sir . . .'

'Absolutely not: I don't want any more children out in the grounds. That's an order.'

'Yes, sir.'

'Asilah, help us with Routon. Everyone else, back to your dormitories.'

Routon was loaded into the passenger seat and the crowd watched as the headmaster's little car bounced off up the drive, Professor Worthington in the back. Sanchez wiped the blood from his face and let his eyes scan the lawns, the lake, and the woods beyond. Millie was out there somewhere. Had Anjoli followed her? They were often together. They might make for the Greek temple, that would give them shelter. He had seen the terror in her eyes. She'd make for the deepest, darkest part of the wood. Or maybe she'd had enough now and was fleeing Ribblestrop completely. Perhaps she was running along the open road right now, hitch-hiking as she'd threatened – if Anjoli was with her, maybe he'd persuade her to come back.

He turned quickly. His nosebleed was bad, but he couldn't stop for it. They were wasting time when they should be out looking. He would have to disobey orders, but then he knew things the headmaster didn't. First job, phone the police. Then search parties, there was no question in his mind. He and Asilah led fourteen boys up to the headmaster's office, hoping it would be empty. It was time to phone his father, evidence or not, and ask for help; he should have done it already. The door was closed and he threw it open without knocking.

Miss Hazlitt leaped to her feet, a cellphone pressed to her ear.

'Captain Routon's hurt,' said Sanchez. 'Millie and Anjoli, we think—'

'Quiet!' she cried. She held the children back with a raised forefinger. They'd interrupted her; Sanchez saw her dentures shift as she fought to regain her composure. Her voice was trembling, and she spoke quietly. There was make-up on the desk, a mirror. 'No,' she said. 'We're going ahead.'

'Miss,' said Sam. 'We need the police! We need the telephone!'

'I have to go . . .'

The children pressed in through the doorway, filling the room.

'I'll call you back,' she shouted, over the noise. Then she turned on the boys, a mixture of anger and panic in her eyes. 'How *dare* you!' she cried. 'That is the height of rudeness! Get away from this desk, get back!'

'We need the police, miss!' cried Sanchez. 'Millie's out in the grounds, she's not even got shoes!'

He reached for the instrument, but Miss Hazlitt was faster. She snatched it up and cradled it against her bosom. 'The police are on their way!' she snarled. 'If you'd just stop for a moment, and let me get a word in—'

'We need to find Millie!' said Asilah. 'We need a search party! For Anjoli, too.'

'I called the police ten minutes ago!' screeched Miss Hazlitt. 'That's my job and I don't need to be told how to do it! I am well aware of what is going on in my own school; *I* am in charge here!'

There was silence.

The children looked at her and wondered why her lips were shaking. Her eyeballs were darting from one face to another, and she held the telephone as if it were a precious thing. 'The call has been made,' she hissed, trying to calm down. 'A description has been issued and everything is under control. So I want you to go back to your rooms and go to bed.'

There was a chorus of dismay and outrage. 'We're not going to bed,' said Asilah. 'We'll find our friends first. Two groups, alright? Sanchez takes one to the lake—'

'No!'

'I'll take the other. She ran towards the lake, so we're going to—'

Miss Hazlitt's voice rose above Asilah's, deep and dangerous.

'No you're not!' she cried. She was backing away, because the children were pressing forward. 'You need to calm down, we *all* need to calm down! Nothing is achieved –' she was breathing hard again, '– by hysteria. Look at you, you're treading muck into the carpet! You're half dressed and it's way past lights-out.' Sanchez tried to speak, but Miss Hazlitt went on, unstoppable: 'The shed has been destroyed and that is an act of vandalism. She did it at her last school; she's done it again.' She had to raise her voice once more: 'If she chooses to run off into the night—'

'You think *she* lights that fire?' shouted Israel. 'She was in our room!'

'Well she shouldn't have been, that's against the rules as well! That girl has had countless warnings, I am issuing an order for her immediate expulsion – you as well, Ruskin, for being drunk and disorderly.'

'She wasn't even there,' said Sam. 'Someone was trying to kill her!'

Miss Hazlitt gaped like a fish. 'If you want to speak to me, Sam, you put your hand up – or you're the next one out!'

'Oh for goodness' sake!' said Sanchez, reaching for the telephone. 'I need to call my father and you've got no right to stop me.'

And it was at this point that Miss Hazlitt did a curious thing. She simply took hold of the telephone cord and wrenched it from the terminal block. It took three strong tugs and there was the wire in her hand, torn and ruined. 'You need to know something,' she hissed. She was in the corner now. 'All of you need to know. *I* am in charge now; *I* have taken responsibility and you will do as you're told. The police are on their way and they will deal with the situation. I am locking all the doors . . .' The children were pressing forwards again. 'I'm going to count to three and I want this room clear! One!' she cried.

Her eyes were darting left and right again, unable to focus. She dropped the phone and turned, hunting for something.

Ruskin, however, had beaten her to it. She yelled and plunged towards him, but the boy was too fast. The ring of keys was there on the desk and he snatched it up before throwing it to Israel, who passed them to Asilah.

'Give them to me!' she screamed. 'I'll count to three!' She lunged again, but stumbled and sprawled – then she found herself rising upwards. Her feet were kicking, but the floor dropped away. The children simply lifted her, the way ants lift a leaf; it was as if they'd been practising. She writhed and screamed but there was absolutely nothing she could do. Her feet went up, her head went down. She saw the waste-paper basket coming towards her at a very strange angle, and then her face was inside it, and she was doing a kind of collapsing headstand. As she fell, the desk was shunted forwards, trapping her into a ball. The sofa was next, crunching down sideways and cutting off the light. The hat-stand, a filing cabinet, drawers opening and paper falling. A coffee-table, a bookcase – she was imprisoned in a pyramid of furniture as books, boxes and documents rained down upon her. She had no time to cry out, the violence was so fast.

Then, as suddenly as it had started, it was all over.

She heard the door close and there was a ratcheting sound. Sam had his toothbrush in his pocket; it was a simple matter to use the key-end to lock the door.

Miss Hazlitt sat on the floor, trembling in both shock and fury. Her teeth were out and her wig was on the carpet. She waited until the last footfall had died away and got to her knees, feeling over her scalp for cuts or scratches. Her left hand had been crushed against the desk, but nothing was broken. She flexed each finger and closed her eyes.

The cellphone bleeped. 'Cuthbertson,' she said. She could barely speak. 'Where are you?'

'Coming up the drive, where should I be?'

'You've got Anjoli?'

'Yes, he's in the chair. Did you find your briefcase?'

'No, I didn't find my briefcase. Just a minute.'

Miss Hazlitt managed to crawl. She found a way under the desk and staggered onto her feet. 'The girl's still alive. I searched everywhere, but she's hidden it – listen. Listen to me! She wasn't in her bed and now we've got the whole pack of them out in the grounds looking for her! They've stolen my keys. Turn your headlights off.'

'Why?'

'Turn your lights off and go right. Get off the drive and head for the lake. You'll get her if you're quick; the children said she was making for the lake. She'll go towards the Neptune statue, or she'll double back to the phone box. Either way—'

'She's by herself?'

'At the moment, yes. That's what I'm saying, you can get her! But the children will be following. She had a head-start of five minutes.'

The policeman thought hard. He'd already swung his car onto the grass, lights off. He drove as fast as he dared and, rounding the copse, he could make out the two humpbacked bridges to the island.

'I can see Neptune,' he said. 'I can't see her. Anyway, what can I do? I can't just—'

'She'll be exhausted,' said Miss Hazlitt. 'Get her in the lake.'

'In the lake?'

'It won't take a lot. Get her in the water and she'll last half a minute. I'll start on the boy.'

The policeman was silent. His thoughts were racing too and he knew Miss Hazlitt could almost hear them.

'She won't last long, Cuthbertson! She's skin and bone.'

'I was trying to save her, was I? And I just couldn't reach.'

'Exactly: it was just too cold. She ran into the lake. You went in after her. It's easy, man – you won't need to hold her under, you just push her out and make sure she stays out. You radio for assistance and it's all over.'

'Has she got a torch?'

'I doubt it.'

'I'll find her. Hang on . . . I've got her. I can see her.'

'Where?'

'She's coming round Neptune . . . Got her.'

'Do it properly, alright? She knows everything. I'm going to the lab, I'll start scanning the boy. Has London arrived?'

'Not yet. I'd better go, she's moving.'

'He's awake, isn't he? You didn't overdo the—'

But the line was dead. Miss Hazlitt clicked off her phone and crawled to the panelling. Would she need her wig or her teeth? She picked them up in case and opened the lift's control panel. It was expertly hidden and a tiny switch turned the mechanism on and off. She clicked it on and heard distant pulleys come to life. In less than three minutes the metal grille was open and she was in the lift-car.

Deep underground, Anjoli heard doors open behind him, but he couldn't move to look around. Leather straps restrained him and his skull was held absolutely still by metal rods. All he could do was blink and breathe. He was aware of vibrations in the floor, coming up through the chair. It was as if a train was approaching, getting louder and louder. He could just open his mouth, but he didn't dare. He was too scared even to whimper.

Chapter Thirty-nine

Millie knew that she would not survive the night without shelter, but she didn't know where to go. She was by the lake, with vague thoughts of hiding under one of the bridges – but her mind was full of fire, arrows and shotguns, and everything swirled in her head until the thoughts became soup. A revenge attack, for the bathroom assault? That was Caspar, of course. But the fire? That was someone who knew she'd been underground.

She winced as another spike of something in the ground tore her foot. She was walking now, damp with perspiration and freezing dew, and there was ice all around her. She wore a thin shirt and shorts, and that was all. She'd die if she didn't find shelter.

She thought of Sanchez. She'd hit him, hard! She'd punched her friend, she'd been out of control. And now she was alone and the cold was so deep, her teeth were chattering. Something cracked, off to her left – a stick or something – and she cried out, turning wildly and crouching. It was silent again.

She had to get to London now, there was no debate. She had to keep moving and find a place to hide, then get to the phone box and the road. If those people from the laboratory came looking for her, she'd be easy prey. But then Sanchez would come looking for her too; he wouldn't forget her, however hard she'd hit him. He'd organise a search party and the orphans would sweep the area, so it was a question of who got to her first and if she could stay alive in this bitter cold.

'Oh!' she moaned aloud, and she could hear her own voice shaking. Her feet were so numb they felt like wooden blocks. She stifled a sob, but another one broke through and she started to shake all over. She was by the water's edge and the first of the bridges was close.

'Millie?' said a voice.

She gasped and swung round. It was too dark. She stepped back and her feet sank into freezing water.

'Where are you, love?' She stepped back wildly, away from the voice, and stumbled. One foot scraped on a rock and she was on her backside in the lake, its dreadful coldness crushing her thighs and spine. She cried out with the shock of it and the voice came louder, 'Millie! Stay where you are!'

She knew the voice, and the terror was like paralysis. She tried to stand, but overbalanced and fell flat. The water seemed to tear the skin from her bones. The shivering came in such a terrible spasm, but she hauled herself upright. She stumbled – and saw the shape of a large man moving towards her. It was a big, black shape coming out of the blackness, emerging from the mist with a policeman's cap and an outstretched arm. He was breathing heavily and walking unsteadily.

'Stay where you are, love,' he said. Reassuring. Kind, even – the voice to talk suicides off high bridges. 'It's alright now, Millie – no need to worry . . .' The mist broke and there he was, striding forwards fast. He had a hangman's step, his arms were out and his hands were huge.

Millie stepped backwards into the lake, up to her knees in water, poised for flight.

'It's me, love! Panic over!'

'No,' she croaked.

310

'What's the matter? You know me – just give me your hand.'

He was so close – his boots were in the water. She couldn't back away any more and there was nowhere to go. A second passed, maybe two, as child and policeman stared into each other's eyes. Then Cuthbertson lunged for her, and it was what she needed to locate that last bit of life. She leaped, and didn't slip. He dived for her again and there was an almighty splash and he tripped into the water. He rose up at once, cursing, and slipped in the mud.

Millie ran, and she was faster than she'd ever been. In fifty metres the rough ground was smooth again and she could run more easily. There was one light ahead, not so very far, and she pelted towards it. Oh, thank God! It was the telephone box. If she could make that, she'd be safe. He wouldn't dare touch her once she'd made a call, he'd know he could not. Her father? But he wouldn't be there. The emergency services? The police were here, but he wasn't the 999 service. Just to log her voice on to the operator's system, that would mean survival: they taped and logged everything, prank calls, accidental calls. Nine. Nine. Nine.

She was slowing down, stumbling. She managed a steady, limping jog, and got to the drive. Running on tarmac was easier, even with wounded feet. There was the phone box, gloriously safe and red. The door so heavy you needed both hands. The black telephone snug in its cradle; that musty smell as if someone slept in it. The number of the box was inked confidently in the centre of the dial and everybody knew the emergency procedure. When you dialled that magic number, everyone came running.

Of course, Millie hadn't heard the slamming of a car door. She didn't hear the car engine either, as a wet Inspector Cuthbertson slipped his vehicle into gear and eased it over the grass behind her.

From his point of view, she was easy meat. She was running in the right direction, so she'd miss her rescue party. If she was making for the drive, he'd pick her up without a problem. He wouldn't use his headlights, because he didn't want any witnesses. He'd get her when she tried to use the phone. Soaked as he was, Inspector Cuthbertson found himself chuckling. The thought of Millie in a disused, broken phone box, dialling for her life . . . It came into view and, sure enough, there she was, just a little black silhouette.

Millie stood with the phone in her hand, unable to believe what she was hearing.

'The number you have dialled has not been recognised. The number you have dialled has not been recognised.'

She put the receiver down and waited three seconds. It was not a difficult number, but she might have misdialled. She put the receiver back to her ear and dialled again.

The same voice. 'The number you have dialled has not been recognised . . .'

She tried to keep calm. There was an operator's number: 100. She dialled that, and waited. She had no coins, so there was no chance of trying anyone else. She heard the clicking of possible connections and then the robot voice again, so frank, so earnest, so apologetic.

'The number you have dialled . . .'

Millie put the receiver down and leaned her forehead on the cold plastic. There was no other number to try.

Inspector Cuthbertson couldn't resist putting his headlights on: he wanted to see the girl's face. A swathe of whitening grass was lit up in front of him, a great swinging triangle that caught trees and the lawn rising to the driveway and then, best of all, the red phone box and the little girl caged inside. She was looking right at him.

He jabbed the accelerator and felt the back wheels skid. But he got the extra speed and was climbing nicely from twenty to twenty-five miles per hour, closing in. He put the lights up to full beam and there she was huddled up in panic, scrabbling at the dial.

He chuckled again. Everyone knew the box was purely decorative and hadn't been serviced for years. Lady Vyner insisted it remain and occasionally there were complaints from frustrated members of the public who tried to use it.

He had a mad idea of ramming the box. He was picking up speed and the child was blinded by his lights. Sheer terror! He'd just pluck her out and drive her back to the water. He could even hear his own voice at the inquest, charged with emotion: 'I did everything I could, sir. I dived three times but it was just too cold.'

He slowed and brought the car to a halt. The poor thing was still holding the phone, waiting for an answer. She was gazing into the lights and her mouth was a little round zero.

As the headlights blinded her, Millie's mind blanked out. Then, from that random mix of stories and numbers Sam had passed on, she remembered Lady Vyner's advice: 1939, the start of the Second World War. One nine three nine. She was shaking so much that she misdialled the first time and got the voice again. But the second time, forcing herself to slow down, she got it right. There was a different kind of buzzing. No voice. The clicks of connection and then, magically, as if a magician had touched the kiosk, a phone was ringing.

Millie's breath was coming out in hoarse gasps. Nobody would answer.

The car was getting closer and it didn't seem to be slowing down. She closed her eyes. She knew she should run, but she had no running left, and the phone just rang and rang, even when she whispered '*Please*' in her sweetest, mud-choked voice. A minute must have passed, because the car had slowed after all and was drawing up alongside her. She was caught. She could see that the inspector was in no great hurry. He opened his door and climbed out, as wet as she was.

'Hello?' said a voice.

'Oh!' sighed Millie. 'You're there!'

The voice said nothing.

The inspector had his hand on the phone box. He couldn't see which side the door was on and he'd gone to the wrong one. He had it now.

'Mr Winston, please,' gasped Millie.

'Who is it?' The voice was young.

'Millie Roads. For Mr Winston, please. Help me.'

Inspector Cuthbertson hauled open the door, just in time to see his prey simply drop away through the floor, down a dark shaft. The telephone was left hanging from its flex and, as he stared, the steel plate slid back into place, so the phone booth was just as it had been. Millie had disappeared.

Chapter Forty

The chute dropped vertically, then smoothed to a long curve. It took Millie slithering downwards on her backside and shoulders. She was rolled right, then left over smooth earth. She kept her elbows in and her eyes closed. After thirty seconds of falling, she landed in a sitting position on soft sand.

There was a rushing noise above her head and something heavy dropped like a stone. It slammed down behind her, brutally heavy, and it barred her retreat. She managed to turn her head and saw that it was a rough kind of portcullis. Someone had lashed together timbers, cruelly spiked so they dug into the sand. Perhaps they'd meant to impale her. She heard the same sound again. Another portcullis, another great mesh of timbers! This one crashed into the sand less than a single step in front of her. The spikes dug deep, and Millie saw she was a prisoner in a cage and that all her running had been for nothing. All that effort to survive, to be caught like a rat in a trap.

She sat and peered through the bars. A little flicker of self-pity rose up and she closed her eyes: did she really deserve to die like this? Yes, she thought. She probably did.

'Are you Millie?' said a voice.

Millie didn't have any words left.

'You are, aren't you?'

She did not recognise the voice of her captor. When she opened her eyes though, she could see him – he'd come close. She'd fallen through time, for it was a caveman kneeling there. Or, more accurately, some kind of caveboy – a caveman's ragged little son. Long hair, tied back from the eyes. A necklace of little stones. He was holding a candle. He was wearing a grey shirt. A hand came through the bars, clean and small, rather delicate in fact. It took hold of her arm and the thumb stroked her. It moved up her shoulder and gently touched her face, where there was a trickle of blood.

'What's your name?' he said.

'Millie Roads.'

'You know my friend,' said the boy. 'You know Sanchez.'

'No.'

'No?'

'I mean, yes. Yes.'

'Ruskin? Henry? All my friends.'

'Who are you?'

The face came nearer and she could see that the hair was tied back by a black-and-gold tie. The eyes were soft and the skin was clean and clear. She was looking at someone no more than twelve or thirteen years old.

'I'm Tomaz,' said the boy.

Millie simply stared.

'I couldn't get home.' The boy laughed softly. 'I found you in the freezer, yes? I showed you the way! Remember? I brought you the food.'

'Tomaz?'

'I saved your life.'

Chapter Forty-one

Professor Worthington and the headmaster were in the hospital waiting room. Routon's wounds were being dressed and they sat there grey with worry. In the background, a radio was playing. It was a local station so, amongst advertisements for Christmas sales and some very mellow seventies music, there were regular news and traffic bulletins. News was breaking of a car crash on the M4 motorway. The pile-up was affecting traffic in both directions and the Intercity line, westbound; it was a delay that was to have a major impact on Ribblestrop Towers.

The problem had been caused by a contraflow system that was in place due to resurfacing between exits sixteen and seventeen. An elderly couple were using this very stretch of road; they had decided to visit the west country, driving overnight to avoid the congestion. They had received a postcard from their young son. Though hard to decipher, it seemed to suggest that he would be representing his school in a football match the following day. Knowing the boy's passion for football, they had decided to support him on the touchline. A bonus had been the recent arrival of his black-and-gold school cap – a cap they had feared lost for ever and a cap they knew he was keen to wear. The railway company had finally located it, so this meant the parents could present it in person.

Sam had confused the dates of the game, of course. The game he was referring to had already happened and, had they got there, Mr and Mrs Tack would have been in for a major disappointment. However, at this point in the journey – 11.20pm – they were crawling along at fifteen miles-per-hour, Mr Tack at the wheel, looking forward to a sporting delight the next day.

Mrs Tack was dozing; Mr Tack didn't want to wake her. He did, however, want to know if he could get out of this slow-moving traffic. Was there, for example, anything to be gained from leaving the motorway at the next junction and cutting down towards Wells? They'd discussed the route at length and that had been an option. He turned the interior light on and groped for his RAC Routefinder in the glove-compartment. As he leaned, he tilted the wheel and his car hit a cone.

His eyes were off the road, but he felt the bump and swerved. He had just one hand on the wheel, of course, so as he tried to right the vehicle, he oversteered and clipped a post-office truck that was slowly overtaking him. Sadly, the post-office truck driver, who'd been driving for years and was highly competent, was at that moment unwrapping a Kit-Kat: he too had one hand on the wheel and he too swerved at the jolt. Seeing the lights of oncoming traffic, he instinctively swerved to the left, which meant he crunched back into Mr and Mrs Tack and sent them onto a whole bank of cones, barriers and bollards. Mrs Tack screamed. Mr Tack braked hard and the car behind slammed into his off-side tail light. Mr Tack lost control totally and ploughed over the hard-shoulder onto grass. The car bounced over a kerb and down a bank. Mr and Mrs Tack came to rest on a railway line.

The post-office truck careered helplessly into the resurfacing works, the driver stamping on the brakes and skidding wildly. Thankfully the resurfacing gang was alert and highly trained.

The men leaped to safety and then moved in to rescue the stranded Tacks. But they couldn't shift the car, the chassis of which was wedged onto the rails.

There were emergency phones nearby and, mercifully, the right messages got through. The Intercity London to Penzance service, that might have run straight into the vehicle on the tracks, was alerted when it was just two and a quarter miles from the incident. This allowed the driver, who was by coincidence the very same driver involved in the terrible incident in the Ribblestrop tunnel, to bring the engine to a controlled halt.

Train services on that line would not resume for two hours.

'What was she thinking of?' said the headmaster, as the bulletin finished. 'She'd been working so hard, all day. What in the world was she thinking of?'

'You really think Millie started the fire?'

'I don't want to, but . . . I'm racking my brains. What other explanation is there?'

'I'm not leaping to any conclusions. Millie Roads has been doing extremely well.'

'I agree! I'd pretty much decided, head-girl next term. If there is a next term.'

'Oh, don't be defeatist, Giles. Routon will be fine and Millie and Anjoli will be found. They're probably sitting in the dorm even now, cocoa—'

'I don't mean all that. It's more serious even than that. Miss Hazlitt won't recommend our licence unless I resign. She told me today and she showed me her report.'

Professor Worthington turned and stared at him. 'That's outrageous! There's no question of you resigning, it's your school! It's your dream!'

'Well, my contract paints a rather different picture. Apparently I signed something to give her rather more power than I meant to. I didn't really read the smallprint, there were so many pages.'

'She's a menace. I cannot see that she's made any improvements at all.'

'She wants Routon out as well. Says he's a liability.'

Professor Worthington gasped. 'That man is a hero! Did you see the way he leaped into Millie's shed? Not a thought for his own safety! I'm going to confront her in person, soon as we get back. Wretched woman . . .'

The two adults sat in silence. The headmaster noticed that at some point, they'd linked hands. They sat there now on the plastic seats, staring at the malaria posters. The radio played on.

'Clarissa,' said the headmaster, at last. 'Why don't you go back?'

'And leave you here?'

'It's silly us both being here, isn't it? We've got two children unaccounted for – I'm uneasy. Miss Hazlitt is the only adult in charge and, well – call me uncharitable, but I'm not always sure she has the children's best interests at heart.' He swallowed. 'Yes. I'd really feel much better if you were at school. I can have a snooze here whilst I'm waiting for the captain and I can ring you when I've got some news.'

'Are you sure, Giles?'

'Yes. The more I think about it, the more I think one of us should be back at Ribblestrop.'

As soon as he said it, Professor Worthington felt a need to move quickly.

She crossed the hospital car park at speed and felt anxious when the first taxi that she hailed swept past her. She had a feeling deep down inside that she was needed at school and she felt like running; she couldn't stand still. She moved briskly down the icy pavements, her head revolving as she searched for another cab. She saw one on the other side of the road, moving away from her, so she shouted loudly. She told the driver she'd double the fare if he made it to Ribblestrop in thirty minutes.

The roads were treacherous, but the driver put his foot down.

Country lanes skimmed by and Professor Worthington gripped the headrest in front until her knuckles were white.

Deep underground, Tomaz released a catch and pulled a lever. Then he hauled on a rope. Nothing moved, so he came back to Millie and kicked the foot of the cage. He hauled again and the bars started to rise awkwardly.

'It comes down alright,' he said. 'But putting it up, it's so hard. Lift, can you?'

They struggled together, though Millie had no strength anywhere. Soon the contraption rose to knee height and she managed to crawl out into the passage.

'Good,' said the boy. 'At least it works coming down.'

He smiled. His teeth were white and even. His long hair was clean and his shirt was fresh, though it had been repaired and washed so often it looked like grey rags stitched together. It was tucked into shorts that were too big. His legs were pale and hairless, and they disappeared into army boots.

'Tomaz?' said Millie. Her voice was little more than a whisper.

'Yes?'

'Are you really the Tomaz that ran away?'

He looked at her, then glanced down. 'I didn't go far,' he said, a little sheepishly.

'Why? Sanchez said . . . Sanchez said . . .'

'I'll show you. When you see, you'll understand. Listen.' Tomaz looked around, as if he thought he might be overheard. 'Nobody has ever been here before. You are the first, I think – for years, apart from me. When I heard the phone, I couldn't believe it.' Millie went to speak; he cut her off. 'I've got some clothes so I can get you dry. I've got a fire also. I'm so sorry about the trap, but . . . nobody must know, Millie. Follow me.'

The tunnel was smooth and ran steeply down, bending to the left as it did so. There were candles burning every few paces: as they passed, Tomaz snuffed them out with his fingers. His hair came halfway down his back.

Millie stumbled; he caught her arm and led her carefully. 'We'll go slow,' he said. 'Most of this I found. The tunnels go everywhere, as you know. I think they go under the lake: there's a way of draining the lake if you wanted to do it.'

Millie said nothing.

'I've mapped most of it, but I don't know how many miles there are. It's quite true what they say: you could be lost down here for ever. You know the train tunnel, where the staircase came down?'

'Yes.'

'That was for smuggling. OK, hold my arm – you're OK. Your feet, Millie! You're bleeding!'

'I'm OK, keep going. What about the staircase?'

'They had a railway that went from there right under the house. The trains brought the goods as far as the tunnel, or the centre of the tunnel. Then the men would unload into a little one, narrow gauge. You saw the engine.'

'Did I?'

'It was one of the old steam-engines. The track's good, but so many of the vents have collapsed, you couldn't run a steam train down here any more. One day though, Millie! I would like to try; we could restore it! You know, the Vyner family were into so many things! Lord Cyril was the engineer. But others, wow! Smuggling guns, antiques – I found so many things! There are secret store-houses: cigarettes, machine-guns, explosives. This way, we're nearly there.'

'You gave me all that food.' Millie had stopped.

'I told you,' said the boy, gently.

'Three meals, you gave me. Why didn't you answer when I called?'

The boy smiled. 'You were going in circles: I thought you were going to go mad.'

'I thought it was a ghost!'

'He doesn't go there!' laughed Tomaz. 'He stays in the Churchill Room. When you know the tunnels, Millie, you can double back very quickly. There are false walls, trapdoors, fox-holes . . . Some tunnels go under other tunnels, when you know where to look. I know I was scaring you, but the thing was I could *not* show myself. Could I? My house is totally, totally *secret*.'

Millie said: 'But how do you live down here?'

Tomaz laughed. 'I live like a king. You wait.' He went left, then right. They climbed briefly. He came to a patch of sand and brushed it: a wooden panel was revealed. It was the lid of a cleverly-concealed box, which the boy opened. There was a powerful flashlight inside. He moved into a recess in the rock and giggled. 'You're my first visitor. I'm a bit nervous. Lucky you're thin.'

He grabbed something above his head and lifted his body. He swung his legs into a hole and eased his torso through, twisting as he went.

'Hold the torch. Trust me.'

He squirmed a little further, chest and shoulders disappearing. Then his smile and his hair were gone too. No adult would ever fit: he was going through a rabbit-hole. Millie passed the torch and followed, hauling her body in somehow. She felt her feet gently pulled and she too was through. It was pitch dark suddenly: Tomaz had turned off the flashlight.

'Where are you?' said Millie.

'I'm here,' he said. He was right beside her. She could feel him, leaning against her. His face was close to hers and his breath smelled of liquorice.

'Are you ready?' he whispered.

'For what?'

'For my house.'

She expected him to turn on the torch, but he didn't. He

pressed a light switch and a glittering chandelier came on. Millie felt her jaw drop and she squeezed her eyes shut; the shock was too great, the light and the vision simply too intense.

She opened her eyes and looked and looked. She tried to think of something to say, and failed. After a solid minute of looking, the only expression she could think of, in all its uselessness, was: 'Oh my goodness.'

Chapter Forty-two

'Do you like it?'

They were on a ledge looking down. The chandelier hung from high up on a chain, lighting up the stone surfaces of a series of grottoes, carved into the rock. Millie could see the folding of the earth. The veins of crystal, the ripples of pinks, silvers and reds. She let her eyes drop carefully, foot by foot. There were caves, columns and bowls. Water must have carved most of it, but there were great shelves and cracks, as if massive heat had split and melted the world. It was a natural palace, with uncountable chambers interlinking. A pot-holer would explore such caverns for years.

The central chamber was the biggest and someone had laid carpets on its floor. She could see pale statues around it – fifty or sixty of them – and she thought of an underground church.

'What do you think?' asked Tomaz.

There were tapestries on the walls. Millie could make out hunting scenes: deer were leaping, dogs were chasing, trees were bending with berries and fruit. She could see birds breaking from their branches.

'Come down,' said Tomaz. 'You won't believe it.'

He helped her to her feet and guided her. There were steps carved into the rock. They went together and she stepped onto a rug.

'Take off your socks, please,' said Tomaz. He was unlacing his own boots. 'I think some of the carpets are about a thousand years old. More, I don't know. Some are from Arabia, India . . .' He started to light candles – there were silver candelabra on chests and in alcoves; there were night-lights at the feet and in the hands of the statues. Soon they were all glimmering and the place seemed a shrine.

Millie went slowly and carefully. There were three vast arm-chairs and two leather sofas. There was a table laid up in white with a silver dinner service for a solitary diner. There was a fat-bellied stove, with a roaring fire inside; it had a long chimney that elbowed its way up, zig-zagging through the rock. There were stuffed animals in cases. There were vases, each holding carefully-cut greenery, with sprays of red and white berries. On a pedestal stood a golden suit of armour, gauntlets resting on a glittering sword. It stared forward, like a guardian. There was a white rabbit on one of the sofas and it looked at Millie. There were bowls of fruit. There was another white rabbit on one of the rugs, a huge tiger-skin. There was a bookcase full of leather-bound books and it led the eye to a further chamber with hundreds more, towering upwards – a complete library.

'Beautiful, uh?' said Tomaz, softly.

The room smelled of good food and woodsmoke. 'You should eat,' he said. 'I didn't know you would be coming, so . . . it's not special. Come and see my kitchen, you'll love the kitchen.'

Yes, there were passages off; Millie could see more of them now, half concealed by the overlap of tapestries and the slabs of interlocking rock. Tomaz clicked on more lights. She could see his wiring too, pinned to the rock, hitched over a picture and the antlers of a stag. It came from a wall of car-batteries.

In the kitchen there was a fireplace, and the fire was small and compact. The pot that hung over it had been winched low: it was almost sitting in the ashes. Hand-made bread sat on a stone nearby. There were baskets of vegetables, jars and bunches of leaves. Knives and other utensils hung from a bar. Further down, the room narrowed into a corridor: the light didn't get there, so Millie could only just make out shelves disappearing. She thought she saw a rabbit hanging and a bird perhaps . . .

'It's just a stew,' said Tomaz, stirring the pot. 'It's winter food now, I'm using up apples. Everything I cook now has to have apples in. I am lucky: I learned to cook in Uzbek, I was a kitchen-boy. Now I improvise with what I have. Do you want to wash your hands?'

There was a toilet with a bath, a basin and a jug. He had soap. He had a fresh, clean towel. 'The water's cold,' he said from outside. 'I can heat it on the fire, or you can wash with what's there.'

'I'll use what's here,' whispered Millie.

She peeled off her soaking, bloody clothing. The water was in fact ice-cold, but she doused herself as best she could, head to toe. The stink of fire was all over her and her flesh was terribly scratched. She got up a good lather of soap and massaged herself. She needed to wake up, tempting as it was to give into the dream. She poured a cup full of water over her head and gasped. More, down her back: she was dancing with cold. She wanted to be alert. If she was to leave – and she had to go, she knew that – if she was to escape, she needed to be wide-awake. She wrapped herself in Tomaz's towel and stepped back into the kitchen.

'Tomaz—'

'Oh!' he cried. 'Sorry!' He turned away, instantly blushing. 'I'm sorry, I brought you some clean clothes.' Comically, he would not look at her. He held out a shirt and a pair of shorts, masking his eyes.

He had served the soup and there was a hunk of bread. He'd lit more candles and opened the door of the stove so the room was hot. He sat opposite Millie, but he wasn't eating. He put both elbows on the table and cradled a glass of wine.

'You like wine?' he said.

Millie nodded.

'It's one of the things I've tried to like since I came here. I have about six thousand bottles, but I have to add sugar. These are Winston Churchill's cigars, I think. I like to think so – he was friends with Lord Vyner, after all.'

Millie looked at the dusty label on the wine bottle. She recognised it from her experience all those weeks ago, when she'd sat cross-legged in a tunnel. It was another Clos de Bouchard 1923. 'This is one of my father's favourite wines,' she said.

'It's my currency. I use it to buy what I need. There's a man in town who does business with me. That's another reason I'm careful, you see. One day he's going to think, "Let's follow him home". Every time I come home I try to come a different way. I tell you, Millie, being on the run is scary: I don't recommend it.'

Millie looked into his eyes and smiled. 'I'm on the run myself. Tomaz, how have you done this?'

'It was all here. I just move things about.'

'You're on your own! Don't you get scared? Tomaz, you said there was a ghost – what did you mean?'

'There's a ghost, of course.'

'Lord Vyner. And you've seen him?'

'He was sitting there, just before you came. He doesn't stay, though – he prefers the Churchill Room. It's a bunker, a bit deeper than this. That's where the phone is and some of the control systems. He's very sad, he spends a lot of time down there; he was there when you called.'

'You're serious, aren't you? You're not making this up.'

Tomaz laughed. 'Of course I'm serious! He's totally harmless, don't worry. I think he used to work down here and it's where he was murdered. People say he committed suicide, but he didn't, Millie.'

'You're living with a ghost – you can't!'

'I don't live with him. He *comes through*; and he's no problem,

328

he's just . . . he can't rest, Millie, I don't know why. If you come again, you'll see for yourself. Anyway, he saved my life. He warned me to get away, and I had a friend—'

'The ouija board?'

'Sanchez told you, yes? About Miles, as well? They were going to kill me, I'm sure of it. So I ran away and . . . found all this. Truthfully, Millie – tell me. Listen! What do you think of my house?'

Millie put down her spoon. The food, the clean clothes, the cold water, the warmth of the stove, the candles – everything was accumulating in a great wave of relief; she was alive, in a magical land! They had tried to kill her *four times* and failed. Someone had tried to kill Tomaz and failed. Life was so intense it was burning in her veins and she was so strong she was indestructible. She took a mouthful of her father's favourite wine and savoured it.

'Tomaz,' she said. 'Your home is the most beautiful place I have ever been. You saved my life – twice. I want to marry you.'

Even in the candlelight she saw the boy blush again, to the roots of his hair. He hid his face. When he looked at her again he was smiling one of the widest smiles Millie had ever seen and he was laughing too.

'Yes,' he said. 'Shall we stay here for ever?'

Chapter Forty-three

Tomaz had a wind-up gramophone, just like the orphans. The records were crackly and a heartbroken soprano sang in a soft, tearful voice. The two children lit their cigars and listened. Millie closed her eyes and sank deeper into her chair. 'What are they doing down there?' she said, lazily. 'Who are they, Tomaz?'

'They've been down there for years.'

Millie laughed. 'And you're the next-door neighbour.'

'I stay away,' said Tomaz. 'I go sometimes, to see if I can get an animal. Otherwise, I stay away. You know,' he said, after a pause, 'it may have been my fault that they were chasing you.'

'*Your* fault? What do you mean?'

Tomaz turned and looked at Millie. 'You know they found your tie? You left it in the ventilation shaft.'

'Of course . . .' Millie's hand had gone instinctively to her throat. She sat there, her hand around her neck, looking stunned. 'That is so dumb. It had my name on it, what a fool. Tomaz, that's the most stupid thing I've ever done!'

'I was in there just before you though. I stole the old man's briefcase.' Millie stared at him. 'I know it's wrong, but I thought it was time I . . . I thought it was time I did something too, but I didn't know what. So I took the briefcase and thought that if I could get it to Sanchez, then maybe he could look at what's inside. They probably think that you have it and maybe that's why they're hunting you.'

'She did say something about a briefcase. Miss Hazlitt.'

'I'm sorry, I didn't think they'd . . .'

'Where is it now? What did you do with it?'

'It's just there.'

Millie looked across the room and got to her feet. On a small table stood the same squat metal briefcase she'd seen almost every day in the hands of Miss Hazlitt. She lifted it gently and checked the locking mechanism. Both clasps had been forced.

'You got into it. What's inside?'

'Have a look. Pictures, files, all sorts of stuff. I took it for Sanchez, you see. I thought I would find a way of getting it to him. They're getting ready for something – and I think it's bad.'

Millie cleared a space and he laid it on the table in front of her. 'Have you read this stuff?' she asked. She was pulling out papers and graphs. Some of the writing was typed, some of it was in the cramped hand of Miss Hazlitt. 'What does it say?' she said.

'I don't know.'

'Tomaz, what have you been doing? This could actually tell us what they're up to . . . If you went to the trouble of stealing the thing, why didn't you read what's inside? It's about – the orphans.'

Tomaz paused and there was another ghost of a blush. 'I can't read, Millie. I was learning with Ruskin, but . . .'

But Millie wasn't listening. She had picked up a sheet and was instantly, instantly absorbed. She put it to one side and picked up the next. A puff of cigar, a swig of wine. She sat down again, and spread out some of the documents. They were medical reports. She saw familiar names: Asilah, Anjoli, Israel, Sanjay, Vijay, Podma, Eric – all the orphans' names, but no sign of hers or Sam's or Ruskin's. Henry wasn't there, nor was Sanchez – but then, only the orphans had been through the tests. She skimmed through, flipping the pages. For some reason

Anjoli's name was heavily underlined in a coloured marker pen. Then, paperclipped together in a buff folder, measurements, graphs, information about diet and weight. It was all Anjoli now, every page. Paper after paper, with data that went into long columns of minuscule, obsessive handwriting.

'What do they say?' said Tomaz.

'I don't know.'

Lists. Data. Photographs. 'It's the stuff she was doing in the mornings,' said Millie. 'Our deputy headmistress was measuring them, all the time . . . Look at this, I don't understand it. What's a *medial prefrontal cortex*? What's an *amygdala*? I can't read half of this. I don't understand: it's cross-referenced with something . . . What?'

She unfolded a zig-zag of paper and revealed a whole cosmos of planets.

'They're skulls,' said Tomaz.

Millie opened another folder and a sheaf of X-rays fanned across the desk. Eye sockets, teeth, and the curve of a child's cranium.

She said, 'We shouldn't be sitting here.' Someone had drawn the most beautiful cross-sections of Anjoli's brain, numbering and labelling. *To maintain a self-regulating oxygen supply, anaesthetic is to be avoided. Administer only the minimum dose of compound 311, methodone base (see footnote 4.4) – subject to be conscious, pressure details subject to . . .*

Millie's world plunged.

The ride wasn't over: she was on a new loop of the rollercoaster and this time she was higher than ever and the drop on either side made her feel faint. 'He wasn't there,' she said, with mounting panic.

'Who?'

'In the dormitory, just before the fire. I can see them all. I was looking at them, I was trying to talk to them. They were playing some stupid game and falling off the beds. Anjoli wasn't there. I said, "Where's Anjoli?" but then we saw the fire.'

Millie stood up. She could feel herself falling, overcome by dread. She grabbed the stove chimney to steady herself, burned her hand and cried out. She held the papers to her chest. Then she read the annotations again, even though her hands were unsteady. Down the side, boxed in neatly, were medical details: blood group, cellular breakdowns, a chart with lists of numbers, little graphs that meant nothing. Then, most horribly, she was back in the lab, looking down at the model child and the needles. They needed a subject. They had the green light. They *didn't* have Tomaz.

'I know what they're doing!' she said suddenly. She was crying. 'They're doing it to *him*.'

'*What* are they doing?'

'They've been feeding them pills, but they don't take the pills. I think she's trying to check for changes in behaviour, side effects, that kind of thing, but it hasn't worked. Oh no, she was always checking him, more than anyone else – and she hated him! Then in the lab, I heard them talking about it, dammit, but I just didn't understand – and that must be what the chair is for and why they had that dummy. They were planning it – they were going on and on about how it couldn't wait, but I thought it was you!'

'How *what* couldn't wait?'

'She's working for that man. Mr Jarman, this . . . surgeon. They must be working together and she's running the school to provide him with children . . . Tomaz!' Millie cried out. 'Tomaz! Sam was saying . . . Some of the things he was saying . . .'

'Hang on, you—'

'They've got Anjoli. Where's the lab? How do we get to it?'

'You have to go up – I blocked the tunnel, so—'

'We've got to find the others, Tomaz! Oh, God, why didn't you give this to us earlier? We're going to be way too late! Is there a quick way up? They'll be looking for me, they'll be round the lake!'

'There's a secret way, I'll get you boots!'

Millie was crying harder now, in terror and frustration. She wiped away the tears. 'They've taken him! I was going to ask, but then we saw the fire!' She pressed her palms to her eyes and sniffed back the mucous. 'She's got him and we've been sitting here, drinking. Tomaz, he's my friend, he's my friend!'

'Shh, it's OK, there's a quick way—'

'It's *not* OK! They're going to do something to him, Tomaz, they'll kill him! They've probably already killed him, we're too late!'

Chapter Forty-four

The search for Millie had been long and the boys were frozen.

Asilah had taken seven boys with him and had gone to the Greek temple. He'd led them clockwise round the lake. Sanchez had taken Ruskin, Sam and Henry, and the rest of the orphans, and had moved counter-clockwise. The group leaders were in radio contact, having grabbed the crane-operators' headsets, which Captain Routon had thoughtfully left on charge. They'd done a sweep right round and found nobody. They stretched out again, getting colder and colder. They would do one more circuit.

'Nothing so far,' said Sanchez into his radio. 'I'm back at Neptune. This is hopeless, over.'

'I can see where you are,' said Asilah. 'Nothing so far. I'll try towards the gates, why don't you go back to the school? Over.'

'She won't go back to the school. Over.'

'Anjoli might, if he didn't find her. I'll try the telephone box, and then the back road. Over.'

'Wait.'

'What? Over.'

'I said wait. Asilah . . .'

His teeth were chattering. Sanchez thought for a moment it was a trick of the mist, but as he stared, Neptune's head appeared to be turning. The giant's nose definitely shifted towards him until they were making eye contact. He was no longer surveying his own lake, he was watching Sanchez.

'What's the problem? Over,' said Asilah into the radio.

Sanchez couldn't utter a sound.

The chin tipped up. Neptune was now staring at the stars. There was a hinge at the back of his neck and his head kept lifting; now the neck was a rather disturbing hole. A figure with long hair was appearing through it, as if from a chimney pot. He was standing on the giant's shoulder, helping somebody else, and that person was Millie.

'She's here,' said Sanchez. His voice was a whisper.

'What? I can't hear, Sanchez! Speak clearly. Over.'

'She's here. I said, *she's here*!'

'With Anjoli?'

'Millie's here! She's OK. Over!'

Everyone raced towards the statue. Asilah's team appeared over the first bridge and bounded round the lake. Then Sanchez stopped again, and this time he was turned to stone. Millie was running towards him, shouting something, but he couldn't hear what and he didn't care. Sanchez had recognised the boy with the long hair and could not believe it; he dared not hope. He found himself backing away. By now Millie had reached the throng, but he couldn't go forward. The long-haired boy looked up and saw him and smiled. Sanchez hesitated; it was the long-haired boy who walked up the bank to his friend. Sanchez was mute, so Tomaz said, 'Hello.'

Sanchez found the words at last. He said simply, 'Hello, Tomaz.'

Words deserted him again, and he strode forward to embrace his friend, and it would have been a deeply emotional and a great lingering, joyous reunion had Millie not dived between them and grabbed Sanchez by his shirt.

'You haven't found him!' she cried. 'Have you?'

Sanchez went to embrace her, but she twisted out of his arms and said again, 'Anjoli's been taken. We don't have any *time*, Sanchez, he's gone. Do you have your gun?'

'No.'

'Get it now. We need it.'

'Why? What—'

'You won't believe me. They're experimenting on the orphans and they've chosen Anjoli.'

Asilah was next to her and the other orphans were muttering, clustering, holding each other. 'He was in the kitchen,' said Asilah. 'He was on duty.'

'I know where he *was* and he didn't come back – I asked you!' said Millie. 'I said, "Where is he?"'

'Where is he?' said Israel.

Millie said, 'Don't you remember? Oh, you're so dumb, I asked you, I *told* you!'

It was Asilah's turn to grab somebody. He put his hands on Millie's shoulders and shook her once: 'Where is my brother?' he said. There was a frightening calm in his voice and Millie felt his hands crushing her collarbones.

'Underground,' said Millie. 'I think the policeman took him; I think he's in the lab.'

Asilah made a terrible noise, half groan, half sob. A child started to cry.

Sanchez said, 'There's a lift in the headmaster's study – we were going to explain all this, but . . . we started playing that game.'

Asilah simply ran and every orphan followed him.

Sanchez and the others watched them sprinting away. 'They don't know what's down there,' he said. 'Millie, this is so dangerous – what can they do?'

'Follow them,' said Millie. 'Give me your radio, I'll go down the ventilation shaft. Follow Asilah and get your gun.'

'Not on your own, no—'

Millie screamed at him, and shoved him so hard he nearly fell. 'For once, Sanchez, do what I tell you! You know the way, he doesn't. Take Tomaz – Tomaz knows the tunnels.'

Millie turned and ran. In half a minute she was over the first humpback bridge, racing to the Vyner monument.

Six minutes it took. Asilah's gang piled up the stairs and along the corridor, and Sam was dragged to the door. The toothbrush sprang the lock and they dived for the wall. Eager hands fluttered over the joins and in seconds the panelling was swinging open, to reveal both metal grille and control panel. They stared into a dark lift shaft. They could hear a motor grinding below them and Asilah smashed at the switch panel with his hand.

Nothing happened.

'Someone might be using it,' said Ruskin. 'Press the button again . . .'

Asilah clawed at the grille and other fingers pressed the button. Deep below in the dark vault, the vibrations stopped. The humming was replaced by silence. Then there was a click and the lights in the panel closed down.

'They've turned it off,' said Sam. 'Does that mean we're too late?'

'We're not,' whispered Asilah. He yanked at the metal grille, but it wouldn't budge. He started talking, in a soft clear voice and Ruskin thought he must be cursing, but he couldn't understand a word. It was the orphans' own language, of course, and the boy was giving instructions. He spoke in rapid bursts, and after every line a pair of boys leaped into action.

In seconds everyone was running again, pouring back out of the room and down the stairs. Henry, Ruskin and Sam ran with them; Tomaz and Sanchez met them in the courtyard.

In the tunnels below, Millie paused for breath. She clicked her radio on and tried to speak clearly and calmly.

'Sanchez, where are you?'

'They can't get down,' he said. 'The lift's dead. Over.'

She was trembling. She'd slid down the rope so fast her hands were burning. Then she'd sprinted all the way. 'What's your plan?' she said.

'I don't know. Asilah's in charge.'

'You have the gun, don't you, Sanchez? Over.'

Sanchez paused. 'No,' he said.

'Get it! For the love of God, get your gun. I'm going to the lab, I'll be there in five minutes. You don't know how dangerous this is, now—'

'Alright! I'll get it!'

Millie clicked off the radio and set off again. She knew she was close, as long as she hadn't taken a wrong turn.

Down on the building site, Henry forced a crowbar behind the bolt-mechanism of the storage unit. He took a deep breath, heaved, and the metal clasp sprang from its rivets.

Sanjay and Israel moved inside, pulling out the grinders and welders. There were gauntlets, masks, tool-belts and – heaviest of all – the chainsaw. They fed them into a queue of willing hands.

Asilah grabbed hold of Ruskin and Sam. 'Go with Vijay, take the van. He'll get the chain. I want you to chain up the park gates, then come back here. If you see any cars – anything – stop them, he might be inside.'

'Right,' said Ruskin.

Israel moved off, dragging an acetylene cylinder behind him. Sam and Ruskin shouldered a burden of pipes, rods and asbestos matting and followed Vijay. The main doors were unlocked still after Millie's flight, so in seconds they were out onto the courtyard. A motor was kicked into life: two small orphans cut down the ornamental chains round the front lawn. They were using the huge slate-cutting tool and it sprayed an arc of sparks over the gravel. As the chains fell, they heaved the machine to shoulder height and ran back to Asilah, who was waving them into the main school.

Round the back, Vijay had climbed into Captain Routon's

339

van. He was twisting wires from the steering column and in seconds the engine was revving. His legs were short, so he pulled at Ruskin. 'Drive!' he said.

'Me?' said Ruskin. 'I'm not sure I can. Have you ever driven a vehicle, Sam?'

'I've done the gears for my father.'

'Come on, go!' shouted Vijay. 'Go! Go!'

'I'll give it a try, I'm sure it's not rocket science. That's the brake, presumably . . .'

The welding gear was loaded. Ruskin revved hard and Sam yanked the gearstick into reverse. The van cannoned backwards into the wall, jarring everyone onto the van floor. Sam plunged into first gear and Ruskin accelerated hard over the grass. He snaked wildly, avoiding a tree by centimetres. Then he saw the long ribbon of tarmac that led to the gates and he managed to guide the screaming vehicle onto it.

'I told you, didn't I?' said Ruskin to Sam. He had his mouth to his friend's ear, but he still had to shout.

'Told me what?'

'These boys! They're good in a crisis!'

Lady Vyner was peering through her window in disbelief. She had heard engine sounds and was now staring down into the quadrangle. A crowd of children had gathered, their torches lighting up the school's main fuse-box.

'We'll cut the electricity,' said Asilah.

Sanchez nodded. The fuse-box was sealed in a metal case and three armour-plated cables, the thickness of Henry's arm, snaked up out of it, clamped to the wall. Henry had worked each one free from its clips with his crowbar, so they stuck out like twisted drainpipes.

'Is it safe?' said Sanchez. 'That's a lot of power, that does the whole school . . .'

The orphans wore thick rubber gauntlets and Wellington

boots; they pulled visors down, and one of them wrenched the cord on the chainsaw. It caught first time and howled. Lady Vyner saw Henry stand back and cover his eyes, then the child with the chainsaw leaned into a savage cut clean through the cables. The explosion cracked windows and a bolt of lightning went from the fuse-box to the floor. The saw screamed louder and another great arc of jagged electricity reared up, swung over everybody's heads like a snake, and whipped into the ground. When the smoke cleared and Asilah shone his torch, Sanchez saw that the fuse-box had melted and a black, bent chainsaw was welded to it.

'Not safe at all,' said Asilah. 'Very dangerous.'

Now the school was in total darkness. The boys' flashlights bobbed madly as they buckled on their tool-belts. They jammed in screwdrivers, hammers, chisels, pliers; and as they set off, they clanked. The grinder was heaved up onto shoulders and in a moment everyone was up in the study again.

Asilah said, 'Let's go.'

Sanchez said: 'Come in, Millie – where are you? We're coming down the lift shaft. Where are you? Over.'

'I'm nearly there.'

'We've killed the power. Over.'

'I know, the lights went out down here. Clever.'

'Be careful, though. I think they might know we're coming. Try to . . .'

Whatever Sanchez thought Millie ought to try was drowned out by the frenzy of the grinder, as its motor screamed. He saw Tomaz in the doorway. 'Did you find it?'

'Yes.'

The boy had a box of bullets in one hand and the heavy black pistol in the other. Sanchez took both and loaded in the torch-light. Israel set the grinder to the metal grille and there was another plume of sparks.

Chapter Forty-five

In the hospital, the headmaster was going through a similar experience to Professor Worthington. He would also wonder afterwards what psychic force was pulling him out of his waiting-room chair and infusing him with such impatience. As soon as he was alone, he'd felt restless and started to pace up and down.

He'd phoned Miss Hazlitt, but the line to his study seemed to be out of service. That decided him. He walked briskly to Reception and asked if he could see the patient he was waiting for. Phone calls were made and he was assured that treatment was continuing and he should wait to be called. The headmaster spoke firmly and was assured again that everything was under control. He grew more assertive. He grew positively demanding. In a short while he was standing in a booth looking at the boiled, anaesthetised form of Captain Routon. Two nurses were halfway through the long process of preparing his burns for dressing. Routon was stable, but would be unconscious for a few more hours.

This freed Dr Norcross-Webb, and that was important. He knew then that there was no reason for staying any longer, so he took the stairs two at a time and ran to the car park. His car was covered in ice and he lost precious minutes hacking away at his windscreen. When he had a hole big enough to see through, he roared out onto the Ribblestrop road, a voice whispering, insistently: *Get back to your school, get back to your school.* The ice meant nothing. He put his foot down and skidded over the lanes.

In the basement, far below, Millie was mystified.

She'd come round the final bend so gingerly, on tiptoe in her army boots. She was in the right place; she could see the door and the air-vent and was ready to go. What stopped her was the fact that the metal door was open.

It had been firmly closed on her last visit, but now it was ajar. She approached it cautiously, not sure what this meant. If she was too late, then maybe they'd done the job and left. Though why they would leave the door open made no sense. Had someone gone to get something? Was it for ventilation, perhaps?

Millie approached, keeping close to the wall. She shone her torch inside. Without electricity, the place had an abandoned look: the power-cut had been a clever idea, it would have turned off every machine and stopped them dead. Perhaps they'd fled? She stepped into the little hallway, and there were the familiar double-doors, the portholes reflecting her beam. Millie crawled towards them and crouched low, waiting for the courage to enter.

Of course, someone might have seen her torch by now. She clicked it off and the darkness closed in all around. If they were in there, they were waiting for her. If they weren't, then it was all over. Anjoli, her friend, would be gone. She could not crouch here for ever wondering. It was Anjoli's life, Anjoli's smile . . .

She clipped the radio into her back pocket so she had both hands free and rose slowly to the glass.

They'd lit candles. She could make out the chair, and cabinets, and glimmering silver tools laid out on long counters. She blinked and tried to see detail. There were candles round the chair and on it – they'd put a cluster on the little tray that swung

343

in close to the chair's headrest. By the light, dim as it was, she could make out a figure, but whether it was Anjoli or the model she could not tell. Around him stood three figures, absolutely motionless. They were in dark silhouette – bending forward, like waiters in a restaurant.

Millie licked her lips, desperate for a bit of moisture. She eased the door open an inch, and as she did she heard someone sob. She waited, her heart in her mouth, and it came again: a lonely, abandoned sob followed by a sniff. She could hear the child breathing, and he seemed to be having difficulty. Then, unmistakable, she heard his voice. 'Please?' he said, very softly.

She pushed her head into the room and listened harder. Nobody moved: the figures were still. They had their hands up by their chests and were holding what looked like trays – yes, now she could see. There were candles on each one, and they were the models she'd seen, the dummies or robots, so similar to what Sam described after his visit to Lady Vyner's home. Now, in the flickering light they looked like statues in a church.

Anjoli sobbed again. 'Please?' he said, louder this time. There was just a quiver of hope in the voice, as if he knew someone was close. It was so forlorn, but it was alive – he could think and speak! It came again, 'Help me . . .' Then the boy started to cry and Millie's heart cracked in half. She drew her head back, let the doors close, and clicked the radio on.

'Sanchez?' she whispered. Her voice was shaking and so were her hands.

'Millie! I can hardly hear you – where are you?'

'I've found him. He's down here. Over.'

'They're down there too, Millie – I tried to say, they were using the lift. They're down there, wait for us—'

'He's alright, I think. They've gone. I'm going to see.'

'No, wait, Millie! We're on our way, stay—'

She snapped the radio off, set it to one side, and entered the room. Crab-like, she scuttled in and waited for her breathing to slow down. She could see Anjoli's cheek, shining wet with tears or sweat. It had to be him, no one else had hair swept back like that.

'Anjoli!' she cried, in a hoarse whisper. 'I'm here.'

Oh, the crying was louder now and it was the loneliest sound in the world. It was desolate, tired and abandoned as if he'd been crying all night. It was so full of longing that it moved things in Millie's guts she never wanted moved again. 'I'm here,' she said. 'It's me – Millie! Be quiet, Anjoli, please!'

She came past the first robot. It was wearing a surgical mask. There were tools on its tray, bright silver in the candlelight. Little picks and knives and tweezers, but she didn't want to look. She glanced up and the second one seemed to be staring at her, over an identical white mask. Cotton wool and towels were piled on that tray.

Millie forced her eyes forward and focused only on Anjoli. He was bound by his wrists and his ankles, and there was a complicated scaffold holding his head still, drawing it backwards. His eyes were wide, bigger than ever, and they were filmed with tears and they weren't focusing. His lips were slightly open too and he was breathing evenly. Deep shock, perhaps?

She put her hands against his face and pushed his hair back. He was warm to the touch. 'Anjoli,' she said. 'Have they hurt you? Have they done anything?'

He stared past her, he didn't know she was there – but the sobbing started again, louder now. It seemed to come not from Anjoli, but from the walls and ceiling. Even as Millie looked up and around, the sobbing started to echo and take on a demented quality, more like mocking laughter.

'He can't hear you,' said a voice.

Millie swung round, and there was Miss Hazlitt, and she too was laughing. She was wearing a white coat. Millie had never seen her in a white coat before. A tape rewound and she heard her own voice, loud and demanding: *'Excuse me, miss? Excuse me?'* Then she heard Ruskin, asking a question, and the laughter of a whole classroom full of children.

'Oh, Millie,' said Miss Hazlitt, sadly. 'Surely you didn't think it would be that easy?' Her voice was different. It was deeper.

'Welcome to our school!' said the voice of an orphan. Children were still giggling in the background. *'We hope you will enjoy . . . we hope you . . .'* The voice dissolved into giggles, and she could hear the Manners and Civilisation class – desks banging, feet stamping. As she stood there, stunned, lights were flashing on. They had generators, of course they did. Monitors were coming on in bright blue and above – on a big screen – there were images of a school corridor, a dormitory. Millie saw children running, walking, fighting . . . *'Can I help you, sir? Are you looking for the office?'*

Millie spun around and around, not sure where to look. One of the robots was straightening up, offering its tray of tools, and she saw long needles. There were men and women emerging too, in those funeral suits she'd seen from above . . . seven, eight – two men in uniform who looked like security guards. She recognised the bowler-hatted man and the one with the ugly moustache.

'Recordings make the process easier,' said Miss Hazlitt. 'It's part of a re-education programme. Listening and watching whilst we stimulate the brain-cells that remain; it's a process we're so close to perfecting.'

'What have you done to him?' cried Millie.

'Such progress! And we're so close to a break-through. Your friend's had the mildest shot of nerotaxodil. He's probably dreaming of you, Millie.'

'You're not touching him!' cried Millie. She put herself between the chair and Miss Hazlitt. 'You leave him alone!'

'I've given him two grams, it's the mildest of sedatives. The last thing anyone wants at this stage is trauma.'

Somebody said, 'Three minutes,' but Millie didn't see who.

Miss Hazlitt had moved to another of the robots and was pressing its neck. The security guards were blowing out the candles and some of the men in suits were arranging chairs. 'Who are these people? What are you doing?'

'She doesn't understand,' said someone, kindly. The inspection lamp above was on now and its light was blinding.

'There's no reason why she should,' said someone else – a woman's voice. 'Millie, you're part of a very special secret.'

'One that must be *kept*,' said a man. 'Having come this far.'

'We have clearance, old boy,' said the man with the moustache.

As he spoke, Miss Hazlitt's cellphone chirped. She keyed in a number and said, 'Everything's signed, we're ready to go.' She looked at Millie and smiled, the dentures huge and white and far too smooth. The face looked older, as if the make-up had been wiped away to reveal something stony, even dirty. 'This has taken years, my dear. You'll never know how long the future takes to construct. Inspector!'

Millie swung round but even as she moved she felt a hand on the back of her neck. She hit blindly and kicked, but a hand caught her wrist and her right arm was wrenched up behind her. Twisting, she lunged with her left, but that too was caught and twisted so she couldn't breathe. He knew the manoeuvres, he'd done this so many times. In a moment Millie was tripped onto her face and a huge, heavy knee rested on her back; the air was driven from her lungs, and her face was pressing into the rubber floor as she coughed and retched.

'I've been waiting too,' said Inspector Cuthbertson. He too was breathing hard, and he smelled of the lake.

'Let me go,' she whispered. He had all his weight on her, his hands were squeezing and she could feel her sinews being torn apart. Was he laughing? She could hear laughter, but her oxygen was going. 'Please!' she cried, with the last mouthful of air. 'Just let us go, please!'

'Don't break her, Percy,' said Miss Hazlitt. Her voice was so cold. 'I was just trying to explain, trauma can complicate the injection process, and as she's volunteered, I think we need to give her the best possible chance. We haven't run tests on you, Millie, so to some extent we're flying blind. You'll be what's known as a *parallel study*. Raise the boy.'

Someone was wheeling a trolley, she could hear the rumbling of castors; then a bell was ringing, and the floor shook as more trolleys were wheeled around her. It was the robots again: they were the nurses. As Millie twisted and looked up, she saw one adjusting a dial; another rolled forward slowly. It had a gun in its hands.

'Nobody's going to hurt either of you,' said Miss Hazlitt. She was checking a screen, as a third robot passed her a tiny glass tube. 'In a very short while you'll be back at school . . . eating your breakfast. You'll be different people, though. That's for sure.'

Another bell rang and something started to bleep. The noise was sharp and penetrating.

Millie gulped some air and thrashed on the floor. She tried to kick but the hands that held her simply lifted her up, and the two guards in uniform were helping so she didn't stand a chance. She found herself on a trolley, and thick restraints were going over her shoulders, chest, ankles, thighs. There was something in her mouth and a bright light in her face. One of the robots was moving, bringing the tray low, close to her ear: Millie saw scissors of all different sizes. Sightless eyes locked onto hers. She tried to scream.

'After this, child, you'll be so co-operative. You'll give. You'll work! And, who knows, Millie?'

'*I like to clean my shoes,*' said a child's voice, clear over the speakers.

'Maybe your father will want you back.'

Millie managed a howl, and the thing in her mouth was pressed deeper.

'If we turn you into a good citizen . . . Look at me. If we burn the revolution out of you, you might find a family that wants you. Don't you want to stop fighting, Millie?'

Miss Hazlitt looked down over her and raised her hands to her head. The tight curls of hair were shifting under her fingers, as the children's voices bleated on: *'No! That's against the rules!'* The woman's scalp was moving and suddenly, like a bathing cap, it was sliding to one side revealing the mottled, grey skin of old age and a tangled mess of white hair.

'This is about transformation, my dear.' The teeth were working loose and saliva dripped. Miss Hazlitt reached between her lips and out they came, handfuls of teeth, so that the skull shrunk and the cheeks flopped in. The make-up cracked like paint on rubber, and Millie was gazing into the eyes of a very old man. 'What you're listening to, is the language of co-operation: *"I do as I'm told"*,' he said, as a child said the same thing. 'My name's Jarman,' he said. 'Miss Hazlitt is no more, not until tomorrow. Shh, my dear, you have to relax now: everything changes. We can all be transformed!'

The old man laughed and there was laughter fluttering round the room on enormous wings, the echoing laughter of children. The smell of cigarette and perspiration was unbearable as he leaned hard on the trolley, coughing and chuckling. She recognised him now – she'd seen that hair from above, and Sam's stories of wartime research were clicking into place with the precision of dominoes falling. The lessons, the cameras, the tapes and the medicals. Miss Hazlitt's slow, insect-like movement along the corridors, locking doors, touching the children with those long slim, fingers – easing himself in, and edging others out.

He'd put on glasses now, with great, bug-like lenses, an inch thick. His posture had collapsed into the skinny, hunched thing she'd observed from above, a man in his nineties.

'I must tidy up my room,' said a child. *'I want to do good things!*

349

No – that's against the rules, I mustn't!' There was a robot at the old man's elbow, hypodermic on its tray; from one of the steel sinks a second robot came slowly forward, bearing a pair of plastic gloves.

Jarman reached behind Anjoli and took the gun from the third. But as he brought it close, Millie saw that it wasn't a gun at all, it was more like a pen or a soldering iron. The old man raised it and took off its cap. There was an electrical flex attached to one end and at the other there wasn't a nib. Jarman was holding a drill.

'You ought to be proud,' he whispered. 'You children really are pioneers – like the Wild West. Speed seven, I think. We don't want to set him on fire.'

There was a squeal of metal and out of the drill came a long, fine sting. It grew in length and Jarman moved a dial so the squeal rose into a scream.

'Everyone ready?' he said. 'We'll do the boy first. It's just five little holes, Millie. I'll create perfection, with just five little holes.'

Chapter Forty-six

Back in the headmaster's study, the chainsaw screech of grinders had obliterated hearing and the children were working by sign language. Asilah had done the locks on the grille, slicing through steel. They hauled it back and played flashlights into the well of the lift shaft. Black cables ran down into an impossibly deep hole. The torches illuminated black space and nothing more, but nobody hesitated. They all had gloves so, led by Sanjay, they leaped for the wires and slid down, down, down into the inky darkness.

Their boots gave good friction, but the journey was long. It was as if they were going to the centre of the earth. Israel landed first and started to help the others onto the top of the lift car. Instinctively now, they worked in silence.

Tomaz had found the trapdoor in the roof and had it open: the hatchway was small. There wasn't room for many. Asilah dropped through with Sanjay, and then they helped Sanchez. In the jumping torches and the crush of boys, he had his gun out. He stared at the lift doors. Another metal grille and a second door, that looked like thin steel. Asilah waved his hand and Podma swung the grinder down towards him. Eric guided it through the hatch.

*

Meanwhile, at the main gate, Ruskin kept the van idling. He was getting more used to it now, and while the orphans clambered out of the back and chained up the entrance, he and Sam successfully manoeuvred the vehicle around.

'Where did they learn this, Ruskin?' said Sam, wonderingly.

'I think a lot of it is instinct. Asilah was giving the orders and it all seemed to come naturally. Do you want to drive back? How's your eyesight these days?'

'Black and white still.'

'I'll do the gears, you have a go at steering.'

As the boys swapped seats, Israel finished wrapping the gates in chain. Vijay lit the burner and in seconds had the pressure right. The rods melted in crackling bolts of lightning, and in less than a minute the chain was spot-welded into an unbreakable mass: the gates were sealed. They dragged everything back into the van and Sam dipped the clutch.

'Go!' shouted Vijay.

'First gear, Sam: go!' yelled Ruskin.

They reversed three metres, and slammed into a gatepost. There was a blast of car horn and Ruskin wrestled with the gearstick. The van shunted forwards this time, in a huge kangaroo leap. They stalled.

'Easily done,' said Ruskin. 'The clutch is more delicate than you think.'

'I think there's someone behind us,' said Sam.

Everyone turned to look out of the rear doors, mashed as they were. A pair of headlights shone dazzlingly bright, glinting through the shattered glass. You could just see the little lamp on the roof.

'Police,' said Vijay. He barked at Israel in his own language and the boy slid under the dashboard for a quick hot-wiring.

'I don't think that's a police car,' said Ruskin. 'No, that's a taxi cab.'

A figure had stepped out of it and Professor Worthington's voice came loud and clear: 'Open this gate!'

'Oh no!' said Ruskin. 'We're for it now.'

'Open it! *What* is going on?'

'She sounds upset,' said Sam. 'I suppose it's way past lights-out.'

They heard the gates rattling and the voice again: 'Who's in that van? Show yourselves!'

Then, as they watched, they saw an amazing thing. Professor Worthington was climbing. She was remarkably good at it too, picking hand and footholds with absolute instinct, and swinging a long right leg up over the top of the gate. She clambered halfway down, then launched herself onto the van roof with a crunch. The vehicle rocked under her. Then she was on the bonnet, staring at the boys with a look of absolute ferocity.

'Professor Worthington,' said Ruskin, leaning out of the window. 'Can we give you a lift?'

'Get out of the van, Sam, you're not driving anywhere!'

'You don't understand, miss!' cried Sam. 'We're on a mission!'

She jumped to the ground and yanked the door open. At that moment, Israel made the connection and the van rattled into life.

'Move over, both of you!'

'Miss, please!'

'I'm on the same mission and *I'm* driving. Now get out of the way!'

'Come in, Millie?' said Sanchez, softly.

He pressed the radio's call button again. 'Come in, Millie – where are you? We're in the lift. Where are you, over?'

'Let's go,' whispered Asilah.

'Millie!' hissed Sanchez.

Podma pulled at the cord of the grinder. It didn't catch.

Sanchez pressed his ear against the metal, hoping to hear something. Maybe it was the noise of the engines earlier, but all he could hear was the high-pitched whine of what sounded like a drill.

Asilah said, 'The grinder's dead. Shoot the lock.'

'If I shoot the lock, the bullet could bounce back—'

'*Shoot the lock*. Then, Henry?' He was talking so softly. 'You get the door open.'

Henry would barely fit through the hatch, but with pulling and pushing from above, they got him in. He filled the car. He pressed his back to its wall, hung from the hatchway, and lifted two giant boots. He would kick the lift apart.

'What are you waiting for?' said Asilah to Sanchez. 'Shoot the lock!'

Sanchez flicked the safety catch and put the muzzle at the first bolt.

Millie had heard a soft gasp of metal and for a moment she thought of the lift. She dreamed it might be rescue, but it was simply the hydraulics under Anjoli's chair because it was rising and tilting at the same time, bringing the child closer to the surgeon's chest.

Jarman pulled a mask down over his mouth, his toe tapped a switch, and the drill moved to a new speed. A high-pitched whine filled the air as if some hornet was loose and furious.

Millie cried out, but she was inaudible. Anjoli, she saw, was blinking and licking his lips. Was he straining in the chair? She couldn't tell. She saw his fingers move.

Jarman laid a gloved hand upon his cheek and held him firm. The noise of the drill soared yet higher, until the glassware was vibrating.

It was at that precise moment that Sanchez pulled the trigger.

The bullet passed straight through the lock, bursting it to pieces. It sang across the laboratory and ricocheted through two metal cabinets. In the fountain of breaking glass and ringing steel, everyone froze. The drill was poised at Anjoli's forehead and two more gunshots followed in quick succession. Sanchez destroyed the final bolts and Henrȳ started to kick.

Anjoli would explain what he saw later, many times, to anyone who would listen. He would explain how, at the first gunshot, it had all seemed like a dream. The noise jerked him awake, just as the hand holding his face tightened. When Sanchez fired a second and third time, Mr Jarman swung round, and some of the crowd around him dived for cover. Anjoli said he saw somebody fall over, bleeding, but that was never confirmed. He said that immediately security guards started to move people out, shouting into radio sets, and a huge door was pulled back – he said he glimpsed a train.

Who was in that laboratory? How many, and what were their roles? None of that was ever confirmed. In the confusion, one thing definitely happened, and Millie witnessed it. In fact, both children were able to describe it in exquisite detail, and Anjoli later drew a picture for the school magazine, a picture that had to be rejected because it was so disgusting. As the doors burst inwards, Mr Jarman turned and lost his balance: he tripped on the foot-switch and nearly fell. Anjoli saw the man's frog-like, panic-stricken eyes looming over him. He felt a thumb pressing against his cheek where the old man's hand rested, trying to steady himself. In the terror of the moment, some instinct took over and Anjoli opened his mouth.

The man's thumb slipped between his teeth.

Unluckily for Mr Jarman – who was still off-balance – his thumb was in up to the second joint, close to the palm. The boy bit hard. He sank his teeth in and squeezed with all his might.

Millie knew, and dimly remembered telling someone or being told, that the jaw is the most powerful muscle in the whole human musculature; it has a ratio of something or other that lets the teeth apply enough sheer pressure to crack nuts, branches and bones. Back to our days as vegetarian leaf-grinders, mixed with our years as flesh-tearing carnivores, Anjoli had evolved with lethal jaws. He bit so hard, he was down on the cartilage in a second. Mr Jarman writhed like a fish on a line, gasping, and then – in what seemed like sudden silence – he screamed. There was a great scattering of tools and bottles. Henry was kicking by this time, battering the doors that would not give. Anjoli just bit harder and harder, till the surgeon ripped his own hand from the bloody mouth and fell against the counter, a geyser of blood not oozing, but pumping from the mutilated stump.

Cuthbertson had dived forward to assist, but now he ran. The doors were giving way. Crowbars and screwdrivers were scratching and levering. Hands, then elbows, then shoulders. There was Sanchez, there was Sanjay and Asilah, and above them all – forcing the doors apart with his mighty hands – was Henry. He was purple with exertion, his haggard face shining with sweat.

Jarman was screaming, like an alarm that could not be silenced. The crowd had gone – vanished! The gate to the underground train was just closing. Still, metal was clattering as the old man fumbled and fell about, his white coat now splattered with red. The monitors played on, as a montage of children tied shoelaces, stood in line, worked at desks, put their hands up and combed their hair.

Israel grabbed the gun from Sanchez and fired two more shots at random, which brought parts of the ceiling down.

There were orphans everywhere and they made straight for the chairs. The struts and straps were undone, the bonds that held Millie were cut. Asilah had Anjoli in his arms and went to crush him to his chest, while Sanchez was lifting Millie and trying to embrace her.

'They're getting away!' she shouted. 'Get them!'

Anjoli spat the thumb from his mouth. It hit the floor and lay there like a slug.

Sanchez got his gun back and everyone raced towards the double-doors.

Chapter Forty-seven

Mr Jarman and Cuthbertson managed to flee before the lift doors were fully open – and that, no doubt, saved them being torn into pieces. They skidded on blood and glass, but stayed upright. Another tray of bottles and jars went skittering under their feet and a robot was knocked onto its back. Then they were out.

Which one of them slammed the door shut? It wouldn't have been Jarman because he was still groaning over his ruined hand, so it must have been the inspector. He even had the presence of mind – or the survival instinct – to whip out his key and lock it. Just in time: as the men paused to get their breath, they both heard the first smack of a child piling into it, smashing against it. Yes, the children were pounding after them. They concertina'd against each other and Sanchez fought for the space to level his gun. He feared a bullet would bounce off and maim the children around him, so he shouted for the grinder. It was burned out, so it was Henry again, who saved the day. He got the edge of a crowbar under the lock, and the children watched in amazement as metal peeled apart around the bending weapon. He exposed the lock and kicked hard.

Everyone spilled out into the tunnel, and there was the great flurry of sandy footprints, clear as an arrow: left turn.

The children ran like they'd never run, but the fugitives were too far ahead. Asilah was in the lead with Tomaz, zig-zagging right and left as the footprints – and the trail of blood – led them.

Jarman was getting weak. His run had become a drunken stagger and he was whimpering in pain. He'd wrapped his mutilated hand in a handkerchief, and that was now so wet and red it couldn't stem the flow. He stopped and leaned against the wall. The shock was taking hold too: he was shivering uncontrollably. He tore off his belt and wrapped it just above the elbow, pulling it so tight he gasped. 'Help me,' he shouted.

The inspector was in shock too and didn't respond. He'd run on ahead, but was cautious now, aware that he didn't know the route as well as Jarman. His career was flashing before his eyes. The suspension, the inquest . . . was it time to move to the back-up plan?

'My arm, Cuthbertson! I'm bleeding to death!' The inspector went back, and took some weight.

'They're behind us, they're following.'

'I don't know the way!'

'Please, go left! There's a staircase to the left . . .'

It was like some awful three-legged race, the crazy staggering waltz down the tunnel. They found the stairs, but it was a long climb. When they got to the iron door they could barely work the keys, and they could hear the children.

They staggered into the car park.

'Get me in. I can drive, if you get me in.' Jarman threw himself into the driving seat; he screamed again as his damaged hand fumbled with the controls.

Cuthbertson backed away. He had to take his chance and be very, very clever now. His own car was round the side of the building; Jarman could make it alone from here and had his own support structure. The engine revved; he heard the cries of children, and dived for the corner of the building.

Meanwhile, Jarman could hardly see for the pain. He reversed at such speed he lost control and smashed a tail-light on the wall, scraping one whole side and losing a mirror. The wheel spun between his hands and he cried out again, his thumb-stump burning, pulsing, bleeding until the wheel was sticky-wet and sliding between his fingers. Revving hard, he cannoned forward in a blizzard of gravel.

Tomaz was first into the car park, Asilah behind him. They just touched the bumper as the car turned. Asilah launched himself at the windscreen, glimpsing the terrified face of an old man, and was bounced off in a somersault. He landed, cat-like, on his feet and the rest of the children piled out into the car park behind him.

'It's her,' said Millie. 'She's him!'

'Shut up, Ruskin!' said Professor Worthingon. 'I was a semi-professional driver! I drove for seven years—'

'All I meant was—'

'Three years on the rally circuit, four on the track: so don't give me advice about driving.'

'No, I was just observing the speedometer—'

'Get your belts on if you have them; brace yourselves if you don't. Get that gear stowed under the seats, Vijay. Why didn't you come to me, you *stupid* boys?'

They'd reached sixty miles an hour. She'd heard the boys' garbled stories as they set off, and she didn't try to understand. Enough details rang with truth. The fire. The endless measuring, the pills and the sacking that the headmaster had referred to. Memories of that chemical on Millie's face, a controlled substance she should have reported – meant to report – but when the child's skin responded to treatment, it slipped from her mind. More than anything, the fears and feelings of the past fortnight.

'Oh, my,' cried Ruskin. 'Lights up ahead, please slow down!'

'I recognise that vehicle,' said Professor Worthington. 'I'd say that was our friend, Miss Hazlitt.'

'You'd think there'd be a police car by now,' said Sam. 'She said she phoned some time ago.' As he spoke, a blue light flashed from round the side of the building.

'There you are, Sam!' said Ruskin. 'Professor Worthington, how fast are we going?'

'Fast,' said the professor. 'But not fast enough. Come on, come on . . .'

She had her head down and knew the van couldn't last much longer. It was time to do something drastic. Memories of the track in South London: if she went for the broadside, then flipped her tail around she could block the Landcruiser before it left the courtyard. The driver had misjudged the exit and was reversing again. She could see children around the headlights, so the driver was panicking badly, maybe she'd stalled? Every second counted now.

'Honestly, I'd slow down. Captain Routon said the brakes on this thing are—'

'Shut up and brace.'

Ruskin said, 'I really think we should slow down. I'm not one to—'

'I'm going to ram her. They're getting away, and I'm taking the near-side. Brace, everybody! Here we go! Brace!'

Jarman saw the van coming, but couldn't believe it would hit. He'd manoeuvred out of the little parking area and was coming round the front of the school aiming for the drive. He was aware of a blue, flashing light; he was aware of children, and stones or fists hitting the car. Now he'd missed the exit because of the vehicle coming at him, the full-beam of its headlights blinding his tired old eyes. It wasn't going to stop. In slow motion it swerved, and its rear end came round like a hammer. Jarman jabbed the throttle in the nick of time, otherwise he would have been crushed where he sat. His Landcruiser leaped and Professor Worthington spun a full circle. She caught the other vehicle a glancing blow, tearing the bumpers off and smashing the other tail-light. Then the van crunched up onto the fountain and came to rest on the great marble surround, front wheels spinning in the air.

None of the children were wearing seat-belts, but at least most had braced themselves.

Sam hadn't. He was flung against the windscreen and his forehead shattered the glass. As the van reared up, he was dropped back into his seat, eyeballs bobbling. The horn was jammed on. Professor Worthington was trying to find reverse gear, but the whole chassis was wedged.

'Sam!' yelled Ruskin. 'Oh, my goodness – not again!'

The words boomed as in an aquarium. There were hands pressing in on him, the doors were yanked open. He saw Sanchez, Millie, Asilah, Anjoli . . . all his friends were there, lifting him out while other voices yelled, 'He's getting away!'

'We're stuck, we're stuck!'

'Get in!'

Tomaz leaped into the front seat and he pressed his foot onto Professor Worthington's. Her cries were lost in the din. Sanchez had dived in, trying to reload his gun. Bullets scattered on the floor. Yet again, it was Henry who saved them. He got under the front wheels and lifted. He sidestepped and threw the van, which crunched with every shock-absorber and spring onto the gravel, the glass bursting out. There was just time for him to grab the door and jump, because Professor Worthington was throwing the van in a tight circle, to resume a limping chase.

'Follow him, follow him!'

More children were leaping on. The back doors were open, so everyone dived in and Sam was rolled onto the floor. The van had a roof rack: children hauled themselves up onto it,

Millie and Anjoli clambering to the front and sitting, clasped together.

A police car was overtaking them, siren wailing, the driver's arm waving from the window, the *Stop* sign shining bright red over the boot. Professor Worthington ignored it.

'Go, go, go!'

She jammed her foot down and Ruskin got a leg through and slammed his foot on top, to be joined by Tomaz again: three drivers and they were off again, their chassis dragging sparks from the tarmac.

'He's turned off his lights,' said Sanchez. 'I can see the car though. Dead ahead, keep going.' His gun was loaded and he managed to get an arm through the shattered windscreen. He shot once, wildly, hoping it would frighten the driver into stalling.

'What's that police car doing?' yelled Millie. 'Go round it, go *round!*'

Cuthbertson had got his vehicle onto the driveway, well ahead, and sat there with lights flashing. His siren was wailing; he could see the van swerving towards him in his mirror, so he opened his door and moved into the centre of the road. He raised his hand, palm flat and stared bravely into the lights. The van smashed past him, tearing the door from its hinges. He watched in disbelief as it bounced across the lawns. He was aware of cheering and then the stink of a burning engine.

'We're going to kill him,' said Asilah. 'I want to kill him, myself, just me! Give me the gun!'

'No!'

'Come on! Faster, faster!'

The boys on the roof were pounding the metal, but everyone was aware of the clouds of smoke billowing from exhaust and bonnet.

'Where is she?' said Professor Worthington.

'It's a him,' said Tomaz. The dashboard gauges could rise no higher – the radiator was still in the fountain, and the oil sump had been ripped out. The engine was melting under her.

'Faster, please,' said Asilah, quietly. 'We'll get him. I want the head, I want the heart . . .'

The bus was losing speed. The vehicle was disintegrating and any bolt not welded for ever in the furnace of metal was shaking loose or sheering off. An off-side front tyre had burst, so the metal rim was rasping. They reached the phone box and the steering went. They hit it hard and the engine simply seized. As the panes of glass burst and the telephone swung, a new set of headlights came round the corner.

The headmaster pulled up gingerly, handbrake on. His interior heater had broken some time ago, so he was wrapped in an overcoat, gloves and hat. He wound down the window, paler than frost: 'Boys. What on earth's going on?'

His door was opening. So were the others. Hands were lifting him and there were children on the bonnet. His little car was rocking and he didn't know who to look at, or who to talk to.

'Move, Giles – get out of the way!'

'Professor Worthington . . .'

Hands were picking up his car. It was turning, like a boat upon the sea. He was facing the opposite direction.

'Go!' shouted the children.

'But what are we doing? Where are Millie and Anjoli?'

'Here, Giles, on the roof. Move over.'

Professor Worthington revved hard and checked the wing-mirrors. Boys were still clambering, she had to wait another few seconds. Sam was being carried and packed neatly in the boot. Then hands were drumming and the chant started: 'Go! Go! Go!'

'What's happened, Clarissa? There's a police car back there . . .'

'Now's not the time, Headmaster – it's got incredibly complicated. Trust me, we know *exactly* what we're doing. Hold on, everybody!'

First gear into second. The car wobbled along at fifteen miles per hour and she knew she'd be lucky to sustain that. This chassis was also scraping the road, but they were moving . . . twenty miles per hour. She saw the Landcruiser in the distance, accelerating away towards the school gates.

Chapter Forty-eight

Of course, Jarman did not know that his exit was sealed. Numb with pain, he concentrated only on losing the lights behind. His cellphone bleeped, and answering it was so hard, he moaned with the pain. It was Cuthbertson.

'I'll try and hold cars off you; that's about all I can do.'

'I'm nearly at the gates,' rasped the old man.

'They're still in pursuit. I've never seen anything like it. Get on the road, and get clear.'

'I'll aim for Bristol, can you radio London?'

'Too dangerous, it's police frequency. You're better getting off the road and calling yourself. I've got to think, there's no way I can—'

'I can't do anything, Cuthbertson! He's ruined my hand! Scupper the lab, scupper me. Now, before anyone goes down there—'

'They'll be doing that now, sir, you can guarantee it!'

'Cuthbertson, the gates are closed. Why are the gates closed? Cuthbertson, help me!'

The inspector hung up and closed his eyes. *Blunder through*, he said to himself. *Brave it out and blunder on*. An urgent voice, a desperate voice was needed. Keep it crisp though: urgent, but efficient. He reached for his radio. 'Charlie-yankee, one-zero.'

The click of static. 'One-zero, go ahead.'

More urgent, with a note of fear – fear for children at risk: 'Cuthbertson, here, reporting. Priority, please.'

'Thought you were on leave, sir – priority's yours.'

'Undercover and requesting assistance. Major incident, Ribblestrop Towers; request immediate back-up, all available units.'

'Roger. Confirm Ribblestrop, that's the school, sir? Over.'

'Ribblestrop Towers, we've had attempted kidnap, suspects have flown, are heading to the B3022 – units towards. Children at risk, repeat, *children at risk*.'

'Confirm details, sir: suspects have children with them?'

'No, I've rescued the child. I am in pursuit, but unit damaged – requesting units towards.'

'Understood.'

Inspector Cuthbertson drove slowly up the drive.

Jarman was nearly defeated. The school gates were shut, which was insane because he knew they usually stayed open day and night. With his hand in the condition it was, he wondered if he could swing them back, but he staggered out of the Landcruiser, determined to try. That's when he saw the chain, shiny and black in the headlights. When he went to untangle it, he saw the welds. He pulled at them with his one good hand and moaned with disbelief, falling against them. Clearly, they would never move. Panic beat around his head, the pain was making him drunk and faint. 'Think fast,' he muttered. 'Stay ahead, stay ahead of them.'

He got back in the car and did a quick three-point turn. His thumb had settled into a deep, sickening throb which went right up to his shoulder, but he was learning how to avoid disturbing the wound. So lucky he had a sturdy car and a tank full of petrol. Anyway, the road ahead was going to be full of children – and they had a gun.

He came over the rise, beam up full, and saw the headmaster's car crawling towards him. It was a parade-day stunt, it had to be – either that or an hallucination. How many children can you fit on a car and still drive? The acrobat team of Ribblestrop Towers, the human pyramid on wheels . . .

He laughed again and suddenly there was a bullet-hole in his windscreen. He heard only the mildest snap, but a silvery web of cracks spread all across his vision. A hole had been drilled straight through the glass, and freezing air was rushing in. The bullet had missed, gone straight past his head: but the next one wouldn't!

He heaved the steering wheel right, then left, and his thumb jarred again on the spokes of the wheel making him sob with pain. The Landcruiser rocked horribly as if waves had picked him up to capsize him. He was bumping over grassland and the low branches of trees were whipping his vehicle.

Professor Worthington slowed down and eased gently off the tarmac too. She could see the Landcruiser bobbing madly, its headlights swaying through the wood. She drove to intercept it, but had to go slow. Some of the boys had jumped and were now running alongside her. They were moving faster than she, fanning out like a pack of hunting dogs. They ran like they'd never give up, as if the marathon had only just started. In fact, when she looked around, she saw that it wasn't just *some* children – *everyone* had deserted. Only she and the headmaster remained bunched into the front seats: the boot and every door stood open, and one of them now smacked against a rock and slammed shut.

The two adults huddled together.

'How did you get in, Giles? The gates were sealed.'

'I came through Mr Johnson's farm. Who sealed them?'

'Our children.'

'Oh. What happened to Miss Hazlitt?'

'That's who we're chasing. But I think she's a he.'

*

367

Jarman was lost. There was a ditch and next to that a barbed-wire fence. His off-side wheel dropped and he knew he was in the ditch, stranded. No he wasn't! Fool, he hadn't even been in four-wheel-drive! He snapped the transmission and the whole vehicle lurched up with a new strength. Foot pressed hard down in first gear, he was away again, sobbing and laughing, the sweat running into his eyes. The trees opened into a bit of park, so he fought the wheel and lurched into it. Then, by pure miracle, he swung round again over a hillock and his tyres found a track. It was stony and rough, like a farm track: he got into second gear and zoomed up to fifteen, twenty miles per hour. But, oh! The little car was on his tail again, its headlights locked onto his mirror.

The track led deep into trees, his speed climbed, and suddenly he knew just where he was. He could have sung! He could have cried out! It was the track to the signal-man's hut. Of course it was, he knew this part of the park after all, and had his bearings.

'The old road,' he muttered. 'We can do it. It's through the tunnel, and you're out. There's no gate, they can't have blocked a train tunnel!'

The Landcruiser gathered speed, faster and faster. The engine sounded sick and there were noises he'd never heard before, but he was on his way. There were no lights in the mirror now and he realised he must be a good ninety seconds ahead of them. And that was all the time he needed, because once in the tunnel he'd be on the smugglers' route, the one old Cyril and all the Vyners before him had used so successfully. He was at the north entry; all he had to do was drive through the tunnel, and at the far end – the north end – he'd pick up the B3113, which led – if you took two lefts and a right – to a sleepy little village called Ringsbury. The old Bristol Road. He could hide out there, make a call, and London would send a car and a doctor. They'd do that fast and fly him out. There was so much at stake.

'You can do it!' he muttered. 'There's the tunnel, on you go!'

He eased towards the rails and butted against them. In a moment, a front wheel was over and he was turning. He nudged the throttle and felt the steady bumping of the sleepers. It was past three o'clock in the morning so there was no fear of trains. He decided to stay in a sensible low gear. The tunnel was less than half a mile: in minutes he'd be safe. His headlights revealed the beautiful brickwork and the metal tracks stretched away to vanishing point. Then he braked, and rolled to a stop.

By coincidence, he was at the exact spot that the children had reached when they'd been exploring, all those months ago. It was the site of the smugglers' pit and it was wide open. To drive over it would be tricky. He could see light from underground; he could see the stone steps leading downwards. Cuthbertson had sealed it shut – yet here it was, yawning open.

More surprisingly, and more worryingly, there appeared to be a man climbing up the steps. It was an elderly gentleman, and he was wearing black evening dress. Jarman could see him rising up out of the pit, the headlights picking out every detail. First his head, then his shoulders, and now his chest, rising slowly. He was carrying a tea-tray. Jarman let the engine idle. He was blinking and blinking, but the hallucination wouldn't go away. The man walked on, into the headlights, and got brighter and brighter. Up close there was no doubt about it at all – it was Cyril Vyner. He wasn't dead, he was standing there large as life. But half his head was missing.

'I shot you,' whispered Jarman.

The old ghost was staring with his one remaining eye. He smiled and licked his lips, as if about to speak. Jarman sat there, stunned, and the seconds passed. The two old men looked at one another through the buckled windscreen.

'I shot you,' whispered Jarman, again. 'You're dead.'

The ghost looked at him and its sad mouth twitched and twisted. The lips stretched, and it was as if the poor thing was smiling. But Jarman's eyes were blinking again, because he was becoming aware of a new and terrible light, sweeping towards him. It was accompanied by the most awful sound. There was a vibration, too, and it was making the whole car tremble. Cyril Vyner's ghost didn't move. Behind him, shadows were curling on the tunnel walls. The noise was building faster and faster – a sound of thunder boiling down the tunnel. The light got mercilessly bright and a headlamp appeared, so white it scalded your retina. It was brighter than the sun and, as it raced towards Jarman, it seemed to him that the ghost of Lord Vyner simply burst into flames and was gone. Was that possible? Or was it simply the impact of the speeding train and the subsequent explosion of fuel?

Chapter Forty-nine

Had you been in the cab of the seriously delayed 20.05 *Queen of Devonia* from London Paddington to Penzance, you would have heard the following conversation:

'Hello, Arthur. Everything alright?'

'No, Darren. There's a lot of very unhappy people back there tonight and they seem to think it's my fault.'

'Well, we've lost hours.'

'I've had the same conversation again and again. I've told them, there'll be taxis at St Austell. We've dished out tea and coffee, and I've said it's nobody's fault – these things happen!'

'Though, technically, Arthur, if you do want to point the finger of blame it has to be at that couple in the car. He was admitting it, he was reaching for a wretched map.'

'I realise that, but an accident's an accident. You can't blame an old boy for getting confused. What worries me is how a little vehicle like that breaks through the fencing and ends up on the track.'

'Now we're getting to it, aren't we? We've lost men on maintenance, we've lost men on signalling. Ten years ago – no, five years ago – this wouldn't have happened. I tell you, there are accidents waiting to happen round every bend. He wasn't hurt, was he?'

'More in shock than anything else. You did a very nice stop, Darren, I hope that's acknowledged.'

'I was taking it easy, actually, because we'd come through Reading a bit quicker than usual. It's lucky that's a straight bit of line.'

'Very lucky. Blow your whistle, mate.'

'You do it, will you? It's above your head. I can get a bit of speed up here, make up a bit of lost time.'

'Sixty-five's the limit.'

'I think we can risk a bit more than that . . . This is the Ribblestrop Pass again.'

'I know where we are. I wasn't going to mention it.'

'I've put it behind me, Arthur. I had two weeks' leave over it and the wife was very good. Her attitude is if it happens once, it won't happen again – lightning doesn't strike twice. Gave me time to sort the garden out as well.'

'Careful, Darren, you're touching ninety . . .'

'Let's get these people home, Arthur!'

'What's that light?'

'Where?'

'There's two. Two lights.'

'I don't know.'

'Slow down a bit.'

'I am.'

'It's a car.'

'It can't be.'

'Darren, it's a bloody car, it's a car in the tunnel! And a man!'

The children heard the devastating crunch and saw the fireball. They too had found the track, so they'd piled back onto the headmaster's car, and Professor Worthington had nosed it carefully forward in pursuit. Alas, they'd had a flat tyre within sight of the train-tracks and, having no jack in the boot, there'd been no way of changing the wheel and continuing the chase. They had sat on the roof and bonnet, rather forlorn, Anjoli in the arms of his brothers, cousins, uncles and friends. Israel had just started to sing a song – one he'd learned from a Himalayan Nomad celebrating the birth of a new llama – and it had a rousing chorus. The children were just joining in when the wreckage burst from the tunnel and passed them at about sixty miles per hour.

'Wow!' said Sam. 'I just saw colours! That blow on the head's cleared my vision.'

Ruskin was next to him. 'It often works that way,' he said. 'A bang on the head's a cure for a lot of things. My father swears by it.'

They sat there, transfixed. The blazing vehicle sent up gouts of black smoke. Soon there was a minor forest-fire. They could hear the muffled cries of train passengers. Then, from behind, lumbering carefully down the track, came a flashing blue light and the moan of a siren.

The white police car pulled up by the headmaster's tail-lights, and a purposeful, desperate-looking man climbed through a non-existent door. He panted up to the headmaster.

'Thank goodness I've found you, sir. Is everyone accounted for?' Inspector Cuthbertson bristled with concern. His face was wracked by worry, but there was a grim professionalism there too: he was a man with a job to do. 'I've got a fire crew at the gates, ambulances on their way. Is everyone safe here?'

'I think so, Inspector.'

'Then I want you to get them back to the school, sir. I've uncovered a very shocking plot. Get all the kids back to school, and do a roll-call. We must not expose them to further risk.' He moved down towards the track. You could hear the static of his radio. 'Come in, control. Charlie-yankee, one-zero: priority, please. The kids are safe, repeat *kids are safe*. We need all ambulances, all fire-crews. Major incident, Ribblestrop Pass. Looks like an Intercity 125, in collision – repeat, *in collision*. I want helicopters, I want hospitals on stand-by, multiple casualties expected.'

There was a burst of urgent crackling.

'Yes, I am *alone* at the scene. I'm going to attempt rescue and first aid, I'm going in.'

'Inspector, this is control – please await support!'

'Negative, control – lives to be saved. Over and out.'

Within fifteen minutes, a police helicopter was hanging low over the school, its searchlight trained on the disaster. Luckily for Inspector Cuthbertson, there was a pregnant woman in carriage four, and when she went into early labour, he was able to assist with the safe delivery of her child.

He was quite a hero.

As for Jarman, four hundred and seventy tonnes of speeding train had shovelled his Landcruiser back down the line at eighty-three miles per hour. The driver had brought the wreckage to a halt in less than a mile. But could the old man be identified? He hadn't been to a dentist for years, so there were no dental records. In any case, only three teeth were ever found.

Epilogue

I

The next few days were spent among swarms of police, detectives, TV camera crews, security guards, men in suits and sightseers. The train smash was big news. Helicopters came and went, and the driveway was jammed with vehicles. Tents were erected over the site and teams of engineers spent days in the tunnels with cutting equipment. The school car park was roped off, and the children watched as bits of door and lift were brought up and laid on the lawn. They waited to see bits of the laboratory and the big black chair, which Anjoli had claimed for the orphans' dormitory. It never appeared. Nor did the robots, which Sam wanted. They'd have to be content with George, the only survivor.

Anjoli and Millie went to the ventilation shaft, hoping to get down to take a look, hoping to get involved. The area was cordoned off. A truck and a JCB were at work, filling the hole with rock and concrete. They had better luck through Neptune, but when they got close to the lab, they found a brick wall had been constructed from the floor to the ceiling. *Government Property*, read a notice. *Strictly Private*.

One of the saddest things was the removal of the red phone box and the filling of the shaft under that. Millie watched them take it away, thinking how it had saved her life. Lady Vyner was furious and put in a massive claim for compensation. This claim was honoured within twenty-four hours and she stopped complaining.

The headmaster hardly left his office. The phone rang incessantly and there were so many visitors. He assumed he would be sacked, but wondered who was going to sack him. Ribblestrop had no Board of Governors. He couldn't be fired, except (he assumed) by the government department that Miss Hazlitt had worked for. He looked through the contract he'd signed and was amazed at how many powers he'd accidentally given away. But when he phoned the department he'd once dealt with, whoever answered found it hard to recall the school's existence or find any previous correspondence. He was assured that no government department had ever officially been interested in or involved with Ribblestrop Towers; no application for a licence had been made, because his school was exempt from the legislation that department handled . . . and he was asked to stop calling.

Then he reminded himself that the Hazlitt 'woman' – or the man, this Jarman – had been *imposed* on him. He phoned again, determined to speak to a manager. But the office he'd once dealt with had suddenly had its phones disconnected. In a strange way, it was as if she or he or whatever it was, had never existed.

He waited to be arrested.

He waited for Inspector Cuthbertson. Inspector Cuthbertson appeared only once at Ribblestrop Towers, and then very briefly for a photo-shoot. He had appeared in national newspapers, the hero of the train disaster. It turned out that the pregnant woman had been a minor celebrity, and there were photos of him carrying her to safety. His grinning face even appeared next to the newborn baby's, and it was predicted that he would be a god-father. The children didn't see him again and there was a rumour he was taking a few weeks' leave.

Everyone got used to big black cars and important-looking people, but one Friday morning a little convoy arrived. A man in a soft trilby, pulled low over his eyebrows, slid quietly into the headmaster's office. He wore a thick moustache and a heavy overcoat. He brought two secretaries, a bodyguard, and a special dog. A great deal of time was spent setting up some kind of satellite telephone, and then a video screen so that a man in a grey suit could be part of the conference. The first man didn't explain exactly who he was and his business card had only a number. He was quietly spoken and had immaculate manners; he seemed to enjoy listening rather than speaking. But after some time and a great deal of nodding, he leaned forward and presented the headmaster with a cheque.

'This is a little gesture, old boy,' he said. 'Call it an investment in your *infrastructure*. We feel . . . the powers-that-be feel, that you have been pretty badly inconvenienced. It's important we anticipate and go beyond any claim for damages, were you to make one – you'll find the settlement is more than generous. Were you to sue for compensation, old chap . . .' The man leaned forward, and smiled. 'You would find that we were obliged to find *legal representation*; the case would be *vigorously* contested through a counter-prosecution, and all monies would be frozen pending the outcome of the case. The case would be lengthy, I'd say. Lengthy. Do you understand?'

'Not entirely,' said the headmaster.

Both secretaries were tapping furiously into their laptops and paused when he said that. A miniature printer squealed and papers uncoiled.

The man in grey on the screen said, 'What did he say?'

The headmaster said, 'I understand.'

The man with the cheque said, 'I am also empowered to

issue Ribblestrop Towers with a licence to continue trading . . .' Another sheet of paper was laid on the desk, stamped and signed. 'This is valid for a year; I just need you to sign *here* and *here*. The press has been briefed, so you'll find certain events are likely to be dealt with sensitively . . . all the lurid material about doctors under the ground . . . ha!' There was a thin smile under the moustache. 'The media have been encouraged to focus on the railway incident, where there's a bit more human interest. Oh, and I should just draw your attention to paragraph 14C – just there – clause two. We're urging you to confine any press statements to simple expressions of *relief*.'

'Certainly,' said the headmaster. 'I *am* relieved. What about Miss Hazlitt, though?'

'I don't understand your question, sir?'

'Miss Hazlitt. Mr Jarman. Would I be right in assuming that—'

'Questions about deceased persons heretofore employed would require notice. You would have to make *formal application* for any response to any such question. These matters are being investigated and it would be . . . unhelpful for me to comment in a forum such as this.'

'What about Cuthbertson?'

'He's in good shape, I believe. The Caribbean, in fact. Soaking up a bit of sun.'

'What's happened to him, though? It seems he was part of a . . . well, a *conspiracy*, though I hate to use the word.'

'No, no, no. Ohhhh, no. Undercover. Different thing entirely. Friend Cuthbertson has been commended. His work was exemplary and many lives were saved. He dealt with events in the most professional way and his work underground, as I understand it, was *bold*. Foolhardy, some would say – but that's what good policing is all about: a duty of care, the preservation of life must come first. He'll be honoured in due course, sir.' The gentleman paused. His eyes hadn't left the headmaster's and his voice had remained firm yet polite. 'Friend,' he said. 'I have to trouble you to make a decision. If I could have your signature *there*, and *there*?'

The headmaster looked at the size of the cheque. It was enough to pay off every debt he had ever incurred. He could put down another term's rent in advance. He could furnish the school, pay for at least two more teachers *and* throw a Christmas party. He sat quietly for a few seconds, looked at the eyes looking at him, and decided he had no more questions.

'Can I borrow your pen?'

The man's smile got broader. 'We have a recording of this conversation,' he said. 'And you have accepted the Crown's settlement. So that is your copy of my copy, and I think we're just about done. You will brief the children, won't you? Discourage anything lurid.'

Lessons had stopped, of course.

Whilst the headmaster dealt with officialdom, the children got into the habit of visiting Tomaz, via Neptune. Needless to say, his house astonished everyone. He cooked huge meals and nobody ever wanted to leave. A small dormitory had to be excavated and furnished. It was the only way to accommodate so many guests, and the work took several days. By the time the children were above ground again, the press and the police had gone.

Captain Routon returned after two weeks to a huge party. He was wheeled in, bandaged like a mummy. The children had pinned a black-and-gold banner to the mansion doors, which said, simply: *Welcome Home Our Hero*. It was an emotional reunion. They ate and drank and danced and sang, and when Caspar crept in wearing specially padded shorts and sat down to join them, nobody teased him.

Tomaz, in fact, now did most of the cooking. There was an emotional scene between him and the headmaster, but emotional scenes were happening several times a day. The boy was readmitted as a pupil, but with the special privilege of maintaining his own, private accommodation.

The return game with the High School was looming. When the big day arrived, the children were throbbing with excitement.

Captain Routon was wheeled to the headmaster's car. It was currently the only Ribblestrop vehicle.

The children changed in their dormitories. As they had no actual strip, it didn't take long. They threaded the black-and-gold tie of Ribblestrop through the belt loops of the grey shorts. They pulled their grey socks nice and high so that the cardboard shin-pads were secure, and they rolled their shirt-sleeves to the elbow. They had voted to forget lunch, because they were too excited. And anyway, they needed speed and adrenaline.

They set off early.

As the headmaster manoeuvred his car carefully onto the drive, a rather smart people carrier approached the other way. Everyone was used to sight-seers by now, so nobody cared; as the headmaster inched round it, the singing started. The man at the wheel of the people carrier, however, seemed to want a conversation. He was elderly and nervous, and he wore a large surgical collar. So did his passenger. He was trying to wind the window down and his hand fluttered anxiously at the headmaster. After some time he found the switch of the electric window.

'This is Ribblestrop Towers, isn't it?' he said.

'Yes, it is. How can I help?'

'I don't know if you can, but I *hope* you can. This is the *school*, isn't it? Ribblestrop?'

'Yes.'

'It's our first visit, you see. Our son attends this school, in the first year . . .'

'Dad!' yelled Sam.

Sam was curled up on the parcel-shelf above the car boot. He had his face pressed to the side window and, though it was steamy, he could just see out. He'd also heard that distinctive voice.

'It's my dad!' he shouted.

Mr Tack didn't hear. 'It's all a bit of a long story,' said the man. 'We've been recuperating after a car accident and the last thing we wanted was to worry the boy. Thing is, though, we haven't seen him for a while, and just wondered . . .'

Sam had now crawled over Ruskin's head and the shoulders of four orphans. He managed to get his nose through the window over the headmaster's arm. 'Dad!' he cried. 'I'm here!'

'Hello, Sam!'

'You're just in time!'

'Time for what?'

'You're just in time for the football. How did you know?'

'We thought we'd missed it . . .'

'Hello, darling!' said Mrs Tack. She had leaned across her husband and she found her voice was wobbling. She couldn't see all of him, but it was definitely her Sam. She had promised herself all day that on no account would she cry or embarrass her son, but here he was and her eyes were swimming in tears, because he looked just the same. A rather unorthodox haircut, but fashions were forever changing. It was, however, the same little lad she'd waved off from Paddington Station all those weeks ago, and he was *radiant* with happiness.

'Mum, can you take the team?'

'What do you mean? Take them where?'

'What happened to your neck?'

'Oh, Lord, that's a long story. You know me and your mum, if it's not one thing it's another. We had a bump on the motorway, and—'

'This is so lucky! Can you get us all in?'

381

'Where are we going?'

'Millie has directions. Millie – get in the front! Can we talk a bit later?'

Within seconds, the headmaster's car was abandoned, and the Tacks' vehicle was brimming with Ribblestrop players. Mr Tack executed a nine-point turn on the drive, and it was full steam ahead for the High School Sports Centre.

II

The High School for Boys was just outside the sleepy town of Ribblestrop. It had been built on an expanse of wasteland and, as you approached, it looked rather like a nuclear power station set in three acres of crumbling army barracks. A high wire fence surrounded it and a man on the gate waved them through, radioing ahead.

The Tacks had got lost, partly due to Millie's erratic directions, so it was lucky they'd set off so early. The Ribblestrop team rolled in just before kick-off.

Another security officer pointed out the road towards 'Recreational Facilities', and radioed ahead. The vehicles trundled round a bend and you could see the pitches laid out below.

The floodlights were on already, it being a dull afternoon. A vast crowd had gathered, surrounding the grass and turning it into an arena. Two thousand? Three thousand perhaps. You could hear their singing, but as the van appeared it rose into an ecstasy of whistling. The High School for Boys had invited the High School for Girls, and they were all corralled together behind high, chain-link fences. Teachers patrolled the touchline nervously as the whistling turned to a monstrous baying.

'Don't be intimidated,' said Ruskin.

'We are the better side,' said Millie.

An official with an Alsatian beckoned the Ribblestrop vehicles onto the pitch and advised the drivers where to park for a quick exit. The children piled out with their one football and spread out towards the furthest goal. The noise of the crowd made conversation difficult. The children kept their heads down, aware that green banners were being unfurled, and they were marooned in a sea of green scarves and painted faces. The pitch was rock hard. A million boots had worn it to brown dust. It was more suited to Christians and lions than to soccer.

'I want a clean game,' said Harry Cuthbertson. The two captains looked at him. 'This is not to be a grudge match, alright?'

'Tails,' said Millie.

'Remember, Darren. We've got a man from Highbury coming down next term, that's the only reason we're keeping this fixture. Fitness training, this is.' He said to Millie, 'This lad'll turn pro, when he leaves us.'

'How's your brother?' said Millie.

'Good. He's looking forward to seeing you. Unfinished business, apparently.'

'Tell him I'll be waiting.'

'You know he's Deputy Chief-Constable, do you? It was announced yesterday.'

'Yes, I heard,' said Millie. 'What I really want to know is who's more bent? You as a ref, or him as a copper?'

Harry Cuthbertson went so red and stiff he couldn't toss the coin. He gave kick-off to the High School and blew his whistle hard and long. Darren clipped the ball forward and there was a tumultuous roar from the crowd that seemed to lift the very dust; it was like playing in a gale. The Ribblestrop players stared at one another in fear. All around the ground, the metal fence was being picked up and shaken. It was the sound of chains rattling.

The High School were on the offensive fast, and their tactics hadn't changed. The boys weren't quick, but they were powerful and hard, and tackling them was always going to be dangerous. The Ribblestrop team were brave but skittish, and concentration in the din of howling was almost impossible. Everyone was remembering the cruel tackles of the last meeting, and it was clear that the first ten minutes were going to be the hardest.

The penalty, when it came, was outrageous. Cuthbertson was in the right place to see what happened, so his decision was cynical and absurd. Henry had moved in firmly, as a High School player tried to break. Henry played the ball; the other lad went down in a theatrical stage-dive, throwing his arms in the air and somersaulting twice. A hurricane of screams and whistles came from all sides, so intense that the referee's own whistle was inaudible. It was the ref's decisive pointing at the penalty spot that confirmed the unbelievable decision. The dive had taken place a good two metres outside the penalty area, but Cuthbertson yellow-carded Henry, and simply walked through the scrum of protesting Ribblestrop players and planted the ball on the penalty spot.

In the visitors' box, which was a small concrete bunker halfway down one side of the pitch, Mr Tack was aghast. Captain Routon – whose face was red anyway due to the blistering – had turned a frightening plum colour.

Sanchez bounced on the goal-line.

The High School captain backed off for the kick. He had a smug smile on his misshapen face, which turned into a glare as he prepared to run. Sanchez didn't see the ball as it smashed into the top left-hand corner of his goal. He didn't even move.

The crowd noise turned into a jet-engine during take-off. One of the metal fence panels was breached, and there was a brief pitch invasion before a handful of hardy teachers linked arms and filled the gap. As Ribblestrop kicked off, it was as if the ground had tilted and they were playing uphill in a tornado.

Five minutes later, Millie was tackled from behind several seconds after she'd passed the ball. Her shoe was torn off in the assault, and she spent five minutes on her back. Her sock was soaked red, but no foul was given.

Just before half-time Asilah was sent off because the ball hit his arm: handball. Sanjay, Sam and Israel all had black eyes from off-the-ball encounters; Vijay had been hit by something – he hadn't seen the missile, but his forehead was cut. Anjoli's shirt was in shreds. The Ribblestrop tempers were bursting; the crowd was baying with glee.

'You can see his tactics,' said Captain Routon at half-time. His voice was hoarse with rage. 'I gave him the benefit of the doubt last time, but this is outrageous!'

Ruskin said, 'I'm going to write a letter. This will not go unchallenged.'

Millie had her head in her hands. She said, 'The thing is, they're so useless! Every move they make is so blindingly obvious, we're ten times more skilful.'

'It's still one-nil,' said Asilah, bitterly.

'What can we do?' said Sanchez. 'Shall we push Henry forward?'

'No, he's much better in defence.'

'We've lost Asilah, though! We've got to do something.'

'Can I say something?' said Mr Tack.

Everyone looked at Sam's father.

'Certainly,' said Routon.

Mr Tack and his wife were sitting in a couple of canvas chairs. They had ham sandwiches and a flask of tea, all of which was being passed among the starving Ribblestrop team, as no refreshments had been offered.

'I don't want to intrude,' he said, 'and I certainly don't want to pretend I have any special skill in this area. But I've seen Sam play a fair bit, and that little chap – what's your name, son?'

'Anjoli,' said everyone.

'He and Sam are working together like a dream.'

'That's true,' said Routon. Anjoli grinned.

386

'If I were you,' continued Mr Tack, 'I'd change your attack and do the unexpected. Sam has a rather stylish touch with his head, and I have a feeling it's a secret weapon. The last things those lads are expecting is aerial bombardment – you've been keeping it so low. What's your name, my dear?'

'Millie,' said everyone.

'You have a *superb* touch when it comes to passing. Instead of trying to get too far forward, I'd push it out to either Sam or Anjoli. Let them play the wings a bit more. Then, depending on who's clear, if you feed it to Sam, he'll cross to Anjoli. If you get it to Anjoli—'

'I cross to Sam,' said Anjoli.

'Try it,' said Millie. 'I'm happy.'

'But you'll have to make space, boys. Then it's hard crosses. Treat them like shots and get them in the goal-mouth. Oh, and – last thing – remember to keep them high. Both you boys can jump, so keep the ball *high*. Their full-backs are as slow as old tanks.'

The Ribblestrop team trotted out with a new sense of purpose. Unfortunately, so did the High School. They wanted three-nil. Darren wanted his hat-trick because it was quite true, a spotter from Arsenal had accepted an invitation for a fixture next term, and would be looking at his score-sheet.

After five minutes, the whole crowd started to sing, 'Easy! Easy!' Encouraged, the High School forwards hacked into the defence. Henry caught an elbow in the throat, and was brought down hard and dirtily five minutes later, stud marks up his calf. He was dazed and bloody, but no fouls were given. They were getting through to Sanchez too: the shots were piling in and the boy rolled and dived, punching the ball clear again and again. The ball seemed permanently in the Ribblestrop half; it was corner after corner.

Looking back at the game, the felling of Henry was the turning point. The High School players were so thrilled to see the Ribblestrop giant on his back that they relaxed. Even the defenders came forward, confident that the opposition defence was broken.

The ball fell in no-man's-land, and Millie won possession with a neat little sliding manoeuvre. She then tricked the ball to Ruskin, who tripped over it, so it fell nicely for Podma. He had the one technique: the forward pass, which he'd been working on every day for the fortnight. He found Sam, who was through before the defenders were aware of the attack. Anjoli was on his left, so he punted the ball right and leaped the lethal swinging foot that tried to chop him down. He steamed elegantly forward and once again the ball seemed to hang in the air asking to be smashed. He booted it as hard as he could and high, just as his father had advised. Anjoli was there in the goal-mouth; he leaped like a salmon and reached twice his own height, a blur of ragged shirt and flying hair. His head snapped at the ball and swatted it down. The goalie was beaten and the crowd were stunned into silence.

One-one.

It was even again. The silence on the pitch was like deafness. Darren looked bewildered but the Ribblestrop players simply trotted back to position, as if they wanted only to press on. Of course, the High School boys reacted. Of course, they were enraged. But the Ribblestrop boys were well versed in dealing with that, and with an even score they were inspired. For the first time they were able to ignore the screaming, jeering crowd. The noise seemed not to matter. There was a new determination, razor sharp. All the passing practice had paid off. They kept the ball moving and, as the High School tired and slowed, Ribblestrop got faster and more dangerous. Yes, they missed Asilah, for Millie could not complete the elegant triangles he'd been part of, she just couldn't run as fast. But the tactic suggested in the interval was a good one, and the High School boys seemed too stupid to anticipate. She kept on moving the ball up to Sam or Anjoli, and it kept getting through.

With ten minutes to go, they had their chance. This time it was Henry sweeping up to Ruskin. Ruskin lunged bravely for his heaviest kick of the game: the ball bounced through his legs and fell perfectly for Millie. Ruskin shrieked for the return pass and ran forward, arms waving. Millie saw him but tweaked it out to Anjoli, who was way over on the left. He danced it round a defender and brought it inside. Sam's father was shouting, 'Shoot!' The headmaster was roaring. Professor Worthington and Mrs Tack were in each other's arms, and Captain Routon was out of his wheelchair, his bandages unfurling. Ruskin made for the six-yard-box, still calling and calling . . .

Was it a shot, or a cross?

It was probably both. Anjoli took Mr Tack's advice again, and smacked the ball hard and high, just like a shot. Sam, like an arrow from a bow, simply flew: he was a mixture of javelin and cat, and he headed the ball hard. Physics took over. The ball slammed into the goalkeeper's elbows and it ricocheted hard to the ground. A defender swept it away in a half-volley, brutally hard, and the ball caught the still-running Ruskin – two metres from the goal – full in the face. His spectacles disintegrated, but the ball rebounded straight and unstoppable into the top left-hand corner of the net.

Two-one.

Ruskin knelt in the mud, utterly bewildered. He was carried off the pitch shoulder high, laid in the recovery position by the Ribblestrop teachers, and quickly subbed. Onto the pitch ran Tomaz, representing his school for the first time. Ribblestrop wanted three, and the High School needed the equaliser. The next goal would be crucial and there was no time to look after the injured.

It all started with Sanchez.

He kicked longer and deeper; Vijay crossed to Millie. Millie was desperate to score and saw at once her opening. She so didn't want to pass. Anjoli had scored and so had Ruskin: it was her right. She feigned a shot and the goalie went left. A High School defender got to the goal-line, closing down the angle. It was almost impossible. Almost, but there was some slim chance, if she could drive it into the top corner – a voice in her head was screaming, *shoot*!

Weeks ago, she would have shot. But this time, she passed.

It was a skilful little flick and it found Anjoli, who took it like a pro. He flipped it sideways and booted it hard and high; there was Sam, rising by the far post, a bald torpedo of a boy climbing higher and higher, way above the bar. He connected. He nodded it down and the High School were beaten. The goal-net swished again, and it was three-one to Ribblestrop.

'They've done it,' whispered the headmaster. The man was on his knees. Professor Worthington had her arms round him, and they were both crying. Harry Cuthbertson blew the final whistle five minutes early and the High School team walked shell-shocked from the field. Their supporters were open-mouthed and speechless. The Ribblestrop players were equally dazed.

The Head of High School Security had been alerted, and he reversed the Tacks' people carrier right up to the centre-line. As the children climbed in, Captain Routon touched every child's head; he couldn't shake hands because of the pain. He was crying too, and he could only squeak their names. As if to mark the miracle, there was a roll of biblical thunder, like the applause of a God – and a breeze washed over everyone.

Professor Worthington saw the first distant crackle of lightning and went rigid.

'Headmaster,' she said.

'Yes, my dear?'

The blood had drained from her face. 'Where's the car? The storm's early. I need to get back, quickly.'

The vehicles rolled out of the High School as the clouds rolled in.

III

Mr and Mrs Tack took Sam off for a cream tea in a local village, saying they'd return him later that evening. They would stay in a hotel for the night, and take him and Ruskin home tomorrow. Nobody had noticed that tomorrow really was the last day of term.

Millie and Sanchez ducked out of school supper. They left the hall quietly.

'You've got blood on your face,' said Millie.

It was late afternoon and the clouds were solid black. Thunder muttered all around the park.

'I know.'

'Why don't you wash it off? Is it your badge of glory?'

'Shut up, Millie.'

They walked in silence.

Sanchez said: 'They're sending a car for me in the morning. Heathrow Airport. I've got to be there at three.'

'Really?'

'It's all over, isn't it? Time to go home. I'd hardly realised it was . . . that time. Christmas.'

'Shall we go and see Neptune?'

They sauntered over the lawn together and watched the thunderclouds. As they got to the lake, the first raindrops fell like bullets.

'I've been burned,' said Millie. 'I've been frozen. I've been chased, I've been tied up and battered. They still can't get me.'

'Maybe you're immortal.'

'If I've got nine lives, I must have used about . . .'

'Nine,' they said together. And they laughed.

'Next time I'll be mashed,' said Millie. 'If there *is* a next time. The High School ref said I'd better watch my back next term.'

'Where will you be?' said Sanchez.

'Me? I'll be here. Where d'you think?'

There was a flash over the lake and an immediate peal of thunder. Sanchez smiled. 'I thought you hated it,' he said. 'I thought you were going back to London.'

'There are worse places,' said Millie. 'You've got to go somewhere.'

'True.'

Millie said, 'How long are the holidays? When are we going to meet next?'

'Four weeks. We have until the middle of January. I need a break! It's going to be so sunny, it's a perfect summer in Colombia. I was telling Tomaz – I wanted him to come, but he still hasn't got a passport. We were going to take a tent, just me and him. Take a stove, some steaks – we have a ranch so we get the best meat, and the horses are beautiful. It's wild country, Millie. You can ride all day and see maybe just a few Indians, right up into the snowline. He really wanted to see it.'

They were quiet for a moment. There was another bolt of lightning, and they saw this one fall: a neat fork, off in the woods. Neptune appeared in a mist of rain, so they sheltered under his shoulder.

Millie said: 'What was the scariest part, for you, looking back?'

'When we saw that doll in the chair.'

The lightning came again and lit the lake up as a dish of silver. The thunderclap seemed to burst from the woods all around.

'Are you scared now?'

'Now? No. I've been in some storms. The worst storm I ever saw was in Colombia—'

'I was scared in the wood, Sanchez. I was scared when Tomaz got me, I thought he was going to kill me. I was so scared looking for Anjoli. Creeping in, when just the candles were lit. Hearing her voice.'

'That woman was bad news. That man.'

'I was really scared when they were getting ready to drill him, but that was like a dream. That was the strangest part.' She licked her lips. 'I'm scared now.'

'Why? Lightning strikes trees or buildings. There's no way it'll touch us.'

'I'm not scared of that. I'm just scared.'

Sanchez sighed: 'I don't get you. You're about to have a holiday. Everything's fine, you should be happy! You're not scared of thunder, are you?'

Millie turned. She looked at the boy and said, quietly: 'Sanchez, what is wrong with you?'

'What?'

'Why are you so dim?'

'Sorry, I don't understand.'

'No. You don't. You never do.'

They stood in silence for a moment. Millie sighed. 'So go on. Tell me more about Colombia.'

'What do you want to know?'

'Oh, everything. How sunny it's going to be. How you and Tomaz are going to eat plums and go swimming in fresh, cool rivers and—'

'But we're not. He hasn't got a passport, so he can't travel.'

Millie shook her head. 'Forget it,' she said.

'What?'

'What!'

'What's wrong? Forget what?'

'You are such a swine!'

'I'm not, I don't—'

'Where do you think *I'll* be for Christmas?'

Sanchez frowned. 'I don't know.'

'Of course you don't,' said Millie. 'You haven't asked, have you? You have never asked me about my family, my home, or my life. You don't know anything about me.'

'No, I suppose it's not my business . . .'

'You just asked me if I was even coming back here. For all you know, this could be the last time we see each other.'

'Well, yes. But—'

'And you don't give a damn. You just asked me, "Where are you going next term?" You don't care!'

'Of course I do.'

'You don't. You don't care!'

'But, Millie, you just said you *are* coming back. So am I!'

'OK, listen: I don't know where I'm going for Christmas. My father's in Germany, alright? My mother's away somewhere, I don't even know where. I got a message from my dad saying to check into a hotel until he gets back.'

'Oh.'

They were silent again. Millie said quietly, 'I've got a passport. I'd like to come to Colombia with you. I was hoping you would ask.'

'I'm sorry, I didn't . . . think. I thought you'd have plans.' He was silent for a moment, and then he said, softly and formally: 'Millie. My father and I would be delighted if you were able to change your plans and maybe join us for Christmas, at our home. I can get a ticket at the airport. We could fly together.'

For the first time in a long time, Millie couldn't speak. Finally, she managed to whisper. 'I'll have to check,' she said. 'But I think that would be very nice.' She said something else as well, but her words were obliterated by a roll of thunder so loud the very earth seemed to tremble.

IV

Professor Worthington had not been popular when she demanded that everyone meet in the Tower of Science. The children were tired and they wanted to curl up in their dormitories and watch the storm. There was a Christmas party at eight and they wanted to rest their aching limbs before it. But they trooped up the winding stairs, obedient as ever.

When they reached the lab, the first thing they saw was a fine mesh of wire stretched over the ceiling, as if for some elaborate network of cable-cars. It had grown since their last lesson. From sockets in the wall thick red cables looped and curled; crocodile clips pegged them to the mesh. There were coils of copper wire dangling from hooks, threaded through beards of silver wool. Electricity had been restored to the school, of course, since the cutting of the main cables. It looked as if the professor had demanded that a rather larger supply be installed.

'I thought we all deserved a treat,' she said. Her voice was trembling.

'Sanchez isn't here,' said Anjoli.

'Nor's Millie,' said Ruskin.

Sam burst in through the door, his shirt-tails trailing from the football match, his cap firmly, proudly, on his head. 'I'm sorry, miss, my parents took me—'

'I know, Sam. No problem.'

'Wow! What are we doing?'

'I thought we all deserved a treat. Shoes off, everybody.' There was a buzz of uncertainty. 'Put them to one side. Yes, I know his feet smell, Israel, you'll just have to put up with it . . . Asilah, press that blue button, would you? Just above the rheostat.'

'Miss, it's raining! Don't!'

'What's the problem with a little bit of rain?'

Asilah pressed the switch and the roof of the tower started to fold away, leaf by leaf. Fat raindrops bounced on the floor and furniture, and a crash of thunder made the glass rattle. It was cold.

'This happens very rarely, it might be one big anti-climax. I don't want anyone getting their hopes up.'

Ruskin said: 'Should we be taking notes?'

'I promised a demonstration . . .' She pressed another switch and the hydraulic probe lifted from its box and started to extend. The children hadn't seen it since that day, weeks ago, when they'd helped build the lab. It nosed up now into the pelting rain, as if to meet the thunderclouds. A gust of wind sent the downpour spiralling over desks and onto the floor. In seconds the children were soaked, their grey shirts clinging to their skins, their hair plastered back.

'Miss, please!'

'I'm going to connect our main circuit, so shut up. Are we ready? Hands off, Vijay, you'll get a nàsty zap if you touch that sheet. Hands off, everyone. Ready? I want to see your hands on your heads. Good, Sam. I'm going up, to gauge the height. Sit here.'

'You're going up?' said Israel.

'Stay back, boys.'

'Miss, I went up last time! Please! You said—!'

'Stay where you are. Get your feet off the floor; hands on heads.'

Professor Worthington had put on a rubber raincoat. She was wearing enormous rubber-soled boots, and her gauntlets were monstrous. She now started to climb the antenna. As she rose, the metalwork narrowed and swayed; it was like a ship's mast, when the craft is rolling in a high sea. The wind was fiercer the higher she got and she had to go very slowly. There was the smell of electricity still, so intense.

She reached the top and she saw two little figures down on the lawn, both were obviously soaking.

The needle was javelin-sized, and you could raise and lower it by easing a neatly-designed spring. She loosened it and pushed up. Oh, there was lightning overhead, it was sailing in from the ocean. You just had to find your spot.

Just another few metres, higher than the south tower and its weathervane. She could see Lady Vyner, staring out of a window. She pulled back the spring and forced the needle higher. One more thrust; she could feel a great vortex of static rolling around her. She pushed another metre, and the whole sky exploded.

At his desk, the headmaster noticed his table lamp dim for a moment. In fact all over the school, the lights dipped as a multiplied voltage whipped around the east tower. Dr Norcross-Webb was finishing the new blazer badge design, his felt-tip pens scratching away at the paper. He was smiling, recalling the moment on Reading station he first designed the uniform.

The lights went out.

He pulled his door to and trekked down to the kitchen. Captain Routon was shifting the tables.

'Routon, what are you doing? You should be resting.'

'I know, Headmaster, but we need the space for party games. Oh, by the way— What was that?'

'What?' said the headmaster.

'I don't know, sir. It sounded like a scream.'

'I heard something a minute ago, from the north tower. I'm sure Professor Worthington has it all under control, she's doing a final science project. I wonder if we should take a look.'

There was another high-pitched cry from above and then a peal of thunder right overhead. It was as if the stones in the wall were moving.

'I heard a scream. I definitely heard someone shouting!'

As he climbed the north tower, the headmaster was aware of a tingling sensation on his upper lip. This soon spread to the back of his hands and then the back of his shoulders. Pins and needles: not unpleasant. There was also a strange vibration. The tower was trembling and he was caught in the frequency. Then he heard a ringing in his ears, as if someone were doing that trick with the glass when you run your finger round the rim and the note sets your fillings on edge. His eyes were watering too, just as he reached the top step, and he was breathless. The oxygen was thin; he was reminded of high mountains.

He put his hand on the door handle and it flashed with sparks. He gasped and wondered what to do. He didn't relish electrocution, but he could hardly turn back.

Bracing himself, he grabbed the handle again and was relieved to find it uncharged. He twisted it and threw the door open.

'Headmaster!' whispered Professor Worthington. 'Captain. Welcome.'

The room was still and silent. Nineteen children had turned to stone, some of them sitting on stools, some of them cross-legged on the benches. Asilah was standing on a desk, his hands clenched together above his head. The light was electric blue and sizzling along a grid of wires above their heads. Glow-worms of light, hundreds of them, were pulsing from one corner to the next; some were detaching themselves and falling with the long, balletic loop of mercury, to basins below. Occasionally, the light flickered in a halo round a child's hair, flashing for several seconds.

'It happens so rarely,' whispered Professor Worthington. 'I've been waiting so long.'

'What is it?' said Captain Routon.

'Take off your shoes! Quickly!'

They did so.

'It's an electric freeze,' said Professor Worthington. 'To catch it first time! Keep still, you can break it so easily. Sit on the bench.'

The headmaster said, 'Is it safe?'

'Look at Israel,' said Professor Worthington. 'Oh, I *told* them they would see! We're charging, Giles, we're charging . . .'

'My goodness.'

Israel, the nine-year-old, was cross-legged on a stool, his hands in his lap. His head was back, his lips were open; there was a ring of electricity round his mouth, crackling noiselessly. The sparks were scribbling the air, expanding as they watched, playing over his eyelids, his ears. Professor Worthington too was suddenly consumed by a cloud of blue, as if a whole shoal of lightning fish had dashed around her, then off again into the lattice of wire.

'What is it?' said Routon.

'Luck, really,' she whispered. 'There are so many variations, so many differentials. This is the best I've ever had it, and it cleans, Giles – it purifies. Look at Millie – she just came in with Sanchez.'

Millie was standing on a book, rooted to the spot. Her arms were raised in a gesture of what looked like rage, a fist was clenched. Sanchez was opposite her, standing on a chair. He was leaning forward, his mouth open – presumably shouting back at Millie. Both children had a luminous blue glow to their arms and hair, as if they were radioactive. Another, massive bolt of lightning hit the needle in the roof and the room flashed like a gigantic camera. Jagged sparks flew from Millie to Sanchez, from Sanchez to Henry, from Henry to Vijay and Caspar. Tomaz was standing with his hands cupped, holding fire: then the sparks were criss-crossing, flying from every child to every child.

'And it really doesn't hurt, or cause damage?' said the head-master. He had stepped up onto a book; Routon had done the same.

'Can you feel any pain?' said Professor Worthington.

'Me?'

'Look at your hands, Giles.'

The headmaster had placed his hands on a desk and Anjoli, sitting upon it, had reached out gently and was holding one of them. Now, from under the man's fingernails came blue sparks, blue talons of electricity. He held his right hand up to his face; the sparks wove a glove of blue light, which stretched even as he stared at it, to the tuft of hair on his head.

'Oh my, it feels wonderful.'

'Believe me, Giles. There's no feeling like it. It purifies.'

'How though?'

'You have to have the right people.'

'But isn't it dangerous? It must be.'

Professor Worthington had taken off her boots and she sat on the soaking desk, the rain beating down over her. Electricity coiled round her legs and waist, and within seconds she was alight and alive, she was crackling. She smiled: the sparks fizzed between her lips. She stretched her arms out.

'What a question to ask,' she whispered. *'Is it dangerous?'* She laughed, and the lightning struck again and the children sighed, flickering. She touched the headmaster with a finger and, again, bolts of electricity ricocheted from adult to child, from child to adult. 'We're at Ribblestrop, Giles, where life *is* dangerous. Are you telling me you didn't know that?'

The headmaster tried to nod. He managed to smile, and tried to speak. But the storm was now directly overhead, and the lightning was almost constant. Like everyone else, he was lost in electricity.

The very next morning Professor Worthington's response to the headmaster's question was accepted as the official school motto:

Life is Dangerous. It would be woven onto blazers and printed on pencil-cases. It would flutter on the flag, with the lion and the lamb. It would form the chorus of the school song, if the head-master had time to write one. After all, Christmas with thirteen orphans was going to be busy, and next term would be busier. He had banked the cheque and framed his licence. He was dreaming of new projects, new buildings, new people. He'd received a letter saying that Miles would be returning, which was good news, if unsettling.

Next term would be amazing.

NEWSLETTER

Dear parent, guardian and friend,

It has been an eventful term here at Ribblestrop, and I am writing to thank you for entrusting your children to my care and that of my diligent staff. Ribblestrop, I believe, is a home away from home, where we provide a secure sanctuary and equip young people with life-skills. To take you through the events as they occurred would be a hard task for any man. Whilst my own motto is 'look to the future', it would be wrong of me to let the year pass without mentioning some of the spectacular achievements of your children.

First of all, we now have a roof. Under the mathematical guidance of our two new members of staff, Captain Routon and Professor Worthington, a substantial amount of last term's fire-damage has been put to rights. This means we have more classroom space, and will be developing a library and seminar room in due course. If you could have seen your children scaling the slopes and working together, you would have been even prouder than you undoubtedly are already. I put it to you that the combination of academic and practical skills that these children have been learning puts them way ahead of the game when it comes to survival experiences. In the arena of sport, Ribblestrop has acquitted itself well; reading and writing are also coming on strong. The choir has made a sound start; some children have developed their skills as drivers, welders and marksmen.

On a sadder note, you will, no doubt, have heard of the premature departure of our deputy headmistress. In her brief time at Ribblestrop, Miss Hazlitt was one of those teachers that made a real difference. She was dedicated – few children will forget the care with which she taught good manners, for example. On a happier note, you will be pleased to know that Captain Routon is making a speedy recovery.

But what of the future?

I am proud to tell you that scarcely a day goes by without some new enquiry from an interested parent. A substantial injection of funding has allowed me to look not just to our infrastructure, but also to the recruitment of new staff. As I said to the children on day one, you have to be builder and dreamer combined at Ribblestrop: and that is what I can promise for the New Year – expansion, dedication to excellence and massive ambition. I hope your children get the rest they deserve over the holiday (our orphans certainly will, because they are staying here) – and I look forward to welcoming them back next term, for more of the same!

Thank you for your support to date. Please don't forget that each child must be equipped with a flower-press for next term, as Nature Study dominates the Spring curriculum.

Dr Giles Norcross-Webb

Dr Giles Norcross-Webb
Headmaster

About the Author

Andy Mulligan was brought up in South London, and educated at Oxford University. He worked as a theatre director for ten years, before travels in Asia prompted him to re-train as a teacher. He has taught English and drama in India, Brazil, the Philippines and the UK. He now divides his time between London and Manila.